How to Find a Duke in Ten Days

Copyright

This book is a work of fiction. Names, characters, places, and incidents are the product of the author's imagination or are used fictitiously. Any resemblance to actual events, locales, or persons, living or dead, is coincidental.

Cover Design by Ivan Zanchetta

ISBN: 978-1-937823-62-7

About How To Find a Duke in Ten Days

Three Historical Regency Romance Novellas

The Will to Love by Grace Burrowes
His lordship has been looking for a rare manuscript in all the wrong places, but he might just find true love!

How to Steal a Duke (in Ten Days, Give or Take a Few Days, But Definitely in Less than a Fortnight) by Shana Galen
A haughty duke and an impoverished lady turned cat burglar travel to the wilds of Cornwall in search of a castle, a mad earl, and an arcane manuscript.

The Viscount's First Kiss by Carolyn Jewel
Viscount Daunt and the painfully shy Magdalene Carter turn friendship into love in their search for a legendary medieval manuscript.

Dedication

If you pre-ordered this anthology early enough, you might have seen a version of the cover with four authors' names on it, and a version of the price that was somewhat higher. Miranda Neville was instrumental in creating the overarching premise for *Ten Days* and in helping us develop the framework for our stories. The timing hasn't worked out to include a story from Miranda in this volume, though we are very much in her debt. If you enjoy these tales of bibliophiles in search of old manuscripts and new love, please know that the concept and early research was Miranda's, and that's why we dedicate this anthology to her.

Table of Contents

Prologue

"I FIND IT untenable, insupportable, and entirely unacceptable that we haven't unearthed a single quire of the *Liber Ducis de Scientia.*"

Dominick Spencer, Duke of Tremayne, had both the consequence and the physical presence to speak in emphatic polysyllables. He was big, dark, decisive, and could accomplish with a single scowl what others failed to achieve in entire polemics. The wiser members of the Bibliomania Club had given up debating with His Grace years ago.

Seton Avery, Earl of Ramsdale, knew for a fact that Tremayne could be wrong. As Tremayne's friend since boyhood, and as a man who valued the present arrangement of his own facial features, he kept that news to himself.

"We've tried," Ramsdale said, topping up Tremayne's brandy. "We'll keep trying. Between the three of us, we have means, influence, connections, and expertise. If the *Duke's Book of Knowledge* still exists, we'll find it."

"Don't forget charm and good looks," Harry Fordyce added from the depths of the library's sofa. "Also grace on the dance floor and stamina in the saddle."

Harry, recently burdened with the Daunt viscountcy, kept a superior intellect well hidden behind humor and stunning good looks. He was tall, brown-haired, and deceptively good-humored—a sleek, self-confident housecat of a viscount, to appearances—while Tremayne prowled and growled around the library's perimeter.

They were equally formidable men, each in his own way, and Ramsdale regarded part of his role in their trio as that of referee.

"Trying won't do," Tremayne retorted. "For two hundred years, the best minds on the Continent have been *trying* to find that manuscript. A compendium of all the knowledge known to the sharpest intellects of the Renaissance doesn't just disappear."

Not only the sharpest intellects of the Renaissance, but those deemed worthy of memorialization by Lorenzo de Medici, often referred as Lorenzo the Magnificent. Under his patronage, the *Liber Ducis de Scientia* had developed as a perfect blend of the scribe's art and the scientist's knowledge.

Harry sat straight. There were rumors about one of the volumes of the lost Duke that involved a fellow bibliophile and friend of his. None of the club members believed Harry's friend had had anything to do with the incident, but rumors did persist.

"Your Grace's patience has disappeared," Harry observed, taking a sip of his brandy and setting the glass on the carpet. "If the Duke has remained well hidden for two centuries, what has you all a-swither now, Tremayne?"

Ramsdale studied his drink, for Harry must be allowed his entertainments. Adjusting to an unwanted title was—appropriately enough—a daunting task.

"I am *not* all a-swither, *your lordship.*"

And Tremayne must be allowed his.

"Daunt makes a point," Ramsdale said. "We've searched, we've sent out correspondence, we've followed up on possibilities. I'm taking another look at my uncle's will, in fact, and I suspect the two of you are also on the scent of yet more clues. Why the urgency now, Tremayne?"

Though with Tremayne, everything was always urgent—except recreation, relaxation, diversion. Those trivialities had ceased to matter long ago. Ramsdale worried that Tremayne had become so obsessed with acquiring valuable books that he'd forgotten the pleasure of actually reading the damned things.

He'd also forgotten the necessity to acquire a duchess somewhere along the way.

"Peebles has announced his retirement," Tremayne said. "He'll step down in less than a fortnight."

"Ambushed us," Harry said, rising in one lithe move, drink in hand. "Damn it."

"If the professor doesn't want any fuss or bother, then we should respect his wishes," Ramsdale said, for fuss and bother surely numbered among the deadly sins.

Peebles had tutored each of them at some point in a difficult public school education. The professor's passion for old books, and his endless reserves of biscuits, patient counsel, and humor had earned him the lasting loyalty of many a lord's heir. The Bibliomania Club would have faltered in its early years, but for Peebles's enthusiasm.

The *Duke's Book of Knowledge,* was the professor's greatest passion, also his greatest frustration. Some claimed to have seen the Duke, or portions of the manuscript, others—an increasingly vocal portion of the club's membership—had begun to claim the Duke was a hoax.

"Peebles retirement will involve a banquet of some sort," Tremayne said. "Imagine how that evening will be for him, if not a scintilla of evidence is produced proving that his life's work is a literary fact."

Harry stood before the fire, an unwitting study in male pulchritude. "Tarkington is saying it outright: The Duke is a hoax, a fable made up by Peebles for his own aggrandizement."

"Tarkington had best not stay that in my hearing," Tremayne replied.

Ramsdale rather wished Tarkington would make that error. Mr. Tarkington, an earl's son, was that most irksome of combinations, stupid and arrogant.

"I might be able to make some progress in the next two weeks," Ramsdale said. "Even a single quire of the manuscript would vindicate Peebles's research."

Tremayne turned a brooding gaze in Ramsdale's direction. "We need all four quires."

No, they did not, but Tremayne must carry every task to its perfect completion.

"All four quires would be the best gift we could give Peebles," Ramsdale said, "and our fellow book lovers."

"My time is spoken for over the next two days," Harry said, expertly plying the poker to re-arrange the coals on the hearth. "I'd have ten days to find the Duke. Those are not good odds."

"Those," Ramsdale said, "are the odds we have. I've already placed a few advertisements, and I promise you gentlemen I will exert myself to utmost over the next ten days to find all or part of the *Liber Ducis de Scientia.* Are you with me?"

Tremayne touched his glass to Ramsdale's, then to Daunt's. "We were Peebles's favorite students, the best of the lot. How hard can it be to find a Duke in ten days?"

He flashed a rare and frighteningly fierce smile, while Ramsdale sipped his drink. Peebles had told every boy that he was the best of the lot. Now it was time to live up to the professor's expectations.

"To finding the Duke in ten days," Ramsdale said, touching his glass to Daunt's. Ramsdale infused his words with confidence, though what he offered was as much a prayer as a toast. The Duke had remained hidden for two centuries. What hope did even the most determined book lovers have of finding such a treasure in a mere ten days?

The Will to Love

BY

GRACE BURROWES

Chapter One

IF YOU CAN read Magna Carta, association with the undersigned could be lucrative for you. Inquire at the Albion.

"How is a lady to inquire at the Albion," Philomena Peebles muttered, "when that blighted bastion of male bloviations refuses to permit a female foot to cross its threshold? Have you seen my cutwork scissors?"

Jane Dobbs peered into the workbasket on Philomena's lap. "How can you find anything in there? Use mine." She passed over a tiny pair of scissors on a silver chain. "Why would you want to go to the Albion Club, other than for the obvious pleasure of shocking the dandiprats?"

Jane was twenty years Philomena's senior, part companion, part poor relation on Mama's side, and all friend. She'd joined the household shortly after Mama's death, though nobody had explained exactly how she and Mama were related.

Philomena hadn't cared then and didn't care now.

She trimmed out the newspaper notice and passed it to Jane. "I can read Magna Carta and am in want of funds to finance my search."

"You always turn up alliterative when you're restless. Are you off to hunt for the Duke again?"

"Of course. All the evidence points to at least parts of the manuscript being right here in London, and Papa's retirement banquet is a mere ten days away."

As Papa's amanuensis, Philomena had memorized every scrap of information known about *The Duke's Book of Knowledge,* or the *Liber Ducis de Scientia.* Papa was considered the international expert on the manuscript, though being an expert on a book nobody had seen for two hundred years was a vexing contradiction. Some said *Liber Ducis* didn't exist, and the good professor had been hoaxing his academic associates for years.

"If the Duke is here in London, what do you need funds for?" Jane asked, giving the notice back to Philomena.

"Research is costly. Everything from cab fare to bribes to the occasional male escort takes a toll on a lady's exchequer."

In Paris, a woman could walk the streets without fear of being either judged for her independence or attacked for her coin. London, self-proclaimed pinnacle of human civilization, was generally considered unsafe for a genteel lady on her own.

Some civilization.

"It really is too bad that nice Tolerman fellow went off to Peru," Jane said, threading her embroidery needle with gold silk. "He let you drag him all over creation and nary a word of protest. The poor man was quite devoted."

"He's off to Egypt, and he wanted to entice me away from Papa because I can transcribe notes in all the classical languages." Beauford Tolerman had been a handy escort, until he'd confessed a violent passion for Philomena's nose.

Not even her eyes—her nose, or in Beauford's words, her pulchritudinous proboscis. She might have forgiven him his outburst, but then he'd tried to kiss the object of his ardor. Philomena had suggested to Professor Arbuthwhistle that Mr. Tolerman would make an excellent addition to the very next expedition to the pyramids.

Beyond the parlor door, a maid welcomed a caller. Visitors were frequent because Papa knew absolutely everybody who took an interest in ancient literature or philosophy, and many were paying calls to wish the professor a happy retirement.

For Papa, *happy retirement* was a contradiction in terms, hence Philomena's determination to find the Duke, or at least the portion of the manuscript that dealt with secrets of the human heart.

The Duke knew all the answers, if Papa's research had any validity. Page by page, the manuscript documented the most sophisticated thinking from all over the Renaissance world, grouped into four subjects: natural science, arcane medicine, fabled lands, and sentiments of the heart.

Philomena wished the entire manuscript would be found, but her personal objective was the treatise on human emotion, *De Motibus Humanis*. That tome was said to include recipes for tisanes for everything from grief, to jealousy, to melancholia. Perhaps she might find a potion that could help Papa attract a companion for his autumn years.

"Ladies, good day." Seton Zoraster Avery, Earl of Ramsdale, bowed to the room at large.

Philomena slipped the little notice into her pocket. Ramsdale was skilled with modern languages and particularly skilled at using the English language to talk about himself. No need for his overly active mind to light upon a lowly newspaper advertisement.

Philomena rang for tea, schooled her expression to patience, and sent Jane a look: *Please be gracious, for in the face of such unrelenting tedium when I have a duke to catch, that sacrifice is beyond me.*

At least Ramsdale was interesting to behold—dark where the usual lord was fair, muscular rather than slim, and possessed of a voice Jane referred to as a *bello basso*—a beautiful bass. Philomena liked that about him.

And not much else.

HAVING DISPENSED WITH the tedium of a social call upon Professor Peebles's household—the professor had literally stuck his head through the doorway, and that head had still worn a sleeping cap at midafternoon—Ramsdale sought out that haven of rational conversation and fine fellowship, the Albion Club. Its appearance was unprepossessing, the location just off St. James's Street ideal.

And the quiet in the reading room was blessedly reliable.

This was a club for grown men, not raucous youths looking to make extravagant wagers or debate politics far into the night. The food was good, not merely expensive, and the service attentive rather than haughty. Ramsdale occasionally took rooms here rather than bide at his own town house, and thus nobody looked askance as he proceeded to the second floor and let himself into a familiar parlor.

"Good day, my lord," said Pinckney, his valet and general factotum at this location. "Three more responses came while you were out. The first of the gentlemen is scheduled to arrive within the hour."

Ramsdale turned so Pinckney could take his greatcoat. "That's five altogether. Only five people in all of London, Oxford, and Cambridge can read medieval law Latin?"

For Ramsdale had advertised at the universities as well.

"Perhaps it's the case that only five people who need coin can fulfill your request, my lord. But surely, from among a field of five, you'll find one who's acceptable."

The Duke's Book of Knowledge was reportedly written in plain, straightforward Latin, which owing to a lack of marching centurions or strutting gladiators, hadn't changed much over recent centuries. The problem was not the long-sought Duke, but rather, Uncle Hephaestus's will. Uncle had believed that medieval monks invented the crabbed, complicated law Latin to save on ink and parchment and that saving on ink and vellum remained a worthy goal.

Hence, he'd written his damned will in law Latin, and in the abbreviated version of the abomination still practiced by elderly clerks and particularly mean judges. Such was the incomprehensibility of that hand that, in the last century, it had been outlawed for court documents.

"Shall I ring for tea?" Pinckney asked.

Ramsdale had choked down two cups of gunpowder while maundering on in the Peebles's parlor. He had no wish for more damned tea. Why did the ladies never contribute anything of substance to a conversation? They smiled and nodded and yes-my-lorded but never *said* anything?

"Order a tray with all the trimmings," Ramsdale said. "If I'm to interview starving scholars, I'd best feed the poor devils."

Then too, Pinckney would help himself to a biscuit and a sandwich or two, and nothing on the tray would go to waste. The footman and groom would see to that when supper was hours away.

The scholars, alas, proved a shabby lot. Two reeked of mildew, two could not fumble through a single sentence of Uncle's codicil, and the fifth wanted a sponsor for yet another expedition to plunder the Nile.

Time was running out, and defeat was unacceptable.

"Have any more responses come?" Ramsdale asked when the Nile explorer had been sent on his way.

"Not a response per se," Pinckney said, tidying tea cups and saucers onto a tray. "There is a gentleman below stairs who said he'd wait rather than make an appointment. Tidy young chap, relatively speaking."

"Tidy and skinny, I've no doubt."

The afternoon was gone and so was Ramsdale's patience. "Send him up, but don't bother with another tray. I doubt he'll be staying long."

Pinckney used a small brush to dust the crumbs from the table onto a linen serviette. "And will you be going out this evening, my lord?"

Ramsdale had been ruralizing in Berkshire for the past month, being a doting godfather to a friend's infant daughter. Had a fine set of lungs on her, did his goddaughter.

"I might renew acquaintances around the corner," he said. "If there's anything to miss about Town, it's the company of the ladies." Though the women who dwelled at the odd St. James address didn't consider themselves ladies.

Ramsdale had spent many a pleasant hour in their company, nonetheless. His favorite chess partner was a madam of no little repute, and he delighted in the linguistic variety her employees brought to an evening. French, Italian, and German were all to be heard in the main parlor, along with a smattering of more exotic languages.

Pinckney withdrew, and Ramsdale gathered up what passed for his patience as a slim young fellow was admitted by the footman.

"My lord." The scholar bowed. He had a scraping, raspy voice. He also wore blue-tinted spectacles that must have made navigating after dark difficult, and in the dim light of the sconces, his countenance was very smooth.

Too smooth. "Have you a card?" Ramsdale asked.

The scholar's clothes were loose—probably second- or third-hand castoffs—and his hair was queued back and tucked under his collar. He passed over a plain card.

Phillip Peebleshire. *Ah, well, then.*

"You look familiar," Ramsdale said.

"We are not acquainted, my lord, though I have tutored younger sons from time to time."

Probably true. "Well, have a seat, and lest you think to impress me with your vast qualifications, let's begin by having you transcribe a few lines from this document."

Of the two seats opposite Ramsdale's desk, Peebleshire took the one farther from the candles. Ramsdale passed over Uncle Hephaestus's first codicil—there were nine in total—and Mr. Peebleshire took out a quizzing glass.

"I have paper and pencil, or pen and ink if you prefer," Ramsdale said.

"This codicil," Peebleshire read slowly, "is made by me, the undersigned testator, Hephaestus George Louis Algernon Avery, being of sound mind and composed spirit, as witnessed in triplicate hereto, and does hereby revoke any previous codicils, but not my will, which document is dated—"

Ramsdale plucked the document from Peebleshire's pale hands. "You can translate at sight?"

"The legal documents all tend to follow certain forms, my lord. The vocabulary is limited, until you reach the specific bequests and conditions of inheritance. A modern holographic will written in such arcane language is unusual, though."

"My uncle was an unusual man." Generous, vindictive, devious, and merry. In life, Ramsdale hadn't known what to make of him. In death, Uncle had become purely vexatious.

Ramsdale repeated the exercise with the second codicil—the only one he himself had muddled through in full—and again, Peebleshire translated accurately at sight.

Bollocks. Ramsdale rose and took a candle from the branch on his desk. "What compensation do you seek for your services?"

Peebleshire named a sum per page—shrewd, that—as Ramsdale lit several more branches of candles around the room. The wages sought were substantial, but not exorbitant for a true scholar.

"How quickly can you complete the work?" Ramsdale asked.

"That depends on how much of it there is."

Uncle's will ran on for thirty pages, and the codicils for another sixty. As near as Ramsdale could fathom, seven of the codicils were rants against the established orders at Oxford and Cambridge, with much ink spilled on the reputation of one Professor Peebles.

"Nearly a hundred pages," Ramsdale said, "and I also have correspondence Uncle wrote to various scholar friends. Can you translate French?"

"Of course, my lord."

"German, Italian, Spanish?"

"German, and all of the romance languages, Greek, Aramaic, Hebrew, Latin. My Coptic is less reliable, and I am not confident of the Norse languages. I'm gaining proficiency in spoken Arabic, but the written language is a challenge."

If that recitation were true, Ramsdale would have to admit to surprise. "Then you are clearly qualified to meet my needs," he said, "but before we discuss the rest of the terms, I have one more question for you."

Because Ramsdale had lit every blessed candle in the room, he could see his guest well. Peebleshire sat forward, apparently eager for the work.

"What is your question, sir?"

"How will I explain to your dear papa, that his darling offspring has taken to parading about London after dark in men's clothing, Miss Peebles?"

LINGUISTIC INSTRUCTION FOR young ladies seldom included curse words, but Philomena's father had educated her as if she'd been one of his university students, and thus she could wax profane in a dozen languages.

In Ramsdale's rented parlor, she remained outwardly composed, while mentally insulting his lordship's antecedents in Low German.

In very Low German.

"If I'm to parade about London with anything approaching freedom or safety, I dare not wear a lady's garb," she said, rising.

Ramsdale stood across the room, looking broody—which he did well—and amused, which made Philomena uneasy.

Uneasier. While waiting downstairs, she'd almost risen to leave a hundred times. A hundred and one times, she'd reminded herself that Papa's reputation hung in the balance, and if he was to have private students to keep his retirement comfortable, if his monographs were to receive a respectful reception, then finding the Duke—any part of the Duke—had become imperative.

"Come now, madam," Ramsdale said, sauntering closer. "All you need to assure your safety is a common fashion accessory."

"Firearms are noisy and unwieldy," Philomena said. "Knives are messy and can easily be turned against one."

Ramsdale peered down at her. "What a violent imagination you have. Merely drape an escort upon your arm and your troubles are solved. I will see you home, for example, and you'll find we traverse the streets entirely undisturbed."

His lordship smelled good, of leather and bayberry soap, and with his height and muscle, he'd doubtless scare off the footpads as easily as he attracted the ladies. Jane had intimated that Ramsdale had a reputation among the demimonde, suggesting his skills in the bedroom compensated for a lack of appeal in all other regards.

Thanks to the bawdy inclinations of the Greeks and Romans, Philomena's literary grasp of amatory pursuits was well informed to an unladylike degree.

"Thank you, no," Philomena said. "I will see myself home. Shall I take your uncle's will with me?"

Ramsdale stepped away and began blowing out the candles he'd just lit. "You recognized the signature?"

"Your uncle accounted himself my father's nemesis. I've seen that signature often enough. Every time Papa published an article regarding *The Duke's Book of Knowledge,* Hephaestus contradicted him, usually with no evidence whatsoever."

Ramsdale pinched out a flame with his bare fingers. "How does one prove a manuscript does not exist?"

Smoke wafted about him in the shadows, giving him a diabolical air—which he probably cultivated. His voice was a dark growl that carried even when he spoke softly.

"One cannot prove a book doesn't exist," Philomena said. "A brilliant scholar wouldn't attempt that logical conundrum, which is why Hephaestus Avery, otherwise accounted an intelligent—if eccentric—man, must have been motivated by something other than a passion for the truth."

Ramsdale's gaze followed the smoke trailing upward. "They collaborated, you know, once upon a time. Traveled the Continent together. Co-authored a review of Parisian restaurants."

Philomena sank back into her chair. "You're daft. They hated each other." And Papa would as soon eat shoe leather as he would breaded sole with truffle garnish.

"Which is why your father attended Uncle's funeral? Why he helped draft the eulogy?"

Papa hadn't told her that. He was often forgetful. "One can respect an opponent."

"One can, but as a gentleman, I am also bound to respect you, madam, and that means you should not be alone with me, in my rooms, at a staid and respected gentleman's club. Your presence risks my reputation and yours, so let's continue this delightful argument while I walk you home."

Philomena ought not to be alone with Ramsdale anywhere. He was an earl, and thus all but impervious to gossip, while she was the spinster daughter of an academic one step above obscurity.

"I've known you for ages," she said. "Seen you wolfing down jam and bread in my father's kitchen and watched him send you on your way with biscuits to hoard until your next tutoring session."

The earl had been a quiet boy—a large, quiet boy. Ramsdale was not academic in the usual sense, but he'd had an ear for languages that had deserved advanced instruction. He'd been among many students whom Papa had taught over the years. They'd all been hungrier for food than for knowledge, and most of them had been easy to forget.

"And here I thought you never even noticed the boys coming and going from your papa's study. I account myself flattered, Miss Peebles. Shall we be on our way?"

Not until Philomena had achieved her objective. "I can't stop you from wandering where you will, my lord, but I am well qualified for the translation work you need. Do we have an agreement regarding your uncle's will?"

Ramsdale leaned back against the desk, a mere two feet from where Philomena sat. She didn't want to look up at him, and she certainly didn't want to gaze at what was immediately in her line of sight.

"You want to see Uncle's will because you're afraid his testament discredits your father once and for all."

Well, yes. Now that Philomena knew the daft old man had left such a lengthy will, she did want to read it.

"Don't be ridiculous, my lord. I came here today not knowing who sought a translation of what document or for what purpose. You doubtless seek to support your uncle's criticisms of my father's work."

Ramsdale settled into the chair beside hers. The furniture was dark and sturdy, like the man occupying it, and yet, the impression he made was one of leisure and grace.

"Your father was the only instructor who saw any potential in me, Miss Peebles, and the main reason I didn't starve my first term. Why would I seek to impugn the reputation of a man I esteem? I'm more inclined to believe that you seek to discredit Hephaestus. He was a thorn in your papa's side, and you want posthumous revenge on him for demanding proof of a text no living soul has seen."

"We are back to the impossibility of proving something in the negative, my lord, for you ask me to establish what my motives are not. Your uncle has been gone these two years. I wish for him only the reward his Maker sees fit to bestow on him."

Philomena rose rather than admit that bickering with Ramsdale was invigorating—debating with him, rather.

Ramsdale rose, yanked a bell-pull, and met Philomena at the door. He prevented her immediate departure by virtue of leaning upon the jamb.

"My preference for the Albion is well known," he said. "You saw the advertisement I've been running in *The Times*, and in a flight of female intuition, the likes of which inspire sane men to tremble, considered that I, who have a known interest in languages, had placed the notice."

Philomena put a hand on the door latch. "As far as I know, the owner of Ramsdale House dwells at that location. Perhaps the Albion is closer to your preferred entertainments, my lord, but that is no concern of mine. If we're not to transact business, I'll be on my way."

He straightened as a servant brought in a greatcoat that could have made a tent for a family of six.

"Shall I wait up for you, my lord?"

"No need, Pinckney."

The older man bowed and withdrew, his gaze barely brushing over Philomena.

The earl shrugged into his coat, one long arm at a time. When he drew the second sleeve up, he got one side of the collar tucked under itself.

"Hold still," Philomena said. "You'll go out in public looking half dressed, and your poor valet will have an apoplexy, and the next thing you know, you'll be a caricature in shop windows with your breeches on backward and your watch fob dangling from your hat brim."

She sorted out his coat, passed him the hat sitting on the sideboard and then a walking stick that weighed more than her father's family Bible.

"I suppose you've had to develop managing tendencies," Ramsdale said. "You have no mama, and the professor grows easily distracted. Shall we be on our way?"

He gestured toward the door, and had Philomena not been so desperate for coin, she might have let his polite suggestion see her right out into the corridor.

"I want the work, your lordship. I can bring that will home with me and start on the translation this very evening."

"That is my only copy, Miss Peebles. Meaning no disrespect for your motives or your abilities, I'm not about to let it out of my sight."

This was merely prudent, also deuced inconvenient. "Then I'll simply wear my disguise, and nobody will be the—"

His lordship laughed, a booming, merry cascade of derision. "Your disguise didn't fool me for two minutes, my dear. In broad daylight, it likely fooled no one."

Philomena wanted to smack him. "I sat downstairs in the foyer for *two hours*, my lord. Nobody gave me a second glance."

He tapped his hat onto his head, then paused before pulling on his gloves. "For two hours?"

"Perhaps longer, and may I say, the chairs are not as comfortable as they look."

Too late, Philomena realized that he was no longer having a laugh at her wardrobe. He stared past her shoulder for a moment, and she could feel him parsing evidence and testing hypotheses.

"You will tutor my sister in French," he said, "starting tomorrow at nine of the clock at Ramsdale House."

"No earl's daughter will be out of bed at that hour."

"Precisely, but my uncle's last will and testament will be available for your perusal in the library. My sister's French is in want of polish, and she intends a trip to Paris later this year."

"I see."

Philomena did not see. His lordship was making it possible for her to translate a long document without risking any harm to her person or her reputation. He must be desperate to know what was hidden in the details of his uncle's will.

The only other explanation—that he'd realized a woman who'd wait two hours for an appointment must be badly in need of—attributed to him both accurate intuition and a generous spirit.

Neither of which Lord Ramsdale possessed.

But he did make Philomena feel safer on London's dark streets. That much, even she could admit.

Chapter Two

"I SHALL BEGIN with the will," Miss Peebles said.

This morning, she was dressed as a female, barely. Her round gown had probably begun life as flour sacking, each finger of her gloves had been mended, and she wore not even a watch on her bodice for decoration.

But the intelligence snapping in her blue eyes sparkled like sapphires, and she moved about the library with radiant confidence. When faced with a linguistic challenge, she was not the drab Miss Peebles of Ramsdale's memory, but rather, some mythical creature who combined intellect, determination, and—confound it, when had this happened?—curves.

"There is no need for you to read the will," Ramsdale retorted. He'd ridden in the park before breaking his fast and should have felt more prepared for this encounter.

This argument. Everything with Miss Peebles had been an argument. She'd debated the best route to take homeward the previous evening, how long she would work per day, and whether her compensation should be paid at the end of the day or the end of each week.

Ramsdale didn't have weeks. He had days to find his assigned portion of *The Duke's Book of Knowledge*, only nine days now.

For every position Miss Peebles put forth, she had reasons by the dozen, in addition to corollaries, theses, supporting statements, and evidence. When on a flight of logic, she used her hands to punctuate her lectures, and twice while strolling down the street, Ramsdale had had to grab her arm lest she march across an intersection in the midst of traffic.

"If I'm reading the codicils," she said in patient tones, "then I must know the substance of the document they refer to."

"Chancery found the will quite valid," Ramsdale said. "The estate has been distributed, and the will itself holds nothing of any import." Except some specific bequests, that made Uncle seem more than half-daft.

Miss Peebles strode across his library, her heels beating a tattoo against the carpets. "The settling of the estate was doubtless uncontested. Chancery waved this document under the nose of one elderly, overworked clerk and took a year to do that much. Let me see the will."

Chancery had taken a mere year and ten months, actually, which meant Ramsdale had seen the will in its entirety only a fortnight ago, when the document had been couriered to him in Berkshire.

And now he was wasting time arguing. "You will not write out a translation of the will," he said. "You will read it for your own reference."

Miss Peebles gave him the sort of look Ramsdale's friend, the Duke of Lavelle, gave his infant daughter. As if His Grace hoped that someday the little mite would speak in intelligible sentences, or at least refrain from bashing about the nursery heedless of her own well-being.

"You have changed your mind, my lord. Last night, you told me the translation effort included thirty pages of the will itself. You also look fatigued about the eyes, suggesting you might have spent the night studying the document yourself when I know your command of the law hand is indifferent at best."

Ramsdale had spent the night losing repeatedly to his friend the chess madam and refusing increasingly bold invitations to take the game up to her boudoir.

Fatigue had doubtless dissuaded him. A remove to Town always taxed his energies, and one didn't acquit oneself less than enthusiastically in the bedroom, ever.

"I spent the night reacquainting myself with the blandishments London offers a peer of means, Miss Peebles. I am quite well rested, and a gentleman does not *change his mind.*"

Her gaze cooled, a fire dying out over a procession of instants. "Then logic compels me to conclude that you are not a gentleman, for yesterday you described the task before me as including a thirty-page will, and yet today—"

"I know what I said yesterday." When he'd been distracted by the degree to which the determined curve of a woman's jaw was revealed when she arranged her hair in a masculine queue.

"You do not trust my motives," Miss Peebles observed, stepping away. "And I do not trust yours. We must get past this, my lord, or your coin is wasted. I can claim the will translates into a recantation of Hephaestus's criticisms, while you could put anything before me and say it's a newly discovered codicil describing destruction of *The Duke's Book of Knowledge* thirty years ago. If Professor Peebles's own daughter translated those words, they'd be credible indeed. We are at *point non plus.*"

She wafted away on the faint fragrances of vanilla and cinnamon, rich scents at variance with her brisk words. Memories of warm biscuits and cold milk in the professor's kitchen stirred, along with the realization that the lady was right.

They either moved past this bickering, or Ramsdale was stuck, searching blindly for a document that had eluded discovery for centuries.

"What's wanted," Ramsdale said, "is a modicum of trust."

He was capable of trust. He trusted the Duke of Lavelle to gush tiresomely about his brilliant daughter and his lovely duchess, for example. He trusted English weather to be fickle. He trusted women to be bothersome, and poor relations to turn up at the worst times with the most pathetic fabrications of misfortune.

"Trust?" Miss Peebles took the seat behind the desk that had belonged to the Earls of Ramsdale for time out of mind. "Perhaps your lordship might explain himself."

She looked good in Ramsdale's armchair, self-possessed, ready for a challenge. Ready to tell a peer of the realm to *explain* himself.

"We will agree," Ramsdale said slowly, "that whatever is discovered or disclosed within these four walls will not be made public without the consent of the other party." Such a term should have been part of any contract for translation services, and yet, he'd not thought to draw up a contract, had he?

Hadn't wanted to involve the solicitors at all, and quite honestly did not have time.

Miss Peebles opened the left-hand drawer—not the right—and took out a penknife. "What do you fear I'll find in the will?"

She tested the blade against the pad of her thumb, then set to sharpening the quills in the pen tray. Her movements were quick and sure, and the parings accumulated on the blotter in a small heap.

"Your turn to offer some explanation, Miss Peebles. What do you fear the will might reveal?"

She swept the parings into her palm, rose, and dumped them into the dust bin on the hearth.

"I am afraid I will find proof that my father has been a fool, or perpetrated a hoax the better to draw notice to himself. I am afraid that Papa's years of research have been for naught, that if he dies without finding proof of at least one volume of the Duke's wisdom, then nobody will take up the hunt in future generations, and a great literary treasure will be lost forever. I am afraid," she went on more softly, "that without the Duke, Papa will be unable to attract pupils to tutor, and his old age will be characterized by penury and despair."

She spoke of her father and of great literature, not of herself, and her concerns were valid.

Which would be worse, having a fool or a charlatan for a father?

Which would be worse, penury or despair?

"What of you?" she asked, remaining by the unlit hearth. "If you don't seek to vindicate your uncle's skepticism regarding the Duke, why go to the effort of translating a hundred pages of what appear to be rambling invective?"

She'd gleaned that much by glancing at one page of one codicil?

Ramsdale closed the door to the library, which was ungentlemanly but necessary if soul-baring had become the order of the day.

"Hephaestus left little to anybody," Ramsdale said. "His legacy was debts, a few books, and several obese felines. He was too poor to even house the tomes he'd collected. You see them here,"—he swept a hand toward the shelves—"but such was the enmity between my father and my uncle that having agreed to shelter Uncle's books, Papa in later years denied his brother access to the premises. Their quarrel was bitter and stupid. I would not want their disagreement to become public knowledge."

"Family linen," Miss Peebles said, packing a world of impatience into two words. "My mother's relations never stopped criticizing her choice of spouse. Mama married down, you see, which surely qualifies as the eighth deadly sin for a marquess's granddaughter."

"Any particular marquess?"

"My uncle is now the Marquess of Amesbury. He and Papa correspond annually at Yuletide."

The lofty title and its proximity to Miss Peebles herself was a surprise. An unwelcome surprise. An exceedingly unwelcome surprise.

For years, Miss Peebles had been one of the myriad figures on the periphery of Ramsdale's busy life. He liked and respected her father—he owed her father—and had continued both a correspondence and a social connection with the professor after leaving university.

As a decent female of humble station, Miss Peebles had occupied the status of nonentity to the young Ramsdale heir. He'd more or less forgotten about her as he'd taken up the reins of the earldom, and she'd doubtless forgotten about him.

To learn that he had something in common with her—family linen, of the wrinkled, stained variety—was oddly comforting. That she was brilliant, devoted to her father, and inconveniently logical made her interesting.

That she was a marquess's niece and had not been presented at court was wrong, and yet, polite society would not have been kind to one of her unique gifts.

"You probably don't like me," Ramsdale said, "which bothers me not at all. I like very few people myself. But can you consent to the terms I propose, Miss Peebles? We keep whatever we learn from the will to ourselves, unless we both agree otherwise?"

"You don't like me either," she replied, returning to the desk to put away the penknife. "That's a credit to your common sense, because I am difficult and overly educated. This has addled my female humors, and the damage is likely permanent in the opinion of Papa's physician."

She crossed the room at the brisk pace Ramsdale was coming to associate with her. Only when dressed as a man had she been capable of a leisurely stroll.

She stuck out her hand, a slim, pale appendage with a smear of ink at the base of her thumb. "We have a bargain, my lord. No disclosures unless we're both agreed in advance."

She expected him to shake hands with her, proof of her addled humors.

Perhaps Ramsdale's humors were a bit addled as well. He took her hand in his and bowed. When he straightened, Miss Peebles was smiling at him, a wonderful mischievous expression as surprising as it was heart-warming.

He did not like her—he barely knew her, and one could not like a woman whom one did not know—but he liked that smile.

He liked it rather a lot. Doubtless, Ramsdale would never see that smile again if she learned he was all but courting the Marquess of Amesbury's daughter.

"PHILOMENA MENTIONED NOTHING to me about tutoring Ramsdale's sister," the professor said.

"She told you last night at supper," Jane replied, taking a pinch of salt and sprinkling it over her soup. Cook had made a wonderful beef stew flavored with a hint of tarragon, but her efforts, as usual, had to compete with some tract or treatise at the professor's elbow.

"Is the Duke joining us at table again?" Jane asked.

The professor—without looking up—took a slice of bread from what happened to be Jane's plate and dipped it in his soup.

"You banished His Grace from supper five years ago. We're not eating supper."

That would be a yes. From some arcane manuscript unearthed by one of the professor's students at a bookstall in Prague, or at an estate sale in Italy, somebody had come across a fleeting reference to that dratted Duke.

"Professor, you are retiring," Jane said, gently moving the pamphlet away from his elbow. "Isn't it time the Duke retired as well, or that a younger generation of scholars debated his existence?"

Phineas Peebles had aged well, if not exactly happily. He still had snapping blue eyes, a thick thatch of white hair, and a posture many a military recruit would envy. He sat up very tall.

"Just because nobody has seen the manuscript for two hundred years doesn't mean it ceased to exist. Britain has many documents that are much older, and Shakespeare folios and quartos seem to turn up every other year. Where's the butter?"

Jane passed him a dish sitting not eight inches from his pint of ale. "Why must you be the one to find him?"

"Jane, you wound me. When Lorenzo de' Medici commanded that the most significant knowledge of his day be set down in a single compendium, by God, you may trust that knowledge was set down. I am the Duke's champion in the present age, and every scholar and dilettante involved with ancient languages and philosophy knows it."

Mostly because they disagreed with the professor. A document of that size and significance would not simply disappear. Rumors abounded—perhaps the French had pilfered it from a Florentine villa, or the Spanish had married their way into possession of the Duke. Perhaps the four quires had been flung to the compass points in an effort to ensure at least one part of the treatise survived.

The professor had followed every hint, every shred of evidence, and they all confirmed—in his opinion—that the Duke of Buckingham had got hold of the entire work on behalf of James I.

"You won't find a document that has been missing for two hundred years in the next nine days," Jane said. "Will you devote the next thirty-five years of your life to the same fruitless cause as you have the last thirty-five?"

The professor buttered another slice of bread, broke it in half, and passed half to Jane. "My career has been distinguished by much scholarship, endless teaching responsibilities, and research into all manner of ancient documents and theories. Why attack the Duke now, Jane? In retirement, I will be more free than ever to track him down."

"Phineas, the Duke is not a person. We speak of him as if he's a distant relation who's wandered off after taking an excess of spirits. Your own daughter wanders off and you take no notice."

This criticism was pointless. Phineas loved his daughter if he loved anybody, but loving somebody and being able to show that love were not the same in his case.

"I noticed," the professor said. "You said she's teaching French to Ramsdale's sister, hardly a dangerous undertaking. Do you intend to eat that bread?"

Jane passed him the buttered half slice when she wanted to upend her soup in his lap. "Phin, you should be taking Philomena to visit her maternal relations. You will have time now. She's too old to be presented at court, but titled relations might help her meet an eligible man, might even see their way clear to—"

The professor held up a staying hand—and a half slice of buttered bread. "If you utter the word dowry, I will not answer for the consequences, Jane Dobbs. The exalted marquess well knows Philomena's circumstances and hasn't invited her to visit her cousins, much less to drag me into the countryside as her escort."

"Because you refuse to ask it of him."

"She doesn't want to go," the professor said, taking a bite of the bread. "She's smitten with the Duke too, though I defy you to explain how a woman can find what trained scholars have been unable to search out after two centuries' effort. Philomena's loyal, though, which is more than I can say for *some* people."

That was… that was the professor's version of a tantrum. For him to retire without finding any direct evidence that his precious Duke existed was turning his usually placid nature sour.

"You're right," Jane replied, pushing away her lukewarm soup. "Philomena is very loyal to her papa, while I am only her paid companion. She's approaching thirty, though, and nobody expects a confirmed spinster from a home of humble means to require a companion."

The professor put down his spoon. "What is that supposed to mean?"

"You are actually looking at somebody with whom you're sharing a meal. I will die secure in the knowledge that miracles occur."

He had the grace to look abashed. "Jane, I am much distracted of late, I know, and I do apologize, but the Duke... A man who unearths a treasure of that magnitude might aspire to a token of royal favor. He might attract the best tutoring prospects. He might be appointed a librarian or special lecturer, or curator to a significant collection. Without the Duke, I am merely another fading scholar, wearing my nightcap at odd hours and tucking scraps of paper where they do not belong."

Jane chose to be encouraged that Phineas was discussing his frustrations, but she could not afford to relent so much as one inch where Philomena's future was concerned.

"You have much to be proud of, not the least of which is your daughter. Can you not take a few months away from your obsession to see her settled?"

"Obsession is an ugly word, Jane."

"So is pride, Phineas. The Duke has waited two hundred years, wherever he's lurking. He can wait another few months."

Jane was angry, but she'd been angry with the professor for years. She'd hoped retirement would inspire him to finally act like a father to his only child, finally make room in his life for something other than scholarship. In Jane's opinion, that scholarship was merely a desperate quest for recognition from a lot of prosy old windbags who dropped Latin phrases into their conversations like debutantes showing off their French.

"The Duke cannot wait, Jane. You recall Mr. Handley."

"I have never met anybody named Handley."

"He's an apothecary with a shop in Bloomsbury. Makes excellent tisanes for aching joints."

Aching joints, such as one acquired when one spent long hours gripping a quill pen.

"What of him?"

"He attends monthly dinners with others of his profession, and he heard Mr. Eagan, of Eagan Brothers Emporium in Knightsbridge, bragging about a new source of recipes for love potions, one written in an ancient hand and stolen from an Italian monastery by the plundering French. That could only be the Duke, or a partial copy of the Duke, for he devoted an entire volume to the emotional workings of the human heart."

While the professor lately appeared to have no heart. "Magic potions are nonsense, particularly where amatory matters are concerned. What's wanted in that case is for two people to have mutual respect and compatibility."

The professor finished Jane's ale. "Such a romantic, Jane. In any case, rumors are based on facts, and while Philomena is off pretending to tutor Ramsdale's sister in French, I will be making a jaunt down to Knightsbridge."

Jane helped herself to the professor's ale. "Shall I hold supper for you?"

"Please. I expect Philomena will be back before I am."

He rose and collected his half slice of buttered bread, though he hadn't finished his soup. "My compliments to Cook. The soup was a bit bland."

Delicate. The soup had been delicate. Jane's nerves were growing delicate. "Philomena said she might not be back until after supper."

"Of course she'll be back," the professor said, picking up his treatise. "Ramsdale's sister spent two years at a French finishing school, and the earl is fluent in French. Her ladyship has no need of a French tutor, much less one underfoot the livelong day."

He resumed reading as he left the dining room, muttering under his breath and leaving a trail of crumbs on the carpet.

Jane drank the last of his ale and clung stubbornly to the notion that the conversation had been encouraging, for it had been a *conversation.* With the professor, that was an accomplishment in itself. He'd also set aside his reading for a good five minutes and noticed the peculiarity of Philomena's scheduled activities.

He had not, alas, noticed the woman who'd taken over raising his daughter more than a decade ago.

Not yet.

THE WILL WAS a puzzle, just barely comprehensible in places, ridiculously satirical in others, and touchingly genuine in still others. Philomena had plowed through eight pages of cramped, slashing prose rife with idiosyncratic abbreviations and odd phrases before Ramsdale interrupted.

"That is enough for the present, Miss Peebles."

"You've taken notes?" His lordship had sat at the reading table, paper, pen, and ink before him, while Philomena had stumbled and lurched through the text from the comfortable chair behind the desk.

Once or twice, Ramsdale had snorted or guffawed, but he'd mostly remained silent.

"I have taken three pages of notes," he said, capping the silver ink bottle and laying his pen in a matching tray, "but mostly, I have enjoyed hearing my uncle's voice in your words. Luncheon should be ready, if you'd accompany me to the dining room?"

He rose and approached the desk. Philomena had the thought that he was about to toss her from the library bodily, then realized he expected to hold her chair.

"I hadn't planned on a midday meal, your lordship, though a tea tray with a few biscuits wouldn't go amiss. I promise not to get crumbs on your blotter."

She offered him a smile, lest he think to lecture her into acceding to his wishes. A day offered only so much sunlight, and Philomena needed to make use of every instant. Thus far, Hephaestus had made several references to "that misguided fool, Peebles," but had said nothing about the Duke.

Philomena hoped Hephaestus would wax eloquent about the volume of the Duke's manuscript that dealt with the secrets of the human heart—*de Motibus Humanis*—a topic Hephaestus had publicly declared Lorenzo the Magnificent would never have troubled over.

Why particularly discredit that one aspect of the ducal manuscript, unless—?

The earl braced his hands on the desk and leaned across. "Please join me for lunch, Miss Peebles. The mind grows dull without periodic rest, and I daresay if you're to make progress this afternoon with Uncle's specific bequests, then you will need more than a few biscuits to fortify you."

What magnificent eyes he had. Very... compelling.

"I am a trifle peckish," Philomena said, which was something of a surprise. "Perhaps you'd send a sandwich with the tea?"

The earl leaned closer. "Perhaps you'd for once let somebody show you a bit of consideration and take a meal with me?"

How many times had Philomena and Jane made small talk over a beef roast, pretending that Papa hadn't once again forgotten to join them for his favorite meal?

"I'll bring this short passage," she said, picking up the first page of specific bequests. "We can work through it while—"

Ramsdale came closer, so he was nearly nose to nose with Philomena. "How can that brilliant and busy mind of yours fail to grasp the concept of respite, Miss Peebles? Allow me to explicate: respite, from the Latin *respicere,* to have concern for, to cast one's thoughts back to; and the Middle French, *respetier,* to save, show clemency to, or delay. In modern English, to rest from one's burdens."

Rather than raise his voice, he'd pitched his little lecture just above a whisper and come closer and closer, until Philomena could see that his eyes were not black, but rather, a sable brown.

He tugged on the page of vellum she held, and Philomena was abruptly aware that she was within breath-mingling distance of an adult male to whom she was not related. She had spent four hours alone with the earl in the library and not given *him* a thought, so absorbed had she been in her task.

"I'll join you for luncheon," she said, surrendering the specific bequests. "But we'll not linger over the meal, sir. Not when my progress this morning has been slower than I'd anticipated."

He came around the desk and held her chair. "We'll not linger over the meal, but we won't rush either, madam."

He offered his arm, another small surprise. Philomena accepted that courtesy, and wondered why her own father never bothered with such a small gesture of consideration.

Chapter Three

RAMSDALE SILENTLY SCOLDED himself for being high-handed—his sister Melissa often called him naughty—but Miss Peebles would have sat at that desk translating at sight until the opening of grouse season, left to her own devices.

Of course, she'd be done with Uncle's will long before that.

"Will Lady Melissa be joining us?" Miss Peebles asked.

The dining parlor table held only two place settings, one at the head, the other at the foot. The silver epergne in the middle of the table was piled two feet high with oranges, limes, and strawberries, and thus neither diner need acknowledge the other.

"Her ladyship will doubtless take a tray above stairs. This time of year, she's abroad at night more than in the daytime."

Miss Peebles wandered to the sideboard. "Who would sip gunpowder in solitude when she could enjoy such bounty instead?"

Better an aromatic gunpowder than the dubious sustenance of a musty document. "We will serve ourselves, and you must not worry about the leftover food going to waste. My staff eats prodigiously well."

Ramsdale gathered up the place setting at the foot of the table and moved it to the right of the head, then carried both plates to the sideboard.

"Have whatever you please and take as much as you please. My late father believed the natural appetites were meant to be indulged joyously."

Miss Peebles was busy inhaling the steam rising from a cloved ham and appeared not to notice any improper innuendo—though, of course, none had been intended.

She took one of the plates from Ramsdale. "I love a creative use of spices, and cloved ham has long been a favorite. Our cook does try, but Papa seldom notices her efforts."

Miss Peebles heaped her plate as if preparing for a forced march, and started for the foot of the table, then seemed to realize the cutlery had been moved.

"Do you and your sister typically dine twelve feet apart, my lord?"

"No, we do not," Ramsdale said, serving himself portions of ham, potatoes, and beans. "We typically dine thirty feet apart, on those rare occasions when we share a table."

The lady took her seat without benefit of his assistance. Ramsdale joined her at the table and poured them both portions of the Riesling. He was about to sip his wine when he recalled that company manners were appropriate, despite the informality of the meal.

"Perhaps you'd say the blessing?"

Miss Peebles looked pleased with that small honor and launched into a French grace of admirable brevity.

"This ham has a marvelous glaze," she said. "Might I prevail upon your cook for the recipe?"

"Of course. We make our own honey on the home farm in Sussex, and in all humility, I must admit it's a superior product."

"Jane loves to collect recipes, though, of course, her treasures are lost on Papa. I do fancy a hearty German wine."

The disciplined, focused Miss Peebles became like a girl in a sweetshop when presented with a decent meal. As she waxed appreciative about everything from the buttered potatoes, to the apple tart, to the cheese, Ramsdale gained a picture of a household awash in intellectual sophistication—Miss Dobbs was learning Russian for the novelty alone—but starving for simple pleasures.

Miss Peebles's chatter between bites revealed a side to Ramsdale's mentor that flattered no one. The professor apparently ate without tasting his food and ignored his womenfolk at table the better to remain engrossed in his treatises. Birthdays and holidays caught him by surprise, and he tolerated their observation with an absent-minded impatience that never shaded into irritability, but had still made an impression on his only child.

"My upbringing emphasized different priorities from yours," Ramsdale remarked as he chose some strawberries and an orange from the abundance on the epergne. "We had diversions and recreations, one after the other."

"One envisions the aristocracy living thus," Miss Peebles said. "I'd go mad in a week."

Ramsdale passed her an orange. "I nearly did. Your father grasped my difficulty. I was a bright lad without adequate academic stimulation. I needed a challenge, and he provided it. Perhaps you'd peel that orange, so we can share it."

She sniffed the fruit and ran her fingers over the rind. "You don't want a whole one for yourself?"

Did she want the entire orange? Would she admit it if she did?

"I would rather share," he said, mostly because her brilliant father would never have said that to her. "A few bites will be enough for me. What do you make of the first eight pages of the will?"

As soon as he asked the question, he regretted it. The animation in Miss Peebles's eyes sharpened with an analytical edge where sheer enjoyment had been previously. She tore into the orange.

"Your uncle knew that document would receive significant scrutiny. My impression thus far is that we're wading through obfuscation, our senses dulled by arcane prose in prodigious quantity. The specific bequests should be interesting, given that you claim he died in penury."

Ramsdale missed the other Miss Peebles, the one who marveled over a ham glaze and delighted in a brie flavored with basil. She was interesting, or rather, that she existed in the same person with the dedicated scholar interested him.

"Not penury—my father would not have allowed that, and neither would I—but obscurity. Uncle was brilliant, never forgot anything, and corresponded with acquaintances in half the royal courts of Europe. Papa got the title, though, and the lands and commercial ventures. Uncle envied Papa his status, Papa envied Uncle his brilliance."

Miss Peebles passed over half of the orange. "Where did the heir to the title fall?"

Through the cracks. "I could not be disloyal to my father, and yet, I had far more in common with Hephaestus. They compromised by sending me off to school as early as possible."

Though, of course, neither man would have called that decision a compromise, and Ramsdale wouldn't have either, until that moment.

"Girls are lucky," Miss Peebles said. "We're not tossed out into the world at the age of six and expected to become little adults by virtue of overexposure to Latin and sums, and underexposure to fresh air and good food."

Her father had likely told her that taradiddle, while being unable to afford a good finishing school for her.

"Speaking of fresh air, let's enjoy a few minutes on the terrace before we return to our labors." Ramsdale put his half of the orange and the strawberries on a plate and rose.

Miss Peebles cast the sideboard one longing glance and allowed Ramsdale to hold her chair for her.

He led the way to the back terrace, which was awash in roses.

"How beautiful," Miss Peebles said. "I don't believe I've ever seen so many blooming roses."

"You've never been to the botanical gardens?" Ramsdale asked, setting the plate of fruit on the balustrade overlooking the garden.

"Jane says we should go, but Papa is busy."

Papa was a fool. Phineas Peebles had loomed like a god in Ramsdale's youth, a brilliant scholar who could make entire worlds come alive through languages and literature.

With maturity had come a more realistic view of Peebles: brilliant, but also burdened with ambition, and the narrow focus ambition required. The professor meant nobody any harm, but he'd taught in part because he loved to show off his knowledge, not because he'd loved to teach.

The disappointment Ramsdale felt in his former teacher should not have been so keen.

"I'll take you to see the gardens," he said, "once we find whatever Hephaestus was hiding. Have a strawberry."

He held up the plate, and Miss Peebles inspected all eight choices before selecting the most perfectly ripe berry.

"You have been unforthcoming about your motives, my lord. I am seeking the Duke, or any part of the ducal treatise, in order to safeguard my father's reputation, add to his security in old age, and delight the scholarly world. What of you?"

She bit off half the strawberry and held the other half in her fingers. The sight was deucedly distracting.

"Your father showed me how to navigate the path between my papa's demands and my uncle's expectations. I could have a lively interest in learning and be an earl's heir. That was a far better solution than turning into the sort of scapegrace lordling I'd have become otherwise. Have another berry."

"You owe my father?"

"I do, and I always pay my debts."

She chose a second berry. "You have no interest in the actual information that *The Duke's Book of Knowledge* contains?"

Ramsdale took the least-ripe fruit for himself. "Tisanes for easing grief? Elixirs to stir the animal spirits? Medieval love potions? I am a peer of the realm, Miss Peebles. I do not want for companionship from the gentler sex and hardly need alchemical aids to inspire the ladies to notice me."

She dusted her hands and marched off toward the house. "We'd best be getting back to work, my lord. For you, finding the Duke might be a matter of settling a debt, but for me, finding that manuscript looms as a quest, and I cannot achieve my objective while admiring your roses."

They were Melissa's roses. Ramsdale left the plate of fruit behind and followed Miss Peebles to the door.

"There's another reason why the Duke's tisanes and potions have no interest for me in and of themselves."

Miss Peebles acquired that testy-governess expression again. "You don't believe in the tenderness of emotion that characterizes the human heart? Don't believe in love?"

"I believe in many varieties of love," Ramsdale replied, "but if the challenge at hand is stirring a young lady's passion, I prefer to attend to the business myself, using the old-fashioned persuasive powers available to any man of sound mind and willing body."

She regarded him as if he'd switched to a language she could not easily follow.

A demonstration was in order. Ramsdale reached past Miss Peebles's elbow and plucked a pink rosebud from the nearest bush. He treated himself to a whiff of its fragrance, offered it to her, then held the door and followed her back to the library.

WORDS HAD MEANINGS, and those meanings might be varied and subtle, but they remained mostly constant in a given age. Philomena's definition of the Earl of Ramsdale was shifting as the day went on, and that bothered her.

He was self-absorbed, arrogant, inconsiderate, and enamored of the privileges of his station—that's how earls went on. They did not trouble over boyhood loyalties, did not insist on small courtesies, and did not engage in whimsical gestures involving spinsters and roses.

And yet... Ramsdale had and he did.

He also showed relentless focus when it came to the task of translating Hephaestus's will. By the time the afternoon sun was slanting toward evening, they'd muddled through the entire will.

The specific bequests had been interesting.

To my niece, Melissa, I bequeath five years to enjoy her widowhood before she allows some handsome nitwit with an enormous glass house to coerce her back into the bonds of matrimony.

To my long-suffering housekeeper, Mrs. Bland, I bequeath the privilege of tossing all of the rubbish that had such sentimental value to me—my old slippers, my nightcap, a lock of fur from my Muffin, may he rest in feline peace.

Ramsdale had sat at the reading table, scratching down a note here and there or sitting for long periods in silence as Philomena did her best to render Hephaestus's commentary into English.

"He paid attention," Ramsdale said when Philomena had finished. "He was not the distracted curmudgeon he wanted people to think he was."

A King James Bible sat on the table on a raised reading stand. The book was enormous and had probably been in the family since the Duke had last been seen. The earl idly swiped at the dust that had collected on the leather cover.

"What do you make of his bequest to you?" Philomena asked.

"Read it again."

The list of specific bequests went on for pages. She had to hunt to find the lines tucked between the life of ease and comfort left to a beloved cat—Muffin's granddaughter, Crumpet—courtesy of that responsibility passing to a neighbor, and a case of piles bequeathed to a retired professor of theology who'd since died of an apoplexy.

"'To my nephew, dear Seton, a bright boy whose potential has been cut short by the dubious burden of an earldom, which will do the lad no good, but some things cannot be helped, I leave the honor of recording my demise in the family Bible, which tome yet rests among good friends I have not visited nearly enough, thanks to the parsimony and stubbornness of the late earl. Seton, you have your father's ability to overlook the treasures immediately beneath your nose, and please do not blame the dimensions of that proboscis on my side of the family, because your Danforth relations must clearly take the blame. In this particular, I wish your resemblance to the late earl were not so marked.'"

Whatever did that mean? Antecedents and pronouns in both the original and the translation were garbled, and Hephaestus had used abbreviations to ensure they remained so. Was it Ramsdale's nose that Hephaestus found regrettable, or a tendency to miss what was to be found immediately beneath that nose?

"I cannot fathom what he was about," Ramsdale said, rising and stretching. "Nor do I think further effort today will be productive. I'll study my notes tonight, and we can resume in the morning."

He moved to the sideboard and regarded his reflection in the mirror above it.

Philomena abandoned the desk to stand at Ramsdale's elbow. "I like your nose."

In the mirror, his gaze shifted from his reflection to Philomena's, who was turning pink before her own eyes.

"I'm rather fond of my nose," Ramsdale said. "At least when the roses are in bloom. Might you elaborate on your observation?"

Was he teasing her? Fishing for flattery? Philomena lacked the social sophistication to decide which, but she could be honest.

"Your nose has character," she said. "It's not a genteel feature. Somebody broke it at least once. Here." She traced her finger over the slight bump on the slope that divided the planes of his face. "I expect that hurt."

"The wound to my pride was severe. I walked into a door while reading Catullus. I was fourteen years old, and the concept of a thousand kisses was both intimidating and fascinating. How long would it take to bestow a thousand kisses?"

"Years, I should think, if the kissing were done properly." Oh, she had not said that. Had not, had not, had not.

Had too. As a slow smile took possession of the earl's expression, Philomena wasn't sorry.

His lordship's smile was merry and conspiratorial and shifted his mien from stern to piratical. He became not merely handsome—most men were handsome at some point in their lives—but attractive. Hard to look away from. Hard to move away from.

Philomena didn't even try. She remained beside him, smiling back at him stupidly in the mirror.

"I knew you had hidden depths," Ramsdale said, the smile acquiring a tinge of puzzlement.

"Perhaps we all do. I'll see myself out." The sun would be up for some time, and Philomena was not Lady Melissa, to be escorted at all hours when setting foot outside her own doorstep.

There went the last of Ramsdale's smile. "You will do no such thing."

"You said we were through for the day, my lord."

"So we are, but you will not travel the streets alone when I am available to remedy that sorry plan. Shall you take your rose with you?"

He plucked the pink blossom from the porcelain bud vase in which it had sat for the afternoon. The rose was only half-open, and the spicy fragrance had come to Philomena on every breeze teasing its way past the windows.

"The blossom is better off here," Philomena said. "That rose belongs in a Sèvres vase, surrounded by learned treatises, velvet upholstery, and Mr. Gainsborough's talent."

Ramsdale sniffed the rose and took out a monogrammed handkerchief.

"Mr. Gainsborough was to my father's taste more than mine, though I do like his equine portraits." He took the vase over to the dust bin and dumped the water over his handkerchief, then wrapped the wet handkerchief around Philomena's rose.

"The blossom should travel well enough if we don't stand about here, arguing over a simple courtesy," he said.

And thus Philomena walked home in the lovely summer sunset on the arm of an earl, who carried for her the single lovely rose.

She realized as her own garden gate came into view that Ramsdale was being gallant, as men of his ilk were supposed to be—when it suited them. Earl, by definition, did include a certain mannerliness toward the ladies, even a lady of humble station.

Which meant the definition that no longer functioned must be the definition of Philomena herself, for she was most assuredly not the sort of woman to stroll along on the arm of a titled lord, conversing easily about bequests, Latin abbreviations, and the joys of translating a language that had no definite articles.

JACK AND HARRY Eagan had learned the apothecary's trade from their father, in whose memory they raised a glass of brandy every Saturday evening as they counted the week's earnings.

Mama had been the family's commercial genius, though, and they recalled her in their prayers each day at supper. She'd been the one to insist her grandson Jack Junior be sent off to Cambridge and her other grandson Harry Junior to Oxford. The expenses had nigh bankrupted their papas, but the lads had acquired polish, connections, and a smattering of natural science that gilded advertisements and product descriptions with credibility.

Mama had also pointed out that ladies preferred the counsel of other ladies when purchasing a tisane for Certain Ailments, and thus the Eagan wives were usually on hand to help customers of the female persuasion.

In her later years, Mama had noticed that each social Season resulted in a crop of young ladies eager to employ any means to secure a good match. She'd watched as those young ladies had become increasingly desperate with the passing weeks, until—by early summer—they would have burned their best bonnets and sworn allegiance to the Fiend's housecat if the result was a titled husband.

The Eagans were all red-haired, slight, and energetic, which Mama attributed to having fiery humors, as evidenced by their coloring. Jack Eagan thought the red hair was indicative of quick wits, and Jack's hair was the reddest of them all.

"Poor dears," Harry said, closing the door after another lady's maid had been sent on her way clutching a bag of fragrant dried weeds. "As badly as they want to speak their vows, you'd think the young men of England would oblige them."

"Young men are fools," Jack replied, for that was the expected response and what dear Mama would have called an eternal verity.

"You were a fool," Harry said, twisting the lock on the shop door. "You should not have mentioned that *King's Encyclopedia* business at dinner the other night."

"*Duke's Book of Knowledge,* and it were Hal Junior who suggested we find it."

Hal Junior had gone to Oxford, which he tried without success to lord over his cousin. Jack Junior had grasped the potential to turn the language of science into coin, while Hal had learned to hold his drink.

"Nobody finds what's been lost for two hundred years," Harry said. "That's not a believable tale. We're more likely to find the king's common sense hiding under a toadstool."

"A good tale is only half believable," Jack retorted, "like a rumor on 'Change." He took a rag from beneath the counter and began polishing the shop's wooden surfaces. Harry would do the glass jars and windows, and thus the shop would be neat and tidy for tomorrow's customers.

"But you shouldn't have told that tale to the other chemists and apothecaries," Harry said, starting on the jars of teas and tisanes. The patent remedies were dusted once a week, on Mondays. Fewer people drank to excess on the Sabbath, hence demand for relief slackened early in the week.

"The other fellows will come up with their own schemes," Jack said, "and old manuscripts will be all the rage before the king's birthday. I do so love the smell of this shop, Brother."

Harry paused in his polishing to survey shelves of jars and bottles, treatises, sachets, soaps, elixirs, teas, pomades, fragrances, and recipe collections. Every product was guaranteed to enhance health or well-being in some regard.

"The smell of a successful family enterprise," Harry said, inhaling audibly. "But if all the other chemists have their old manuscripts, then ours won't be special."

Harry was a hard worker, and he took the welfare of the customers to heart. Jack was thus left to deal with more practical matters, such as parting those customers from as much of their coin as possible.

"You are worried about *The Duke's Book of Knowledge* because of that rumpled old fellow who came in here earlier asking about it," Jack said. "That fellow was none other than Professor Phineas Peebles himself."

Harry used his elbow to shine up the glass lid of a large jar labeled Fine English Lavender, though a small quantity of grass clippings might have strayed among those contents.

"What's a professor to me, Jack Eagan?"

"He's our pot of gold. Your own son studied under Peebles at university, and it's from Peebles that Hal Junior learned of *The Duke's Book of Knowledge.* The manuscript is famous, among them as studies manuscripts. Peebles has got wind of our tale, and he'll spread the word, and our shop will soon be the most popular apothecary in London."

Popular being a genteel version of profitable.

Harry repositioned a series of jars sitting on a table in the center of the shop, so they were lined up in exact rows.

"How does one old gent make our shop popular? He didn't buy anything, best as I recall, but took up a good twenty minutes poking about and asking questions."

The next part of the discussion had to be handled delicately, for Harry had inherited Papa's logical mind—logical, Mama had said, as if logic ever moved any faster than a funeral procession.

"Our Elixir of Aphrodite's Joy will be the one everybody buys," Jack said, "because it was discovered by a woman."

"Have you been nipping from the Godfrey's Cordial, Jackie, my lad?"

Lovely stuff, the cordial. It had doubtless soothed the nerves of many a frustrated wife.

"Peebles has a daughter—Hal Junior noticed her, said she's her father's right hand. She reads over everything the professor has published, lives for all that Greekish nonsense."

"Galen was Greek. Don't you be insulting our Galen."

Galen's Goodbody Elixir was a perennial favorite with the housemaids and stable boys.

"And the duke fellow," Jack went on, "who had this manuscript writ down was from Florence. The Florentines were powerful clever people, and the professor's daughter is clever too, says Hal Junior."

"He was probably sweet on her."

Hal Junior was sweet on anything in skirts, bless the boy. "So we put it about that the professor's own daughter dreamed that she'd find the recipe beneath the tallest tree on the Lover's Walk at Vauxhall, put there for her by the goddess Aphrodite, to be shared with every unmarried woman of good name in the most important city in the civilized world."

Harry started on the shop window, though most of the smudges and dirt would be on the outside. He cleaned the outside in the morning, the better to greet everybody who happened by and the better to show off the merchandise throughout the day.

In winter, a window cleaned at sunset would be dingy by dawn.

All of these small touches of genius Mama had devised, and Jack abruptly missed his dame. She would have seen the potential in *The Duke's Book of Knowledge,* and she would have concocted a better story than some goddess cavorting among the soiled doves of a London night.

Harry spit on his rag and went after a long streak. "You say Hal Junior studied under this Peebles fellow?"

"Your own dear boy, and Peebles is obsessed with this manuscript. Nobody has seen so much as a page of it since Good King James took the throne long, long ago."

Harry finished with the long streak, and the window sparkled in the evening sunshine.

"Seems to me that Cupid might have left something beneath that tree for the gents," Harry said. "Nothing sorrier than a young man's pangs of unrequited love."

Never underestimate the power of a logical mind. Mama had been right about that too.

"Just so," Jack said, fraternal affection warming his heart. "Gifts from the deities of old to the lovelorn of today, bequeathed to a scholar's plain-faced spinster daughter."

Harry tossed the rag in the air and caught it. "Is she plain-faced? Not like Hal Junior to pay a plain-faced girl much mind."

"She's a scholar's daughter," Jack said, taking a pencil and paper from beneath the counter. "They are always plain-faced. We need product descriptions, Brother. Even the gods benefit from effective advertising."

Harry got out the brandy—stored in a bottle labeled Hungarian Nerve Tonic—and poured two full glasses. Advertising was thirsty work.

Which great wisdom had not come from Mama, but from Jack's own modest perceptions.

Chapter Four

"BUT WE KNOW that what we imbibe, what we eat, even what we touch and smell, has an effect on our mood," Miss Peebles said. "Why is it outlandish to think that in former times, when folk were more attentive to their natural surroundings, some perspicacious monk noticed that a particular concoction resulted in a greater sense of affection for members of the opposite sex?"

Ramsdale and his translator strolled along in the lengthening shadows as clerks made their way home and shopkeepers closed up for the night. The earl was seldom abroad at this time of day, but he liked the sense of tasks completed, rest earned.

No chess for him tonight. He was too fatigued by his hours in the library with Miss Peebles and her relentless intellect. Then too, Lord Amesbury was a sharp fellow. Ramsdale would allow himself a nap before dressing to join the marquess for dinner.

"You know little of monks, Miss Peebles, if you think they needed a magic potion to increase their awareness of the ladies. The average monk wasn't supposed to be anywhere near the fairer sex, and thus he'd remark each woman he met with great… fondness."

Especially if he was a young fellow and the lady was comely.

Miss Peebles's brow knit, as if the habits of celibate males were one topic beyond the grasp of her brilliance.

"An apothecary, then," she said. "A man happily married, children frolicking at his knee of an evening. He notices that the ginger tea with rose hips he's made to combat sore joints or a bilious stomach also results in a mood that ladies find attractive."

She was passionate about her science, passionate about her languages, passionate about finding the Duke, of whom they'd seen neither word nor phrase. Would she be passionate otherwise?

By virtue of their linked arms, Ramsdale prevented Miss Peebles from charging headlong into the street as a fishmonger's empty wagon clattered by.

"I cannot imagine that ginger and rose hip tea would predispose me to anything other than profanity," Ramsdale said.

"And yet that ungracious observation might be the effect of the rotten-fish stink that came to you as yonder wagon passed us. Admit that the theory of a love potion is sound."

"The theory is not sound," Ramsdale countered, flipping a coin to the crossing sweeper. "You leap, my dear, from a potion having an effect on the person who imbibes it, to that same potion having an effect on the persons in the vicinity of the imbiber. Where is your supporting evidence?"

He cared little for her supporting evidence. He simply enjoyed watching her mind work, watching her free hand gesture for histrionic emphasis, watching the looks of passersby who were amused by a young lady discoursing at volume about Florentine monks and alchemical theories.

"Consider," she said as they turned down the side street that led to her back garden, "the intoxicating effects of spirits."

"My very point," Ramsdale replied. "One drinks to excess, one becomes intoxicated. One's companions do not, unless they too are drinking."

"Is this truly the case, my lord? Is it not more a matter of one man drinks, and his good spirits and bonhomie, his humor and garrulousness, inspire others around him to join him? He's drinking, and soon they are too?"

How could she know—? But of course, she'd know how university boys gathered round a barrel of ale or hard cider.

"That proves nothing. One man's sociability will result in others joining him. That doesn't prove the sociability was the result of..."

"Yes?"

The happy drunk was a fixture in any pub or gentleman's club, and few responded to him with anything other than good will, or at least, tolerance.

"You spout nonsense, Miss Peebles. The spirits work upon the one drinking them. Have you ever become inebriated by association with one consuming spirits?"

Her steps slowed. "No, but I am in company with only my father and Jane when spirits are on hand, and they never consume to excess. Papa would as soon drink ginger tea as wassail or sip flat ale as wine. You must, though, concede that when a lady wears perfume, that does have an effect on the gentlemen in her ambit."

Damn, she was relentless. "You're suggesting the *Motibus Humanis* is more about perfumery than intoxicants or tisanes?"

"You enjoy the scent of that rose, my lord. Most women and men of your strata would not dream of going out of an evening without first splashing on their fragrance of choice. They do so with the express intent of creating a more favorable impression. Who's to say that the impression created isn't..."

They'd reached the little alley running behind her father's modest dwelling. Venerable oaks arched above, and the racket and clatter of the street faded.

"You were saying, Miss Peebles?"

She looked around as if surprised to find herself a half-dozen streets away from where the conversation had started.

"*The Duke's Book of Knowledge* is of interest on a scientific basis, my lord. The ancients grasped the movement of the heavens more clearly than did our nearer ancestors. The same might well be true regarding scents and potions that stir the emotions or plants that aid the cause of medicine."

In the quiet of the alley, Ramsdale realized that the damned manuscript had inspired foolish hopes in an otherwise sensible young woman. Miss Peebles expected wisdom to flow from *The Duke's Book of Knowledge,* valuable insights, genuine science.

"You are daft," he muttered, setting the rose on the nearest stone wall. "Men and women have no need of magic elixirs or exotic scents when it comes to taking notice of each other."

"Beautiful women," she retorted. "Handsome, wealthy men, perhaps. What of the rest of us? What of the plain, the soft-spoken, the shy, the obscure? Do you begrudge them the benefit of science when their loneliness overwhelms them?"

Good God Almighty. She sought the Duke for *herself.*

"Madam, it is often the case that a woman attracts a man's notice, and because that man is a decent fellow and would not press his attentions uninvited, she remains unaware of his interest. She doesn't need the dratted, perishing Duke, she needs only a small demonstration of the fellow's interest."

Another demonstration. Miss Peebles regarded the rose resting on the stone wall a few feet away, the stem wrapped in Ramsdale's damp white handkerchief. She seemed puzzled, as if she'd forgotten the flower, and possibly the man who'd carried it halfway across London for her.

"Miss Peebles—Philomena—you will attend me, please."

Ramsdale took her by the shoulders. Her expression was wary and bewildered, and thus he schooled himself to subtlety. No one would see them in this quiet, shadowed alley, but by the throne of heaven and in the name of every imponderable, Miss Peebles would take notice of *him.*

He framed her face in his hands and kissed her.

RAMSDALE'S PALMS AND fingertips were callused, while his kiss was the essence of tenderness. Philomena was so stunned by the earl's attentions, so utterly unprepared for such intimacy, that she wasted precious seconds searching for words to describe sensations.

Gentle, teasing, delicate, daring... oh, the adjectives flew past in a jumble as Ramsdale shifted, and a debate ensued between Philomena's mind and her body. Her intellect sought desperately to catalog experiences—his thumb brushing over her cheek, his body so tall and solid next to hers, the imprint of his pocket watch against her ribs—while her body railed against words and labels.

And her body was right: This experience was beyond her ability to describe. Rejoicing sang in her blood, while a great emptiness welled too—the unfulfilled longings of a woman invisible for too long, invisible even to herself.

She startled as Ramsdale's tongue flirted with her upper lip. So soft, so intimate that single touch.

He eased his mouth from hers, and Philomena sank her hand into his hair.

Don't go. Not yet. Not so soon. This experiment isn't over.

He wrapped an arm around her, and Philomena leaned into him, breathing with him and gathering her courage.

All day, she'd remained steadfastly loyal to her missing Duke, droning on and on about cats, nightcaps, megrims, and mulligrubs. She'd puzzled out abbreviations, resurrected forgotten vocabulary, and deconstructed sentences that were the grammatical equivalent of London's Roman wall.

Her mind was tired, her soul was lonely, and her body was clamoring for more of Ramsdale's kisses.

He apparently considered that little taste of intimacy enough, a mere pressing of mouths and bodies, a single flirtation of the tongue, and this half embrace in twilight shadows. Indignation organized itself from among the welter of emotions silently racking Philomena.

Indignation that her only experience of a pleasurable kiss should be so brief, so quickly over. Years ago, a few of the university boys had tried to steal kisses from her. Their larceny had been hasty, inept, and so very disappointing.

Philomena's history of kisses had nothing in common with the raptures Catullus had written of, and Ramsdale's kiss hinted of greater joys than she'd glimpsed. He ran his hand down her back, a slow caress that spoke of competence and confidence.

He drew a breath and slowly let it out, her cheek riding the rise and fall of his chest. "Philomena, I did not intend—"

No. No, Ramsdale would not apologize, reason away, or explain his kiss, not when he'd shared such a fleeting, paltry hint of what Philomena suspected a kiss—with him—could be. She took a firm grip of his hair, gave him one instant to stare at her in surprise, then joined her mouth to his.

He remained passive, drat him to the bowels of the British Museum, did not repeat that caress to her back, did not sigh against her mouth, but remained stoically enduring her kiss, as if some other man had shown her the cherishing tenderness he'd lavished on her moments ago.

Philomena did not know what to do, did not have a vocabulary of caresses or love words, so she resorted to imitation, to dancing her tongue across his lips, once, twice... To running her hand over his chest in a slow exploration of masculine contours. She pressed closer, until she could feel the mechanism of his watch moving in a tiny, mechanical march beneath her heart.

Do not leave me to wonder for another ten years what a kiss might be. Do not abandon me to uncertainty and ignorance. Do not set me aside, ignore me, or assume that you may determine all the parameters of our dealings.

All of this she put into her kiss. She conveyed to Ramsdale the longing and loneliness, the outrage and frustration, on a soft groan. He lashed his arms about her and lifted her bodily, bracing her back against the wall.

He plundered, she invaded. He lectured, she rebutted. He took her captive, and she declared victory, until they were both panting. Ramsdale braced a hand above her head against the wall, and Philomena let him support her.

Her mind would not work, her body would not calm. Not in any language did she have words for what she'd just experienced.

With Ramsdale before her and the wall at her back, Philomena occupied a small world filled with the scent and heat of him, and with her own sense of vindication. There was more to life than Latin and mending. She had both hoped and feared it was so, and silently thanked Ramsdale for confirming her suspicions.

"I hear Catullus laughing," he said, straightening enough to trace a finger down the side of Philomena's cheek.

The earl was all self-possession and wry amusement, while Philomena felt as if she'd walked into a door. What mortal could survive a thousand such kisses, much less write poetry about them?

"Laughing at me?" Philomena asked.

The amusement in his eyes faded, replaced by what might have been sadness. "No, love." He straightened and ran a hand through his hair. "Should I apologize?"

"I will kick you if you apologize, my lord. Kick you in a notoriously vulnerable location."

He stepped back. Moment by moment, he was assembling his earl-lishness. Sardonic half smile, proud bearing, distant gaze, subtly unwelcoming expression... Philomena wanted to weep, to take his hand and place it against her cheek, to prove by touch that a man, not merely an aristocrat, shared the alley with her.

"Do you agree," he said, taking her rose from the top of the wall, "that one need not resort to potions or magic formulas to engage the attentions of a member of the opposite sex?"

Philomena took the rose from his grasp and brought it to her nose. He'd tried for lordly amusement and failed. His question had been flung too carelessly in her direction, his gaze remained too steadfastly on the cobblestone path they'd trod.

Philomena unlatched the gate to her father's back garden. "No, I do not agree. A wound might heal without medical attention, but heal faster if properly treated. You might attract a lady through your appearance, wealth, or skills, but capturing her heart could happen more easily if you had the Duke's secrets. We can discuss this at greater length when I resume translating tomorrow."

She was grateful for the deepening shadows and steeled herself for a witticism that would cut, for all it amused. Ramsdale hadn't meant for that kiss to become so passionate, and that bothered him. Philomena liked that he was bothered on her account, and that was foolish.

He bowed. "I'll bid you good evening."

A curtsey was in order. Philomena instead kissed the earl's cheek, then latched the garden gate behind her. She sat in solitude long after the earl's steps had faded, until darkness had fallen and the air had grown chilly, and still, she had no words for what that kiss meant to her.

"IF YOU GENTLEMEN will excuse me," Lady Maude said, "I'll bid you good evening. Do enjoy the port."

She curtseyed and aimed a demure smile at Ramsdale. The angle of her curtsey was such that a view of her décolletage was also aimed his direction.

"You're fond of chess," the Marquess of Amesbury said as his daughter quit the dining room. "Let's repair to the game room, shall we?"

"A fine notion."

Was Ramsdale fond of Lady Maude? Of all the young ladies on offer this year, he'd thought her the most appealing. She was sensible, of an appropriate station to become his countess, played the pianoforte well but not too well, and enjoyed apparent good health.

"How did you find His Grace of Lavelle?" Amesbury asked, taking a seat on the black side of the chessboard.

The game room was the most masculine domain in the entire town house, with fowling pieces, dress swords, and hunting portraits sharing equal space on the walls. A billiards table dominated the room, and the card table would seat eight comfortably.

The chess table had been set up by the fireplace, with screens positioned to reflect both light and warmth.

So why did the chess set feel like a metaphor for an elegant ambush?

"I found Their Graces well," Ramsdale said. "Their daughter thrives too. Berkshire is pretty at any time of year, and Lavelle's ancestral pile has benefited from having a duchess in residence."

Amesbury tidied up his forces, putting each piece at the exact center of the square. The marquess was a spare, dapper fellow with thinning sandy hair and an avuncular air that masked a keen interest in politics.

Ramsdale was not interested in politics, any more than most schoolboys were interested in sums. One endured, one did what was necessary. One did not pretend to a propensity one lacked.

"Lavelle's choice of duchess was unusual," Amesbury said. "But then, His Grace is without parents or elders to guide him on such a matter. Perhaps the duchess, being of gentry stock, will be a good breeder."

The comment was distasteful. Lavelle had married a neighbor of long-standing from a respectable family. More to the point, he'd married a woman with whom he was wildly in love.

Ramsdale moved a queen's pawn.

"Their Graces were well acquainted before the marriage," he said, "and the duchess comes from respectable family on both sides. Lavelle chose deliberately and well. Your move, sir."

Actually, Ramsdale was the one who should have been making a move. The purpose of this gathering, despite the meal served and the chess in progress, was for him to ask permission to court Lady Maude.

He'd made that decision in June, as the Season had ended. An earl needed heirs, and Ramsdale had no interest in entangling himself in that great drama known as the love match.

The marquess moved his king's knight, which usually presaged a slow march across the field.

"Lavelle chose expediently," Amesbury said. "His duchess, being of common stock, won't expect lavish entertainments or London extravagance. She'll be content to manage her nursery, but she'll hardly be a political asset."

While Lady Maude would be the perfect political hostess.

Ramsdale moved his bishop. Bishops covered a lot of ground in a single move and tended to be overlooked as weapons.

"I hope every mother would take an interest in the denizens of her nursery," Ramsdale said. "My own mama certainly did."

Amesbury sat back, as if the game had progressed past opening moves, which—where Lady Maude was concerned—it should have.

"Times were different," Amesbury said. "My own late marchioness knew better than to meddle where the boys were concerned, but she lavished the best governesses and tutors on our Lady Maude. My daughter had a different instructor for watercolors and pastels, a voice teacher, and a teacher for the pianoforte. She's quite accomplished."

Could she insult a man in Low German? Work at the same document for four straight hours? Make a feast of a simple luncheon and kiss as if she were promising her whole soul to the one who kissed her back?

Ramsdale pretended to study the board, though in his mind's eye, he was seeing Philomena seated at his desk, twiddling a goose quill while she sorted various possibilities for an obscure abbreviation.

Philomena gesturing enthusiastically as she explained the intricacies of the vocative case to Ramsdale along the length of Oxford Street.

Philomena grabbing him by the hair and kissing him so passionately he'd nearly started unbuttoning his falls.

"Your move, Ramsdale."

He advanced another pawn, a random, dilatory maneuver that fit into no larger strategy.

"How fares your bill?" Ramsdale asked. Amesbury always had bills churning about in the House of Lords.

"Which one? My bill for the establishment of a board to oversee the turnpike trusts is meeting with significant opposition, but then, we knew it would. I'll not be worn down by a bunch of pinchpenny barons who can't see that roads are the key to the realm's commercial success. Yes, we can ship a great deal by sea or canal, but how do the goods get to and from port, I ask you?"

As the game wandered along, Ramsdale lured Amesbury from one political diatribe to the next, though the marquess occasionally tossed in references to Lady Maude's attributes as a hostess, waltzing partner, and musician.

Before his lordship started mentioning how many teeth the lady possessed, Ramsdale brought the chess game to a close. The marquess played without guile, simply moving pieces about in reaction to Ramsdale's initiatives.

Such a man was easy to manage, and thus Ramsdale made the game look much closer than it was. Ramsdale did not, however, allow the marquess an unearned victory.

"Will you be attending Professor Peebles's retirement banquet?" Ramsdale asked, returning his pieces to their starting positions.

The marquess put the black queen on her square. "Phineas Peebles? Why do you ask?"

"I was under the impression he was a family connection. Am I mistaken?"

Amesbury considered the queen. "You are not mistaken, though Peebles disdains to recollect that notion. Academics can be eccentric."

The marquess, who'd waxed loquacious about turnpikes, excise taxes, and the economic implications of imported French soaps, said nothing more.

"Peebles has a daughter," Ramsdale said, setting the white king on his square. Ramsdale had looked for a resemblance between Philomena and her cousin Lady Maude and found little. Lady Maude was dainty, blond, and graceful.

Philomena was substantial, plain, and ferociously passionate.

"Peebles has a daughter, as do I," Amesbury said. "A pity Maude could not play us a few airs while we enjoyed our chess. She's very skilled."

Skilled, not passionate. A proper lady had no use for passion, and if asked a week ago, Ramsdale would have approved of that view.

But then Philomena had shown up at the Albion, wearing those ridiculous blue glasses, waiting two hours for a chance to earn some coin.

When all the pieces had been positioned, Amesbury turned the board so he had the white pieces. "Shall we play again? I'll not be distracted this time by your parliamentary questions. You can fool me once, Ramsdale, but I'm wise to your tricks now."

Amesbury shook an admonitory finger at Ramsdale, the gesture intended to be playful.

Ramsdale was not charmed. The moment had come to raise the topic of paying addresses to Lady Maude, and Ramsdale wasn't charmed by that prospect either.

"The hour grows late," he said, the most trite of clichés, "and I'm not entirely recovered from ruralizing in Berkshire. I'll thank you for a fine meal and a good game, my lord."

Amesbury was too much the parliamentarian to show his dismay at this abrupt departure. He rose and accompanied Ramsdale to the stairs.

"You were hoping to spend more of the evening with Lady Maude, I venture. How can the chessboard compare to a young woman's accomplishments? Perhaps next week you'll share another meal with us. I'm free on Wednesday, and I know Lady Maude will rearrange her schedule at her papa's request."

Such an obedient female, was Lady Maude. Obedient, and... dull, bless her soul. Ramsdale would not have to exert himself to win her or woo her, wouldn't have to compete with Catullus or the mysteries of medieval law Latin to gain her notice.

"My schedule is as yet unsettled," Ramsdale said, making his way to the front door. "Perhaps I'll see you at Peebles's retirement banquet?"

This question was the equivalent of moving a pawn to distract from a larger strategy, a random exploratory gesture that amounted to nothing.

"Not likely. Why don't we plan on Thursday if Wednesday doesn't suit?"

"Perhaps the following week," Ramsdale said as the butler handed him his greatcoat. "I'll send 'round an invitation when I've sorted out my current obligations."

"And gained the permission of your cook," Amesbury said. "I know how the bachelor household is run. The right countess could spare you all that."

Hunt season had begun in the shires and apparently here in London as well.

"I'll bid you good night, my lord, and thanks again for a lovely evening."

Ramsdale did not run down the steps, though he set a brisk pace—a very brisk pace.

Chapter Five

"THIS IS THE worst codicil so far," Philomena said. "I'll need to start a list of terms I can't translate and have Jane help me with them."

Ramsdale had taken to wandering the library rather than making notes. That's how convoluted and hopeless the sixth codicil was. Philomena had been able to translate the first three at sight, the fourth by consulting a few references, and the fifth by consulting every reference Ramsdale's library boasted.

Five days remained before Papa's banquet, with three codicils to go and not a Duke or *de Motibus Humanis*—the portion of the work Hephaestus referenced most often—in sight.

Ramsdale peered into the lens of a telescope that was aimed at the leafy canopy of the square across the street. "You'd consult Jane rather than your father?"

"Papa thinks I'm teaching your sister French." That scheme had been Ramsdale's own invention, though for the past few days, the earl had been distracted—taking very few notes, mostly staring into space, while Philomena stumbled and thrashed her way through Hephaestus's verbal puzzles.

"Teaching Melissa her French, right." The orrery gained his notice next. He gave Venus a gentle nudge with one finger and set the planets in motion. The solar system had been crafted mostly of copper, and midday sunshine pouring through the window turned the heavenly bodies to fire as they traveled in their orbits.

"My lord, if you're bored, I can struggle on here without you. I'm sure you have better things to do."

Better things to do than distract Philomena from her Latin, which Ramsdale did without even saying a word. The pull and stretch of his breeches over his thighs as he paced the library was a declension Philomena had never noticed before: need, want, desire, yearning, longing.

Ramsdale's mouth had become a conjugation of possibilities: I kiss, you kiss, he kisses, we kiss…

He halted the sun, moon, and planets. "I shall be going out. I can have your luncheon served here or in the breakfast parlor."

Philomena was certain that "going out" had not been on his lordship's agenda two minutes ago, but getting rid of him would be a relief.

Mostly. "In here will suffice. We are running out of time, and so far, I can't see a single clue among all of Hephaestus's rantings."

He'd gone Old Testament on them with the fourth codicil, pearls before swine, a dog returning to its vomit, all quite graphic and unpleasant, and much of it an exhortation in Ramsdale's direction.

"I'd rather you not consult with Jane, if you can avoid it."

"I can avoid it."

He crossed to the door, then paused and scowled at Philomena. "You are working too hard. You are tired, and I'll not have it said I was inconsiderate of your welfare."

Sleepless nights spent alternately regretting and reliving certain kisses and long evenings consulting Papa's reference books had cost Philomena much rest.

"While you have grown snappish, my lord. Be about your business. It's not as if I'll make off with your uncle's will."

Philomena had offered, daily, to take the will home with her, where those references would be closer at hand and the distractions fewer. She'd have to hide her work from Papa, and that didn't sit well, but her concern was moot.

Ramsdale was adamant that she work in his town house. He had latched on to the notion that further clues to the Duke's whereabouts lurked among his uncle's small collection of rare tomes, all of which were housed in the earl's library.

"You've tried to make off with the will," Ramsdale said. "You pester me daily to make off with that document, when you expressly agreed to do the work here."

Philomena rose, her back protesting even as other parts rejoiced to be free of the chair.

"I had no idea how complicated your uncle's prose would become. I had no idea you would be perching at the reading table like a mother cat at a mousehole. I had no idea..." Philomena stood before Ramsdale, truly looking at him for the first time that day. "*You* are tired, and you see your own fatigue when you look at me."

"Too much waltzing, one of the hazards of my station." Still, he didn't march off to his appointment, if any appointment he had.

"Do you want to kiss me again?" Philomena hadn't planned to ask the question, though it had filled every corner of her mind not already crammed with Latin.

Ramsdale's expression became very stern. "What I want doesn't matter, Miss Peebles. I should not have taken liberties with a young woman who has enjoyed a sheltered existence and, in a temporary sense, could be said to be under my protect—"

Philomena kissed him, mostly to stop him from spouting a lecture about propriety, deportment, and the temptations of the flesh.

Also, because she'd thought of little else but kissing him for days.

The experiment was a failure. Kissing Ramsdale in his library, Philomena found none of the surprise, none of the tenderness and wonder that she'd experienced in the shadowy alley. She might as well have been kissing the planet Saturn, warmed by the sun but inert metal for all its fiery—

Ramsdale's arms stole around her and pulled her close. "Drat you—" He drew the pencil from Philomena's chignon and tossed it over his shoulder. "All week, I have tried..."

That was encouragement enough. Philomena resumed kissing him, her pace more leisurely. Ramsdale was not indifferent, but he was held hostage by gentlemanly scruples, for which Philomena had to like him.

"All week, my patience has been tried," Philomena said against his mouth. "Are you truly indifferent to a woman whom you've embraced so passionately?"

Jane said men were like that. Their pleasures did not involve their finer feelings, but Jane was a spinster, as best Philomena knew.

Ramsdale twisted the lock above the door latch. "Are you truly more interested in a lot of damned Latin than you are in my kisses?"

Philomena answered him without words, until tongues tangled, the world fell away, and she had the earl pressed up against the door. Delving into great books was a fine pastime for a lively mind, but as the mind gorged, the heart could starve.

Ramsdale had shown Philomena that with a single kiss.

"You are interested." Philomena glossed a hand over Ramsdale's falls. "I grew up in a house full of biological treatises and rude university boys. You are interested, my lord."

Ramsdale captured her hand and kissed her knuckles. "Ladies aren't supposed to *be* interested, and regardless of your father's reduced circumstances, you are a lady."

Amid the joy and desire coursing through Philomena, confusion blossomed. Papa's circumstances weren't reduced, though compared to an earl's, they were humble. Comfortably humble.

Too humble for Philomena to have designs on a peer of the realm. "I am a spinster, my lord, and you spoke in error. I did not enjoy a sheltered upbringing, I *endured* one. My situation was all the more frustrating because I had access to the best literature penned here or on the Continent. The French have a far more enlightened view of women than we English do, and their women are doubtless happier as a result."

Ramsdale sidled away from the door and picked up the pencil he'd tossed aside earlier. "The French women you call happy I call left to fend for themselves, unprotected, even disrespected."

Nothing killed a tender moment as quickly as a philosophical disagreement.

"I'm sure the ladies of France would rather we'd killed fewer of their menfolk in the recent hostilities, instead of quibbling about the respect the women are owed now."

Ramsdale slid the pencil back into Philomena's coiffure. "I concede that point. I will also admit that, on the one hand, my knowledge of Hephaestus and his life will prove invaluable if we're to identify clues to the location of any part of the Duke. On the other hand, if I sit here any longer staring at your mouth, or your hands, or your other attributes, I shall go daft. We are at another impasse, Miss Peebles. As a gentleman, I apologize for my blunt speech. As a man, I owe you honesty. This arrangement is not working."

Philomena took the pencil from her hair—it was pulling at her scalp—and set it on the blotter.

"This arrangement is working well to get the will translated. Not another scholar in all of London, save Jane or my father, could undertake this exercise half so expediently as I have, and they'd charge you—"

Ramsdale put a finger to her lips. "Miss Peebles—Philomena—I am trying to be a gentleman. You agreed to translate the will in exchange for coin. I would be the basest scoundrel imaginable if I parlayed that agreement into an exchange of favors no gentleman would ask of a lady."

That finger slid across her lips, down her cheek, down her neck, to trace along the décolletage of Philomena's day dress. One touch, and she was muddled beyond speech.

Ramsdale was propositioning her.

No. He was trying *not* to proposition her.

"You don't even like me," he said. "I know well that kissing a man out of curiosity or boredom isn't at all the same thing as liking him. We have... an animal attraction. I've been attracted before, doubtless so have you. It doesn't have to mean anything."

Had he spouted off in some obscure eastern dialect, Philomena could not have been more befuddled.

"I do like you," she said. "You are honorable, you are considerate, you are patient and determined. You are... I like your voice. When all I knew of you was the strutting earl, I did not care for your company. Now I know the man who keeps the fire built up, who insists on escorting me, who makes sure I eat and refuses to let me toil until all hours. You gave me a rose."

He studied the floor, a complicated parquet of blond oak. "Nobody gives you roses?"

"Nobody gives me roses, violets, or even daisies. Nobody fixes my tea just how I like it. Nobody demands that I put my books aside to take a pleasant stroll in the early evening sunshine. Nobody listens to me spout off about the lesser-used Latin cases."

"You are passionate about the vocative."

Also the locative, which everybody forgot. "I like you, my lord. I like you."

Happy surprise accompanied Philomena's words, because they were utterly true. The last, grumpy, lonely part of her still didn't entirely trust Ramsdale—he'd had years to hunt for the Duke, so why take on that challenge now?—but she did like him.

And his kisses.

"HE'S NO LONGER interested in offering for me." Lady Maude sounded about eight years old, while her papa felt closer to eighty-seven. Late nights arguing politics took a toll, and young people these days were given to needless drama.

"Ramsdale will certainly not offer for you if your mouth becomes set in that unattractive pout, my dear. He's been back in Town but a fortnight, and he was most attentive to you when he took a meal with us."

"I am a marquess's daughter," Maude said, opening the cover over the pianoforte's keys. "He can't think to do better."

Amesbury set aside his morning newspaper, for he'd get no reading done once Maude started on her finger exercises.

"Don't put on airs, my dear. Ramsdale could well marry the daughter or sister of a duke. The earl has ever been close to the Duke of Lavelle, for example." Ramsdale and Lavelle had met under Phineas Peebles's roof, of all places.

Maude placed a sheaf of music on the rack, though after all these years of diligent study, she ought to have every drill and scale memorized.

"Lavelle's sister is married. Why must men be so fickle, Papa? Ramsdale showed me marked attention last Season. Everybody said so. Then he disappears to Berkshire, and it's as if he forgot all about me."

In all likelihood, given the blandishments available in the countryside, he had. A man of Ramsdale's robust nature didn't hare off to Berkshire to watch birds.

"If it's any comfort, Ramsdale could barely give me his attention for the duration of a single chess game. Once you left us, he was incapable of focusing."

Or he'd been bored.

"I adore a rousing game of chess."

Rousing game of chess was an oxymoron, even with Ramsdale, who enjoyed deep stratagems and wily ploys. A pity the earl wasn't much inclined toward politics.

"One of your many fine accomplishments," Amesbury said, wishing for the thousandth time his marchioness had not abandoned him for the celestial realm. Her ladyship would have known what to *do* with Maude, who seemed one Season away from becoming shrewish and demanding.

And the poor lady was barely twenty years old.

"A countess must be accomplished," Maude said, beginning on an infernally gloomy minor scale at an interval of a sixth. This was one of her favorite exercises, one she could execute in every key.

"My dear, might you start off with a graceful air? I'll repair to the library, and the happy strains of your pianoforte will lighten my mood as I deal with the day's correspondence."

Amesbury started for the parlor door, while Maude brought her scale to a close in the bass register.

"Papa, I can't lose Ramsdale. He's not charming, he's not friendly, he barely makes conversation when he stands up with a lady, but he's an earl and well-to-do."

"So you've mentioned." Several dozen times a day for the past six months.

"He also singled me out last Season. I can't allow him to go strutting on his way, or I shall become an object of pity. You must make him offer for me."

Never had a stack of correspondence beckoned with such a sense of succor. "His lordship won't be marrying me, Maude Hermione. He'll propose to you. If you've set your cap for him, then you must be the one to inspire his addresses. He said he'd invite us to dinner when he was settled here in Town, but nothing is stopping you from enjoying the carriage parade at the fashionable hour or enjoying a quiet hack first thing in the day."

Ramsdale would never subject himself to the carriage parade. Maude would never leave her bed in time to ride at dawn.

"Everybody takes the air in the park," she said, embarking on the same lugubrious scale at an interval of a tenth. "I must be more bold."

"No, you must not. In my day, if a couple was thought to suit, their mamas would have a friendly chat, their papas would nod agreeably, and the young fellow and the lady would be given a few opportunities to get to know each other. Nobody grew desperate, nobody engaged in unseemly fits of pique. If Ramsdale senses that you have become so lost to dignity as to pursue him, then I assure you, he'll decamp for the shires without a glance in your direction."

Amesbury wanted to decamp for the shires, and Maude was his only begotten daughter.

She increased the tempo of her scales, and her fingers stumbled. "Mama was eighteen when she married you. I'm twenty, Papa. Twenty years old, and everybody knows it. Marilee Newcomb is plain, common, and only modestly dowered, and she's engaged to a marquess."

Maude's litany of indignities could go on for hours.

"The press of business does not allow me to discuss this topic at greater length, my dear, but lamenting and comparing gain you nothing. If you are interested in Ramsdale, then you must be where he will notice you in a favorable light. Show off your new bonnet, show off your French. He's known to be a fine amateur linguist, and I'll warrant Marilee Nobody can barely wish her marquess good day in any language but English."

Maude always had a new bonnet, also new shoes, new reticules, new gloves. She was nothing if not well attired.

"That's it," she said, leaving off in the middle of a scale. "My French. I'm quite clever at it. All of my tutors said so. Tomorrow, I'll pay a call on Lady Melissa, and we'll chatter away in French until Ramsdale is quite besotted. Thank you, Papa. It's a fine strategy, and when next we dine at the earl's home, he'll be smitten."

That was no sort of strategy at all. Ramsdale wasn't even likely to be home, much less at his sister's elbow when she entertained callers.

"Very clever, my dear. I'm off to tend to my parliamentary business. A keyboard serenade wouldn't go amiss, if you're in the mood to indulge me."

Maude set aside the book of finger exercises and laid her hands on the keyboard. A sinking sensation accompanied the pretty picture she made, for if she wasn't using music, that meant Amesbury was about to endure one of her party pieces.

He withdrew, leaving the door open, because Maude would notice if he closed it. As he sat down to work at his desk across the corridor, strains of some sonata or other reverberated through the house, the tempo too fast, the dynamic too loud.

As usual.

NOBODY GAVE PHILOMENA Peebles roses—or violets or daisies. This struck Ramsdale as a great wrong, beyond an injustice. Of all ladies, a woman whose imagination dwelled in ancient Rome, while her nose was in a book and her person stuck behind walls of treatises and tomes, deserved posies.

He held out a hand. "Come with me, Miss Peebles."

She crossed her arms. "I have work to do."

He dropped his hand. "And if you are to do that work efficiently, you must rest your eyes and your mind, take sustenance, and permit an occasional change of scene."

Her gaze went to the desk, where the dratted sixth codicil lay in its crabbed, arcane glory. Hephaestus was waxing dire about Sodom and Solomon, admonishing his nephew at length about abuses of titled power, as best Ramsdale could figure.

Or possibly, Uncle had been going on about the House of Lords. For the first time in days, Ramsdale didn't care.

"Miss Peebles, that will isn't going anywhere. You will work more efficiently for allowing me to divert your attention to a different topic."

She studied her hands, the right one bearing various ink stains. "You might try asking."

Ah. *Of course.* "May I show you something?"

"Yes, you may." The mischief in her eyes transformed a modestly pretty woman into a siren. Ramsdale's imagination galloped off in unruly—*unclothed*—directions while he held open the library door.

"Where are we going, my lord?"

"Up to my office," he said. "I keep some references there rather than here in the library, this being a public room."

"Latin references? Histories?"

He accompanied her up the stairs, pausing only to ask a footman to have luncheon served on the back terrace.

"I work up here," Ramsdale said, ushering her into his private office. "Meet with my factors, tend to correspondence, and hide from my sister. She would no more disturb me here than I'd intrude on her sitting room."

Miss Peebles stood peering about near the doorway. The library was on the ground floor, the windows looking out on the street. Propriety was skirted when Ramsdale was alone with an unmarried woman there, particularly with Melissa in the house and the library door open.

Or mostly open.

The office, by contrast, was private and much smaller. When Ramsdale had invited—ordered, asked—Miss Peebles to join him here, he hadn't considered what the chamber said about him or how intimate the closer quarters might feel.

"You are tidy," Miss Peebles said, "and you like to have beauty around you."

Landscapes rather than portraits, a few roses in a Venetian glass vase. "Yes."

"And you are attached to your comforts."

Worn slippers sat by the reading chair near the hearth. An afghan had been folded over the hassock, and Uncle's youngest cat, an enormous gray specimen named Genesis—the only tangible bequest from uncle to nephew—lay curled atop the afghan, his chin on his paws.

"I'm not half so attached to my comforts as that dratted feline is."

"Oh, isn't he splendid?" Miss Peebles advanced into the room and knelt by the hassock. "Such a handsome fellow and so soft."

Genesis began to rumble—he claimed nothing so refined as a purr—and Miss Peebles stroked his head and back as if she'd never before had such a privilege.

Genesis squinted at Ramsdale. *This lady can visit any time.*

"I'd give him to you," Ramsdale said, "except he'll eat you out of house and hanging hams without catching a single mouse. Genesis enjoys a contemplative existence."

Miss Peebles cuddled the cat against her chest. "You'd give away such a fine, handsome beast? You'll hurt his feelings with such jests."

Genesis rubbed his cheek along Miss Peebles's décolletage, then squinted at Ramsdale again.

Some expressions needed no translation, not even between species.

"By virtue of Uncle's final arrangements, Genesis and I are stuck with each other. If you can tear yourself away from his abundant charms, there's a book I'd like to show you."

She carried the cat with her to stand beside Ramsdale as he took a volume bound in red leather down from the shelves.

"You are in want of flowers," he said. "This is an herbal of sorts, published by Professor Axel Belmont. The illustrations are exquisite because the professor's discourse is on the medicinal use of common ornamentals."

Miss Peebles set the cat on Ramsdale's desk and took the book. "He dedicated it to his wife. How lovely." She leafed through the pages, and lovely became a woman standing in Ramsdale's office, her bodice adorned with gray cat hairs, a pencil sticking out of her chignon.

"If the book appeals to you, I want you to have it." *I want you to have me.*

That thought was like the solution to a chess riddle. Ramsdale had spent the past few days pondering, considering, cogitating—and lusting—when he ought to have been attending to Miss Peebles's translations of various codicils.

He desired her. That sentiment—those sensations—had been easily categorized. He wanted to join his body to hers and bring her pleasure as no ancient poem or elegant translation could. He wanted to make her burn and laugh and forget every word of every language she'd ever learned save pure physical expression.

He'd desired other women. She'd probably desired other men. Nothing profound there, though the attraction he felt for Miss Peebles bordered on the ungovernable.

Desire, however, wasn't the entire definition of Ramsdale's feelings where Miss Peebles was concerned, and thus he'd devoted his attention to that riddle while she'd devoted her attention to Uncle's will.

What, exactly, did he feel for her?

She looked up from the book. "You are giving me this herbal? The illustrations belong in an art collection."

"Nobody gives you flowers," Ramsdale said. "These are flowers that will never fade, with descriptions that include the Latin names as well as the practical uses of each blossom. The book suits you."

She clutched it to her chest. "Because I am practical?"

He took the herbal from her and set it on the desk. "Because you have an attractiveness that will not fade, a luminous spirit that's as much passion as intellect, as much of the soul as the body, and I must kiss you in the next instant, or I will descend into bad verse and maudlin quotations."

He did not kiss her, but rather, waited for her verdict.

Desire could be as impersonal as it was intimate. A randy fellow sought a willing wench, a lusty wench sought a willing fellow. Beyond a few details of physical preference, the particular party on the other side of the bed in such an encounter didn't matter. Fondness might play a role, but attachment need not.

Ramsdale wanted Philomena Peebles to desire *him*—not the earl, not a willing, randy fellow—but Seton Avery, a man better than some, by no means a saint, who very specifically valued her. He wanted her respect, not simply her desire. He wanted her to enjoy his company, of all the daft notions, to look forward to being with him as he looked forward to being with her.

In some language or other, these inclinations of the heart likely had a name, probably among the incurable ailments and afflictions.

"You look so serious," she said, smoothing an ink-stained finger between his brows. "And so kissable."

She pressed her lips to his, gently, as if he needed coaxing, and yet, she was right. This kiss was different—premeditated, prefaced with what amounted to a declaration, for him—and a headlong descent into passion wasn't all that he needed from her.

Ramsdale took Philomena in his arms and rejoiced.

And then he kissed her back.

Chapter Six

"WHERE ARE YOU off to?" Jane asked.

"Knightsbridge," the professor replied. "I don't suppose you'd like to come with me?" He posed the question casually, without much hope of an affirmative response. Jane was a pragmatic soul, and toddling about London hardly amounted to a productive use of her time.

Jane straightened the folds of his cravat, which were forever getting wrinkled into the creases of his jacket and waistcoat.

She took down a bonnet from the hooks beside the porter's nook. "Hold still."

Next, she extracted a nacre hatpin from the bonnet, repositioned the trailing ends of Phineas's cravat—he could never tie the damned things correctly—and used her hatpin to put his linen in order.

"Thank you."

She remained where she was, a woman no longer young for all she was still handsome and had a fine figure. Phineas wasn't young either, and he hoped Jane regarded that as a point in his favor.

"One doesn't want to presume on Dora's memory," she said. "But I can't have you going out in public looking half dressed."

"Mrs. Peebles left me to dress myself," Phineas said. His late wife had left him very much to his own devices, particularly after Philomena had arrived. Theirs had been a mésalliance, an act of rebellion on Dora's part, a fit of lunacy on his.

He'd not been able to keep her in the style she deserved, and she'd not been able to hide her disappointment.

"What is your errand in Knightsbridge?" Jane asked.

"I was not satisfied with my interrogation of the Eagan brothers. They professed to have no knowledge of the *Liber Ducis de Scientia*. I had occasion to press Mr. Handley for details regarding his confreres, the Eagans, and he reiterated his tale of old manuscripts and secret potions."

Jane passed Phineas his hat, which he'd been known to leave the house without. "You think a pair of scheming shopkeepers have found a manuscript that has eluded your lifelong search?"

"I don't know what to think. Why would they come up with this notion now, Jane? Why, when my retirement is imminent, should anybody profess to have found even a single page of the document?"

Jane tied her bonnet ribbons in a soft bow. "My cloak, if you please."

Phineas obliged by draping her cloak over her shoulders, though he would not have assumed such familiarity was welcome. Jane was a grown woman, capable of asking for assistance when she needed same. She turned and raised her chin, as if Phineas was to...

He fastened the frogs of her cloak and, for a moment was distracted trying to recall a Latin word for the color of Jane's eyes. Periwinkle-ish with a hint of gentian was as close as he could come in English.

"Your gloves," Jane said, passing Phineas a clean pair. "We can cut through the park and enjoy some greenery while we're out, but when we get there, you let me talk to these shopkeepers, Phineas. You'll lecture them straight into the arms of Morpheus."

Jane took Phineas by the arm and led him into the bright midday sunshine. He'd not invited her to walk out with him in all the years they'd shared a household, which was remiss of him.

The birds sang more sweetly, the breeze blew more benevolently, and the city was more cheerful with Jane by his side. Why was it he never appreciated the women in his life until it was too late?

PHILOMENA HAD SPENT too many hours—too many days—shut up in the confines of Hephaestus's will. Her mind buzzed with secondary meanings and literary allusions, while her head ached.

But her heart... her heart was caught up in the possibility of actually finding the Duke or at least a portion of that great manuscript. Reading through the will's cramped, complicated writing, she had a sense of negotiating a briar patch. If only she were careful, if only she paid relentless attention to every detail, she'd find the ripe fruit of a clue, a hint, a solution to the mystery the Duke had posed for ages.

And every morning, when she arrived to Ramsdale's library, another sort of fruit awaited her—a bright gold sovereign, reverse side up on the desk blotter, so that even her remuneration included a few words of translation.

Honi soit qui mal y pense. Shame upon him who sees wrong in it...

Philomena saw no wrong in parting Ramsdale from his coin, just the opposite. She gloried in knowing that her years of study were worth bright, shiny coins, that her skills were not only admirable but *valuable.*

She loved the idea that she need not entirely rely on her aging father for security. The possibilities were heady, a whole new dictionary's worth of meanings and opportunity.

Why shouldn't a woman's mind merit the same respect as a man's?

Why shouldn't a woman find the Duke?

Why shouldn't a woman kiss whom she pleased to kiss, rather than waiting for the fellow to take the notion to kiss her?

So in the privacy of Ramsdale's office, she kissed him the way she'd longed to, slowly, savoringly. As she had rendered Hephaestus's ramblings into coherent English, Ramsdale's steady regard had been working a similar transformation of *her*, from bluestocking spinster daughter to a woman of highly trained abilities, a lady both admirable and desirable.

And she desired him.

Ramsdale was sentimental about a cat. His mind was drawn to beautiful landscapes, the movements of the heavenly bodies, and Latin poetry.

His body *was* poetry. His arms stole about her, and Philomena relaxed into an embrace both secure and cherishing. She could shelter in his strength and glory in her own. Ramsdale was far above her touch, he was not above her passion.

Philomena pressed nearer and realized that Ramsdale was growing aroused.

"We should stop," he whispered, the words tickling her neck.

She put her lips to his ear. "We should lock the door."

Ramsdale drew back to rest his forehead against Philomena's. "If we lock that door, what follows will have consequences, Philomena. Serious consequences, and I do not take that step lightly."

He was so wrong, so innocent of Philomena's reality. If Professor Peebles's plain spinster daughter stole an interlude with a wealthy earl, nobody would know, nobody would care. Philomena was not like her cousin, one of polite society's pampered darlings, raised in a gilded cage of manners, gossip, and pretty frocks.

And Philomena would never again be simply a plain spinster daughter.

"I would take that step with you." Philomena had never been tempted by passion before, never had more than an idle curiosity about erotic intimacy. She would trade everything—trade even the Duke—for this chance to become Ramsdale's lover.

Ramsdale looped his arms around her shoulders and kissed her forehead. "So be it."

He remained entwined with her for a lovely moment, then he put the cat out and locked the door. The cat's expression had been indignant, while Ramsdale's smile was lovely—intimate and naughty, a lover's smile.

And Philomena smiled right back.

SO BE IT.

Ramsdale had plighted his troth, and like everything else about his relationship with Philomena Peebles—soon to be Lady Ramsdale—the proposal had been unconventional and the acceptance more unconventional still.

Perhaps he was his uncle's nephew more than his father's son—or he was both.

"We have options," he said, surveying his office with new eyes. "My desk, for one, upon which I will likely spend the next fifty years tending to correspondence. A memory made with you there would shine through that entire half century."

Philomena looked at him as if he'd spoken in the lost Etruscan tongue.

Not the desk, then. "Perhaps the reading chair," he said, "which—given your literary interests—has a certain appropriateness."

"The chair seats only one, my lord."

My lord was not good, though Ramsdale would soon show her how that chair could accommodate two very agreeably.

"The sofa is a bit worn, but I've dreamed many a dream there nonetheless." Perhaps they'd conceive their firstborn on that sofa, in which case, the battered old thing would become an heirloom.

"I bow to your choice in this," Philomena said, "and I would like to bow to it *soon*."

Her gaze drifted over his face, his shoulders, down, down, down, and then back up. He thought she might have lingered particularly on his hands, which were at his sides, or possibly...

"We'll improvise," he said, the notion striking him as appropriate for the couple they were about to become. He was not the typical earl, and she'd be a magnificently different countess.

He spread the afghan from the reading chair over the rug before the hearth and followed with the pair of quilts from the sofa. Next, he sent several pillows sailing to the makeshift nest on the carpet, while Philomena's expression became bemused.

"The floor?" she said.

"I'm told the chair seats only one. On the floor, we'll be comfortable with room to spread out. The carpets in this house are kept spotless, and I promise I'll do all the work."

"If there's work involved, we'll share it. Does one undress?"

She was *adorable*. "Two do, unless you'd rather not."

Philomena advanced on him as if he'd threatened to steal her favorite Latin dictionary. "If we're to be lovers, then I want to be *lovers*, Ramsdale. Deal with me as you would any other woman to whom you've taken a fancy. I'm not a schoolgirl, and I intend to be very demanding."

Which, of course, made her blush, stare at her hands, and settle herself on the hassock more regally than a queen.

Ramsdale wanted to assure her that this was no mere fancy. Instead, he stowed the pretty words and knelt at her feet.

"Boots off," he said, gesturing toward her hems.

Philomena inched her hems up to just above her ankle. "They're worn. Practical. Not elegant."

Her self-consciousness might have a little to do with her boots, which were indeed far from new, but Ramsdale knew what she wasn't saying.

He'd trysted with any number of perfumed and proper ladies who would allow him to roger them witless for the space of a quadrille, but who'd be horrified at the thought of him seeing them in a pair of old boots. In unlit parlors, such a lady would lift her skirts and pant in his ear like a winded hound, but heaven forbid that a cat hair should touch her bodice.

Ramsdale pitied those women, and he spared a bit of pity for himself, rutting and panting right along with them, then stuffing himself back into his satin knee breeches in time for the supper waltz.

What an ass he'd been. "My field boots are the most comfortable footwear I own," he said, undoing Philomena's shoelaces. "I'd wear them everywhere, except that would cause a scandal."

She brushed his hair back from his brow, and he knew why Genesis purred.

Ramsdale drew off her boots and set them aside, then reached under her skirts to untie her garters.

Philomena surprised him by drawing her skirts up to her knees—but then, he suspected she'd frequently surprise him. Still, he denied himself more than a glance. The feel of her ankles and calves clad in nothing but silk…

"Are you always so…?" She fell silent as Ramsdale undid the left garter.

"Behold, my lady is already at a loss for words. My confidence swells apace." His confidence—among other noteworthy articles.

He drew off her stockings and tossed them in the direction of her boots. To unhook her dress and unlace her stays, he moved to the reading chair.

The pencil protruded from her chignon, and Ramsdale knew himself to be a man in love. He silently slid the pencil free and tossed it to the desk—a memento to be treasured in years to come.

Philomena's nape required some kisses, as did the soft flesh where her neck and shoulder joined. Ramsdale rose from the chair, the better to indulge himself, and she turned, pressing her cheek to his thigh.

"I'm in a hurry," she said.

Ramsdale stroked her hair, which he'd soon free from its pins. "Afraid you'll lose your nerve? You'll have nothing but pleasure from me, Philomena, as much pleasure as I can give you."

She peered up at him, as inscrutable as the cat. "And if you lose your nerve?"

His falls were about to lose their buttons. Ramsdale pushed aside that pleasant urgency to consider her question, because Philomena's queries mattered.

They would always matter.

He knelt before her, so they were face-to-face. "If you shout erotic Latin poetry when at your pleasures, I will answer in Middle French. When you publish your first treatise on alternative translations of the Magna Carta, I will buy a hundred copies to donate to universities the world over. Your brilliance doesn't intimidate me, your sense of focus sparks only my admiration. If your father's colleagues or students feel threatened by your capabilities, that's a reflection on their petty conceits, not on you. I can't wait to play chess with you."

He'd given her plain truths, and he'd upset her, for Philomena—who could glower at the same curmudgeonly document for hours—wiped a tear from her cheek.

"I like chess," she said.

Ramsdale enfolded her gently, cursing Peebles for a dunderhead, cursing all the learned men whose cowardice and bigotry had tried to crush a bright spirit. The lot of them were purely frightened of her, and someday, she'd see that.

"If you get me out of these clothes," he said, "we can play chess naked."

Philomena started on his cravat, and even that—a mundane, almost impersonal assistance—fueled his arousal. His sleeve buttons and watch went next, and from there, matters accelerated, until Philomena stood in her shift and Ramsdale in his breeches, their clothing strewn over the sofa in a merry heap.

"Now what?" She ran a hand over his bare shoulder. "You are quite fit."

He captured her hand in his own. "To the blankets."

She sat and drew her knees up, and Ramsdale came down beside her. He'd locked the door perhaps ten minutes ago, but they'd been a long and self-disciplined ten minutes. In fifteen seconds flat, he had Philomena on her back amid the blankets and himself arranged over her.

When they had their clothes back on, and he could again form a coherent sentence, he'd offer her a proper proposal—bended knee, pretty words, the promise of a ring.

Now, the time had come to make love with his intended.

PHINEAS WAS A surprisingly companionable escort, once Jane got him away from his treatises and tomes. He set a sauntering pace through Hyde Park, which was reaching its full summer glory, and he'd spared Jane any exhortations regarding his infernal Duke.

Jane hated that Duke, which was very bad of her. "Does any part of you look forward to retirement, Phineas?"

He tipped his hat to a pair of schoolgirls out with their governess. "Yes and no. Being able to settle here in Town, rather than haring up to Oxford or Cambridge, will be welcome. The best collections are here. Many of my colleagues are here."

"But?"

They came to a divergence of the footpath, which ran parallel to Park Lane, though beneath the towering maples of the park itself.

"But Lord Amesbury is here."

"What has his lordship to do with…?"

Phineas had spoken literally. Amesbury was driving a high-perch phaeton down the nearest carriageway, his daughter at his side. His lordship either did not see or chose not to acknowledge his brother-in-law.

Lady Maude was chattering at a great rate, exuding the forced gaiety of a young woman who had only her papa to drive out with.

"Every time," Phineas said quietly, "I see that strutting dunderwhelp with his pretty little barmy-froth of a daughter, I grow angry. The marquess might have done something for Philomena, might have eased her way. Now she's to be a spinster, no household of her own, no children. All of the scholars and lecturers I've paraded before her haven't gained her notice, nor she theirs. Amesbury hasn't lifted so much as a gloved finger."

The words vibrated with indignation, also with veiled bewilderment.

"You have written countless letters of recommendation for your former students," Jane said. "You've invited younger professors to serve as guest lecturers. You will read a draft treatise for any colleague. Your nature is kind and generous. Amesbury wasn't given your charitable spirit or your intellect. I suspect he's been waiting for you to ask for his help, Phin."

The phaeton disappeared around a bend in the path.

"Waiting for me to *ask*? Waiting for me to ask Philomena's only titled, wealthy relation to toss her a crumb of recognition? To invite her to a family gathering at the holidays? A house party or a musicale?"

Jane drew him gently along the walkway. "Does Philomena have a wardrobe that would allow her to attend those entertainments in style, or would she be shamed by comparison to her cousin?"

"Philomena has frocks."

"So does that nursemaid," Jane said, nodding in the direction of a young woman in brown twill leading a small boy by the hand. "If you don't know the state of Philomena's wardrobe, how can her uncle know? If she was asked to play a tune on the pianoforte, could she oblige without stumbling over the keys when earls and baronets were in the room rather than schoolboys and scholars?"

Phineas remained silent as they crossed from the park into Kensington. That he was annoyed on his daughter's behalf was a pleasant surprise. That he hadn't done anything to address the problem was to be expected. Amesbury was a marquess, and his neglect of his niece shameful.

"The Eagan Brothers' Emporium makes a good impression," Phineas said as they approached a sparkling shop window. Dried bouquets, groupings of patent remedies in colorful bottles, and artfully displayed herbals and sachets all enticed passersby to drop in.

"And what on earth are they advertising?" Jane asked.

For in the middle of the window sat a placard lettered in an extravagant hand: Secrets of the Ages! Your Heart's Desire, from the Long Lost Duke's Book of Science! Found by Wisdom's Handmaiden Right Here in London!"

"The flat-catching, bat-fowling scandaroons," Phineas spluttered. "They lied to me!"

"They're lying to every customer they can fleece," Jane replied. "But if we're to learn anything beyond the obvious about their swindling, then you will wait right here until I come back."

Before Phineas could gainsay her, she marched up to the shop and swept through the door.

THE TIME HAD come for Philomena to take her first lover—very likely her only lover, ever, for Ramsdale engaged not only her curiosity and her desire, but also her esteem. He'd said he did not embark on this interlude lightly, and neither did Philomena.

However much regard Ramsdale brought to this lovemaking, Philomena brought more.

Nonetheless, she had no applicable experience.

"Do we resume kissing?" she asked. "Or is there something more?"

Ramsdale was braced above her, the sight of him shirtless making her itch to touch his arms and chest.

"There's more of whatever brings you pleasure, Philomena."

Certainly, there was more of *him*. He'd fit himself against the juncture of her thighs, and his weight felt good—and frustrating.

"When will you remove your breeches?"

Ramsdale closed his eyes, as if taking a moment for prayer. "Would you like me to tend to that detail now?"

Getting him naked was not a detail. "Yes."

His weight was gone, and then his breeches were sailing across the office to join the pile of clothing on the sofa. He stood over Philomena, a dark version of the aroused masculine ideal viewed from an interesting perspective.

"Boni di."

"You resort to Latin," he said, resuming his crouch over her. "Was that a happy 'good gods,' or a dismayed—?"

Philomena lashed her arms and legs around him, wanting to envelop him bodily. She hushed his prattling with an openmouthed kiss, because the sight of him—fit, strong, and aroused—sent a wild boldness singing through her.

She—boring bluestocking, entirely unremarkable—was to have a lover, and *such* a lover.

Ramsdale laughed against her mouth and tried to hold himself away, but Philomena had locked her ankles at the small of his back, so he took her with him.

"Now, Ramsdale," she said. "Immediately. You promised me pleasure, and I'm holding you to your word."

"This instant? Where is the woman who will spend an hour noting every possible meaning for an obscure term? The woman who becomes so absorbed in the possibilities of the genitive case that she forgets to eat?"

"She's here, and she's absorbed with you."

Ramsdale hitched delectably close—why did that feel so lovely?—then brushed Philomena's hair back from her brow. "This is too important to rush. Please trust me, Philomena."

Trust him. He was in complete earnest, almost grave, when he'd been laughing a moment ago.

And he was right. This moment was important, not in the sense of ridding Philomena of virginal ignorance, though she was happy to be free of it, but in the sense that the experience should be savored, and Ramsdale knew better than she how to go about that.

"In this, I trust you."

He shifted so he was more over her, all around her, a blanket of warmth and wonder. As he pressed soft kisses to her lips, brow, and throat, she closed her eyes and explored him with her hands.

She learned textures—smooth, bristly, crinkly, velvety, silky—and tastes. A touch of salt, a hint of lavender. His palms where callused—Ramsdale was a noted equestrian—and his hair was thick and soft.

And she learned a new vocabulary. Ramsdale let her know that he liked her fingertips gliding over the slope of his back, liked her teeth scraping his earlobe. He sighed, he growled, he laughed, and when she glossed her hand down his belly, he drew in a swift breath, but made no move to deter her.

So she learned him, *there,* where he was most masculine and most vulnerable.

He bore her exploration silently, his head bowed, his mouth open against her shoulder, until Philomena positioned him against her sex.

"There's more," she said. "I know there's more you would show me, but Ramsdale, I cannot be patient. Not in this. Not any longer."

He shifted to meet her gaze. "My name"—he pushed forward the first inch, and the union was begun—"is Seton."

Seton. My Seton. My lover Seton.

Philomena might have made up a whole glossary of singular possessive endearments, but sensations crowded her intellect into silence. The intimacy was strange and new, the pleasure complicated. To join this way was an exquisite relief. Ramsdale somehow knew the tempo, the touches, the *everything* to satisfy her bodily cravings.

When to slow down and kiss.

When to gather her close and sink deep.

When to go still for a moment, so Philomena could revel in the intimacy and swallow past the lump in her throat.

And then he turned his attention to her breasts, and simmering desire became a wildfire of need. His hands were diabolical, until Philomena began cursing in a low, steady stream of French—modern French, which was all she could manage.

He answered in the same language. "Hold on to me, Philomena. Stay with me."

To hear that silky, sinuous tongue rendered in Ramsdale's night-sky voice destroyed the last filament anchoring Philomena to reason. She became pleasure, an incandescent spirit where a quiet, bookish woman used to be.

The physical experience was beyond words and ebbed barely short of too much. Philomena sensed Ramsdale's consideration in that intimate mercy, for the emotions flowed on unchecked even as he withdrew and spent on her belly.

Joy and tenderness swamped her, as did an inexorable undertow of sadness. She would have these moments with Ramsdale, but that's all she could have—moments.

Precious, wild, unimaginably intimate moments. The inspiration for poetry that endured for millennia, but still, for her there could be only moments. She could give Ramsdale her whole heart, and likely already had. She could love him without limit, but eventually—he was a peer, he needed legitimate heirs—she would have to let him go.

"I can feel that great, elegant brain of yours pulling you back to the damned library," Ramsdale growled. "I account myself proud that for all of twenty minutes, I could tempt you away from your quest."

Twenty minutes that would change the rest of Philomena's life, and she was not sorry.

She ruffled his hair. "Our quest. I feel as if an idea lurks in the shadows of those codicils, an insight that refuses to come into the light."

He rested his cheek against her temple. "A pattern that won't emerge. I know what you mean. Hephaestus is laughing at us. Don't move."

He was on his feet and rifling the pile of clothing in the next instant. Philomena lay on her back amid pillows and blankets, her shift undone and bunched beneath her ribs.

"What a glorious picture you make," he said, using a handkerchief to swab at himself. He was matter-of-fact about the whole shockingly personal business, handling his own flesh with brisk familiarity.

While Philomena felt as if she'd been reborn in another woman's skin. *I know so many languages and so little that matters.*

Without putting on so much as a shirt, Ramsdale knelt beside her and used the handkerchief on her belly, then tugged the shift down over her thighs and gave her a pat between her legs.

"Lest the sight of you tempt me to excesses my conscience forbids. Take a soaking bath when you get home tonight, please. I was not as restrained as I'd hoped to be. Next time…"

His gaze traveled over her, and a world of passionate possibilities blossomed in the silence. Philomena stretched up and kissed him.

He kissed her back, gently cupping her right breast, and a few of those possibilities crept nearer.

A soft scraping sound at the door intruded.

"I will make the damned beast into a pair of gloves," Ramsdale said, going to the door and opening it an entire six inches.

Genesis strolled in, tail held high, nose wrinkling.

"'A righteous man regardeth the life of his beast,'" Philomena quoted, "'but the tender mercies of the wicked are cruel.' I doubt Proverbs contemplated such a creature as Genesis."

Ramsdale pulled a shirt over his head as the cat stropped itself against his bare legs. They'd clearly done this often—the man donning clothing with the cat in casual attendance—and Philomena was jealous of that cat.

"I'm sure my breeches are somewhere…"

Philomena rose and passed Ramsdale his breeches. "Why did Hephaestus name his cat Genesis?"

Ramsdale took the breeches, shook them once, and stepped into them. "Because that cat is the originator of all mischief, perhaps? Perhaps he's the runt of a litter of seven, all of whom were named in alphabetical order. I don't suppose you could locate—"

She passed him his waistcoat, and with each piece of clothing, Philomena yielded a little more to the pull of the library. Her heart wanted to linger here, where she and Ramsdale had become lovers. Her mind sought the safety of the linguistic challenge Hephaestus had bequeathed her, because she needed a refuge from her emotions.

"Your hair," Ramsdale said when the pillows and blankets were all put to rights and he was dressed but for his coat. "Your coiffure has been disarranged."

Philomena looked over at him between lacing up her left boot and the right. "By the wind, perhaps?"

Ramsdale slung his cravat about his neck and blew her a kiss. "By a mighty tempest."

Hephaestus had prosed on in several places about tempests. *With the flame of a devouring fire, with scattering, and tempest, and hailstones,* was his favorite quote.

"Was Hephaestus particularly religious?" Philomena asked as she tied Ramsdale's cravat.

"Hardly. Uncle had contempt for what he called the pious hypocrites of proper society. I want you again already, Philomena. I thought if we indulged our passions, I might have a prayer of—"

She kissed him and ran her fingers through his hair, which the tempest had also left sticking up on one side. "We have work to do, your lordship. Why so many biblical references from a man who disdained religion?"

Ramsdale caught her hand and kissed her palm. "Am I already back to being a lordship, Philomena?"

That one small kiss caused inconvenient, lovely stirrings. "When we leave this office, you will most definitely be a lordship, and I will be a Miss Peebles, sir. On that topic, I will brook no discussion."

He kept hold of her hand, leaned back against the desk, and drew Philomena between his legs.

"'She is more precious than rubies,'" he said, kissing her knuckles this time, "'and all the things thou canst desire are not to be compared unto her.'"

Some of the most beautiful words in the Bible, and Ramsdale looked like he was about to offer her more lovely quotes.

Philomena wanted to hear them, but *later*, because her imagination chose then to leap upon a potential connection.

"That's *it*," Philomena said. "The biblical allusions. Hephaestus uses them frequently, more than any other reference, almost to the exclusion of any other reference. For a learned man to limit himself to a single source of literary comparisons makes no sense."

"Philomena, might we discuss dear Uncle and his daft—?"

"Come along, Ramsdale. We must list every biblical reference in the will, because if I'm right, this could be a clue to the Duke's whereabouts."

The cat resumed his place on the hassock, and Ramsdale pushed away from the desk. "To the library, then, but let me see to your hair first."

Her—Philomena put a hand to her head—*hair*. Her thoroughly mussed hair. "Of course. I'm as bad as my father."

A gallant lover would have argued with her. Ramsdale smiled, tidied up her braid, and escorted her to the library.

Chapter Seven

THREE DAYS REMAINED until Peebles's retirement banquet, and little remained of Ramsdale's sanity.

Philomena had hastened through the remaining codicils for the sole purpose of listing biblical quotes or allusions, while Ramsdale had done his paltry best to aid her. The family Bible—an enormous tome of ancient pedigree—probably hadn't seen this much consultation in all its decades of gathering dust.

Nor had the library been the scene of so many kisses.

Only kisses, alas. Ramsdale had ordered a ring for his intended, though he'd yet to settle on an inscription.

The front door banged and Genesis, who'd taken to supervising his owner, was startled from his napping place to the left of the desk blotter.

"My sister is apparently going out," Ramsdale said. Meaning the person most likely to intrude had considerately left the premises.

Philomena sat at the desk, petting the cat and staring out the window. She stared out the window often, and looked lovely doing it too.

"Her ladyship isn't off to pay calls," she said. "She must have a visitor. A coach and four have pulled up out front, very fine. Matched grays in harness."

Ramsdale went to the window, which had been cracked to let in the fresh air. Amesbury's crest adorned the coach door, though Philomena likely hadn't noticed that. She went back to scrawling quotations from the will, intent as ever on finding any trace of her Duke.

Ramsdale had found his countess and wished the dratted Duke were not still such a matter of urgency for her.

"If Melissa is entertaining, I'd best put in an appearance," he said, because he was nothing if not a dutiful brother. "Will you manage without me?"

Philomena waved a hand, not even looking up. "There's a pattern here, Ramsdale. I know there's a pattern. I can feel it."

The pattern was he longed to visit the office with her again, and she longed to find the Duke. Gentlemanly scruples weighed in favor of offering the lady a formal proposal—or at least chatting up the professor—before another such interlude.

If Philomena had to choose between spending one of the next seventy-two hours in her intended's bed or pursuing her Duke, he suspected she'd choose the Duke.

Ramsdale paused, his hand on the door latch. "You want to find the *Liber Ducis* for yourself, don't you? Not only for the professor."

The pen stopped moving across the page. Philomena looked up slowly. "Would that be wrong, my lord?"

"You need not my-lord me when we are private." More than her polite address, the caution in her eyes annoyed him.

"Would it be wrong for me to want all my years of study and scholarship to result in accomplishing what my father could not? Would it be wrong for me to claim a small portion of the respect and deference he's been shown his whole life?"

Ramsdale's every instinct told him to answer carefully. Philomena was tired, frustrated, anxious, and facing significant changes to a future she'd thought well settled.

"I understand that ambition, Philomena, but some quests take more time than we can allot them. My regard for you does not depend on your achieving the impossible."

As far as Ramsdale knew, none of his fellow bibliophiles had located so much as a page of the missing manuscript.

She stroked the quill over the cat's nose. "Is that why you neglected to pay me today? Because you don't think we'll find the Duke?"

Her gaze was as inscrutable as the damned cat's, and Ramsdale was abruptly at sea. They were no longer employer and employee. They were a couple all but engaged. But then, a woman raised without wealth was likely incapable of treating money casually, and they were not *quite* engaged.

"An oversight on my part," Ramsdale said. "I'll correct my error tomorrow." He crossed the room to kiss Philomena's cheek, though the gesture was awkward when appended to a discussion of wages.

He left the library for the formal guest parlor. When a marquess came calling, only the formal parlor would do, of course. If Lady Maude had accompanied her dear papa, then Ramsdale was doomed to take a cup of tea.

To his relief, only the marquess graced the pink tufted sofa in Melissa's parlor.

Amesbury rose, a tea cake halfway to his mouth, when Ramsdale made his bow.

"Amesbury, a pleasure, though I'm afraid my schedule does not permit me to linger. I do hope you'll be able to join us for dinner on Wednesday next?"

Almack's held its assemblies on Wednesdays, and Lady Maude would be well motivated not to linger over dinner when she might instead be waltzing. Melissa's slight smile said she knew exactly why Ramsdale had chosen the date.

"Dinner would be lovely," Amesbury said, finishing his tea cake. "Just lovely, though Lady Maude and I will soon be removing to the family seat. Only a fool remains in London during summer's heat, eh?"

A fool or a man intent on avoiding matchmaking papas.

"More tea, my lord?" Melissa asked, sending Ramsdale a you-owe-me glance.

"Until Wednesday," Ramsdale said, sketching a bow and nearly running for the door.

Melissa was a widow, and the occasional gentleman did call upon her, though why Amesbury, who was old enough to be her godfather, would trouble himself to pay a—

"My lord!"

Ramsdale had been halfway down the stairs, rounding the first landing, and thus he hadn't seen Lady Maude coming up the steps—or lurking below the landing. She clung to his arms, her grip painful as she sagged against him.

"You gave me such a fright, sir! My heart's going at a gallop. To think I might have tumbled to my death!"

For pity's sake. "Hardly that. The stairs are carpeted, my lady. I'm sure you'll catch your breath in a moment."

She'd chosen her opportunity well, because this flight of stairs was in view of the front door. Callers came and went all afternoon, and somebody was bound to see her plastered to Ramsdale's chest, panting like a hind.

The first footman remained at his post by the porter's nook, earning himself a raise by keeping his eyes firmly to the front.

"You are uninjured," Ramsdale said, trying to set the lady at a distance on the landing. "We didn't even collide."

Though not for want of trying on her part.

"But I am feeling quite faint," she retorted, refusing to stand on her own two feet. "I vow and declare I might swoon."

A door clicked open below—not the front door, thank the benevolent cherubs—the library door. Philomena emerged and, of course, moved toward the stairs.

She stopped at the foot of the steps, staring at the tableau above her.

Ramsdale knew what she saw: her almost-betrothed with a sweet young thing vining herself around him like a vigorous strain of ivy, and not just any sweet young thing—Philomena's titled, unmarried, younger, wealthy cousin.

RAMSDALE WAS HIS usual attentive escort on the way home, and he made a few attempts at conversation, but Philomena could not oblige him.

How sweetly Lady Maude had nestled against his lordship's chest. How delicately she'd clung to him—and how tenaciously. Ramsdale had grumbled about presuming women and scheming misses, but to Philomena's eye, he hadn't been trying very hard to dislodge Lady Maude from his embrace.

Not very hard at all.

Thank heavens that Lady Maude had not seen Philomena gawking like a chambermaid at the foot of the steps.

"You're very quiet, Philomena," Ramsdale said as they turned down the alley.

"I'm tired, also pondering the Duke. Tomorrow I'll make a list of the objects Hephaestus is referring to when he makes his biblical comparisons."

"Hang the damned Duke. I know what you think you saw, Philomena."

What she *thought* she saw? "We are not private, my lord. I am Miss Peebles to you."

"You will never be Miss Peebles to me again, dammit. We have been gloriously intimate, need I remind you."

The alley was deserted, else Philomena would have delivered his lordship a severe upbraiding for his careless words.

"You need *not* remind me, nor do you need to tell me what I *did* see with my own eyes. A comely, eligible young lady in your embrace in a situation where you and she had every expectation of privacy."

"The footman was at his post in the foyer, and she was not in my embrace."

Philomena stopped walking long enough to spare the earl a cool perusal. Footmen were no source of chaperonage whatsoever. Even she knew that much.

"Then Lady Maude wasn't in your embrace, but you were certainly in hers, and it's of no moment to me in any case. Polite society has its rules, and I grasp them well enough even if they don't apply to me. I'll bid you good evening, my lord."

Philomena had too little experience arguing to make a proper job of it. She never argued with her father, never argued with Jane. She accommodated them and then found some other way to accomplish her ends.

With Ramsdale, that meek course would not do, even if he was an earl.

Even if his uncle's will did hold the key to finding the Duke.

"Philomena, please don't bid me farewell when we're quarreling. Lady Maude ambushed me. I've stood up with her from time to time, and she's gone two Seasons without attaching a suitor. I consider her father a friend and would not avoidably hurt a lady's feelings."

Philomena did not want to have this stupid disagreement. Ramsdale owed her nothing, save for a few coins. He'd made her no promises, and even if he had, she wouldn't have believed them.

"I don't seek an apology, my lord, or an explanation. I'm tired, peckish, and cross. I'll see you tomorrow."

He put a hand on her arm. Just that, and tears threatened.

Philomena wanted to be the only woman nestling against his chest. She wanted to wear pretty frocks that would catch his eye. She wanted her hair styled in a graceful cascade of curls artfully arranged to show off her features, not a boring old bun that also served as a pencil holder.

"We'll find your dratted Duke," Ramsdale said. "The damned manuscript has put you out of sorts, but if anybody can find him, it's you. Until tomorrow, Miss Peebles."

Philomena would have fallen sobbing into his arms, except he gave her cheek a lingering kiss, and that... helped. The *earl* had put her out of sorts, but so had the Duke. She'd never felt this close to success, or this assured of failure.

She'd also spoken honestly. She was exhausted from successive sleepless nights, hungry, and frustrated.

"Until tomorrow, my lord."

He bowed. She curtseyed and mustered a smile.

He touched his hat brim, and Philomena slipped through the garden gate, latching it closed behind her.

Jane sat on the bench near the sundial, her expression as thunderous as Philomena had ever seen it.

"Don't you *dare* remonstrate with me, Jane Dobbs. I'm eight-and-twenty years of age, my father stopped seeing me as anything but a free translation service fifteen years ago, and my dealings with Ramsdale are my business. If you'll excuse me, I haven't had any supper."

She would have swept past the bench, except Jane began to slowly applaud.

"If his lordship has finally put you on your mettle, he'll get no criticism from me, but a certain apothecary in Knightsbridge claims you've found a portion of *The Duke's Book of Knowledge*. They've put that story about to lure young ladies into buying love potions, which—I can assure you—are flying off the shelves at a great rate."

Chapter Eight

THE COINS ON the blotter winked up at Ramsdale in a shaft of morning sunshine, while the cat silently mocked him.

"She isn't coming," he informed Genesis. "Miss Peebles—I am to call her Miss Peebles—says she has an urgent matter to see to involving the Eagan Brothers' Emporium in Knightsbridge this morning. She will resume her duties tomorrow."

Ramsdale set Philomena's note—he *thought* of her as Philomena—before the cat, who gave it a sniff.

Knightsbridge was a hodgepodge of shops, taverns, inns, the occasional newly built mansion, and lodging houses more famous for the highwaymen who'd bided among them than for hospitality. What would matter so much to Philomena that she'd use the next to last of the Duke's ten days *shopping* and in such surrounds?

Genesis rose from the desk, leaped down, strutted across the library, and affixed himself atop the family Bible, which was closed for once.

"Blasphemer. Philomena is about the least-mercantile female I've ever met." Unlike Lady Maude, who likely kept half the shops in Mayfair in business.

Genesis circled twice and curled down into a perfect oval on his cushion of Holy Scripture. Ramsdale had the peculiar sense the cat was telling him to have done citing Proverbs and quoting Isaiah and *go after the lady.*

"It's a fine morning for a jaunt about Town. Guard the castle, cat. I have a countess-errant to find."

Purring ensued. At least somebody was having a good day.

Ramsdale's morning deteriorated as he cut through the park. Everywhere, couples were taking the air—happy, devoted, new couples, who had sense enough to enjoy each other's company without the interfering presence of a chimerical Duke.

"I must court my countess," he muttered, crossing south into Knightsbridge proper. "I wouldn't mind if she were to court me a bit too."

He would have gone on in that vein, except a dog nearly tripped him—one of the many strays running about London—and thus he looked up in time to see Philomena striding along ten yards ahead of him.

No maid, no footman, no handy aunt. Because the next Countess of Ramsdale was once again dressed as a young man. She'd changed her walk, changed her posture, queued her hair back, and donned the blue glasses along with a fancy cravat, top hat, and walking stick.

Marriage to Philomena would be an adventure.

She marched into the Eagans' shop, and thus Ramsdale had no choice but to march in right after her.

One of the proprietors, a spare leprechaun of a fellow, totaled a ledger behind the shop counter, his fingers clicking away on his abacus. A book bound in red leather sat at his elbow, while his pencil trailed down a single page of foolscap. An older woman in a bonnet sporting four different stuffed birds inspected shelves of patent remedies, and a young lady all in pink—two pink birds amid her millinery—sniffed at the tisanes stored in large glass jars.

Philomena went on an inspection tour, studying the shop shelf by shelf. She was very likely waiting until the other patrons left, and when they did, her gaze met Ramsdale's.

By God, she was good. Her perusal of him was exactly what a young gent would spare an older fellow of means. Brief and neither disrespectful nor envious.

"May I help you gentlemen?" the proprietor asked. "Jack Eagan, at your service. I believe you were first, young sir."

"He was," Ramsdale said.

"These Tears of Aphrodite," Philomena said, taking a blue bottle down from an arrangement on the shelves. "They're quite expensive." She uncorked the bottle and held it under her nose. "Rose water, cheap brandy, perhaps a dash of cloves. I hope you don't expect the young ladies to drink this."

The shopkeeper took off his glasses, a man prepared to be patient with a difficult customer.

"Have you any idea, sir, how unhappy the young ladies become when you gents fail to show them proper attention? When you dismiss all of their efforts to please you, put up with your conceits, flatter you, and endure your indifference? If I could sell my fair customers strong spirits in the name of medicine, I would, but that bottle you hold contains nothing less than a miracle of mythical proportions."

Ramsdale was uncomfortably reminded of Lady Maude—of all the Lady Maudes—and of Philomena's question about respect.

"I'm well aware of those tribulations," Philomena replied. "Does your elixir claim to end the young ladies' suffering?"

The shopkeeper folded his page of foolscap. "It can, indeed. Sometimes, what we need to see us through a challenge is a drop of hope. That bottle can give a young lady hope. My sainted mother believed that half of an apothecary's inventory was hope and the persistence it yields. How many problems can be solved by application of those two intangibles?"

Philomena jammed the cork back in the bottle and brandished the label side at Eagan. "You imply the recipe for this potion was discovered by the daughter of

Professor Phineas Peebles. How did she come by her discovery, and why would she share it with you?"

Unease crept into Eagan's eyes. "You know the good professor?"

"And his daughter." Philomena's tone brought the temperature in the shop down considerably.

Eagan grasped his lapels with both hands. "Then you know that she's exactly the sort of young lady—a plain spinster, overlooked for years, no hope of marriage—who would have sympathy for others similarly situated, though I daresay her circumstances are none of your affair."

Ramsdale strode forward, shamelessly using his height to glower down at the shopkeeper.

"Miss Peebles is neither plain nor overlooked. She is brilliant, tenacious, passionate about her scholarship, and honorable to her beautiful bones. You slander the next Countess of Ramsdale at your *everlasting* peril. My intended would live on crusts in the meanest garret before she'd take another's coin under false pretenses. You either erase all evidence of your vicious scheme from this shop in the next hour, or expect a call from my man of business."

Eagan scuttled back behind his counter. "And you would be?"

Ramsdale dropped his voice to the register that carried endlessly even when he whispered. "Your sainted mother's worst nightmare."

Philomena came up on Ramsdale's side. "You behold the Earl of Ramsdale in a *mild* temper, sir."

"Mild..." Eagan cleared his throat and slipped his sheet of foolscap into a slit in the ledger's binding. "Mild temper. I see. Well. Then."

He kept two sets of books, and he swindled young women. Probably swindled old women too, and anybody desperate enough to rely on his pharmaceutical products. He did not sell hope and persistence.

He sold lies.

Except for Eagan and Philomena, the shop was empty. Would she truly mind if Ramsdale indulged in a bit of pedagogic violence?

She was staring at the ledger, at the barely discernible slit in the red leather binding into which Eagan's foolscap had disappeared. Staring more fixedly than she stared out of windows, into fires, or at her tea.

Not more fixedly than she'd regarded Ramsdale in the office, though.

"What is it?" Ramsdale asked.

"I know where the Duke is. Ramsdale—or at least where the *Motibus Humanis* is, *I know.*"

"We've no need to involve a duke," Eagan sputtered. "I'll happily relabel—I mean, remove the offending bottles. Cupid's Tears would sell quite well, or Cupid's Revenge. I rather like—"

Ramsdale grabbed Eagan by his neckcloth. "No tears, no revenge, no more profiting from the false hopes of the lovelorn with your greed and dishonesty."

He gave Eagan a slight shake—a minor, almost gentle shake, truly—but didn't let him go until Philomena flicked Eagan's cravat.

"Every bottle," she said. "Gone, before the next customer sets foot in this shop of horrors. I have it on good authority that the professor is about to unveil the contents of the real manuscript, and your paltry scheme will be similarly unmasked."

Eagan changed colors, from pale to choleric. "No more love potions. I understand. I do understand, my lord. Sir. I mean—I understand."

"Come," Philomena said, taking Ramsdale by the arm. "We have a Duke to set free."

RAMSDALE HAILED THEM a hackney. As a female in polite society, Philomena would have traveled with him in a closed conveyance at risk to her reputation. She had never occupied anything but the tolerated fringe of good society, and to all appearances, she was not a female.

"I wanted to hit him, Ramsdale. I wanted to ball up my fist and plant him a facer. Draw his cork, put up my fives. He lied. His whole shop is a lie."

Ramsdale kissed her cheek. "The soaps and sachets seemed genuine enough. I wanted to do more than hit him."

How Philomena loved the menace in Ramsdale's voice and the affection in his kiss. "The soaps and sachets are lures for the unwary, and when we're upset, we're all unwary."

Ramsdale took her hand. "I can bring a lawsuit for the way he maligned you, and that would be the end of his chicanery. I should have taken that execrable sign with us as evidence. To think that my future countess's scholarly research was bandied about as fodder for shop-window gawkers. Perhaps I'll threaten him a bit, give him a few sleepless years."

Frightening the little toad within an inch of his larcenous wits had probably already accomplished that aim.

"Ramsdale, be sensible. You lied too." All in good cause, but the nature of those fabrications dulled the golden lining from the morning's adventure.

Ramsdale turned a lordly scowl upon her. "I am not prone to dissembling, Philomena. Unlike some people, I present myself as I am in all particulars at all times."

How did he make the hackney's interior shrink? How did he fill the entire space with two indignant sentences?

"I've seen your particulars, Ramsdale, and I'd like to see them again soon, but you told that scoundrel I am your prospective countess. I doubt he'll be gossiping about your conversation, but you did misstate matters."

Though Philomena had dreamed. Despite all common sense and logic to the contrary, she had dreamed. She knew where the Duke was, though, and thus her dreams, and even her time with Ramsdale, were over.

How ironic, that finding the Duke meant losing the earl.

"Shall I kneel in the dirty straw of a moving conveyance, Philomena? Shall I go down on bended knee now, when the ring I ordered has yet to be delivered and your infernal Duke has revealed his whereabouts to you?"

Two realities collided as Philomena searched Ramsdale's gaze.

At this moment, she didn't care one whit for the Duke. Let Papa's reputation rest on decades of sound scholarship and inspired teaching. He didn't need the Duke to polish his academic halo.

Philomena didn't need the Duke either. She needed the earl.

And apparently, the earl needed her. "You aren't jesting."

"When do I jest?"

"When you haven't any clothes on. You tickled me. That's a jest of sorts. You truly want a bluestocking spinster for your countess?"

He did not lie. He did not dissemble. He did not... well, he did embrace pretty young women on staircases, or they embraced him. Philomena had done likewise at the first opportunity, so she couldn't really blame Lady Maude for attempting to secure Ramsdale's notice.

"Spinsters are fine company," Ramsdale retorted. "They are fearless and direct, also given to independence and blunt opinions."

"You've just described yourself, my lord."

He kissed her on the mouth. "So I have, but it's not a spinster to whom I offer my hand in marriage. I plight my troth with a brilliant, dauntless, wily, unstoppable, beautiful, passionate woman, with whom I'd consider it the greatest privilege of my life to be married. What say you, Philomena?"

The hackney swayed around a corner, pushing Philomena away from Ramsdale, and yet, he held her hand. She mentally searched for words—any words, in any language—and found only one.

"Yes. I say yes, and yes, and yes. I will be your countess, your wife, your lover, your greatest privilege."

"And if I haven't any connection to His Perishing Literary Grace?" Ramsdale asked. "If all of Uncle's maunderings are only that and no part of the Duke lies in my possession?"

That this bothered him gave Philomena's conscience a pang. "What matters the Duke when I can possess myself of the lover, the husband, the companion?"

The hackney slowed.

"You're not enamored of the earl?"

"Let's repair to your lordship's office," Philomena said. "I'll show you just how enamored of the earl I am."

THANK GOD FOR the servants' half day and for a widowed sister with a sense of discretion. Ramsdale had taken "Mr. Peebleshire" not to the office and not to the library—so there, Your Grace—but to the earl's private sitting room.

Which adjoined the earl's bedroom, of course.

The midday sunshine turned the skin of Philomena's shoulder luminous as she slept on Ramsdale's chest. Her hair was a chestnut and cinnamon riot tumbling down her back and her breath a soft breeze against his throat.

They'd worn each other out, twice.

Ramsdale was determined that their next bout of passion would wait until after the vows had been spoken, so that his bride—and her groom—could fully enjoy the wedding night. Philomena would probably poke eight holes in that strategy before next week, and what pleasurable holes they'd be.

"You're awake," Philomena said, pushing up to straddle him.

"I'm engaged, also in love."

She blushed, which on a naked woman was a fascinating display. "As am I."

For a polyglot, she could be parsimonious with her declarations.

Ramsdale patted her bottom. "You're shy. No matter. I will earn your passionate devotion, and soon you'll be declaiming panegyrics in my honor from the—"

"Dining parlor," Philomena said. "I'm hungry. Your passionate devotions have put an appetite on me."

Also a rosy flush and a smile. Ramsdale's whole body was smiling in response. "I could order a tray."

"We'll go down to lunch. Do you suppose your sister might lend me a dress? We're of a size."

Melissa made that loan without a question, though it would likely come at a high rate of sororal interest. Ramsdale played lady's maid, Philomena served as valet, and a composed and proper couple descended to the dining parlor.

"You wouldn't rather stop by the library first?" Ramsdale asked.

"The Duke has waited two hundred years," Philomena said. "He can wait another hour."

"A fine notion."

Philomena did justice to the food, Ramsdale did justice to the wine, and the afternoon was half gone before they joined the cat in the library.

"I should put him out," Ramsdale said, lifting feline dead weight off the Bible. "He's overdue for a trip to the garden."

"Let him stay," Philomena said. "We can all admire the roses together once we've found what we came for."

She was eyeing the Bible, and chess pieces rearranged themselves in Ramsdale's head. "All those biblical references and allusions."

"But only when your uncle was discussing you or your father. For everybody else, Dante, Chaucer, Voltaire... but for you, always the Bible. For the cat, a book of the Bible. Your uncle would have been in this room, probably alone, on those few occasions when he was allowed to visit his books."

Philomena carried the Bible over to the desk and sat.

"I'd examine the front first," Ramsdale advised. "He named the cat—my first bequest—Genesis."

Said cat began to purr.

Philomena took up Ramsdale's quizzing glass, peering at each edge of the front cover. "Here, right along the edge. The stitches are so fine, I can barely see them even with your glass. It's here, Ramsdale, but I'd best not wield a knife when my hand is shaking."

Something lay beneath the binding covering the front of the family Bible. When Ramsdale joined Philomena at the desk, he could feel the slight bump beneath the leather and feel the lack of a corresponding bump under the back cover.

The cat sat on the blotter, as if having called the meeting to order himself.

"It might be a map or a letter," Ramsdale said, "or another codicil."

"We can give it to Papa to translate, then, something to occupy him in retirement." She sent Ramsdale a look that promised he'd be too busy to aid the professor—and so would she.

Ramsdale tested the edge of a penknife against his thumb. Sharp, not too sharp. Stitch by stitch, with Philomena holding the quizzing glass for him, he worked his way down the binding.

"Do you suppose Uncle enjoyed taking a knife to an heirloom?"

"Not at all. He knew that of all your possessions, the one you'd likely carry from your home in case of fire or flood, the one you'd safeguard against mobs or invading armies, was this Bible."

Philomena's confidence was comforting, also convincing. Uncle had been eccentric, not unhinged.

"Something has been secreted in here," Ramsdale said when the last tiny stitch had been cut.

"You do it," Philomena said. "Do it carefully."

Little care was needed. The old leather was supple, and a document about a half-inch thick and maybe seven by ten inches otherwise, slid easily from behind the Bible's binding.

"That's it," Philomena said softly. "Don't open it. Give it a chance to adjust to the air and light, but that's it."

The weight of the volume suggested vellum rather than paper pages. No glue had been used to fasten the pages to the leather protecting them. A Latin title had been scripted onto the leather in a handsome hand: *Liber Ducis de Scientia—de Motibus Humanis.* Below the title was an ornate numeral 4 and golden shield bearing three fleurs-de-lis on a blue circle with six red balls beneath.

"That's the Medici coat of arms," Philomena said. "The number of red balls tells us this cover is dated from..." She fell silent, a tear meandering down her cheek.

Ramsdale set the manuscript aside, out of reach of the cat, and took Philomena in his arms. "You found your love potions. You put together the clues, you did the translations, you had the combination of knowledge, dogged persistence, and inspiration to find the treasure, Philomena. The world is in your debt, and I am *obnoxiously* proud of you."

Tears intended to manipulate could not move him, but honest tears—of relief, joy, gratitude, and exhaustion—earned his respect. Philomena shuddered in his embrace for a time, the cat stropping himself against her hip all the while.

"You helped," Philomena said at last, stroking the cat's head. "You perched on the Bible, you kept us company. I want to be married in this room, Ramsdale."

"And shall we travel to Florence on our wedding journey?"

If he'd given her the other three volumes of the *Liber Ducis*, Ramsdale could not have earned a more brilliant smile from his countess.

They were married in the library, and they did travel to Florence—also Rome, Siena, Paris, Budapest, Berlin, Vienna (the professor and Jane, also on a wedding trip, met them there), Copenhagen, St. Petersburg, and Amsterdam.

And Philomena eventually had an opportunity to study the entire compendium of *The Duke's Book of Knowledge*, but the stories of those other three volumes involve other members of the Bibliomania Club and are tales for another time.

What did Ramsdale inscribe on his beloved's engagement ring?

Amor omnia vincit—of course!

To my dear Readers,

So who was that Duke of Lavelle fellow? I know him as Philippe Ellis, who comes a cropper for true love in ***His Grace for the Win***, a story in the novella duet, ***The Duke's Bridle Path***.

My most recent full-length Regency novel is ***Too Scot to Handle***, the second book in the Windham Brides series (excerpt below). ***No Other Duke Will Do*** (November 2017) is the third story in that series, and my first romance set in Wales—but not my last! Because the Duke of Haverford is a very persuasive gentleman, I've also included a sneak peek from his courtship of Miss Elizabeth Windham.

If you'd like to stay up to date with all of my new releases, sales, and special deals, but you aren't keen on receiving yet another newsletter, please considering following me on Bookbub. Those folks will send out a short email alert when one of my books is listed for pre-order or on discount, and unsubscribing is easy. If you're more the newsletter type, I only publish those when I have illustrious doin's to pass along, and I will never convey your information to third parties, ever.

Happy reading!
Grace Burrowes

Read on for an excerpt from ***Too Scot To Handle***:

C OLIN MACHUGH AND *Miss Anwen Windham share an interest in a certain Home for Wayward Urchins. After a morning gallop in the park, they tarry on a bench, discussing the children, and touching on a few other topics...*

Anwen unpinned her hat, or whatever the thing was. A toque, maybe. Her wild gallop had set it slightly askew.

"You think the boys will consider working on the grounds a reward?" she asked. "I thought house servants ranked above the outdoor servants?"

Colin took her hat from her, examining the collection of pheasant feathers and silk roses that had probably cost a footman's monthly wages.

"I think we do best that which we enjoy most." He enjoyed kissing and that which often followed kissing *exceedingly*. "If a boy is to spend his entire life at a job, it had better be a job that he has some aptitude for. Let the fellow with a passion for horses work in the mews, and the fussy young man who delights in a perfectly starched cravat become a valet. It's all honorable work."

He was being a Scottish commoner with that sentiment.

"That's sensible," Anwen said. "Sense is what the orphanage needs. Not good intentions, or idle talk. Common sense. What are you doing with my—Lord Colin?"

He'd pitched the thing with feathers into the bushes five yards off, so it hung from an obliging branch of the nearest maple.

"Come," he said, taking her by the hand. "The squirrels have no need of such fetching millinery, and the grooms are busy with the horses."

"Right," Anwen said, rising. "Enough serious talk, for now. I'm full of ideas, and can't wait to put them into action."

"Exactly so," Colin said, leading her into the deep shade beneath the tree. "Time to put a few well chosen ideas into action."

Also a few foolish ones.

He made sure they were safe from view, drew the lady into his arms, and kissed her, as a snippet of her earlier words settled into his imagination. She'd said he'd given her hope.

She'd given him hope too.

NOTHING PENETRATED ANWEN'S awareness except *pleasure.*

Pleasure, to be kissed by a man who wasn't in a hurry, half-drunk, and all pleased with himself for being brave enough to appropriate liberties from a woman taken unawares by his boldness.

Pleasure, *to kiss Lord Colin back*. To do more than stand still, enduring the fumblings of a misguided fortune hunter who hoped a display of his practiced charms might result a lifetime of security.

Pleasure, to feel lovely bodily stirrings as the sun rose, the birds sang, and the quiet of the park reverberated with the potential of a new, wonderful day.

And beneath those delightful, if predictable pleasures, yet more joy, unique to Anwen.

Lord Colin had bluntly pronounced her slight stature an advantage in the saddle—how marvelous!—and what a novel perspective.

He'd *listened* to her maundering on about Tom, Joe, John, and Dickie. Listened and discussed the situation rather than pontificating about her pretty head, and he'd offered solutions.

He'd taken care that this kiss be private, and thus unhurried.

Anwen liked the unhurried part exceedingly. Lord Colin held her not as if she were frail and fragile, but as if she were too precious to let go. His arms were secure about her, and he'd tucked in close enough that she could revel in his manly contours—broad chest, flat belly, and hard, hard thighs, such as an accomplished equestrian would have.

Soft lips, though. Gentle, entreating, teasing…

Anwen teased him back, getting a taste of peppermint for her boldness, and then a taste of *him*.

"Great day in the morning," he whispered right at her ear. "I won't be able to sit my horse if you do that again with your tongue."

She did it again, and again, until the kiss involved his leg insinuated among the folds and froths of her riding habit, her fingers toying with the hair at his nape, and her heart, beating faster than it had at the conclusion of their race.

"Ye must cease, wee Anwen," Lord Colin said, resting his cheek against her temple. "*We* must cease, or I'll have to cast myself into yonder water for the sake of my sanity."

"I'm a good swimmer," Anwen said. "I learned very young, and one doesn't forget. I'd fish you out." She contemplated dragging a sopping Lord Colin from the Serpentine, his clothes plastered to his body….

"Such a sigh," he said, kissing her cheek. "If ye'd slap me, I'd take it as a mercy."

"I'd rather kiss you again." And again and again and again. Anwen's enthusiasm for that undertaking roared through her like a wild fire, bringing light, heat, and energy to every corner of her being.

"You are a bonfire in disguise," he said, smoothing a hand over her hair. "An ambush of a woman, and you have all of polite society thinking you're the quiet one."

He peered down at her, his hair sticking up on one side. "Am I the only man who knows better, Anwen?"

She smoothed his hair down, delighting in its texture. Red hair had a mind of its own, and by the dawn's light, his hair was very red.

"No, you are not the only one who knows better," she said, which had him looking off across the water, his gaze determined.

"I'm no' the dallyin' kind," he said, taking Anwen's hand and kissing it. "I was a soldier, and I'm fond of the ladies, but this is… you mustn't toy with me."

Everlasting celestial trumpets. "You think I could *toy* with you?"

"When you smile like that, you could break hearts, Miss Anwen Windham. A man wouldn't see it coming, but then you'd swan off in a cloud of grace and dignity, and too late, he'd realize what he'd missed. He wouldn't want to admit how foolish he'd been, but in his heart, he'd know: I should ne'er have let her get away. I should have done anything to stay by her side."

I am a bonfire in disguise. "You are not the only one who knows my secret. *I* know better now too, Colin." She went up on her toes and kissed him. "It's our secret."

Order your copy of ***Too Scot to Handle***!

And read on for an excerpt from ***No Other Duke Will Do***!

*E*LIZABETH WINDHAM IS *attending a house party hosted by Julian, Duke of Haverford. His Grace has done the unthinkable and disagreed with a lady, and then—in an effort to further elucidate his position, he offers an argument by way of demonstration.... Or something.*

Elizabeth hadn't meant to rant at Haverford much less confide in him, hadn't meant to disclose her past, or even discuss Charlotte's inchoate schemes with him. The dratted man listened, though. He was a duke, and yet he was also like no kind of aristocrat Elizabeth had met—or kissed—before.

Haverford was trying to convince her he was a lazy kisser, but he was lazy like a prowling lion, bringing infinite patience and focus to his advances. His lips moved over Elizabeth's in gentle brushes, and she scooted closer, the better to grip him by the lapels.

He came closer as well, spreading his knees, and sliding a hand into Elizabeth's hair.

His kisses were lovely. Tender, teasing, maddeningly undemanding.

"I want—" Elizabeth muttered against his mouth.

His tongue danced across her lips. She braced herself for an invasion, for a crude imitation of coitus, but Haverford surprised her by pausing to caress the nape of her neck.

"If you don't like it," he said, "you show me what I'm doing wrong. You are gifted at chiding and correcting. Chide me."

Oh, gracious. *Oh, yes.* Elizabeth explored the shape and texture of his mouth, the contours of his lips, the arch of his eyebrows. His jaw was only slightly bristly—he must have shaved before dinner—while his eyebrows were soft.

Elizabeth took a taste of him, and his every movement, from his breathing to the susurration of his clothing, to his slight shifts on the hassock, stilled.

"Again," he said. "Please."

Elizabeth liked the sound of that, liked the feel of the word *please* whispered against her mouth.

And as the kiss deepened and became a frolic followed by a dare, punctuated by a challenge, she rejoiced.

I was wrong. I was so very, wonderfully wrong. Every man wasn't an inconsiderate lout. They weren't all monuments to self-satisfaction. At least one bachelor could kiss and kiss and kiss....Elizabeth took one more taste of pleasure, then drew back enough to rest her forehead on Haverford's shoulder.

"I need a moment, Your—Julian."

He stroked her hair, his cheek resting against her temple. "Take all the time you need. I'm in rather a state myself."

Elizabeth hugged his admission to her heart. He'd restored her faith in something—perhaps in herself. The fault had lain not with her, but with the men she'd chosen, and if she could be wrong in this, she might be wrong about the joys of marriage, about her own dreams, about anything.

Elizabeth sat back and smoothed the duke's cravat. "My thanks. You deliver an impressive counterexample. You've given me something to consider."

One mink-dark eyebrow quirked. "Such effusive praise will surely turn my head, Miss Windham."

"Elizabeth. If I'm turning your head, you may address me as Elizabeth when private."

They shared a smile, conspiratorial, sweet, and a bit dazed. This was how it was supposed to be between a man and a woman, both comfortable and daring, a private adventure...

Order your copy of ***No Other Duke Will Do***!

How to Steal a Duke

(in Ten Days, Give or Take a Few Days,
But Definitely in Less than a Fortnight)

BY
SHANA GALEN

About How to Steal a Duke

Dominick Spencer, the Duke of Tremayne, is a powerful man used to having his way. When he and two other members of the Bibliomania Club set out to find the lost volumes of The Duke's Book of Knowledge to present to their favorite Oxford professor, Dominick takes his task seriously, even hiring a cat burglar to help him gain entry to a remote castle in Cornwall inhabited by a mad earl.

Rosalyn Dashner knows accepting the duke's assignment is dangerous, but her impoverished family and sick brother need the money. The daughter of a gentleman, Rosalyn is not impressed by titles. She's not impressed by the haughty duke until she comes to know the kind but lonely man under the gruff exterior. The duke might be looking for a manuscript, but she's found a man she loves. When Rosalyn must risk her life to obtain the manuscript, will Dominick choose her or his quest for the Duke's Book?

Acknowledgments

Thanks to Kelly Snyder for suggesting the title of this novella.

And much appreciation to Grace Burrowes for saving me from sickening readers with my original plot. (And no, I won't tell you what it was. Well... I might if you write to me and ask.)

Of course, thanks goes to Carolyn Jewel as well for being such a fabulous co-author and to Miranda Neville for her help with the book's theme and concept.

And I want to acknowledge Joyce Lamb for her stellar copyediting. She tries to make me perfect, but if there are any mistakes, they're still my own. Same goes with Sarah Rosenbarker, who proofed the manuscript. I always send her what I think is a flawless manuscript, and she always finds more mistakes. Thanks, Sarah.

Chapter One

"WHAT DO YOU mean you don't have it?" Dominick Spencer, the Duke of Tremayne, slammed his fist on the desk, rattling the tea cup perched on its delicate blue and white china saucer.

"I'm s-sorry, Your Grace," the agent stammered, shrinking back as though he wished he could blend into the wood paneling of the duke's London town house. "I have exhausted every avenue—"

"Damn and blast your *every avenue.*" Dominick stood and stalked around the large oak desk that had been his father's and his grandfather's and his great-grandfather's before that. "You didn't exhaust every avenue, or you'd have the book in your hands by now."

"Yes, Your Grace." The man hung his head, staring down at the hat he had crumpled in his hand. "I will keep trying—"

Dominick waved an arm. "Get out."

The agent looked up quickly.

"Get out of my library and my house, and while you're at it, get out of my employ. Mr. Jones, you are relieved of your position."

"It's Jarvis, Your Grace."

Dominick took two more menacing steps. He was a large man, three or four inches over six feet, with brawn he had cultivated from fencing, pugilism, and riding. He did not drink spirits. He did not gamble. He did not socialize.

He had a half-dozen estates to oversee and thousands of tenants, servants, and others relying on him. The Duke of Tremayne was one of the most powerful men in England, and he ruled his dominion with an iron fist. Either an employee did as he or she was hired to do, or he was out.

Dominick glared down at the agent. "I don't bloody care what your name is. You are through." He pointed to the door, and Jones or Jarvis or whoever the hell he was scurried out.

As soon as the agent was gone, Quincey entered. The secretary was a man of about sixty, of average height and build, with white hair and small, round spectacles. He knew not to speak until addressed, and so he waited patiently while Dominick leafed through several papers on his desk. They were in a neat stack precisely in the center of the desk and arranged alphabetically. He found the one he wanted easily and removed it, straightening the stack again before turning to his secretary.

"Tell Fitch I want my hat and coat."

"Yes, Your Grace. Shall I inform the butler you will not be dining at home? He will want to notify Cook."

Dominick waved a hand without looking up from the paper. "Fine." He didn't care about food. He cared about the book. He and two other members of the Bibliomania Club had pledged to find the four volumes of a manuscript known as *The Duke's Book of Knowledge*. Dominick didn't need another book. He had a library full of rare and extraordinary books, as did the other members of the club. They were all collectors, usually in competition for the ancient volumes. But this was not about his own library. Not this time. This was about Professor Peebles, who had been his instructor at Oxford. Peebles's literature class had inspired Dominick's love of rare and unusual books. And for as long as Dominick had known the professor, he'd been searching for *The Duke's Book*.

Now Peebles was an old man and ready to retire, his one regret that he had never found any of the volumes of *The Duke's Book*. Three members of the Bibliomania Club, Peebles's students at Oxford, had agreed to find the four volumes, and they planned to present them all to Peebles on the eve of his retirement. Even now, Viscount Daunt or the Earl of Ramsdale might have a volume of the manuscript in hand. Dominick had nothing, and the professor would retire in a little more than a fortnight.

Unacceptable.

"Is there anything else, Your Grace?" Quincey asked.

"Yes." Dominick folded the paper neatly and slid it into his pocket. "Make a note that I have fired Mr. Jarvis."

"Yes, Your Grace." Quincey's lined face betrayed no emotion. "I assume Mr. Jarvis did not manage to find the volume."

"He did not. It appears if I want something done, Quincey, I will have to do it myself."

"Your Grace?" Now Quincey's brows rose, and he managed to look both composed and slightly alarmed.

"That's right, Quincey. Jarvis is the third man I've hired, and not a one of them has found the volume. I don't have any time left to waste. Have Bateman pack me a valise. Tomorrow I leave to find the volume on my own."

Once at the club, Dominick climbed the wide stairs to the second floor, which housed a drawing room, where the members often met to discuss their acquisitions, and an extensive library, full of books about... well, books. This was the room members visited if they wanted to research a particular book to ascertain its value. Some books were valuable because of their content. Others were exceedingly rare. Still others were not so rare, but were volumes any bibliophile worth his salt would have in his collection.

Dominick opened the door to the research library and inhaled the smell of leather, ink, and old parchment paper. It was an intoxicating scent. The room was dark, as no fire or sconces were allowed inside, and Dominick took a lamp from the table just outside the doorway, lit it, and stepped inside, closing the door after him. He set the lamp on the polished oak table in the center of the room and strode to the medieval section of the library.

The Duke's Book of Knowledge had been commissioned by Lorenzo de' Medici in the fifteenth century. The volume Dominick sought was filled with arcane medical knowledge. He had consulted experts in the field, but thus far, all of their suggestions as to where the medical volume had been hidden had proved fruitless.

He pulled a book off the shelf, one he had perused many times, and read silently under a section titled *The Duke's Book of Knowledge.*

> *... secretly commissioned book of knowledge to be assembled from the greatest scholarship, written in a fine Italic hand by a team of Florentine scribes, and illustrated by great artists. Very few eye-witness descriptions of the book exist.*

Dominick skipped ahead. He didn't care where the eye-witness descriptions might be chronicled. He knew those descriptions from memory at any rate. There were four bound volumes, each with a Roman numeral on the spine. His finger slid down the page.

> *... in the possession of François I of France, Philip II of Spain and, finally, the Duke of Buckingham, James I's favorite, who was said to have brought the volumes to England. After the Duke was assassinated in 1628, the manuscript disappeared from view...*

Dominick knew all of this. He replaced the tome and pulled down another. This one stated that the Villiers family, Buckingham's surname, did not possess the manuscript upon the duke's death. The scholarly author suggested the four volumes had been dispersed.

"Oh, I beg your pardon, Your Grace. I did not mean to intrude. Just making my rounds."

Dominick glanced over his shoulder at the elderly man in the doorway. "You are not intruding, Mr. Rummage. In fact, I am just about through here."

Rummage, who served as the club's Master of the House, had been in that position ever since Dominick had joined. It was impossible to tell how old the man might be. He could have been sixty or eighty. His hair was gray and rather unruly, sticking up at all angles. His beard was just as bushy, but his watery eyes were sharp and keen. He was a tall, thin man, who dressed in black and who seemed to wander but always managed to be where he was needed. "Did you find what you were looking for, Your Grace?"

"Not exactly."

"Might I be of assistance?"

Dominick almost shook his head, then reconsidered. Rummage had been here a long, long time. Mightn't he have overheard a conversation or perhaps read a passage in one of these books that could be useful to Dominick?

"What do you know about *The Duke's Book of Knowledge?*" Dominick asked.

"Professor Peebles's manuscript?" Rummage stepped inside the room and closed the door behind him. "I know there are several of you searching for the volumes. You seek the medical volume, do you not, Your Grace?"

"I do, and I'm having a devil of a time finding it."

"I can well imagine, Your Grace. That's the one—well, I doubt I can be of use."

But Dominick had seen the hint of something in Rummage's eyes—a memory that caused a flicker of a smile and a slight crease in the older man's brow.

"I would not be so quick to dismiss you," Dominick said. "Come. Sit with me a moment and tell me, do you recall ever hearing anyone speak about *The Duke's Book*, specifically about the volume on medical knowledge?" Dominick took a seat at the oak table, but Rummage remained standing.

"I don't think it would be proper for me to sit, Your Grace, but I will say that I remember many, many conversations about *The Duke's Book.* The professor used to speak about it at length."

"Yes. I've consulted him, and I've had every location on his list searched to no avail. There must be somewhere else." He resisted the urge to scrub his hand over his tight jaw, which he assumed was darkening with stubble by this hour of the night.

"Then it wasn't in that old keep on the Cornwall coast?"

Very deliberately, Dominick straightened. "Cornwall, you say?"

"Yes. The Temples. To hear the professor talk about it, it sounded like a setting from one of the Gothic novels the ladies like to read. It always seemed more like a myth than a possible location for *The Duke's Book.*"

Myth or not, Cornwall was not one of the locations Dominick had searched.

"But you did search The Temples, Your Grace?"

"No, Mr. Rummage, I have not. And now, I insist you sit right here and tell me all about it." He held up a hand. "Do not argue. I will call for tea, and we shall take our time going back over the conversation as best you recall it."

"Yes, Your Grace." Rummage sat, and Dominick went to the bell-pull to summon a servant.

The Temples. This was it. He could feel it, the same way he knew when a horse was of the best stock or an investment was sound. Dominick believed heartily in books and documents and research, but there was something to be said for instinct as well. The Dukes of Tremayne had been famous for their instincts for centuries. Instinct was how they'd known who among their vassals were traitors, which side of the War of the Roses to fight on, and which women to take to wife to ensure the bloodline.

Dominick trusted his instincts, which meant The Temples was where he would find that lost volume.

❧

MISS ROSALYN DASHNER had been called a cat more than once in her life. She'd first climbed out of her crib at the tender age of ten months, whereupon she then proceeded to crawl across the room and claw her way onto her toy box to retrieve the doll she wanted. Her nanny had returned to the nursery to find her charge scaling the railing to return to her crib.

And this was before Rosalyn could even walk.

As she grew older, she climbed bookshelves, trees, and even a trellis or two. But by the time she was fifteen, she was no longer climbing for fun. Her father had died, leaving her mother and her three siblings in dire straits indeed. Then Rosalyn's youngest brother, Michael, had become ill. The cost of doctors and medicines had been exorbitant. The once genteel family had fallen deeper and deeper into debt. They'd had to sell their small country house and move to the unfashionable Cheapside area of Town.

Rosalyn did not mourn the move. She adored London. London was alive. It reminded her of an enormous beehive that had hung from a tree on the path she liked to walk back in country. When she'd been five or six, she barely noticed it. But by the time she was twelve, the hive was so large it bent the branch on which it hung. Rosalyn had worried that a stiff breeze would send it tumbling to the ground, angry bees swarming about.

That was London. Year after year, it seemed to grow and expand until it became so dense and so large the mass of people within could barely be contained. And just like that beehive back home, London buzzed and hummed with constant activity. Rosalyn never felt alone in London. There was always someone awake and about, and usually their intentions were as dishonorable as her own. But now that summer was upon them and with it warmer days, tempers were shorter and foreheads damper. It seemed everyone was on edge, waiting for that stiff breeze that would dislodge the hive and catapult the city into violence.

Rosalyn had seen it before—brawls that turned into riots, riots that created mobs. London was woefully unprepared for such lawlessness. There was no centralized police force, and the watchmen snoozed more than they patrolled. Rosalyn had long thought she was fortunate to be a cat. Cats could tiptoe away when violence erupted, looking down on it all from the safety of a high branch.

Her branch tonight was the roof of Thomas & Sons on Canterbury Lane. Her older brother, Stephen, was beside her, lying on his back and smoking a cheroot, the smell of which reminded Rosalyn of her father's pipe. Stephen was more of a raven than a cat. He had sharp eyes and could pick a lock as though he'd been born to it. With his light brown eyes and dark black hair, he perched in shadows and moved through alleys so quickly it seemed he flew.

Daniel, on the other hand, could neither slink nor fly. He was a year younger than Rosalyn, and the two were often mistaken for twins. They both had dark hair, like Stephen, but their eyes were green, not brown. Rosalyn was shorter than Daniel, but Daniel was shorter than Stephen. Daniel and Rosalyn were both thin and wraithlike. Rosalyn used her small body to advantage, slipping into spaces most adults could not manage and hanging on pipes or clotheslines that would have bent or broken if someone with more weight had relied on them.

But for all the grace she had been given, Daniel had only awkwardness. He was gangly and clumsy, forever knocking over small tables and breaking Mama's few remaining china plates. For this reason, Daniel served as lookout, loitering below the shop, ready to signal when the shop owners had finished locking up for the night or if the watch happened by.

"It shouldn't be long now," Stephen said, blowing smoke into a sky already gray from coal fires.

"Not long," she agreed, peering over the edge of the building to keep her eye on Daniel. He slouched against a shop across the street, hands in his pockets, looking half asleep. But she caught the glint of his green eyes under the brim of his hat. He was alert and ready.

"You know what you're after?"

She glanced at Stephen, annoyed to find his dark eyes fixed on her.

"If you mean, do I remember how all of you voted against me, the answer is yes. I lost. No jeweled cameo. Instead, I'm to swipe a simple silver chain." Even she could hear the bitterness in her voice.

"We can sell the chain easily. Any of the popshops will take it. They can turn around and sell it again the next day. Who do we know that will have the blunt or the customers to pay for a jeweled cameo?"

Rosalyn had heard this tedious argument before. Stephen was probably just as tired of her response. "Then we find a buyer for the cameo. Or, forget the cameo. When I cased the shop last week, I saw rings and brooches. I could swipe one of those. We find the right buyer, and we're done thieving for a year or more."

Stephen raised a brow at her. "And here I thought you liked thieving."

She did like it. "That's not the point. Mama does not approve, and she's probably right. No matter how good we are, eventually we will be caught."

"You mean Danny or I will be caught. It would take another cat to catch you, Ros." He tousled her hair, which she'd pulled back into a long tail and tucked under her coat. She wore men's clothing because it was easier to move in. She'd often thought she should chop her hair off so she would not have to worry about it getting in the way or spoiling her disguise, but her hair was the only womanly thing about her. She was otherwise as thin and straight as a boy.

"I don't like to worry about you and Danny, but I also miss having some security. Having a little money would buy us security."

"And taking something that valuable would hurt the shop owners. They'll hardly miss a silver chain, but a ring worth thirty pounds might mean they go out of business. I hardly want to get rich by stepping on the backs of others trying to earn an honest living."

Rosalyn sighed. How could she argue with that? She had always been inclined to take the every-man-for-himself view. But she had gone in the shop, and the older gentleman who had offered assistance had been very kind. She didn't want to see him unable to pay his rent or feed his family.

"Fine." She peered over the roof again and then ducked back just as quickly. Danny was consulting his London guidebook, which was her signal that the owners were about to depart. "He has the guidebook," she whispered to Stephen.

Stephen stubbed out the cheroot and rolled onto his belly. Both of them listened intently to the street noise below. Gradually, she heard the jingle of bells as the door to the shop opened. The passing carriages and general hum of the hive that was London kept her from hearing the actual clicks of the keys in the locks, but she could imagine the sound. Then, after at least ten minutes had passed, she rose up on her elbows and peered over the roof again.

Daniel had put his guidebook away and was setting his pocket watch. She and Stephen knew the watch did not actually work, but it was a convenient signal.

The shop owners had departed.

"Still too light," Stephen said.

"I hate these long summer days," she replied. She'd loved them when she'd been young and carefree in the country. She'd been able to go for long walks after dinner down to the pond or the stables. But now that life had ended, long summer days meant waiting for the sun to creep low enough that she could melt into the shadows. And so much for dinner. Her mother would have some broth waiting for them when they returned. Perhaps bread as well. But it would barely quell the rumbling in her belly. And if she was hungry, she could only imagine how much worse it must be for Stephen, who was bigger and taller than she.

But the sacrifice was worth it for Michael. Sweet little Michael, who had been so ill and whose medicines and tonics and doctor's calls were so very expensive. Michael was fourteen now, but he looked much closer to the age of nine. He was so small and so pale. Rosalyn would have given her brother all of her dinner if it would have made any difference.

But nothing seemed to help. She did not like to admit it, but her brother was growing worse, not better. Rosalyn did not like to imagine life without Michael.

"Ros, it's time."

Shaken out of her dour thoughts by Stephen's voice, Rosalyn peered over the edge of the building and looked down. Indeed, the streets were gray and shadowed. She could barely discern the glow of Danny's cheroot.

She looked at Stephen. "Pull out the rope."

Chapter Two

"TELL ME ABOUT The Temples," Dominick said, leaning over the hot cup of tea he did not want. Rummage had added cream and sugar to his, and Dominick judged he'd waited long enough for the information he wanted.

"I have never been myself, Your Grace," Rummage said, "but to hear the professor tell it, the place is more like a fortress than a home. It was a medieval keep at one time and had been heavily fortified at one time. It is located on the coast of Cornwall, high on the cliffs. It sounded a dark and treacherous place."

"Is it abandoned?"

"No. The professor went to The Temples and was refused entrance by the servants. It is said a mad earl lives there."

"Which earl?" Dominick knew his Debrett's, and he could think of no earl associated with a family estate called The Temples.

"Let me think. This conversation was at least a decade ago, perhaps more." Rummage sipped his tea, and Dominick refrained from tapping his fingers on the table.

"Ah, I have it. Verney. The Earl of Verney."

"Any idea how old this mad earl might be?" After all, if the professor had traveled to meet him a decade before, mightn't the earl be dead by now? Perhaps his much saner son held the property now, and if he needed blunt—and what noble with a crumbling cliffside structure did not need money?—might he be persuaded to sell the volume to Dominick?

"I couldn't say, Your Grace. Shall I consult Debrett's for you?"

"I can do it." Dominick rose to fetch the book, which was located near the door. "Tell me more about what you know of the professor's visit."

"He was turned away by the staff, and he always intended to go back. But he rather doubted the volume was located at The Temples, so he preferred to search elsewhere first. But I think he knew if the manuscript was lodged at The Temples, it was lost forever."

Dominick looked up from the page where he scanned the names of the peerage. "Why is that?"

"Not only was the earl mad and unreasonable, the structure itself was all but impregnable." Now Rummage lowered his voice. "I don't think it would surprise you, Your Grace, if I said the professor was not above actions some might consider rather shady to achieve his aims."

This did not surprise Dominick in the least.

"The professor said that one would have to be a monkey or a cat to scale the walls of that keep, and a surefooted cat at that, what with the wind buffeting you."

"Hmm." Dominick supposed he would have to do what he always did—order his way in. He was a duke. He outranked an earl. But using his power didn't always have the best results. He might have used charm—if he'd had any. But what if...his finger slid over the entry for Verney. He frowned. Unless the earl had died in the last year or so, he was very much alive and very much ensconced, a recluse it seemed, in The Temples.

And that meant the volume was very much out of Dominick's reach.

ROSALYN LOWERED HERSELF over the side of the building and took a moment to find purchase for her feet. She wore thin gloves that kept her hands warm but allowed them the freedom of movement. She'd changed from her boots into the sort of slippers a dancer or a tightrope walker might wear. These gave her toes a better grip.

She'd removed her coat and descended slowly in shirt-sleeves and trousers. Her fingers gripped the fine but sturdy rope Stephen had dropped down. Since they couldn't risk him standing on the street picking the lock of Thomas & Sons, she would descend to the window and enter on the shop's first floor. The family's residence was elsewhere, and though she did not know what the first floor might house, she knew from her observations that no one slept on the premises.

The rope was secured about her waist, but Rosalyn wrapped a length of it loosely around her hand and used it to begin her descent. She kept close to the brick of the building, staying small and tight lest anyone happen to look up or out from one of the other windows. She was dressed in all black, which helped her to blend in. Above her, she could hear Stephen huffing. Now that night had fallen, the heat had begun to dissipate, but it was still hot and strenuous work to support all seven or eight stone of her over the side of a building.

She lowered herself carefully, picking her way delicately across the landscape of the bricks until she found the safest. Finally, she reached the lone window on this side of the upper story. She inched down until she was even with the sill, then positioned herself on the narrow ledge, sideways so her shoulder and thigh pressed against the glass. Now she released the rope she held in her hands, but should she fall, she had the protection of the knot at her waist.

Not that she would fall. She never fell.

Still, she hoped Stephen hadn't become complacent. If he wasn't gripping the rope, this could be the one night she tumbled to the hard ground below.

Rosalyn took her time to catch her breath, listening for Danny's whistle. The whistle was the sign everything was clear. When she heard it, she took a deep breath and attempted to slide the window open.

It didn't budge.

She hadn't expected it to open easily, but there was no reason not to try. It was too dark for her to see whether the window was secured by some sort of lock, but given that it wasn't the ground floor, she doubted it. No reason to lock a window on the first floor, especially when one might wish to open it and allow air to circulate. But it was still early in the summer, and perhaps no one had needed to open it since last fall. The painted wood might be stuck to the casement at the sill.

She reached into her boot and unsheathed her knife. It had a long, thick blade. She had never used it as a weapon, but it was wonderful for prying open recalcitrant doors or windows. If her blade didn't work, she'd have to break the glass. But given that the glass was thick, breaking it was her last option.

Adjusting her position so she didn't slip backward, Rosalyn slid the blade between the sill and the window casement. The fit was tight, and it took some wriggling to wedge the blade all the way in. Keeping her balance under such conditions was a fine art of knowing just how to shift one's weight and when. Rosalyn gritted her teeth and pressed the blade up, trying to free the casement from the sill. This too was a tricky endeavor, because she did not want to break the blade. Finally, she felt the wood of the casement give, and she twisted the knife vertically, forcing space between the two pieces of wood.

She withdrew the knife and stuck it back in her boot, then tucked her small fingers into the space she'd created. It was a beastly tight fit, but she managed it, then pushed up with all her strength.

With a creak, the window lifted. She didn't need much space, and as soon as she had it, she slipped one leg inside, then the other. When she was standing inside the dark chamber, she grasped her knife again and cut the rope from her waist. There was no point in attempting to untie it. It would be knotted too tightly. She tugged on it twice to let Stephen know she was free of it, then left it dangling inside the half-open window. She'd need it on the way out.

Rosalyn surveyed the room she stood in. It was an open chamber, running the entire length of the small shop below. A table with chairs sat near the other window, which would receive the morning light. On the table were small instruments that she did not know the names of but that she associated with jewelry making. This was obviously the place where the family repaired broken jewelry as well as made the jewelry patrons requested.

There was also a large safe in the far corner, and it was closed and locked. This might have been a short night if someone had left a silver or gold chain lying out. But thieving had never been so convenient for her. She'd have to make her way downstairs and find a suitable piece. She had an idea of the one she wanted—not too showy but a good piece nonetheless.

She wove past a chest of drawers and a desk and padded silently over the carpet until she reached the steps. They had been designed in an L-shape, which meant she would go down about half a dozen, then have to turn on the landing and finish her descent. There was something about the landing she didn't care for, though. It was too...light. Had someone left a lamp burning? Was that where the light filtering up from the ground floor to the landing originated?

If the steps had been straight down, she would have been able to see what she was moving toward, but as it was, she was blind.

Daniel had definitely signaled that the shop owners had departed and locked the door. No one was here, so the light must have been a forgotten candle or lamp. Still, Rosalyn paused and waited for a long moment, listening. She heard nothing but the thud of horses' hooves a street over and a hawker attempting to sell pies.

She put her foot on the first step and slowly lowered her weight onto it. Then she did the same with the other. Her progress was slow, but she could not be too careful. Now was the time when she really must prowl. She'd descended four of the six steps to the landing and was just placing her foot on the fifth when she heard a slight cough. The sound startled her, and she would have pulled her foot up, but it was too late. Her body's momentum was forward, and she ended up lowering her foot harder than she would have liked.

The step creaked. Loudly.

"Who's there?" a man's voice called.

Rosalyn froze.

DOMINICK LOOKED UP from the notes he'd taken of his conversation with Rummage and frowned. His carriage was not moving. How long had they been sitting still? He'd been reading by the light of the carriage lamps and hadn't really taken note when they'd stopped. He'd been so engrossed that they might have been sitting here for an age. Dominick parted the curtains, saw very little in the darkness outside, and rapped on the roof with his walking stick.

John Coachman opened the hatch. "Yes, Your Grace?"

"Why are we stopped?"

"Terribly sorry, Your Grace. There's a line of carriages on the way to Covent Garden."

Some play or other was doubtless debuting, and the *ton* wanted to be present. Not to watch the performance, but to be seen in attendance. Ridiculous. When Dominick attended a play, he went to see the play, not ogle the audience with opera glasses. "I am not attending the performance," he said.

"No, Your Grace," the coachman agreed.

"Then move us out of the line of conveyances."

"I would, Your Grace, but it would mean taking a more roundabout route home."

"I don't care. Just get us moving again." Dominick used the handle of his walking stick to slam the hatch closed. The carriage began, slowly, to move again, and Dominick tried to go back to his reading, but his focus had been interrupted. Instead, he parted the curtains and peered out.

There wasn't much to see—the usual carts full of coal or firewood, a flower girl attempting to sell her last few wilting daisies, and a few couples making their way, on foot, toward Covent Garden. None of which shed any light on his current dilemma. How the devil was he to gain access to the library in The Temples? If the mad earl was as much a recluse as everyone seemed to think, Dominick might push his way in, but how would he be able to confront the earl and persuade him to relinquish the manuscript? He certainly couldn't scale the crumbling walls and climb inside the earl's chamber. Rummage had laughed about needing a cat. Where was Dominick to find a cat?

Just then, something large and heavy thudded on the roof of his carriage. John Coachman called to the horses to stop, and Dominick stuck his head out. The sight that greeted him shocked him.

Then it made him smile.

"WHO'S THERE?" CALLED the voice again.

Rosalyn pushed down a surge of panic. Someone was here! A man, by the sound of the voice, was still in the shop, and he'd heard her. Even now, he was listening for her to move again.

Rosalyn didn't have time to wonder how Daniel had made this mistake, or to think how they might find another way to acquire the blunt they needed for Michael's medicine. All she could think of was escape. And the one avenue of escape she had was the open window. She turned on her heel and raced back upstairs.

But she was well and truly caught now. She could hear the man coming after her, his hard-soled shoes thumping on the steps as he went up. Rosalyn was quick and nimble, but she didn't have time to secure the rope around her waist again. Nor did she want Stephen caught at the other end of it if she didn't manage to get away. She skidded to a stop before the window, grasped the rope and tugged it three times. That was the signal for Stephen to pull the rope up and fly away.

She'd never had to use this signal before, and there was a moment's hesitation before the rope started to rise. No doubt Stephen hadn't wanted to leave her, but he knew as well as anyone that she didn't need a rope to escape. Plus, as a woman, she would be treated with much more leniency than he or Daniel. She heard the whistle that alerted Daniel to run just as her pursuer stumbled into the upper chamber.

"I knew it!" he yelled in triumph. He was a young man, probably twenty or so, close to her own age. He had rusty hair and a profusion of freckles, visible in the light of the candle he held in one hand. A clerk, she thought. He'd stayed behind to do...whatever clerks did...and they hadn't accounted for him. The shop owners had locked the front door, but what if there was a back door they'd instructed the clerk to use when he'd finished for the night?

And why hadn't she considered this before she was standing in front of him?

He reached out a thin hand, pointing a long finger at her. "Thief! Watchman! Thief!"

Oh, blast it all. He was one of those. She'd hoped he might take her on himself. She could defend herself with a well-placed kick, but if he insisted on bringing all of London down on them, she had only one option—climb out the window.

Rosalyn ducked through the open window and immediately dropped down so her hands held on to the sill but her feet dangled freely below. She wouldn't bother trying to climb up. It was slow and difficult work. It would be much faster to use gravity to her advantage and climb down. Of course, she would need to do so quickly, before the watch did make an appearance.

She moved her feet, feeling for any sort of ledge or nook. When she found a small outcropping, she braced one foot on it and then trailed her other foot until she found another.

In the meantime, the clerk had stuck his head out the window and screamed for the watch.

The clerk's screaming bought her time to lower herself below the casement. Her arms shook when she released the sill, out of fatigue and fear. She was balanced on the thinnest of perches and would have to climb all the way to the ground this way. Since she'd been on only the first floor, she wouldn't have to climb far before she could drop down to the ground and run, but the descent was in no way easy.

She imagined from below it might look like she was clinging to the sheer brick wall, but what most people didn't realize was that almost every structure had irregularities, and one could use those as foot- and handholds if one was small and nimble.

She found another outcropping, big enough for most of her toes, and perched on it. One of her hands slipped, and she tried to ignore the panic that came with the possibility of falling. She found another place to put her hand, a bit flatter than she would have liked, and held on.

Thus, slowly, very slowly, she began to climb down. She was so intent upon her work that she didn't notice the clerk any longer. At least not until he hurled a book down at her. He missed, but not by much. She looked up and scowled. She hadn't even stolen anything, and he was trying to kill her?

A glance down told her she still had some ways to go before she could jump. She also saw the book land on the top of a passing carriage. The coachman paused, his mouth dropping open as he spotted her. Rosalyn went back to the task at hand. She couldn't hurry, much as she wanted to, and so forced herself to take her time finding the next outcropping and balancing on it before lowering herself another foot or so.

Another book sailed toward her, bouncing off her shoulder. She bit her lip to stifle the flinch of pain and maintained her tenuous hold.

"You there!" came an imperious voice. "Stop that at once!"

Rosalyn could not help but look down. There, emerging from the carriage that had halted, was a tall man dressed in dark breeches, a white shirt and cravat, and a dark coat. He looked up at her, his bright blue eyes peering out from under the shadow of his beaver hat. His eyes were striking, and he would have been handsome if his expression hadn't been so severe. Those turquoise eyes were hard, his lips a thin line, his jaw tight, his cheeks sharp slashes. Rosalyn had the urge to climb right back up again. She rather thought she might fare better with the book thrower than this man.

He was a noble. She didn't even have to look at the cut of his clothes or the shine of his carriage to know that. Everything about him spoke of nobility—and the imperiousness that came with it. She'd moved in those circles once, perhaps not such exalted circles as this man must occupy, but she was familiar with the look of privilege and hauteur.

"Watchman!" the clerk yelled above her. "Stop this thief!"

"I haven't stolen anything, you dolt!" Rosalyn yelled back. Her shoulder still stung from the impact of the last tome he'd thrown.

"You there!" the nobleman called. "Climb down here."

Rosalyn looked down at him, then back up at the clerk. She couldn't hang on forever. Her arms ached, and the muscles still shook with fatigue. Her toes were numb and would soon cramp from clinging to the small foothold.

"Lad, climb down," the nobleman ordered. "No harm will come to you."

As though she believed that, but she didn't have the strength left to climb back up, so down seemed the way to go. Besides, once the nob realized she was a woman, he might be more likely to give her clemency. Still taking care, she began to descend again. The clerk disappeared from the window above, and Rosalyn assumed he would be waiting on the street below when she landed on solid ground. Her hands had begun to cramp, and her arms and legs shook so badly with strain that she almost lost her grip. But she held on, descended another foot, then glanced down. The drop was not so far. She could make it.

Releasing the building's wall, she jumped, landing in a crouch. She stayed down, swiveling to face the nobleman and the clerk, who stood beside him. "Watch!" the clerk called.

"Stubble it," the nobleman ordered, coming toward her. Rosalyn might have shrunk back, but she had nowhere to go. Instead, she rose fluidly to her full height, quite a few inches shorter than he, and stared up at him defiantly.

"What is your name, boy?" he asked.

"They call me The Cat," she said.

His eyes widened with interest. "I can see why. You're not a boy either."

"And I'm not a thief." This was not completely true, but she hadn't stolen anything tonight. "I didn't take anything from that man." She nodded to the clerk. With some dismay, she noted a watchman was approaching, waddling as quickly as he could manage.

"Then what were you doing in the shop?" His gaze shifted to the sign above the door. "The jewelry shop, after it had been closed for the day?"

She met his gaze, feeling very much like a schoolgirl under the critical eye of her governess.

"What's this about?" the watch demanded. "What is happening here?"

"He's a thief!" the clerk said, pointing to her. "He picked the lock on the shop, and if I hadn't stopped him, he would have robbed Mr. Thomas blind."

"Is this true?" the watch asked her.

"No," she said. "He has it all wrong. I'm not a he. I'm a she. And I didn't pick any lock. Go ahead and check them if you don't believe me. I don't know the first thing about picking locks." That wasn't precisely true either.

"Then how was it you managed to be crawling out of the shop's window?" the nobleman asked.

"Now see here," the watch said, his face growing red with annoyance. "I am asking the questions, Mr.—"

One of the footmen who had been riding on the coach stepped forward. "You will address the duke as Your Grace."

The watchman's small eyes widened. "Duke? I'm terribly sorry, Your Grace. Do forgive me."

Duke. Wonderful. She had somehow managed to not only attract the notice of a clerk and the watch but also a duke. Her mother had always said one day she would be caught. This appeared to be the day.

"As I was saying," the duke continued, looking at her, "can you explain how you came to be crawling out of the shop's window?"

"Of course," she said with a decisive nod. "I fell into it by mistake. I was making my way to the ground floor to ask for assistance when this man"—she looked at the clerk—"began yelling and accusing me of theft. Naturally, I ran."

"Naturally."

She couldn't tell whether the duke believed her or not. His voice and expression betrayed nothing. The sky was darkening as night came upon the city, and she could barely make out his features.

"Did you hear that?" the clerk spluttered. "How did she fall into a closed window?"

"Are you certain it was closed?" the duke asked, never taking his gaze from her. The longer he looked at her, the warmer she felt.

"Well, no, but it's always closed."

"But you can't be certain," the duke said.

"I'd like to know how the chit fell." The watch waddled up to her, hands on his hips. "Do you claim you can fly, girl?"

"I like to walk on the roofs," she said. "It's much safer than the streets for a woman like me."

The three men stared at her, the watch and the clerk clearly incredulous. The duke's expression was still unreadable. Rosalyn blew out a breath of air. This was the end, then.

"That's the most ridic—" the clerk began.

"That makes perfect sense to me," the duke declared.

"It does?" The watchman's eyes bulged.

Rosalyn's own eyes felt like bulging as well. It was, as the clerk had no doubt been about to point out, a ridiculous story.

"Clearly, she isn't a thief," the duke declared. Rosalyn fumbled to turn out her pockets in illustration. The duke looked at the clerk. "Has anything been taken?"

"I-I don't know." The clerk eyed her empty pockets. "I would have to inventory everything."

"Do that, sir. In the meantime, I will escort this lady home. If you discover something has been stolen, appeal to my solicitor for compensation." He reached into his coat and handed the clerk a card. "If you will excuse us."

A footman opened the door to the carriage, and the duke gestured for her to climb inside. Rosalyn looked at the clerk, the watch, and then the duke. Her choice was clear. She could stay and go to prison, or enter the duke's carriage and... and she knew not what might happen. Prison or a duke's carriage... She took the footman's hand and climbed into the carriage.

This night had not ended at all as she'd planned, but one thing was clear. The duke had just rescued her.

The question was why.

Chapter Three

SHE WAS A small thing—petite was how his mother would have put it. But she wasn't a child. He'd seen the lift of her chin and the flash of determination in her green eyes. No, she was a woman, and an intelligent one at that.

She was also a thief. When he'd seen her scaling the wall of the shop, he'd known exactly what she'd been about. She probably deserved to be left to the mercy of the watch and whatever magistrate she was brought before.

Except Dominick needed someone who could scale walls, and this woman was a veritable cat.

"What's your name?" he asked as he settled back in his seat across from her.

"The Cat."

"Your real name."

She blinked at him, her eyes large in the dim light from the carriage lamps and her lips clamped shut.

"Very well. Where do you live?"

"Here and there."

He crossed his arms. "I fear my coachman needs more specific directions than that."

"Then you do intend to take me home?" She sounded surprised, as well she might. She had no idea what he meant to do with her. And she probably wouldn't like it when she found out.

"Of course."

"There's no need, Your Grace. I can make it on my own."

Oh, now she was referring to him as *Your Grace.* He smiled thinly. "I wouldn't want you to risk your welfare on the dangerous streets or chance… falling into any more open windows."

"No risk of that, Your Grace. My mother and brothers are waiting for me, so I'll just be off." She reached for the door, and he closed his gloved hand over hers.

"I said I would take you home, and that is what I plan to do. Now, Miss… Cat. We can sit here all night, or you can tell me where you live and we can be on our way. I prefer the latter."

"I prefer none of the above. Unhand me, please."

He ignored her. "I wonder at your identity, Miss Cat. Your accent is that of an educated person, and correct me if I'm mistaken, but you are not from London."

"You are not mistaken."

"I never am."

She rolled her eyes at that remark. He was almost offended. He could not remember the last time anyone had dared roll their eyes at him. Perhaps one of his siblings had when they'd been in the nursery.

"Then might I assume that you were intent upon stealing from that jewelry shop—no, I do not believe your absurd claim to have fallen into the window—because your family has fallen on hard times?"

She said nothing, but her expression was full of suspicion. She might not have been raised in London, but she knew enough to be wary.

"You mentioned a mother and brothers, but you did not mention a father." He knew this story well. A woman was widowed and then taken advantage of by unscrupulous sorts. Soon, she was destitute and forced to move to London to find honest work and cheap housing. Neither were to be readily found, and the widow was forced to take on less-honest work. In this case, it appeared her children had gone that route.

Dominick would help them. Not because he cared, although it couldn't be said he didn't care—he gave to various charitable organizations—but because aiding her would serve his purposes.

"I have a proposition for you, one that will ensure neither you nor your family want for funds in the near future."

She stiffened. The hand that had lain docilely beneath his jerked away. "You mistake me, Your Grace. I am no doxy you can buy for a night."

He stared at her, at this thin, small woman dressed in men's clothing. She was about the furthest thing from the sort of woman he'd want in his bed as he could imagine.

"Now open this door, or I shall scream until someone comes to rescue me."

He leaned forward. "First of all, no one will come to your aid no matter how much you scream. I am the Duke of Tremayne. I have more money than, if not God, certainly the king. You leave when I say you leave."

She opened her mouth to protest, but he held up a hand.

"Secondly, *you* mistake *me*, Miss Cat. I do not want your body. You hold absolutely no appeal for me. I want to buy your skills as a thief. I have a... job, so to speak, and I need someone with your abilities. You acquire the object I need, and I pay you. We part ways and never need meet again."

She stared at him for a very long time, so long, in fact, that he realized he'd been disingenuous, inadvertently, when he'd said she held no appeal for him. Her eyes were really quite beautiful, and her skin looked far softer than it should have, considering her "profession." Then there was her mouth, plump and red—

"I accept."

He snatched his gaze from her lips. "I beg your pardon?"

"I said, I accept."

"Of course you do." He sat back smugly, ignoring her eye roll. Two in the space of a quarter hour. The next dozen days would be a trial indeed.

"Where is this object?" she asked.

"I will tell you more as you need to know. Suffice it to say, the object I seek is not in London. You and I will have to travel to reach its location."

She bit her lip, seeming to consider this. He watched the way her small white teeth seemed to sink into the lush flesh.

"I need half the fee up front, then."

"I see." He'd been expecting this. "What is your fee, might I ask?"

"It's hard to say since you won't give me any details."

"Shall we say fifty pounds?"

Her mouth dropped open. It was almost comical the way she gaped at him. He hadn't been this amused in a very long time.

But she closed her mouth and narrowed her eyes. "If you are willing to give me fifty pounds, what you have planned must be dangerous."

"It could be, but from what I have seen, it will be nothing you cannot handle. Do hurry up and make your decision. I plan to leave first thing in the morning, and there are arrangements yet to be made."

She gulped, like a fish struggling to breathe out of water. "I said I accept, and I do. Give me the twenty-five pounds now, and I will meet you at your town house at first light. Where do you live?"

"I don't think so, Miss Cat. Once I pay you, you are mine. I don't allow you out of my sight. That's a protection on my investment."

"I cannot simply disappear. My family will be frantic with worry."

"Which brings us right back to where we began. Where do you live? I will take you home, you may collect what you need, say your farewells, and we will be off."

"And you will give my mother the money, the twenty-five pounds?"

"I will press it into her hand personally."

She closed her eyes tightly, reminding him of someone about to leap off a very tall cliff. When she opened them again, he saw that determined glint again. "My name is Rosalyn Dashner. If you summon your coachman, I'll give him my address."

THIS WAS A mistake. This had to be a mistake. Why on earth had she agreed to this ludicrous plan? Her mother and brothers would never agree to it. She couldn't run off to God knew where with a duke. But as the carriage sped closer and closer to the small flat her family rented, and the moment approached when she would have to explain to her mother and brothers the bargain she had struck, Rosalyn couldn't summon the will to tell the duke she'd changed her mind.

She *hadn't* changed her mind. This was their chance to break the chains of poverty that had been taking an ever firmer hold. With fifty pounds, they could pay the doctor's fees, the rent, and buy food and coal to see them through the winter. The little her mother earned from sewing could be put aside for the future, and her brothers could look for work instead of spending all day plotting burglaries with her and all night carrying them out.

And she could... Well, she could finally be a help to her mother. She might nurse Michael or help with the sewing or even take in some washing. This fifty pounds would mean they could finally get ahead, instead of always struggling to catch up.

She glanced at the man seated across from her. He sat facing the rear, which was the less desirable seat. Even though he'd not known her father was a gentleman, he'd treated her as a lady. He probably wasn't aware she understood his show of regard. He stared out the curtains she had parted earlier, his face impassive. Now that he'd struck his bargain, he was silent. He was no fool, then. He wouldn't risk saying anything that might make her change her mind. And she had enough questions to fill a library. What did he want her to steal? Why did a duke even need to steal? And what would happen if she failed? Not that she planned to fail. But, of course, she hadn't planned to fail tonight.

"How did you come to be outside Thomas & Sons tonight?" she asked.

His eyes never left the window. "I told my coachman to take a different route to my town house. The streets around Covent Garden were crowded."

A new show was opening. She'd seen the pamphlets. "But how did you know I would be there?" she asked. "Have you had me followed?"

His gaze touched on her briefly. "Our paths crossing was merely coincidence. Until the moment that book landed on the roof of my carriage, I had no idea you even existed."

She studied his face, which remained stoic. He didn't look as though he was lying. "Your Grace, I am a thief, and you need a thief. That seems a rather large coincidence."

He shrugged. "I didn't need a thief. I happened to see you, realized what you were, and decided I could use a thief. Perhaps I misspoke when I said our meeting was coincidence. I should have said it was an opportunity—one I think will be mutually beneficial."

He looked like a man who made use of opportunities. He was probably a man who had opportunities fall in his lap, so to speak, every day. At one time, she had felt like her life was charmed. Not any longer. Now it seemed anything could go wrong and usually did. "What if I fail?" she asked. She didn't want to bring up the possibility, but she had to know. He might ask the impossible of her. With his rigid posture, perfectly pressed clothing, and carefully chosen words, he looked like a man who had high expectations.

His eyes were not as bright blue in the glow of the carriage lamps, but his gaze was still intense when it rested on her. "You won't." It was an order.

"I appreciate your faith in my abilities, but I like all my threads knotted. If I fail, does my mother have to give back the twenty-five pounds?"

He leaned forward. "Miss Dashner, if you fail, you will have much larger worries than what happens to the twenty-five pounds." The carriage slowed to a stop. "Ah, we are here."

JOHN COACHMAN OPENED the door, and Dominick stepped out into a street full of shops that were closed for the night. He didn't recognize it, but the address she had given was in Cheapside. He supposed her living situation might have been worse. This wasn't Seven Dials, with its gangs of pickpockets on the streets and prostitutes on the corners. But the shops here were shabby, the street muddy and in disrepair, and the gin shop just opposite them seemed to be doing a brisk business.

Miss Dashner climbed out. It was difficult to think of her as a *miss* in her men's clothing, especially when he'd seen her dangling on the side of a building, but in his travels around the world, he'd seen stranger things. "Lead on, Miss Dashner," he said.

She gave him an alarmed look. She seemed to have a large store of them, and she chose one to toss to him every few minutes. They were mostly similar in that her mouth dropped open or her eyes widened or she blinked at him with horror. This time, her brow furrowed, and she stepped back. "You needn't come in, Your Grace. I live just above that shop there. I'll go speak to my mother and return in a quarter of an hour."

He had no doubt she could be halfway across London in a quarter of an hour. "I told you that from now on you do not leave my sight."

She frowned, that supple mouth turning down at the corners. "But surely you cannot watch me every single moment. I must have privacy to sleep or attend to personal needs." She flushed at the last, reminding him very much of many of the young ladies he met in Society.

"If I am not able to be with you, someone else will be. But at the moment, there is no one acceptable save me. So lead on."

"But—"

"Miss Dashner, I tire of arguing each and every point with you. It grows irksome. Kindly follow my orders the first time I give them, and we will waste far less time."

Her eyes flashed emerald fire, which was a nice change from her expressions of alarm. He would have called her appearance one of outrage. It interested him, as most people didn't have the backbone to show him any outrage, but her look didn't faze him.

Hands on her hips, she leaned close. "Your Grace." She practically spat the courtesy. "If you think I will follow your orders like one of your servants, think again. You may pay me for one job, but I don't work for you."

He watched her lips move, those red full lips, and hardly listened to her words. Finally, she stopped speaking, and he had to pause to think about what she'd said. He obviously took longer than was customary, because she prodded, "Did you hear me?"

"I heard you," he said.

"And?"

And he had no intention of bowing to her demands. He was the Duke of Tremayne. His way was the only way.

Except he needed that damn volume, and he wasn't at all confident he could acquire it without her special skills. It was a rare thing for him to need anyone, and he was not quite certain what to do about it. His instinct was to walk away that moment. She could go her way, and he'd go his. But he fought against that instinct. "I hired you, and I give the orders. That much should be obvious. Now, shall we stand about in the cold, or shall we collect your belongings, say your good-byes, and be on the way?"

He saw the struggle in her face—the way she pressed her lips together—and her body—the way she clenched her hands into fists. She needed him every bit as much as he needed her. "I propose a compromise," she said, though her voice sounded strained, and she spoke through teeth locked together.

"I am a duke. I don't compromise."

"Then I walk away." She spoke confidently and without hesitation. He knew she'd do it.

"I'm listening," he said.

"I will take your orders into consideration on all matters up and until the actual"—she glanced at the coachman, who appeared very interested in the horses—"job. Then I take over as general."

"You don't even know the details."

"I know you've never so much as picked a pocket. You have your areas of expertise. I have mine." She stuck out her hand. She'd removed her gloves, and he stared down at her long, slim fingers. Did she want him to kiss her knuckles?

"Shall we shake on it?"

He almost chuckled. Shake on a deal with a woman? This was certainly proving to be an interesting evening. But he stuck out his hand and took her small one into his. "Now will you lead the way?"

She sighed. "Yes."

A few moments later, he saw why she had been hesitant to show him her home. It wasn't any shabbier than he'd expected. Though he was a duke, he had spent his share of time engaged in charitable endeavors or sitting with tenants in their simple cottages. And Dominick had spent enough time in London to know how the poor lived. Miss Dashner lived better than many. Still, it was a shock to duck his head and enter the small room crammed full of people. At least it seemed so. As soon as Miss Dashner opened the door, her mother was there, then her brothers. Upon seeing him, their questions ceased and they moved back as Miss Dashner led him inside. There was barely enough room for he and Miss Dashner to fit in the room, full as it was with the mother and her two brothers—three brothers, actually, he noted when he saw the young boy on a pallet in the far corner.

He scanned the room quickly, taking in the cold fireplace, the clothing hanging on lines from one side of the room to the other, and the furnishings, which he could see had once been lovely. Everything was clean, but the place had the lingering odor of potatoes and onions he always associated with the poor.

All eyes flew from him to Miss Dashner, and she held up a hand before what he assumed would probably be an onslaught of questions. Miss Dashner indicated the woman he assumed was her mother. "Mother, may I present the Duke of Tremayne. Your Grace, Mrs. Dashner."

Dominick was surprised the thief knew the proper form of introductions and then even more surprised when her mother dipped into a well-practiced curtsey. He nodded. "Ma'am."

"Your Grace," she said in the unmistakable accent of the upper class. His brows rose. "Might I introduce my sons, Mr. Stephen Dashner"—she pointed to a man who looked about five and twenty—"Mr. Daniel Dashner"—this one was younger and might have been the daughter's twin—"and Mr. Michael Dashner." He was the one on the pallet. He had the dark hair of the rest of the family, but he was very pale and scrawny.

"Your Grace," he said, his voice thin and reedy. "Forgive me if I do not rise."

"Pray, do remain seated, Mr. Dashner," Dominick replied. The boy was obviously ill. And what was even more obvious was that this family was not what he had expected at all. He should have expected it. The signs had been there—in the way Miss Dashner spoke and carried herself. But he'd been blinded by her masculine clothing and—truth be told—her very feminine lips.

"I see you have met my daughter," Mrs. Dashner said. "To what do we owe the honor of your presence?"

"His Grace saved me tonight," Miss Dashner said before Dominick could answer.

"How kind of the duke," Stephen Dashner said. "Mama, I told you, we were separated on our way home."

Mrs. Dashner sighed. Clearly, she did not believe her son. And the fact that the man saw the need to lie to his mother about his sister's—and possibly his own—illicit activities solidified Dominick's theory. This was a noble family who had fallen on hard times. As there was no father present, the mother had probably done the best that she could with what meager money she had. But the sick child had drained their provisions quickly, and the other children had turned to thieving, an occupation of which their mother did not approve.

"Stephen, it's no use," Miss Dashner said, then turned to her mother. "We were out attempting to pilfer a shop."

"Rosalyn!" Her mother inhaled sharply.

"I'm sorry, Mama, but that is the truth. It went badly, and in the course of my escape, I encountered the duke. If not for his intervention, I would be in the hands of the watch at this moment."

Mrs. Dashner clutched the white apron keeping her dress clean. "Then we owe His Grace our gratitude. May we offer you tea?"

"No, thank you, ma'am." If they had tea, he would certainly never dream of taking any for himself.

"He has no time for tea, Mama," Miss Dashner went on. "The duke saw my—er, unique skills and offered me a position."

The mother's hands stilled, and she went very rigid. "What sort of position?"

"I've asked her to assist me in acquiring an object I've been seeking," Dominick said. He had allowed Miss Dashner to tell her family the first part as she saw fit, but he could speak for himself. "The object is quite valuable, and I may have need of someone who can, shall we say, access difficult places."

"And you agreed to this?" Mrs. Dashner said, looking at her daughter.

"He will pay me fifty pounds."

Mrs. Dashner put a hand to her heart. "No. Absolutely not. This sounds not only illegal but also dangerous."

"I assure you it is not illegal." Dominick didn't intend for Miss Dashner to steal the volume. He would need her only if he could not gain access to the earl, in which case he'd have her—what had she said happened at the jewelry store?—*fall* into The Temples and persuade the earl to grant him an audience.

Perhaps the plan was slightly illegal.

"It might be mildly dangerous," he admitted, "but no less so than the activities your daughter was engaged in earlier tonight."

"But fifty pounds!" her mother said, backing toward one of the chairs and lowering herself slowly into it. "That is a great deal of money."

"The object is not in London. I will need Miss Dashner to travel with me for several days."

Mrs. Dashner's hand dropped from her heart. "I see."

"I will, of course, provide a chaperone. I will have one of my maidservants travel with us."

Miss Dashner glanced at him, clearly interested in the information he gave.

"She will be safe, or as safe as I can make her. Now, I don't mean to rush you, but time is of the essence. Miss Dashner, if you could collect your things?"

"Of course," she said. "But don't you have something for my mother first?"

He gave her an incomprehensible look and then remembered he'd promised payment up front. He took out his card. "Do you have a pen?" he asked. The Dashner who looked like the thief's twin indicated a quill and inkpot on a small table on the other side of the room. Dominick crossed to it in three strides, bent, and scrawled his vowels and twenty-five pounds on the back along with the name of his solicitor. "This is half the fee," he said, turning to give the card to Mrs. Dashner. "Take it to my solicitor, and he will give you the blunt."

Miss Dashner shook her head. "You said you would put it in her hands."

He gave her mother the card. "It is in her hands. I do not have that much on me."

"Surely this card will satisfy," Mrs. Dashner said, "but I don't like the idea of you leaving."

"I know, Mama. Come with me, and we will discuss it while I pack. Excuse me."

Finally, Miss Dashner went to gather her things. There was apparently another room, because she disappeared through a door. He could hear her voice and that of her mother's, though they spoke low enough that he could not make out the words. Dominick felt the gazes of Miss Dashner's three brothers and wished she would hurry.

"If you need a thief," Stephen Dashner said, "why not take me? I can pick locks, and I have the eyesight of a hawk."

Dominick shook his head. "I don't need locks picked or good eyes. I need someone who can climb." He glanced at Daniel Dashner. Perhaps he had his sister's skills, but Dominick didn't want to find out. He'd made his decision. He wanted Rosalyn Dashner. "I have already hired Miss Dashner, and she has agreed."

"You will understand if we are concerned," Daniel said. "She is our sister, and I'm afraid we do not know you very well, Your Grace."

"I understand completely, and I assure you your sister is perfectly safe with me."

"This is my fault," came a weak voice. They all turned their attention to the boy on the pallet. "It's because of me she has to go."

"Michael, no. This isn't your fault," Stephen Dashner said, going to his brother.

"Yes, it is. The doctor and the medicines cost too much. I begged Mama to simply let me die, then you would all be better off."

Dominick did not want to feel sympathy for the boy, but he felt his heart clench.

"Don't be a fool," Daniel Dashner said. "No one would be better off without you. And now we have enough money to pay for the doctor, the medicines, and more besides."

"But we lose Rosalyn."

Dominick cleared his throat. "Sir, I will bring her back." He didn't know how he could make that promise. After all, how could he prevent her from falling onto the rocky shoreline of Cornwall and smashing her head in? "You will see her in less than a fortnight," he said.

Michael Dashner looked at Dominick for a long, long time, his eyes large and dark. "Thank you," he said.

"If you don't mind my asking, what ails you?" Dominick asked. He had noted the bowl beside the couch and recognized it as the sort doctors often used to bleed patients. Personally, he didn't see the value in bleeding a person who was sick. It tended to weaken rather than strengthen him or her. Michael Dashner certainly looked weak.

"I have asthma."

"Which means?"

"I have trouble breathing. Sometimes I cannot catch my breath at all. I have always had difficulty, but—" He began to cough and wheeze.

Daniel Dashner moved forward and handed his brother a handkerchief, then poured liquid from one of the vials near the pallet into a cup and helped Michael Dashner swallow a bit.

"His condition worsened when we moved to London," Stephen Dashner finished. "The air isn't as clean here as it was in Surrey."

That was an understatement, Dominick thought. He moved closer to the table with the vials and peered at them. There must have been eight to ten. "What does that one do?" he asked Daniel Dashner as he capped it.

"It opens the lungs to allow more air inside."

Dominick sincerely doubted that. "Who is your doctor?"

"Doctor Banting. He's the best in the city," Daniel answered.

Dominick would see about that. A movement caught his eye, and he turned to see a pretty young woman walk out of the room where Miss Dashner and her mother had disappeared. Mrs. Dashner followed, and Dominick waited for Miss Dashner. When she didn't appear, he took another look at the woman in the pale blue dress. "Miss Dashner," he said, his voice sounding more strained than he'd intended.

She gave a quick curtsey, hardly even polite. "I'm ready, Your Grace." She indicated a battered valise she held in one hand. Dominick knew he should probably take his leave or offer to carry her valise or…something, but he couldn't seem to tear his gaze from her. She no longer looked like a boy. She was petite and slim, but in the faded blue muslin dress she wore, there was no mistaking her femininity. Her breasts were small but round where they pushed against the fabric of her bodice, and though her waistline was high, when she moved, he could see where it might dip in at her small waist. She had a long, pale neck that looked all the paler with her ebony hair piled on her head. The plain style left her face bare and accented her high cheekbones, her full lips, and those large green eyes fringed with black lashes.

Cat's eyes, he thought, and just as mysterious and beautiful.

"You didn't expect the dress," she said, breaking the silence.

"No."

She glanced at her mother and raised a brow, an expression he had seen many times from his siblings. It said, *I told you so.*

"It's for propriety," Mrs. Dashner said. "Rosalyn insisted on bringing her…other clothes for the work."

Dominick thought of the manuscript again and straightened. That's why he was here. He needed *The Duke's Book,* and the thief would help him acquire it. He didn't care about sick boys or struggling families. He couldn't throw a rock in London without hitting one of those. "Good. Shall we depart, then, Miss Dashner?"

She nodded and started forward, but her mother dragged her back and hugged her fiercely. "Be careful, my love. Come back to us safe and sound."

"I will, Mama," Miss Dashner managed, despite her mother's tight grip.

Watching the scene, Dominick had the urge to do more. Twenty-five pounds was not enough to help this family, not really. Instead, he opened the door and escorted Miss Dashner out.

Chapter Four

"WHY DID YOU ask that man to investigate Doctor Banting?" Rosalyn asked the next morning as soon as they were in the large traveling carriage. She'd spent the night at the duke's town house, whereupon arriving, she'd been whisked off to guest chambers, brought tea and an assortment of sandwiches, and offered a bath. She'd also been assigned a maid, who had not only fussed over her but had cleaned and ironed her dress. It was her only dress, and she wore it again this morning.

She should have slept well, all things considered, but she had worried about her mother and brothers and fretted as well about the job to be done. What did the duke want her to steal? How long would they travel? And then, as she'd been coming down the stairs, she'd heard the duke tell his secretary to look into Doctor Banting and to send him a report. What was that about?

"It doesn't concern you," the duke said, settling back on the squabs. Besides overhearing the duke ask his man to investigate Doctor Banting, she'd also heard him confirm that a groom had ridden ahead to ensure that fresh horses would be waiting at each posting house so they wouldn't be delayed and could therefore travel as quickly as possible. The duke was obviously in a hurry to reach their destination.

"As Doctor Banting is my brother's doctor, I think it does concern me," she said.

He gave her a long, hard look. He'd shaved this morning, his jaw clean of the stubble that had grazed it the night before. He'd removed his hat when he'd entered the coach, and in the daylight she could see his hair was light brown with streaks of chestnut and gold. But his eyes were what held her attention. They were still the prettiest shade of blue she had ever seen.

"I'm a curious man," the duke said at last. "I wanted to know more about Banting."

"He's one of the best in London," she said.

"So he says. I merely wondered what others might say."

She closed her mouth. It was true. She had no idea of the doctor's reputation, other than the praise he'd heaped on himself. But Michael did seem to improve under Banting's care. Didn't he?

The maid—her name was Alice—gasped as the horses started forward, and Rosalyn glanced at her. The poor girl was white as a sheet and wide-eyed. She was young, perhaps even younger than Rosalyn, with white-blond hair and pale blue eyes. She looked like she had come from Druid stock, if the old tales of Druids were to be believed. Even more important, she looked as though she had never been in such a grand conveyance before, or seated across from a duke.

Come to think of it, Rosalyn had never been in this situation either.

"Are you well, Alice?" she asked.

"Oh yes, miss." She stared out the window, then turned quickly back to Rosalyn. "Do you need anything, miss?"

Rosalyn shook her head. Just to be finished with whatever it was the duke wanted from her and to go home. "Now that we are under way," she said, leveling a look at the duke, "can you tell me where we are going?"

"Cornwall," he said.

"Cornwall? But that will take days to reach!"

"That's why I wanted to leave first thing this morning."

"And what is it you want in Cornwall?"

At this question, Alice looked away from the window. Apparently, the maid knew no more than she.

The duke looked at Alice then back at Rosalyn. "We'll discuss it later."

"When?" she pressed.

"Later."

But later, once they were outside of London, the duke vacated the carriage and rode his horse. Without the duke across from them making her nervous, Alice fell asleep, and Rosalyn stared out the window at the countryside racing by. It had been so long since she'd been out of London, she'd almost forgotten what green fields and white sheep looked like. And the air was cool and fresh, even under the heat of the summer sun.

They stopped routinely to change horses, and if time permitted, Rosalyn didn't even wait for the footman to open the carriage door before climbing down. She simply stepped away from the carriage, found a small patch of grass, and lifted her face to the sun. She could remember doing this as a child back at her home in Surrey.

"You'll freckle if you keep that up," said a male voice from behind her.

Rosalyn resisted the urge to lower her face and turn to face the duke. "I don't mind."

He was silent so long she finally did look at him. "I've never heard a woman say she doesn't mind freckles."

She shrugged. "That's because the women you know have nothing else to worry about. Freckles are not at the top of my list. Besides, I might look half alive again if I get some color on my cheeks."

"You look alive as it is."

She studied his face, but his expression gave nothing away. "Was that a compliment, Your Grace?"

"Just an observation."

"Good. Because if it was a compliment, it wasn't a very good one." She thought his lips might have quirked just slightly at that remark. "What is in Cornwall, Your Grace?"

His face clouded. He did not like this line of questioning, and the more he avoided telling her about the job he'd hired her to do, the more concerned she became. "You have to tell me at some point," she said.

He looked dubious.

"Don't you?"

"It's a book. A manuscript, to be precise," he said, surprising her. She'd thought she would have to do much more wheedling and cajoling, skills she had in abundance, as she'd finely honed them on her brothers.

"You want me to steal a book?"

"Possibly."

"Possibly? What book is it?"

"An old and valuable book."

"I didn't think it was the latest copy of Byron."

He frowned. "You have a flippant nature."

"Some people call it amusing. I like to smile, laugh, tease. I don't see the point in frowning all the time. It gives one lines." She touched his cheek to the side of his mouth. "Right here." And then she walked away, smiling because the shocked look on his face was the most amusing thing she'd seen in a very long time.

SHE'D TOUCHED HIM. She'd worn her gloves, so it hadn't been skin-to-skin contact, but nevertheless, she'd touched him. The sensation had jolted him, made him wonder how long it had been since someone else had touched him—someone besides his valet in the course of dressing.

Oh, he kissed his mother on the cheek when he saw her, a formal, perfunctory kiss as befitted a duchess. Nothing like the stifling hug Mrs. Dashner had given her daughter. And of course, he shook hands with men in the Lords. And there were women. He was a duke. He did not have to look very hard for a willing woman, but he had not looked in some time. And no one had touched him in any way that wasn't obligatory or dutiful in longer than he cared to remember.

That was until Miss Dashner. She'd touched him and she'd smiled up into his eyes, and his heart had jolted. He didn't quite know what to think, and so he mounted his horse and kept his distance the rest of the day. But it was impossible to keep his distance that evening. They stopped at an inn for the night, and he must dine with her, else she would have to eat in her room alone. He reserved a private room and sent word to her maid when Miss Dashner was to join him. He was in the room at the appointed hour, sitting at a table. But then he rose because his foot kept tapping. But he couldn't manage to stand still either, so he ended up pacing the room, pocket watch in hand. She was late, which annoyed him. But what annoyed him even more was that he could not seem to stop pacing. Dukes did not pace. Dukes made others pace and wait and worry.

Finally, the door opened and Miss Dashner stepped inside. She gave him a bright smile, and the annoyance he'd felt at her tardiness fled.

"Good evening, Your Grace." She looked just as fresh and pretty as she had this morning. "Have you chosen a table?" She gestured to the three empty ones in the private parlor.

"You go ahead."

"This one, I think. It's close to the hearth, but not so close as to overheat us." She passed him, and he caught the clean scent of her. She smelled of mint mingled with something floral, a clean country scent that was miles away from London. She sat and adjusted her skirts.

"Will your maid be joining us?" No one else had entered after her.

"I told her to eat with the other servants. I didn't think we needed a chaperone here. It's not *that* private. Besides, I want to continue our discussion about this book I'm to steal."

"Keep your voice down." He leaned close. "You never know who might be listening." As if to prove his point, the door opened again and the innkeeper entered. He was a pleasant enough man, tall and broad-shouldered and wearing a clean apron.

"Your Grace." He gave a slight bow. "Miss." Another. "Welcome to The White Hart. Shall I have your supper brought in?"

Dominick glanced at Miss Dashner, and she nodded.

"Very good. I'll return promptly with the tea you ordered."

He departed, and Miss Dashner raised a brow. "Tea? No ale?"

"Tea," he confirmed. He needed all his wits about him to deal with her. A moment later, the innkeeper returned with the tea and informed them it would be a few minutes until their meal was prepared.

Dominick sipped his tea, watching with amusement as Miss Dashner added three small blocks of sugar. "Shall I request more sugar?" he asked.

"Why?" She sipped her sugar laced with tea and smiled. "Did you want sugar?"

"No, but you obviously have a taste for it."

She shrugged. "I can't remember the last time I had sugar in my tea. I've missed it." She sipped again, then leaned forward. "Tell me about this book I'm to steal." Her voice was low enough that he couldn't chastise her, but he still glanced around to be certain they were alone.

"I prefer to say that you may need to assist me in acquiring the manuscript."

"I'm certain you do. Which book is it, and why do you need me to assist you?"

"Have you ever heard of the Bibliomania Club?"

"No, but I know enough Latin to understand it's a group who love books. And judging by what I know of most London societies, it's full of men so wealthy they don't have anything better to do with their money than spend it on rare volumes. Is that the gist of it?"

Dominick frowned. "We allow women."

"How progressive." Her tone was laden with sarcasm. "As I assume you only admit wealthy women, I don't suppose you want me to acquire this manuscript so I can become a member. Do you need it to retain your membership?"

"No."

"Then it's part of a competition."

"Not exactly." If he were being honest, Dominick would admit he did not want to be the only one of the three searching for the volumes of *The Duke's Book* to fail.

"Then it must be—"

"Miss Dashner."

She scowled, obviously annoyed that he'd interrupted her.

"If you will stop talking for a moment, I will explain."

"Of course!" She sat back.

Dominick opened his mouth.

"Please do explain, Your Grace," she said.

He tried again.

"I am all ears."

"Miss Dashner, if you were indeed all ears, I would have already said what I needed to say."

"Do forgive me."

It was the most insincere apology he'd ever heard. If he'd known she'd vex him this much, he would have offered her only forty pounds. "While at Oxford, I studied under an extraordinary man. He was my sponsor for the Bibliomania Club and taught me much of what I know about rare and valuable books."

"What was his name?"

He blew out a breath at this interruption. "I don't see why that matters."

"I'm only trying to make the tale a little more interesting."

"Are you implying that I am boring you?"

She opened her mouth, paused, then pointed to the door. "Oh, look! The food is here. How lovely!"

The innkeeper and a woman Dominick assumed was his wife bustled in with a tureen of soup, bread, and a variety of fresh fruits and fragrant vegetables. As soon as they departed, Miss Dashner filled her plate and bowl. Dominick supposed he should take advantage of her full mouth to speak while he could.

"The professor's name is Peebles, and he has spent his life searching for what is commonly known as *The Duke's Book*. More properly, it is referred to as *The Duke's Book of Knowledge*."

She ate bread and nodded encouragement.

"The book was commissioned by Lorenzo de' Medici sometime in the fifteenth century." He told her the history of the manuscript and about the professor's years of fruitless searching and his own discovery about his volume's possible location the night they'd met. "And so the three of us vowed to acquire the volumes as a gift to celebrate the professor's retirement. That's in about eleven days, so I need to move quickly to secure my volume."

"What is your volume about?" She put down her fork and pushed her plate away. It still held a remarkable amount of food, but her eyes must have been bigger than her stomach. "You said one was a volume on natural history and another matters of the heart. What is the one you seek?"

He was surprised she had actually been listening. "Medical knowledge. I suppose it's all rather arcane by our modern standards, but it's not the content that's important."

"I disagree. I think what's really important is your reputation. I can't think why else you would hire me to steal a book away from an old, mad earl who has nothing and no one else in his life, just to present it to a man who isn't satisfied with all he already has."

With that, she rose and walked away.

ROSALYN THOUGHT STEPHEN would have laughed at her if he'd been here. She was usually the one who argued for taking more and her brother the one who was hesitant to steal from anyone who might be hurt by the theft. But once again, she saw Stephen's point. The duke did not need this volume. He had all he'd ever need and more. The Earl of Verney, however, was a mad recluse who lived in the wilds of Cornwall—at least, that's how Tremayne had described it. What honor could there be in taking something from such a man only to give it to a man, who, though he might appreciate it, had more than enough in his life?

She was disgusted by the situation and disgusted with herself for accepting payment. Even worse, she knew she would go through with the job because Michael mattered more to her than an insane old man.

She marched for the door of the parlor, intent on returning to her room. She'd wanted to know what the job entailed, and now that she did, she'd rather not hear any more or have to look at the man who'd hired her to do it. But just as she lifted the latch, the duke's hand slammed the door closed again.

"What are you about, sir?" She rounded on him.

"I haven't given you leave."

Of all the pompous, asinine... "I didn't ask for leave. I took it. Now, kindly remove your hand from the door and allow me to return to my room."

His hand didn't budge. "You wanted to know the details of the job you'd been hired to do. Now you know."

True. And now she was forced to think how to bring the duke's plan to fruition. How to convince him of its inefficiency without raising his ire—raising it further?

"Well, I wish I didn't know these details. There's no honor in what you're asking me to do."

"You're a thief. You don't possess any honor anyway."

She inhaled sharply. A cold rage settled like a lead ball in her belly, and she stepped away from the door. "I have more honor in my little toe," she said, her voice quiet and steady, "than you have in your entire body."

"Don't be ridiculous."

"You think money or a title makes you honorable? No, it's who you are inside"—she tapped his chest—"that makes you honorable. It's what you do when you lose your money, when you lose your title, that shows your true mettle."

"So I suppose that means your true mettle took the shape of a thief." He grasped her hand and pushed it away from his chest. "Everyone knows there's no honor among thieves."

"And that shows just how *little* you do know. Now, out of my way." This time when she lifted the latch, he didn't stop her.

The next morning, she didn't speak a word to him or even glance his way. She simply climbed into the carriage and slammed the door behind her. Alice jumped. "Is anything wrong, miss?"

"Why would anything be wrong?" she said with false cheer. "It's a beautiful day to do evil."

And, in fact, the day had dawned bright and clear. The sun shone from a cloudless cerulean sky, and a mild breeze kept the afternoon from becoming too warm. Tremayne did not stop at a posting house for a midday meal. He had ordered food from The White Hart to be sent along, and they ate as they traveled. By three in the afternoon, the night she had spent tossing and turning and the novelty of a full belly meant her eyes crept closed. Alice lay sprawled and snoring on the seat across from her, and Rosalyn didn't see any reason not to emulate the maidservant's example. She sank down and was almost asleep when she heard the loud whinny of a horse and the words no traveler wants to hear.

"Stand and deliver!"

Rosalyn caught her breath but resisted the urge to spring up and peer through the open curtains. She heard the rumble of hoof beats, and then the carriage slowed, and she knew there could be only one explanation. The highwaymen had surrounded them, forcing the carriage to halt.

"What is this about? Move aside and allow us to pass, or I will make you sincerely regret it." The duke spoke loudly and confidently, but in her opinion, not altogether intelligently. Now that the carriage had stopped, she slid to the floor and pressed herself against the door. If anyone peered inside from the side where the bandit's voice had come from, they would see only Alice, who was still sleeping. If one of the highwaymen looked in from the other side, he'd see her, of course. From the angle where she crouched, Rosalyn couldn't see any men outside that window, but the shadow of a man—whether the duke or a highwayman, she didn't know—spread out over the floor of the carriage.

"Give us your valuables, and no one will be hurt," the same man who'd spoken initially ordered.

Please just give him what he wants. Don't be a fool.

"You are the one who should worry about injury. I will say it one last time. Turn around and go back the way you came." Obviously, the duke was a fool.

Rosalyn flinched when she heard the sound of a cocking pistol.

"Hand over your valuables, or I put a pistol ball in your head."

Rosalyn couldn't allow this to go on. The duke would be dead if she didn't intervene. Not that she cared about him, but how would she claim her remaining twenty-five pounds?

Stealthy as a cat, Rosalyn crept across the floor of the carriage and pressed the door latch down. The door clicked open, and she parted it just enough to peer out. There were two highwaymen on this side of the carriage, but one pointed a rifle at the coachman, and the other was in the rear, his attention on the duke and the bandits' leader. She could see why the highwaymen had chosen this spot for an ambush. Trees grew thickly along the road, creating a dense canopy overhead and making this stretch darker than most they'd traveled thus far. But the landscape also worked to her advantage.

Pushing the door open a little more, Rosalyn squeezed out, hands first, and slipped underneath the carriage. Reaching up, she closed the door with a soft click.

"What do you have in that carriage?" the highwayman was asking now. She'd evacuated just in time. From under the conveyance, she spotted his horse's hooves moving closer to the window where she'd hidden. He was peering inside and seeing only Alice. "Who are you?"

"J-just a maidservant," Alice answered. Her voice was thick from waking from sleep.

"Are you traveling alone in there?"

The pause lasted impossibly long. Rosalyn closed her eyes and held her breath until Alice said, "Yes."

"Good girl," Rosalyn muttered, then slid across the dirt road. She had only one dress, and it would be ruined after this. The things she did for this idiot duke. Reaching the edge of the carriage frame, Rosalyn reached for the nearest horse's leg and pinched it hard. Just as she'd expected, the horse startled and reared.

"What the devil?" the highwayman called. But the distraction proved enough for the duke. She saw his horse move close to the leader's, and then the duke knocked the man off his animal, jumping down after him, punching him hard, and then hauling him up to use as a shield. Rosalyn snaked forward until she was just beneath the coachman's box, then wedged herself slowly into the space to the side and waited.

"Lower your weapons," the duke called, "or I shoot him."

Rosalyn's brows rose with appreciation. He'd obviously managed to snatch the highwayman's pistol. He wasn't as much of an idiot as she'd thought.

"Go ahead!" the man with the rifle pointed at the coachman called back. "I'll shoot you right after."

The rifle swung toward the duke, and Rosalyn jumped up, landed with a crouch on the box, then leaped forward and knocked the rifle out of the bandit's hands. She fell forward, rolled, rose to her feet, pivoted, and scooped the rifle into her hands. Pointing it at the two bandits still seated on their horses, she strode forward.

"Hello, gentlemen. How lovely of you to provide me targets for my daily practice."

Chapter Five

DOMINICK WAS HALF afraid he'd hit his head. He could not be seeing what he was seeing. Miss Dashner had just appeared from nowhere and disarmed the highwayman who'd held a rifle to his coachman's head. And now she strode along the road, rifle cradled in her arm and at the ready, as though she knew exactly what she was about.

Perhaps she did.

All was silent for two heartbeats, and then one of the highwaymen swung his pistol in her direction. Dominick felt his heart stutter as though a pistol ball had been driven into it.

"Put that down, chit, before I blow it out of your hands." He cocked the hammer.

Dominick swore when she paused and then did as he asked, lowering the muzzle of the weapon.

"Now bring it here," the highwayman called, while the others chuckled.

"You want it?" she asked. "Get it yourself." She tossed the rifle aside, and then, so quickly he could barely follow her movements, she scampered up a tree and disappeared into the foliage.

"Where did she go?" the bandit called, while the man she'd disarmed dismounted and went for the rifle. A shot rang out, and everyone froze.

"Hands in the air!" John Coachman called out, raising the rifle he always kept tucked under his box. Immediately, the man who'd leaped off his horse closed his eyes, clearly regretting his rash behavior. He'd not only lost his rifle but he was without a quick means of escape. Assuming the rifleman also had a pistol, the odds were now even—two armed highwaymen against Dominick and the coachman. Dominick still held the leader, so he would make a poor target. But if anyone fired at the coachman, it would take time for Dominick to shove the leader away, aim, and fire. He didn't have the advantage.

The leader must have been thinking along the same lines. "There's no need for anyone to die today. Give us your money, and we'll be on our way."

"How about we keep our money and none of you have to die?" Dominick answered. One lesson he had learned from his father was to never admit defeat.

Dominick heard a hammer cock and glanced wildly about to try to determine if another highwayman had been in hiding and might be about to fire, but all he saw was a blue blur drop down from the trees. The highwayman nearest him tumbled off his horse, and John Coachman shot the one in the road, who was reaching in his coat, in the arm, causing him to fall to his knees. Dominick didn't stop to think. He shoved the leader aside and ran to Miss Dashner. The highwayman she'd landed on had shoved her off, and she'd rolled away into an immobile heap. Panting, the bandit she'd taken down rose to his feet and stumbled toward his fallen pistol, but Dominick grabbed his shoulder, spun him around, and punched him hard in the jaw.

"Let's get out of here!" the leader called and ran for his horse. The other followed suit. Only the man the coachman had shot still lay in the road.

Dominick knelt beside Miss Dashner, who hadn't moved. He placed a hand on her arm. "Miss Dashner? Miss Dashner?"

Slowly, she turned her face toward him and opened her eyes. "Am I shot?" she whispered.

"I don't think so. I think you hit your head when you tumbled off the horse with him." She had a small red bump on her forehead.

"That explains why my scalp feels as though a dagger is lodged inside. Too bright out here." She closed her eyes again.

The outriders ran to Dominick's side. "One of you check on that bandit." Dominick indicated the man who now lay in the road. The coachman hadn't moved from his box, focused as he was on keeping the team calm and still. "And you, open the carriage door. I want to put Miss Dashner inside." Dominick reached to lift her.

"I can carry her, Your Grace."

"No." He lifted her, noting she didn't weigh much more than a child. She batted his hands away at first, then laid her head on his chest. He placed her in the carriage, and the maidservant, who'd been cowering on the floor, lifted her head.

"Your Grace! Are they gone?"

"Yes. You're safe, but your mistress has been injured."

"I'll see to her."

"Good." Dominick wanted to move again as quickly as possible. There was no knowing when or if the highwaymen might return. The man the coachman had shot was bleeding from the arm. The outrider had tied a tourniquet about the injury. "Bind his hands and put him in the coach. We'll take him to the mayor in the next town."

The horses were checked, the bandit placed in the coach, and Dominick sat beside him. He wouldn't leave the ladies alone with a highwayman. An hour later, they'd deposited the would-be thief with the mayor and Dominick had reserved rooms at an inn called The King's Rest. It was much earlier to rest than Dominick had wanted, but they'd all had enough for the day.

After supper, which he'd eaten alone, as Miss Dashner hadn't been well enough to come down, Dominick went to her room and tapped on the door. His brows rose when Miss Dashner opened the door herself. When she saw him, she opened the door wider and moved aside, an indication he was free to enter. "Come to chide me for climbing trees?"

Dominick peered into her small chamber. "Where is your maid?"

"I sent her to have supper with the other servants. I couldn't stand her fussing anymore. Are you coming in, or shall we converse in the doorway?"

It would have been more proper to converse in the doorway, but she was in her night rail—at least, he thought that was what she wore under the large wrapper she tugged about herself. He didn't want everyone to see her in her wrapper. Not that he should see her either, but now that he'd already seen her, a few more minutes seemed inconsequential. Not to mention, from what he could see, the night rail was a thick, voluminous white sack. Not much to see.

"I'll come in." He stepped inside, and she closed the door then indicated two chairs. A teapot sat on the small table between them.

"Would you like tea? I have sugar left." She gave him a mischievous smile and sat.

He couldn't help but smile back. "No, thank you." He sat across from her. The red bump on her forehead had faded to a dull pink. "How is your head?"

"It feels like it did when one of my brothers whacked me when we were children, but I'll survive. The tea helped."

"Then would you care to explain to me what the devil you thought you were doing?"

She rolled her eyes. "I wondered when the lecture would come. You can't even wait until I'm well again."

"You're well enough."

She scowled. "No sympathy. You're as bad as my brothers."

"You might have had plenty of sympathy. You almost died." He realized he was practically yelling and lowered his voice. What was the matter with him? He never raised his voice.

"That is a gross exaggeration. I bumped my head. Nothing more."

His jaw dropped. "Miss Dashner, you snatched a loaded rifle from a man intent on using it, faced highwaymen with firearms, then jumped from a tree onto the back of another armed man. You should have stayed in the carriage."

"Then we'd all be much poorer."

Oh, he resented that implication. "I could have handled the highwaymen. My men and I have done it before."

"I had the element of surprise on my side. Besides, you didn't hire me to cower on the floor of the carriage."

He rose. "I didn't hire you to get yourself killed!"

"Because then you might never acquire the book."

"No! Yes. I mean, you frightened the hell out of me today."

She studied him as though she were a painter and he the subject. "Are you saying you care about me?"

"Of course I care about you."

She set her tea cup down and raised her brows playfully. "Really? Your Grace, this is all so sudden."

He realized what he'd said and had to qualify the statement. "I mean, I care about you as an employer cares for his employees. I don't want any of my people injured."

"I see. So if Alice had done what I did today, you would be lecturing her."

"Alice would never do what you did today."

She rose and stood before him. "I think that's why you like me. I surprise you."

He took a step back. "I don't like you." But he remembered how his heart had seized when he'd feared she'd been shot, and it hadn't all been because he'd hired her to get him the manuscript. There had been genuine fear and a need to protect her.

"Not even a little?" She took a step closer to him.

"This conversation is inappropriate." He moved back again.

"It is. If I told you that you impressed me today when you grabbed the leader of the highwaymen, would that also be inappropriate?"

"I—" He'd impressed her?

"It wouldn't be suitable for me to mention how handsome you looked, how dangerous."

"Miss Dashner." But he didn't know what to say. Heat radiated from his neck to his cheeks, and he feared he was actually blushing.

"Have I embarrassed you, Your Grace? Surely you know you are handsome."

He fumbled for the door latch behind him. When had he turned into a bumbling schoolboy? "I should go so you can rest. We'll leave at first light tomorrow."

"I'll be ready."

He opened the door, then hesitated. "I owe you an apology." He looked back. Her brows were high and her expression one of surprise. "Yesterday I insinuated you had no honor. I was wrong." Dominick stepped out. "Good night." Closing the door, he walked quickly to his own chamber. There, he closed the door, leaned against it, and took a deep, deep breath.

THE MAN SHE'D teased and made blush the night before, the man who had apologized to her for insinuating—ridiculous, he was not so subtle—she had no honor had disappeared in the morning. He'd been replaced by a stern, demanding oaf who rattled off a litany of orders. As most of them didn't have to do with her, Rosalyn climbed into the carriage, shut the curtains, and closed her eyes. She hadn't slept well the night before. She blamed it on the dull ache in her head and the lumpy bed, but her overactive mind had been part of the problem as well. Why had the duke blushed? She'd been teasing when she asked if he liked her.

What if he did like her?

Did she like him?

Of course, she didn't like him. But several hours later, when she couldn't quite stop herself from opening the curtains to peer out at him, she had to admit she was at least attracted to him. And she hadn't lied when she'd said he'd impressed her. He was more competent than she'd thought, and whether or not she'd placed too much emphasis on his lecture the night before, he did care enough to check on her.

That afternoon, the duke ordered they have a picnic lunch, as he didn't want to take the time to stop at an inn and dine. He'd had The King's Rest pack food for them to eat, and one of the footmen laid it on a blanket in a sunny field a little ways off the road.

"Join me, Miss Dashner," the duke said. It wasn't a question.

She sat, straightening her now stained blue dress. Alice had tried to clean it, but she'd been unsuccessful. They dined on cheese, apples, bread, and a very good wine, and there were more bundles to unwrap. Rosalyn wasn't particularly hungry, though.

"How did you come to love books?" she asked.

The duke paused and looked up from the glass he was refilling with wine. "I always enjoyed reading. It filled the long hours in the country."

She held out her glass for more wine. "I never read in the country, only when we came to Town. It seemed there was never enough time to climb all the trees or chase all the butterflies I wanted when I was in the countryside."

"I was never one for climbing or chasing. The heir to a dukedom is expected to behave with decorum, even at a young age."

That sounded awfully tedious. "But surely you had friends you might ride with or plan battles. My brothers would spend hours lining up their toy soldiers when we were young."

"My brothers are quite a few years younger than I. My sisters are closer in age, but they were only interested in dolls."

"And what of your friends?"

He sipped his wine. "I didn't have many friends growing up. The other children seemed to think I was..."

"Dictatorial?" she offered.

"No." He frowned.

"Overbearing?"

"No."

"Arro—"

"Miss Dashner." His voice held a sharp edge. "I was about to say they considered me too staid. I actually preferred reading."

He looked so offended, she put her hand on his arm. "I was only teasing. My brother Michael is a great reader as well. I think there is no better pastime, as literature not only entertains but educates."

Slowly, he pulled his arm away. "I do think you are the only person who has ever teased me, Miss Dashner."

"That is a tragedy, Your Grace. You should be teased more. Anything that makes you smile is to be encouraged. You have a very attractive smile."

His expression was one of absolute shock, and before she could laugh or he could say something to annoy her, she rose and strode back to the carriage. She had never met a man she could so easily surprise or whose reaction she enjoyed as much.

Several hours later, when they'd stopped at another inn and finished dining in the private parlor, the duke informed Rosalyn they would reach Cornwall and The Temples on the morrow. He had stubbornly resisted her attempts to make him smile all evening, even blushing at one point, but she couldn't resist trying again.

"And when we arrive, do we charge the keep immediately, or do we attempt negotiation first?"

"This is not a game, Miss Dashner. I will call on the earl, and if I cannot persuade his staff to allow me to speak to him, then I will request your assistance."

"And that's when I'm to scale the wall of the fortress, breach its defenses, confront the earl, and persuade him to meet you in the drawing room."

"More or less."

"Why don't I just find the library and steal the volume? It seems more efficient."

They were seated across from each other at a small table near the hearth, and he leaned forward. "I don't want to steal the volume."

She leaned forward, so close they were almost nose-to-nose. "Then why did you hire a thief?"

"I like to be prepared for all eventualities." He hadn't moved back to put distance between them as she'd expected. And now she was the one who felt heat rising to her cheeks. "In any case, our time together is quickly coming to an end."

She nodded. "Then I suppose if you want to kiss me, you should do it soon." Rosalyn couldn't have articulated why she'd said it. She hadn't planned to say such a thing. She hadn't even known she wanted him to kiss her, but as soon as the words were out, she both regretted them and hoped he would act on them. What would it be like to watch this carefully controlled man succumb to passion? And wouldn't she like to be the one with whom he succumbed?

Ridiculous thought. Now she'd only made things awkward between them. She started to move back, but he lifted a hand and ran a finger along her cheek. The light, simple gesture made her freeze. Perhaps things were not quite so awkward as she'd feared.

"I have been wanting to kiss you since..."

"Since you first met me?"

"No."

"Since you first saw me in a dress?"

"No." Before she could speak again, he placed his finger over her lips. "Since I watched you stroll down the middle of a road, facing armed highwaymen."

"Oh, that," she mumbled, his finger still on her lips.

"I've never met a woman like you. I think I can hardly be blamed for wondering what it might be like to kiss such a woman."

She wrapped a hand around his wrist and drew his finger down. "I think you should try it and see."

"Here?"

"Yes."

"Like this?"

"Yes. No choreography required."

"But—"

She kissed him. All she had to do was lean forward and press her lips to his. Yes, the table between them was inconvenient. Yes, someone might enter at any moment and interrupt, but Rosalyn did not intend to lose her opportunity.

His mouth was warm and soft, and the act of placing her lips on his was quite nice. Initially, he seemed frozen in shock, but then he kissed her back, and that was quite nice as well. She didn't have much experience kissing. She'd kissed a few boys here and there, but never a man. Never a duke. Now she'd have something to tell her grandchildren one day.

She drew back, smiling, but her grin faded when she saw the intensity of the duke's look. "Did I do something wrong?" She rose. He rose as well and rounded the table. Now she was the one who took a step back. "Shouldn't I have done that?"

"It was a bad idea."

"Why?"

He stepped closer, and she stepped back again.

"Because now I want more."

"More?"

"More."

She stepped back again, but this time, he caught her arm and hauled her forward, against his chest. "Any farther back and you'll step into the fire," he explained.

She glanced over her shoulder and saw she'd almost backed into the hearth. "Thank you."

"It was no trouble." He was solid and warm against her, his strong arms enveloping her. "And since you are here." He bent, and though she could see he intended to kiss her, she couldn't quite believe it until his lips took hers. This kiss was not at all like the one they'd shared a moment ago. Then, she'd been teasing, testing him, really. But he was not teasing. His mouth took hers with a fierceness that surprised her and made her body catch fire all over. She half feared she had stepped into the hearth after all, because quite suddenly she felt so very, very warm.

His hand skated up her back and cupped the curve of her head, where her hair was pinned, then he deepened the kiss. She knew what he wanted, though she'd never done this herself. But she'd seen others do it. She opened her mouth to allow him entrance, and when his tongue licked inside, she gasped.

He pulled back, his blue eyes large and dark. "Should I stop?"

"Why would you stop?"

"I don't want to scare you."

"I assure you, Duke, the only thing I fear is that you won't kiss me again." The staid duke had hidden stores of passion.

With a smile that made her insides melt, he kissed her again. This time, she ventured into his mouth, her tongue tangling with his. It was his turn to catch his breath. He pulled back and looked down at her. "My name is Dominick."

"Lovely." She kissed him again, not caring what his name was, only wanting to feel his warm lips on hers again. His mouth slanted over hers, and she was not disappointed.

Until he pulled back again.

"May I call you by your Christian name?"

She rose on tiptoes to kiss him again, but he held her back, waiting for her answer.

"Yes, call me Rosalyn. And if you still feel like calling me Miss Dashner, I must be doing something wrong."

His laugh turned to a groan when she took his head in her hands and kissed him deeply. Somehow, they had moved backward, and she felt the wall press against her back. She was relieved to have something to support her. Her legs felt wobbly, and her feet had lost all sensation. There was only the two of them and the way their mouths met, lips teasing and tasting.

And then the dratted man pulled away again. He braced a hand against the wall and, panting, looked down at her. "Rosalyn is a pretty name."

Did he want to have a conversation? "Dominick is pretty too," she said, then reached up again. But he took her shoulders in his hands and held her back. "This is not the time for a conversation, Dominick."

He smiled, making her want to kiss him again. "I'd argue it's exactly the time for a conversation. Otherwise, we may do something we'd both regret."

She wasn't so naïve she didn't know what he meant, but she hadn't considered the possibility that what had begun as an innocent kiss might turn into something much, much more. And if she enjoyed kissing him this much, then how much more might she enjoy what came after? But she was no wanton, and she neither wanted to be ruined by a duke nor bear his bastard. So she lowered her arms and took a fortifying breath. "You're right. I should go to bed."

"As should I. We have a long day tomorrow."

"In that case, sleep well…" She wasn't certain what to call him now that they were no longer touching. Your Grace? Duke? Dominick? "Sleep well."

"You too, Rosalyn," he said, as though he knew her dilemma.

She nodded and made her way on unsteady legs to the door. But she didn't go immediately to her room. First, she stepped outside and pressed her hands to her cheeks and gulped the fresh air. But it would take more than a hay-scented breeze to take away the memory of his hands on her. And it would take sheer willpower to keep from kissing him the next time she saw him.

Chapter Six

DOMINICK STARED AT the ancient structure looming above them. They'd traveled through Cornwall all morning, until they'd finally reached what Dominick assumed must be the most remote area in all of England. The road—if one wanted to call it that—was flanked by cliffs on either side, and below the cliffs, the ocean slammed hard against craggy rocks worn and weathered by the centuries. Rising above it all at the end of a narrow peninsula was a gray structure with towers looming from all four corners and keyhole arrow slits cut into the stone.

"There it is. The Temples, Your Grace," John Coachman announced, sitting back when he'd halted the carriage and an outrider had opened the doors.

"Why have we stopped here?" Dominick asked. The carriage stood a quarter mile or more from the entrance to the old building.

"It's too narrow up ahead, and I don't trust the ground. Could be dangerous for the horses, Your Grace."

Dominick stepped down and surveyed the road himself. The coachman was correct. It would be dangerous for the horses and the carriage to continue. He turned to see Rosalyn descending the carriage steps. She wore a long cape that hid the male clothing she wore underneath, but he knew she was prepared to climb the wall of The Temples at his mere command.

"We walk from here," he said, turning away from her. He waved off the outriders who would have accompanied them, as well as the maidservant. The fewer people who approached the mad earl the better. In fact, Dominick would have left Rosalyn at the carriage too, but she would need a close view of the building if she had to climb it later.

Of course, now, as he walked ahead of her along the rocky path, he was rethinking that plan. He shouldn't have kissed her. He'd known it was a bad idea the moment he'd considered it, but he hadn't been able to convince himself when she stood before him. But in the cold light of morning, when he'd been apart from her for hours and able to evaluate the situation, he knew becoming personally involved with her had been a mistake. She was a servant, little more. He couldn't afford to worry about her safety. If every time he looked up at the high steep walls of The Temples, he imagined her plummeting to her death on the wet rocks below, he would never allow her to scale them. And then he might never acquire the manuscript.

The manuscript was everything, not simply because he wanted to be able to present it to Professor Peebles, though that was important. The man had searched for the volume his whole life. There was no one more deserving. But the search was about more than that. It was about proving himself as a member of the Bibliomania Club. The club stood for truth and knowledge, and Dominick wanted to contribute to those lofty purposes by acquiring a volume that would shed light on the truth and knowledge as it had been viewed in the time of the book's conception.

And, of course, he did not want to be the only one who failed. A Duke of Tremayne never failed.

Dominick glanced at The Temples again. He had to crane his neck to look up at the towers. The climb would be dangerous, and any mistake could mean a long, long fall. If Rosalyn made one false move while climbing that wall, he would never kiss her again. He would never hold her in his arms or inhale the fragrance that was hers alone.

He tried to remind himself there were plenty of other women who smelled just as sweet and felt just as good in his arms. But it wasn't any use. He'd kissed other women, touched other women, and he'd never felt the way he felt when he held Rosalyn and pressed his lips to hers.

"What shall we do now?" she asked, coming to stand beside him. Dominick realized he'd been standing before the massive oak door of the castle for several moments.

"We knock." He eyed the knocker, a tarnished gold ring fashioned into a design of a snake eating its own tail.

"Do you suppose anyone is at home?" she murmured. "It looks completely uninhabited."

"There is but one way to find out." He lifted the knocker and lowered it on the metal plate three times. The hollow sound that echoed back at them made Rosalyn shiver. Dominick resisted the urge to pull her close and reassure her. She was a servant. He was paying her to do a task. He had to remember that.

Five minutes or more passed, neither of them speaking as they stood before the door. Dominick reached for the knocker again, but Rosalyn put a hand on his arm. "Listen," she whispered.

He listened, shook his head, and then froze. He'd heard what she must have as well. A distinct shuffling sound came closer and closer. Rosalyn's hand tightened on his arm, and Dominick did exactly what his mind told him not to—he put his own hand over hers to comfort her.

Or, if he was being brutally honest, perhaps the action comforted him.

The clang and creak of locks turning and latches lifting echoed into the sunlit day behind them. But as the door scraped open, clouds seemed to sweep across the sun, casting everything and everyone into a gray gloom.

In the doorway stood a man of medium height with dark hair and dark eyes. He was dressed in black, his clothing tailored and clean. He looked every inch the typical butler. In fact, he looked so typical that Dominick did not hear him when he spoke.

Rosalyn poked him, and Dominick started. "I beg your pardon."

The butler smiled as though he were used to this response. "I said, good afternoon and welcome to The Temples. I am Payne. How may I be of assistance?"

"I've come to pay a call on the Earl of Verney." Dominick held out the card he had ready. "You may tell him the Duke of Tremayne and his companion are here."

Mr. Payne did not seem as impressed by a duke coming all this way to call as Dominick might have hoped. The butler looked at the card then back at Dominick and Rosalyn. Finally, he stepped back, opening the door wider as he did. "Won't you come inside and out of the rain?"

Dominick frowned. It was not raining. But as soon as he thought it, a raindrop plopped on the back of his neck and the boom of thunder rent the quiet. Rosalyn was staring back the way they'd come, and he turned to follow her gaze. Rain poured in sheets, soaking the horses and the outriders. Lightning flashed in the angry skies over the churning water.

"Storms arise quickly over the water," Payne said. "Does your traveling party require shelter? I'm afraid we have no stable. It washed away several years ago."

That meant Dominick would either have to let his party stand in the rain or send them back two miles to the last vestiges of civilization. He faced Payne. "They'll be fine."

Rosalyn gave him a disapproving look but didn't speak. She stepped into the grand foyer just ahead of him, her neck craning to look up at the vaulted ceiling. The foyer was easily two stories, a massive chandelier hanging from the highest point. It was not lit, but the sconces burning around the chamber meant that the chandelier shed a wide shadow over the center of the floor. Though dark and musty, as many old buildings were, The Temples looked clean and well-kept. If a madman did indeed reside here, his madness had not interfered with basic housekeeping.

"This way," Payne said, lifting a candelabra. He led them out of the foyer and through a dark, windowless passage. The passage ended before an arched wooden door. Payne extracted what looked like a skeleton key from his waistcoat, fitted it in the lock, turned it, and opened the door. The interior was dim, and when Rosalyn began to enter, Dominick grasped her shoulder, holding her back. He wasn't certain whether this was a prison cell or a parlor, and though it might be customary to allow a lady to enter ahead of him, he felt the need to protect her.

Dominick strode into the room, noting the hearth had been lit, warding off some of the chill. It was not a prison cell, but a small parlor, furnished with tapestries and ornate wooden chairs that would have looked at home at the table of King Henry VIII. Rosalyn entered next, followed by Payne with the candelabra, which he set on a side table. "Would you care for refreshment?"

"No," Dominick said. "We'd like to speak to the earl as soon as possible."

"Of course." Payne smiled. "If you will excuse me for a moment, I will see if the earl is at home."

He left the room, closing the door behind him.

"Why do I have the urge to check whether he locked us in?" Rosalyn whispered.

"This isn't a prison, Miss Dashner," Dominick said, reminding himself as much as her.

"It looks quite normal on the inside," she said, moving about the room to examine the tapestry. "I thought there would be spider webs and rusty suits of armor."

Dominick wouldn't admit it, but he'd envisioned far worse. "You are allowing your imagination to get the better of you."

"I don't have an imagination," she countered. "And I didn't imagine that storm that was summoned when you knocked on the door."

"There is nothing supernatural here, Miss Dashner. My family owns at least one castle almost as old as this one, and though it is dark and crumbling, there are no ghosts."

"Oh, that's comforting. Now you have me worried about ghosts," she grumbled. He almost smiled, then caught himself. He must treat her as a servant. Not as a woman he found clever and amusing.

"What is your opinion of the outer walls?" he asked, bringing his attention, and hopefully hers as well, back to the problem at hand.

She looked away from the tapestry and met his eyes with her lovely green ones. "I can climb them," she said, sounding confident. "They're not smooth or sheer. There are plenty of bricks that might serve as hand- and footholds. The problem is that there are no outer windows, only embrasures, and even I am not small enough to squeeze through one of those."

"Then there was no reason for you to come." He felt a sense of relief. She couldn't enter The Temples by climbing the outside. She would not have to risk her life doing so.

"I didn't say I couldn't do it," she snapped. "I only said there are no entrances on the walls. The roof is another matter."

"What do you mean?"

"This was a fortress meant to repel attacks coming from land or sea, correct?"

He nodded, beginning to see where she was leading him.

"There must be turrets along the roof where archers could stand and rain arrows down upon invaders. That means there is a way in from the roof. I only need to climb that high."

Dominick did not want her to climb that high. He did not want to watch her small body dangle above him, while he stood on firm ground below and watched in safety. He couldn't allow it. "Rosalyn," he began.

Someone tapped on the door, and Dominick spun around, expecting to see the old earl, but he was greeted by an ancient woman carrying a silver tray. The tray looked heavy and the woman small and frail, and Rosalyn immediately raced to the servant's aid. "Let me assist you!"

"I have it," the old woman said in a papery voice. "I can still carry a tray or my name isn't Clothilde Wright."

Rosalyn glanced at Dominick, and he strode forward, taking a table with him. "Set it here, Mrs. Wright," he said, placing the table directly in front of her.

"Thank you, sir." She smiled, lifting the mass of wrinkles on her face. "Are you certain this is convenient? You should have tea by the hearth—" She made to lift the tray again, and Dominick shook his head.

"This is perfect. Please do not trouble yourself."

She wiped her hands on her apron. "Very well. Is there anything else you require?"

They hadn't asked for the tea and sandwiches on the tray. "Just the earl, Mrs. Wright. Can we expect him soon?"

"The earl?" The old woman looked confused. "I don't know. I was told to fetch tea for our guests. So nice to have guests. And what a handsome couple you make. Is this your honeymoon?"

Dominick felt his cheeks heat. "No," he said at the same time Rosalyn all but shouted, "No!" He scowled at her. "We came to call upon the earl."

"We have so few guests. The last couple was touring Cornwall on their honeymoon. Such a nice young man and a pretty lady. They didn't stay long."

"Did they meet with the earl?" Rosalyn asked.

"Oh, no. They wanted to tour the castle, but we don't show The Temples."

"Why not?" Dominick asked.

"Oh, too many ghosts, I suppose."

Rosalyn's eyes grew wide, and she moved closer to him.

"Just ring for me if you need me." Mrs. Wright indicated the bell-pull. And then she was gone.

"Do you think she was serious about the ghosts?" Rosalyn whispered when they were alone.

"No. I'm sure she's trying to scare us away. Stories like that will deter other travelers from stopping by and expecting a tour."

"But we don't want a tour. We want to speak to the earl."

"And I am afraid that is not possible," a voice said from the doorway. Payne was back. "The earl is unwell today and will not see visitors."

Dominick had been expecting this. "Did you tell him the Duke of Tremayne is calling? I've come a long way."

"I did, Your Grace. The earl sends his regrets."

"I'll return this evening."

The butler nodded. "That is your choice, Your Grace."

Dominick extended his arm to Rosalyn, and the two exited. Outside, the rain still poured. "May I offer you an umbrella, Your Grace?" Payne asked. Dominick glared at him.

"Don't bother."

When the door to The Temples closed behind them, Rosalyn huddled under the scant protection provided by the overhang. "The lightning and thunder have stopped," she said. "If you make a show of walking out to the carriage, I can slip around to the back."

"Why would you do that?"

"You hired me to scale the walls if you couldn't speak to the earl."

Dominick had to resist the urge to pull her close and protect her. "The rain is coming down in sheets. It's too dangerous."

"I've climbed in the rain before. I can do it."

"You'll wait," he ordered and, taking her hand, pulled her to the carriage with him.

ROSALYN DID INDEED wait. She waited three days. The duke went back to The Temples time and again, but was turned away regardless. They had taken lodgings in the only inn within ten miles, and as there were only two rooms, she and the duke shared a wall. She could hear him railing to his servants that time was running out and he was no closer to acquiring the book than he had been.

Soon, they'd return to London empty-handed. Then what would happen? Michael's declining health required that she earn the rest of her fee, and she wouldn't receive it if she didn't make certain the duke acquired the volume he sought. The duke hadn't said as much. In fact, he'd said very little to her the past few days. She was relatively certain he was avoiding her. They hadn't taken a meal together since the night they'd kissed. Did the duke worry being alone with her would be awkward, or did he simply not want to see her again? Perhaps she was the only one who thought again and again about the kiss they'd shared and wished for another.

Truth be told, she wished for more than that. The duke was a good man. He could be rigid at times, but he could also soften and make her smile. He was good to his servants, the horses, and the innkeepers. He was a kind man. A good man. Letters arrived from London, and he took hours each day to pen responses addressing every concern his stewards might have on any of his vast properties. Yes, he might be mad for this book, which to her seemed rather unimportant, but as hobbies went, collecting books was far less detrimental than gambling or whoring.

When she heard him return from The Temples on the third night, heard the disappointment in his voice as he addressed a servant, she knew what she had to do. The duke might very well feel obliged to pay her, even if she didn't acquire the book for him. She didn't want his charity, didn't want to take advantage of his goodness.

Rosalyn pulled the shutters open and looked out. A half-moon sat in a partly cloudy sky. She might have wished for more light, but it was not raining and it was the best she could hope for. Rosalyn dressed in her male clothing, slipped down to the stables, saddled one of the horses, and made her way to The Temples.

She tied the horse far enough back that he would not be spotted, then approached the narrow, treacherous path alone. The Temples was dark. No lights burned in the windows, and she relied on the light from the moon when it wasn't buried behind clouds. Finally, she'd made her way to the rear of the building. A path wound around the castle, but it was less than a yard wide and ended in a sheer, rocky drop down to the tumultuous seas below. Peering over the edge and into that churning black water, Rosalyn knew if she fell, no one would ever know what had become of her. Her lifeless body would be washed away and never seen again.

So she would not fall.

She extracted her gloves from her pocket and pulled them over her shaking hands. These were one of the tools she'd packed in her valise. Then she changed into her special shoes, leaving her worn half boots at the base of The Temples. She walked along the edge of the building, feeling for handholds, and when she found a likely spot to begin, she took a deep breath.

"For Michael. Always Michael," she whispered to herself, calming her racing heart. "And this time for Dominick too."

When she was calm and steady, she reached up and began to climb. It was difficult work, and she was perspiring within minutes, but it was also familiar. Her body knew what to do. Her hands sought alcoves or outcrops even without her having to think about it, and her toes curled and wrapped around ledges too small for anyone but the most astute to note. She climbed without looking up or down, without wondering at the passage of time, without any thought but of the next place for her hand or foot. When it began to rain, she did not think of the weather. She took more care, now that the stone was slick, but she did not hesitate.

Several times, she lost her footing and dangled above the crashing waves below. Rosalyn wouldn't allow fear to enter her mind. She held tightly with her hands and slid her foot along the wall until she found a better foothold. Then, when she'd regained her balance and caught her breath, she inched upward.

She had no idea how long she'd been climbing when she felt the turret at the top of the building. It might have been minutes or hours. The important thing was that she'd made it. She grabbed the edge of the stone wall circling the top of the building and hauled herself up, her arms shaking with the effort. But the section she'd grabbed began to crumble under her hands, and she realized she'd made a novice mistake. She'd been so relieved to see the end in sight, she hadn't tested the strength of the next handhold. She slipped down, and stone scattered past her, falling for so long she did not hear it land. She had one chance to grasp the next closest section of wall. If it too was weak, she'd go sliding into the sea like the loose rocks.

Her hand slipped as more of the wall dissolved, and she grasped for the section above her. She caught it with the tips of her fingers and closed her eyes, praying it would hold. When it didn't disintegrate, she pulled up. This was the hardest part. Her arms were tired, and now she had to haul her entire body up and over this wall. With a grunt of effort, she lifted herself high enough to release the footholds. Sweat poured down her face, and her arm muscles felt as though they might ignite from the fiery pain lancing through her. Though there was little to give her traction, she tried to use her feet to give her more leverage. Gradually, she worked one elbow over the wall, then the other. She rested for a moment, then swung her legs over and fell onto her back.

The rain felt good on her face, cooling her skin. She didn't know how long she lay there, but when she rose and checked the location of the moon, she realized she had probably been climbing no more than an hour.

Standing, Rosalyn tucked her gloves back into her coat and pushed her wet hair off her face, securing the loose pieces into the queue at her nape. She spotted a doorway and started for it.

Time to meet the mad old earl.

Chapter Seven

DOMINICK BLAMED HIMSELF for not knowing she'd left earlier. It was his own fault for not prioritizing his correspondence, as was his usual practice. But the servant who'd delivered the letters had placed one from the bailiff of his property in Yorkshire on top, and Dominick had not looked at any others in his haste to read that one.

As matters in Yorkshire were still tenuous, he had replied at once and only glanced through the rest of the letters when he'd finished with the most pressing issues. That was when he'd spotted the letter from his secretary in London and one from Mrs. Dashner. It was addressed to him, not Miss Dashner, which he supposed made sense, as it was easier to find a duke than a young lady of no real name or fortune.

He opened the one from his secretary first and read it quickly, nodding the entire time. It seemed Dominick had been right to question the credentials of Doctor Banting. The secretary wrote that the man had few if any credentials and had a reputation for being a fraud and a cheat. In the opinion of the men the secretary had interviewed, consulting with Banting would do a patient more harm than good. Dominick would show it to Rosalyn—Miss Dashner, he had to stop thinking of her so informally—immediately. When they returned to London, she could dismiss the fraud and engage the services of a doctor who could provide real care for her brother.

Dominick supposed the letter from Mrs. Dashner was to ask for more money. These were the sorts of letters he was used to receiving. He only hoped the woman didn't attempt to threaten him with some lie, like he'd stolen her daughter away. He would not show this letter to Miss Dashner. She had not once asked him for so much as a ha'penny. She didn't appear to have any designs on him. After that kiss, he'd worried he'd opened himself up for a seduction ploy. Would she try to repeat it when they'd both be discovered, then force him into proposing marriage? But she'd made no attempt to be alone with him or to steal into his room at night, even though it would have been incredibly simple, as their doors were but a foot apart.

He certainly hadn't slept well thinking about her on the other side of the wall they shared. He could hear her conversing with Alice, her maid, and he tortured himself, wondering if she was dressing or undressing. She might be petite, but he had held her close enough that he knew she still had a woman's figure. He would have liked to explore those curves and dips at leisure.

Pushing his lustful thoughts away—again—he opened Mrs. Dashner's letter and then stood. He couldn't have been more wrong about the reason the woman had written. It wasn't any sort of scheme. It was a notice that Michael Dashner had taken a turn for the worse. Mrs. Dashner did not expect Rosalyn to rush home, as she knew her daughter had given her word to the duke, but would he ask Miss Dashner if she wanted to pen a final note to her brother in case he passed away in her absence?

"What rot!" Dominick said and swore. He'd do far better than asking Rosalyn to pen a note. She needed to see her brother in the flesh. He'd take her home immediately. Tonight. And he'd pen a note now to have the best doctor he knew, his own, sent to tend to Michael.

He was almost to the door when he realized that leaving now meant he would not acquire *The Duke's Book* in time for Professor Peebles's retirement. The volume on arcane medical knowledge would not be among those presented to the man. Dominick would be the only one who failed in the quest to reunite the complete set.

And he didn't care a whit.

The revelation stunned him. He'd rarely cared for anything more than he cared for his collection of books, but he had come to care for Rosalyn. He'd come to anticipate her smile, look forward to her morning greeting, long for her kiss. Dominick couldn't imagine seeing the light go out of her eyes if her brother died. And it wouldn't happen if he could prevent it.

He could find *The Duke's Book* another time. But at the moment, it was as useless as the medical knowledge it contained.

A moment later, he tapped on Rosalyn's door. When her maid opened it, he realized he hadn't thought what he would say. But he wasn't given time. The maid looked as though she had been crying. "Your Grace, thank the Lord you are here. I cannot find her."

"Miss Dashner? You mean, she isn't in her room?"

The maid shook her head. "No, Your Grace. I left for a few minutes to bring the tea tray down to the kitchen, and when I came back, she was gone."

"How long has she been gone?"

"An hour at least, Your Grace."

Dominick clutched the door's casement. "Why didn't you tell me sooner?"

The maid shrank back at his harsh tone. "I-I'm sorry, Your Grace."

Dominick wasted no more time. He all but ran down the stairs and into the common room. A few questions told him no one had seen Miss Dashner in the inn. In the stable, no one had seen her either, but a quick check showed that one of the horses was missing, as was some tack.

She'd left. She'd taken the horse and left.

And since she didn't know about her brother, there was only one place she would go. The image of her battered and broken body lying on the rocky ground beneath The Temples flashed in his mind.

"No!" he yelled and began to shout orders.

ROSALYN DESCENDED THE narrow, stone steps leading into the castle keep, then spent some time at the base working to wedge the door open. If she'd had to guess, she would have estimated it had been at least a century since the steps had last been used and the door was stuck closed. Fortunately, it wasn't locked. And when, with bruised shoulders, she finally opened it, she stepped into a small, dark corridor. The door was at the end of a short, bare hallway with a wooden floor. Closing the door behind her, she made her way along the hallway and encountered another set of stairs. These were wider and cleaner, and she descended them, electing to explore the first landing she reached rather than continue into the bowels of the keep.

The landing led to a small antechamber, which was ornamented with rugs, dark wooden furnishings, and tapestries. No fire burned in the hearth, and with her wet clothing, she shivered in the chill. But she could feel a warmth emanating from the door at the other end of the chamber. A light shone through the sliver of an opening, and she could hear the crackle of logs in a hearth. She tiptoed to that door and peered inside.

A figure sat near the fire, small and clad in black. The woman—Rosalyn surmised it must be a woman—was bent over with concentration. It was a posture she knew well from watching her own mother sewing by firelight. As though sensing she was being observed, the woman turned. "You should have stayed away," she said.

DOMINICK FOUND THE horse Rosalyn had ridden some little ways from The Temples and tethered his own beside it. The rain made the rocks on the path slick, but he ran at full speed, his eyes scanning the stone walls of the structure for any sign of Rosalyn. When he didn't see her on his approach, he ran around to the back, slowing to take more care on the narrower path. But he did not see her. Holding his breath, he looked over the cliffs to the ocean below. In the darkness and rain, it was impossible to discern anything about the shapes below. They might be bodies or boulders. If she'd attempted to climb the building and had fallen, she was certainly dead.

His heart clenched as he considered that possibility. He didn't care about the damn *Duke's Book* any longer. He wanted only to see Rosalyn smile at him again. He wanted only to know she was alive and well.

Dominick ran to The Temples's entryway and hammered the knocker on the door. After five minutes, his arm ached, but he wouldn't give up. If he had to break the door down, he would gain entry. He had to believe she had made it inside. Finally, Mrs. Wright opened the door. She looked white-faced and wide-eyed. "Your Grace, may I help you?"

"I'm looking for the woman who accompanied me on my first visit. Have you seen her?"

The housekeeper's eyes lowered. "You will have to return later, Your Grace. There's been a disturbance." She began to close the door, but Dominick wedged his shoulder against it.

"I'll not come back later. If she is here, I demand to see her."

"No one is to be admitted," she said, as though repeating a refrain. Dominick had heard enough. He took the older woman by the shoulders and gently moved her aside before shouldering his way in.

"Where is she?" he asked. "Tell me."

Mrs. Wright looked up.

Dominick took the steps two at a time.

"I SUPPOSE IT was too much to hope that I would get away with it," the woman said, setting her sewing aside and rising. She was perhaps sixty, slim, with gray hair and a straight spine. She was only a few inches taller than Rosalyn, but her rigid posture made her seem taller. "I do wish you would have listened to Payne and gone away."

"I'm sorry," Rosalyn whispered. "I don't mean to bother you, but I need to see the earl."

The woman sighed. "You cannot. He's dead."

Rosalyn took a step back. The woman's words rang in her ears like a warning. *I suppose it was too much to hope that I would get away with it.* Had she *killed* the earl?

"Now you know my secret," the woman whispered.

Rosalyn shook her head. "I don't know anything. I can leave now. No one has to know I was here."

"I wish that were true," the woman said sadly, "but you will tell someone. I don't know how I kept it a secret this long."

"I won't tell your secret." Rosalyn began to back into the cold, dark antechamber. "No one need ever know I was here, Mrs.—"

The woman raised her steel-gray brows. "I am Lady Verney, and you have no need to be afraid. I didn't kill him."

Rosalyn let out a long sigh. Thank God. This was the earl's wife, and she hadn't murdered her husband. But then, why did she keep his death a secret?

"Payne!" the countess called. A moment later, the butler stepped out of the shadows behind Rosalyn, making her jump. "Please bring us tea. This young lady must be cold and wet. Miss—?"

"Dashner," Rosalyn said.

"Miss Dashner, do come sit by the fire with me."

With Payne blocking her only escape, Rosalyn did not see how she had much choice. She entered and sat in a chair not far from the one the countess had occupied when sewing. The countess sat as well, and Rosalyn fidgeted, unsure what she was to do next. "I am sorry for your loss," she said to break the silence.

The countess raised her brows. "I'm not! The man was mad, had been mad for twenty years. His death was a blessing, I will tell you that. He used to run about here babbling nonsense. Half the time, he was dressed in rags or wore nothing at all. We couldn't keep any staff and spent a fortune on doctors. Nothing helped."

Rosalyn could understand that feeling.

"The last doctor wanted to take him away, put him in some sort of institution." The countess shook her head. "I wouldn't allow that. He died at home, in his own bed, among people he knew."

"That is a blessing," Rosalyn murmured.

"Yes." The lady's eyes sharpened. They were a pale blue, rimmed with gray. "But you didn't come to hear about my late husband's last days. You are here on behalf of the heir, that awful, awful boy."

Rosalyn blinked in surprise. "No. Actually, I don't know anything about any heir. I'm here for a book."

"A book?"

"Yes, a manuscript, actually. It means a great deal to a friend of mine. He's willing to pay for it. He's a collector of sorts, you see."

"I see." She rose. "Come with me, Miss Dashner."

Rosalyn's belly clenched. "It doesn't matter anymore. If you just let me go—"

"You'll want to see the library," the countess said. "Come with me."

Rosalyn saw no option other than to follow the countess out of the room and down a stairway. The lady descended, then paused, indicating Rosalyn should precede her when they reached the next floor. Rosalyn's heart thudded in her chest. She was so close now. Could the countess really possess *The Duke's Book*? In a matter of seconds she could acquire it and give it to the duke. Then he would pay her the remainder of the fee. Her family would be safe for a little while. And the duke would have what he wanted. She knew how much this manuscript meant to him.

Rosalyn veered in the direction the countess indicated and paused before a closed door. The lady extracted a long key from a chain at her waist and unlocked the door. Then she lifted the burning sconce at the door and shone it into the room. Rosalyn gasped just before she heard the shout.

"ROSALYN!" DOMINICK CALLED. "Are you here? Rosalyn!" Dominick ran up the stairs, his voice echoing off the stark walls. Suddenly, he heard what sounded like a woman's voice. He paused, listening.

"I'm here. In the library."

The library? Dominick took several more steps, pausing at a landing where light flickered from the open door of a chamber. He moved toward it, pushed the door open, and there stood Rosalyn and another woman, an older, handsome woman.

Behind them was a large library filled with dozens of gleaming shelves, all empty. Not a single book or piece of furniture inhabited the room. It was completely empty, shining from recent polish and echoing hollowly at the sound of his footsteps.

Dominick ignored the room and strode to Rosalyn.

"May I present—"

He took her into his arms, pulling her tightly against him. She was wet and shivering, but she was whole and she was alive. He held her close, his eyes closed as he rested his chin on the top of her head. "You're alive," he murmured. "I thought I'd lost you."

"I'm alive," she murmured. "But the earl isn't so fortunate."

He pulled away from her, looking down at her face. She looked so pale and cold. "Tell me you didn't climb the walls to gain entrance. Tell me you knocked on the door like a sane person."

Her dark brows drew together. "You really have no faith in my abilities, do you? Of course I climbed the walls."

He wanted to laugh and to shake her all at the same time. "Of course you did. Never again, do you hear me? I don't want to lose you."

"But I did it for you. I know how much the book means to you—"

"Nothing," he said. "Nothing compared to your life."

"Should I leave you two alone?" asked the woman.

Dominick stepped back, and Rosalyn made the introductions. "Lady Verney, this is the Duke of Tremayne. Duke, the Countess of Verney."

"I am terribly sorry to inconvenience you like this," Dominick said. His gaze drifted back over the library. The very empty library.

"I suppose there is nothing for it now," the countess said. "I am found out, but you will at least allow me to explain before you contact the proper authorities."

"There's really no need," Dominick said, thinking of the letter from Mrs. Dashner.

"Please," the countess said. How could Dominick refuse?

They were led to a drawing room and served tea and biscuits. With the rumble of thunder in the distance and the flash of lightning at the windows, the widow began her tale.

"I married very young," she said. "Younger even than you." She nodded to Rosalyn. "The earl was quite sane then, and we were fortunate to have many happy years. But there was sadness as well. We had no children, and we always knew The Temples would go to a virtual stranger, especially as time passed and nephews and brothers passed away, some of them meeting sad ends. When the earl's real descent into madness began, I had the lawyers discover the identity of the next heir. It took almost two years to unravel the lineage and follow each branch to its conclusion. Finally, they located a cousin, a third or fourth cousin to my husband. I summoned him here, and one meeting told me all I needed to know."

"What was that?" Dominick asked, drawn into the story despite his impatience to be gone.

"The man was worthless. He'd spent his life and his fortune on women and gambling. He had the gall to ask me for money when he came, and when he looked at The Temples, all he saw was what he could sell to finance his liaisons. I told him no and sent him back to London. I would have prayed for the earl to live forever if it would mean that awful man never inherited."

"But he didn't live forever," Rosalyn said.

"No." The countess was steely-eyed again. "He died a year ago."

Dominick could not quite stop the quick intake of breath.

The countess closed her eyes in shame. "It is shocking, I know. We told no one, Mrs. Wright, Payne, and I. We buried him ourselves and told visitors he was not well."

"But you must have known you could not keep his death a secret forever," Rosalyn said. Dominick was glad she'd spoken, her voice soft and full of understanding. He was rather less understanding. As a duke from a long, prestigious line, he considered the countess's actions a shocking betrayal of her rank and station.

"I knew, but I needed time. Time to put The Temples's finances in order, time to make sure that it would stand, no matter what that awful man tried to do to it. And I confess, I took that time to sell some pieces I should not have, pieces that by all rights should go to the next earl. But I couldn't allow paintings I loved or the books the earl had collected to fall into that man's hands. I couldn't!"

Now Dominick did understand. He too felt a kinship with his books. He would not want them sold off or ignored should anything happen to him. "What did you do with them?"

"I sold them to a W. Stanley & Co. I researched dealers, and he has a very good reputation. I know he will see they are well taken care of."

Dominick knew the man, and he could not fault her choice.

"But my actions were not wholly unselfish," the countess said. "Because of the sad state of our finances, I was left with very little when the earl died. I have a niece I can live with, but she is not wealthy. I would hate to be a burden to her, and I will admit I took some of the money and put it away for myself."

Dominick felt Rosalyn's gaze on him, and he knew she saw her own mother in this woman. Here was another widow who would be thrown out, through no fault of her own, and all but left to her own devices. Well, Dominick had no desire to bring any further misfortune on the countess. "My lady," he said, "I cannot say I agree with your actions, but neither do I have any desire to reveal them. I believe I speak for Miss Dashner and myself when I say that your secret is safe with us."

She stared at them for a long moment. "Bless you. You will not have to keep it long. That I promise you."

Dominick held up a hand. "I want no details, my lady. As far as I am concerned, we never gained entrance to The Temples." He rose. "And to that end, I think we had better take our leave."

The countess rang the bell. "I'll have Payne see you out."

Dominick bowed and took Rosalyn's arm. As he left the drawing room, he felt his dream of acquiring *The Duke's Book* slip away. He could find W. Stanley. He could instigate a search for the manuscript there, but the thought gave him no pleasure.

He no longer had any appetite for *The Duke's Book*. It was as though *The Duke's Book* had been a child's sweet, and Dominick's palate had matured. He couldn't understand why it had ever meant so much to him.

"His lordship loved the library," Payne said as he escorted them through the foyer. "He spent hours inside."

"I can see it would have been impressive," Dominick said. "I think the earl would be pleased that his books are now in good hands." He could feel Rosalyn staring at him in shock, but he'd explain later. Now he wanted her safe and at his side.

Chapter Eight

WHEN THEY'D RETURNED to the inn and she'd changed into dry clothing and been warmed with brandied tea and a blazing fire, the duke knocked on her door. Alice answered, and Tremayne indicated the maid should stay. Rosalyn began to rise, but he waved her down. "I know you want to talk about what you saw at The Temples and what we should do about it, but we don't have time for that right now."

A cold shard of worry pierced the warm calm she'd settled into. "What do you mean?"

He held out two letters, and she recognized her mother's handwriting on the first immediately. She ripped it from his hand and began to read, even as he explained. "We leave for London tonight, as soon as you're able. We'll travel straight through, only stopping to change horses. If we're fortunate and make good time, we can be there in two days."

"Michael," she murmured. Then, "Yes. I need to go. Now." She tried to rise, but the duke put a restraining hand on her shoulder.

"Alice, pack Miss Dashner's things and your own. We are leaving as soon as you are ready."

Rosalyn nodded, relieved Alice was there. Her thoughts were in turmoil. She could think of nothing but Michael.

"There's something else," the duke said. "The doctor Michael has been seeing is a fraud." He handed her the other letter. "If you'll allow me, I'll send my man to you. He's excellent."

She shook her head. "I doubt we could afford—"

The duke held up a hand. "You needn't worry about payment. I'll take care of it."

It was a refrain she heard often in the next hours. Once underway, she thought to ask what they should do about the dead earl. The duke told her he would take care of it. Indeed, he took care of everything, for which she was grateful. She could do little but fret about her brother. She'd never felt so helpless. The last leg of the journey was particularly trying, as she knew they were close, but she feared she wouldn't arrive in time. And then she was home, falling into her mother's arms.

"Michael?" she asked as her mother hugged her tightly.

"He's fighting, darling," her mother whispered. "We haven't given up hope yet."

The duke's doctor was there, and Rosalyn was disturbed to see that he'd thrown away all of Michael's tonics and potions and eschewed bloodletting. He ordered the boy fed nourishing broth and given fresh air and sunshine.

"You want us to take him from his bed?" Mrs. Dashner asked.

The doctor, an older man, with a thick head of white hair, nodded vigorously. "These small rooms fill with coal smoke, which is why his condition worsened when he came to Town. The boy needs fresh air and food. The countryside would be perfect. In the meantime, the steam from a bowl of hot water and mint leaves will help open his lungs."

Rosalyn and her mother exchanged looks. They would not be able to take Michael to the countryside, but Rosalyn had long believed that the meager diet Doctor Banting had prescribed made Michael weaker, not stronger.

In the next few days, Rosalyn had little time to think of anything but nursing her brother. Stephen and Daniel carried him outside and walked him around, while Rosalyn and her mother heated water and made broth. After a few days, the duke's doctor returned and pronounced the boy looking better already.

Rosalyn agreed. Michael was sitting up and able to stay awake longer. His breathing was still labored at times, but his cheeks had regained some color.

A knock sounded on the door, and when Stephen opened it, the duke was there. He bowed and greeted everyone, his eyes never leaving Rosalyn. She felt herself blush and had to look at the floor so no one would notice.

"Ah, Your Grace," the doctor said. "I was just telling the family that Master Michael seems somewhat improved, but the real improvement will only come if they take him out of the city for a time. He needs fresh air."

"And we do appreciate all you have done for us, Doctor Cavender," Mrs. Dashner said, "but I'm afraid we don't have the means to leave London at present."

"I'll take care of it," the duke said.

Rosalyn's head snapped up at the same time her mother said, "Pardon me?"

"I'll take care of it. My Hampshire estate is the closest. I can send a coach and attendants first thing in the morning."

"But we couldn't possibly impose on you to do such a thing!" Mrs. Dashner argued.

"It is no imposition at all," the duke said. "In fact, I insist." He bowed again, and after the doctor took his leave, the two men departed. Rosalyn waited all of fifteen seconds, then raced after them.

"I'll be back in a moment, Mama!"

The doctor had climbed into his gig, and the duke was striding toward his own conveyance when Rosalyn reached the street. "Your Grace! Wait!"

He turned toward her, then motioned to the footman to close the door. He approached so they stood under the awning of the printing shop below her flat. "How can I possibly thank you for your kindness, Your Grace?" she asked. "It's too much."

"It's not nearly enough," he said. "I should have offered sooner. I should have sent Cavender to your family sooner. Rosalyn." He cleared his throat. "Miss Dashner, I know speaking now, with your brother so ill, might be impertinent, but once he is well again, might I have the pleasure of calling on you?"

She frowned. "You're calling on me now, Your Grace." He was acting so strangely.

He shifted. "Then might I have the privilege of courting you?"

Rosalyn's jaw dropped. "Courting?" she said, before her throat closed in.

"You needn't answer now. And your answer has no bearing on my earlier offer. Your family is welcome at my Hampshire estate regardless, but if you do not wish it, I will not trouble you there with my presence."

It had taken her a moment—several moments, in fact—to understand him. She supposed it had been too long since she had been in such genteel company, and she'd forgotten some of her social graces. But she understood now. The duke wanted her. The duke... Was it possible he admired her as much as she did him?

"Are you saying you want to court me?" she asked.

"I want to marry you."

Her jaw dropped.

"I apologize if my frankness offends you." He stepped back.

"But you are a duke!" she spluttered.

"And you are the daughter of a gentleman."

"Yes." Rosalyn smiled. "I am." She closed the distance between them.

Seeming bolstered by her smile, he took a breath. "I thought perhaps you might need some time to know me better, to come to care for me, before we discuss marriage."

"I'd like that. But what about the manuscript? Don't you need to make inquiries?"

He waved a hand. "That's all settled. It is not worth my time if you are amenable to my presence in Hampshire."

Her breath caught at the thought of seeing him in Hampshire, walking with him, talking with him, teasing him...

"I am amenable, Your Grace. Would it be forward of me to say I am eager?"

"I like it when you are forward," he murmured.

"Then might I add that, far from finding your affection offensive, I welcome it and return it, Your Grace."

"Dominick," he said.

She smiled. "Dominick. I have only hoped you might feel the same."

He smiled back, a true smile that lit his entire face. Lord, but he was impossibly handsome when he was happy. "Then I will call on you when you and your family have settled in at Hampshire." He took her hand and kissed her knuckles.

"I'd like that, but I have one request before you take your leave."

He arched a brow.

"I want more than a kiss on my hand, Dominick. You will think me wicked, but I haven't forgotten the kiss we shared at the inn."

"Nor have I."

"Will you kiss me now?"

He looked about. "Here? On the street?"

"Exactly."

"I thought you'd never ask."

He took her into his arms and kissed her, and though it was brief, it was every bit as perfect as that first kiss. When they parted and he looked into her eyes, Rosalyn knew they would share many, many kisses in the years to come.

About Shana Galen

Shana Galen is the bestselling author of passionate Regency romps, including the RT Reviewers' Choice The Making of a Gentleman. Kirkus says of her books, "The road to happily-ever-after is intense, conflicted, suspenseful and fun," and RT Bookreviews calls her books "lighthearted yet poignant, humorous yet touching." She taught English at the middle and high school level off and on for eleven years. Most of those years were spent working in Houston's inner city. Now she writes full time. She's happily married and has a daughter who is most definitely a romance heroine in the making.

Books by Shana Galen

If you enjoyed this story, read more from Shana. Her most recent release is Traitor in Her Arms, an exciting book inspired by the Scarlet Pimpernel and the first in a new series.

In November, Shana launches a new series with Third Son's a Charm. Read the excerpt below and pre-order your copy now.

London, 1816

EWAN MOSTYN, THIRD son of the Earl of Pembroke, prowled the main room of Langley's gaming hell like a golden-maned lion stalked the savannah. Ewan moved through the ornate room with its red and black damask walls, gilded moldings, and glittering chandeliers as though he owned it. He owned a share in the club, so his proprietary air was not wholly without merit. The illusion that he belonged among such opulence and fragility was somewhat less warranted.

As his feet sank into the scarlet rugs, his gaze passed over the club's dealers—men who straightened at his mere glance—over the courtesans—bold women whose eyes dipped, nevertheless, when they met his—and over the patrons—wealthy, powerful men who studiously avoided garnering his attention.

Unless they were idiots, like the two men Ewan approached now.

Charles Langley had politely ordered the anemic son of the Duke of Suffolk out of the club. The pup's debts were mounting, and his frequent bouts of inebriation were becoming tiresome. But since the lad had not taken his leave, he had become Ewan's problem.

Ewan did not like problems.

"She's mine for the night," Suffolk's son said loudly, poking another man in the chest and hauling a painted tart to his side.

The other man was somewhat older than the duke's son and rather more sober. "And I told you, sir, that I have already paid for the lady's charms. Kindly unhand her and scamper home to your father."

Ewan planted his long, muscled legs beside the two gentlemen and crossed his arms over his chest. The older man widened his eyes until his eyebrows all but reached his graying sandy brown hair. "Sir," he said with a quick bow. "I-I-I'm terribly sorry for the disruption. Lord Pincoch and I were having a slight disagreement."

Ewan looked past the older gentleman and fixed his eyes on the duke's son. All around them, conversation ceased or dimmed to mere whispers.

"Get out," Ewan said. He was a man of few words, which meant those he spoke now carried even more weight.

Pincoch was too deep in his cups to realize the danger he faced. "I'll leave when I damn well please, and no half-wit with more brawn than brains will give me orders."

Ewan felt a muscle in his jaw tense. Not personal, he told himself. But it was too late. The old fury bubbled inside him, and he struggled to contain it. His face betrayed none of the struggle, which must have been why the pup swaggered forward, pulling the tart with him.

Ewan took quick stock of the situation. The lad's friends stood behind him, uncertain what to do. The older man had his allies as well. And the tart was gasping for breath beneath Pincoch's tight hold. Ewan's course of action was clear, though Langley would undoubtedly complain about the damage later. Hell would freeze over before Ewan allowed a man to call him a half-wit and walk away in one piece.

With a speed that belied his size, Ewan grasped Pincoch's free hand and wrenched it behind his back. Pincoch immediately released the whore, who sank to her knees and gulped in a breath. Pincoch screeched for help, and that was the signal for his friends, similarly inebriated, to jump into the fray. The four men charged Ewan, who rammed Pincoch up against a gilded mirror with one hand and tossed a man back by the throat with another.

The older man grabbed the woman and pulled her under a green baize table, where several other patrons had taken refuge. Those still out in the open regretted their decision when one of Pincoch's friends heaved a chair at Ewan. It crashed into his back, and he growled with annoyance. Still holding the lad in place, he turned to see another chair sailing toward him. Ewan reached up, caught the furnishing in midair and thrust it back. It crashed into a faro table, overturning table, chairs, and chips.

Bereft of chairs, Pincoch's friends manned a frontal assault. Ewan finally released Pincoch, and when the boy sank to the ground, Ewan shoved a booted foot against his chest to hold him in place. Both hands free now, he threw a punch with his right and slammed one of his attackers back with his left. Something crashed, but Ewan didn't have time to note what it was before the next man hurtled into him. He struck Ewan in the jaw, and the offense landed him a blow to the breadbasket and an elbow to the throat. When he was on the ground, wheezing for air, another man took advantage of the lull to dance before Ewan.

Ewan almost rolled his eyes. This one thought he was Gentleman Jackson or another renowned pugilist. If there was somewhere Ewan felt at home, it was in the boxing ring. This man danced more than he fought, and while he did his fancy footwork, Ewan slammed a left hook into his jaw.

Heaving for breath but not willing to show weakness, Ewan turned his head to take in the room. "Anyone else?"

No one moved.

With a nod, Ewan lifted Pincoch's limp body by the arms and dragged him past the broken tables and chairs, past the shattered mirror, and past the cracked marble statue. Ewan winced. That statue was new, and he fully expected Langley to opine about it for hours. A footman opened the door of the club, and Ewan tossed Pincoch out onto the street.

He turned and saw several other patrons donning coats and wraps, preparing to depart as well.

That was just what Ewan needed—for Langley and the club to lose blunt because Ewan had scared the patrons away. Goddamn it. Ewan couldn't do anything right. He tried to do his job as the muscle of the club, but it seemed he was always making some misstep or other. He'd already broken the statue. He couldn't be responsible for a mass exodus as well. Ewan positioned himself in front of the door and pointed back to the gaming tables. "Inside."

"But I..." A man who had just donned his beaver hat tried to move toward the exit.

Ewan pointed to him then at the main room, and the man put a hand to his throat. "Very well. If you insist, I could play a game or two."

He turned back to the main room, followed by the rest of the crowd.

One man, however, stood his ground. He looked as though he had recently arrived and seemed in no hurry either to step inside or flee back out the door. Instead, he leaned on his walking stick and cocked his head. He was a tall man—not as tall as Ewan but taller than average—and he had a thin form and dark hair under a beaver hat. His great coat was fine quality as was the ebony walking stick with a silver handle and tip.

"You are one of the Earl of Pembroke's, are you not?" the man asked.

Resigned, Ewan leaned against the doorjamb, where the footmen welcomed patrons and took their coats. Some of the patrons liked to talk. Ewan had found he was not required to answer.

"Not his heir or even the spare. I know those two well. You are the soldier. The third born—or is it the fourth? I know you have a sister."

Ewan cut his eyes to the man, and then disguised his interest by focusing on one of the flickering candles in a chandelier over a table where a group played piquet.

"Well, no matter. I had heard you were strong. You fought with Lieutenant Colonel Draven in the war."

Ewan kept his eyes on the candle. It was an ordinary candle, sputtering and fighting to stay lit. In this world, even a candle fought for light, resisted being snuffed out.

"Now that I see you, I'm not surprised you survived," the man went on as though the two were having a conversation. "You are uncommonly strong. And you do not like to be called stupid."

Ewan turned his head sharply toward the gentleman, who held up his hands. "For what it is worth, I do not think you stupid. No man with less than all his wits about him survived the war against Napoleon. In fact, I would like to hire you."

Ewan narrowed his gaze, almost disappointed. It was not the first time he'd been propositioned. Men had tried to hire him to perform in entertainments or to box for them. Women wanted him for bedsport. Ewan liked his place at Langley's just fine. He enjoyed the modest income his portion of the club afforded him and parted with very little of it to rent a room on the second floor. As his father would not deign to step foot in a gaming hell, Ewan need not trouble with unwanted visits from the earl or any other member of his family.

"I suppose this is not the place to discuss such matters," the man said. "Would you come to my residence?" He removed a card from a silver case and passed it to Ewan.

Ewan barely glanced at it. The light in the vestibule was too dark to read anything anyway. He put the card in his pocket.

"Right. The day after tomorrow at ten in the morning then, if you are interested. It is honest work, and I will reward you handsomely. I will give you more details when you call."

Ewan moved aside and the gentleman passed. A footman opened the door so the yellow lights and bright sounds of the gambling hell spilled into the dark street. When he was alone again, Ewan withdrew the card and moved into a rectangle of light.

"Rrr—Iii—D," he said slowly, staring at one of the words on the card. "Rid." His head hurt as the letters moved and jumped. He stuffed the card back into his pocket and crossed his arms again.

When the last patron had left the tables and the sun was peeking over the horizon, Ewan did one last turn about the club. Maids swept and dusted. Sweet girls, most of them smiled at him when he passed. Ewan headed to the kitchen. Another perquisite of living here was the food. For as long as he could remember, he'd always had a voracious appetite.

In the kitchen Mrs. Watkins had a plate ready for him, the mountain of food buried under a thick slab of buttered bread. "Now, Mr. Mostyn," she said, wiping her red hands on her apron. "You sit down right here. I have some nice potatoes and a stew."

The kitchen was comfortable and inviting, and Ewan sat, feeling the chair creak under his weight. He drank deeply from the ale in the glass before him, but he did not shovel food into his mouth as he usually did. Instead he reached into his pocket and laid the card on the table. He hadn't been able to stop thinking about it.

The cook frowned at it and picked it up. Her kitchen maid, a mousy girl who couldn't have been more than fourteen, glanced his way timidly then continued scrubbing the pots. The cook held the card close to her round face, red and glistening from the heat. "It's the card of the Duke of Ridlington." She put a hand to her heart.

Then she laid the card on the table again and pointed to the words. "See, it says *His Grace the Duke of Ridlington.*"

Ewan nodded slowly. He was surprised a duke wanted his services. This was no mere request for an exhibition of strength then. It might be legitimate work. Ewan pointed to the other words on the card.

The cook turned the card and peered at it. "That's his house—*2 Berkeley Square.*"

"Thank you." Mildly intrigued, Ewan lifted the card and stuffed it back in his pocket. Now he dug into his dinner. His mother would have fainted if she had seen him eating thus. But his mother was dead, and Mrs. Watkins only cared if he enjoyed her food, not if he used the correct fork or a napkin to dab his mouth.

"I wonder why the Duke of Ridlington gave you that card," the cook said, wiping the table where he sat, although it was already clean. "I think he hopes to steal you away."

Ewan wondered the same, but he didn't want to show his interest. He lifted one shoulder then ate another helping of potatoes.

"Seems like you could do better than this." She gestured to the kitchens, which were as nice as any Ewan had seen. "Surely your own father could find a place for you."

And this was why Ewan hadn't wanted to show interest. He didn't always like where such conversations led. Talk of Ewan's father soured his stomach. As the third born son, he was expected either to become a soldier or enter the clergy. Ewan had done his part for his country. After Napoleon was defeated, Ewan had sold his captain's commission and left without a backward glance. His father had probably wished he'd died in the war, but Ewan had lived. Now, no one and nothing could ever force him to join the army again.

As for the clergy—that prospect was laughable. Ewan couldn't even read the Bible, much less stand up every Sunday and drone on about it. If God had wanted Ewan to enter the church, He shouldn't have made him such a lackwit.

No, Ewan liked working at Langley's just fine. Ewan had the money he had made from his days in the army and the sale of his commission, but a little more never hurt and it gave him something to do. He didn't exactly belong, but then he'd always been a misfit. He didn't belong anywhere—anywhere but The Draven Club.

Ewan shoved the last bite into his mouth, nodded at Mrs. Watkins, and carried the plate to the kitchen maid so she could wash it. Then, ducking his head so he wouldn't bang it on the low lintel, he left the kitchen and made his way through the club's back rooms, with their gilded mirrors, mahogany tables, and red velvet chairs and couches. His mother would have called it garish, but Ewan rather liked it. After ensuring all was as it should be, Ewan climbed the stairs to his room. Using the small key, he opened the door and stepped inside, locking the door after him.

He sat on the bed, removed his boots and coat, set Ridlington's card on the floor, and flopped down on the bed. In addition to the bed, the room held a wardrobe and a table with a basin for washing. The room had one small window, which

Ewan had covered with black cloth to block the sun. The room held nothing else—no books, no papers, no personal mementos. The walls were white and unadorned with paintings.

The room, simple in purpose, was just as he liked it. Nothing to confuse or distract him. He closed his eyes and slept.

When he awoke several hours later, it was to the rumbling of his belly. He might have gone down to the kitchens and found bread and cold stew, but when he sat up and dropped his feet onto the floor, they landed on Ridlington's card. He still did not know what to do about it, but he knew who could tell him. Neil Wraxall would know what to do. Neil always knew.

And Neil would be at their club.

Ewan stripped, washed, and dressed again in one of his finer coats. He didn't don a cravat. He didn't like anything tight on his neck. The club didn't require a cravat. The club didn't require anything except that the members had served in Lieutenant Colonel Draven's special unit.

The suicide unit, as Neil called it.

The survivors called themselves The Expendables. They called Ewan The Protector.

Ewan might have taken a hack to The Draven Club, but it was a sunny, though unseasonably cool, spring afternoon and the walk from Langley's on Piccadilly and St. James's to King Street was short. Besides, he liked to pass Boodles. The ancient lords hobbling inside always hobbled a bit faster when they caught sight of him.

He hadn't walked very far when he was surprised by a streak of brown and white bounding past him and into St. James's, which was crowded with carts and carriages at this time of day. The creature barely avoided being trampled by a horse pulling a cart filled with produce. It scurried away from the large hooves and wheels and then huddled, frozen, in the center of the street.

"Watch out!" a woman's voice called right before she barreled into him. But as he was large and she was womanish in size, the impact sent her reeling. He might have caught her and set her on her feet if she hadn't scrambled away, heading directly into the street.

Ewan watched in disbelief as she stumbled directly in the path of a coach and four, whose driver had obviously given his horses free rein. She looked up, saw the approaching conveyance, but instead of jumping back onto the curb, she ran into the coach's path and scooped up the little brown and white scrap of fur. Now both she and the furry creature would be trampled and run down.

Ewan didn't think. He acted. Heart pounding in his suddenly tight chest, he jumped into the street, crossing to the woman in two huge strides. He yanked her out of the path of the coach and four, feeling the breath of the horses on his neck as he shoved her to safety on the other side of St. James's. His heart thudded painfully against his ribs with what he recognized as fear and panic. They'd almost died. For a moment, St. James's became a blood soaked field, the clatter of hooves the sound of rifles. Ewan closed his eyes and drew a slow breath. And then he shook the memory off and came back to the present.

But his hands were still shaking.

Ewan had shoved the woman a bit hard, and she'd fallen to her knees. He would have to beg her forgiveness, though she should really be the one groveling at his feet with gratitude. But instead of looking up at him with appreciation in her eyes, she scowled. "I almost crushed Wellington."

Ewan looked right then left for the duke. Not seeing the general, Ewan glanced in confusion back down at the woman. She pointed to the fur ball. "My dog. You pushed me so hard I almost crushed him."

So the dog was named Wellington, and she blamed Ewan for the danger to the animal. Ewan frowned at her. Was he supposed to apologize for saving her life and that of the beast? Perhaps she had become momentarily disoriented by the tumult. "You ran into the street," he pointed out. Anyone could see the street was busy and dangerous.

She waved a hand dismissively, as though the fact that she had almost been flattened under the hooves and wheels flying past them was but a small matter. "Wellington escaped his collar and leash at Green Park. I have been chasing him all this way."

That explained why she had been on St. James's Street, which was typically the domain of men, and why the dog was running. It did not explain why she did not thank him, but he'd come to expect women to be difficult. Ewan grasped her arm and pulled her to her feet. Belatedly, he realized he should have offered her his arm, but now it was too late. "Where do you live?"

Now it was her turn to frown. She had light green eyes framed by delicate brows, which slanted inward in confusion. Then she blinked. "Oh, dear no. You must not escort me home. You look like some sort of Viking warrior or Norse god. My mother would...well, best not to discuss what my mother might do."

Ewan crossed his arms and stared down at her. This pose usually elicited tears from those of the fairer sex. But this one shook her head again, in defiance. "My maid is probably wringing her hands at the park. I must return."

He hadn't looked very closely at the woman, but now he noted her fine quality dress and spencer. Both were soiled with dirt and animal hair from the fur ball. She was a lady. Now the lack of gratitude made sense. He'd known many such ladies. They looked down their nose at everyone. This time Ewan made certain to offer his arm. She looked at it in horror. "Do you want my mother to confine me to my room?" she asked.

Ewan did not know the answer to this inquiry, so he merely continued to stand with his arm crooked. She pushed it down—or rather he allowed her to push it down. "No, thank you, sir. I am perfectly capable of returning to the park on my own. If I encounter any difficulty, Wellington will protect me."

Ewan glanced at the fur ball. The dog wouldn't have scared a flea.

"Good day." She hoisted the fur ball in her arms, cradling it like an infant. She must have been completely daft. That was the only explanation for her delusions.

Or perhaps she was just a woman. He did not claim to understand women. He left that to Rafe. The daft woman marched off, thankfully looking both ways before crossing St. James's, and disappeared into the hawkers and vendors on the other side. He could have gone after her, but if he did it would only be to protect anyone else who happened to fall into her path.

Ewan stared after her for a long moment before being jostled back into motion. The remainder of the journey was uneventful, and Ewan arrived at the club just as Jasper, the best tracker Ewan had ever known, was leaving. Porter, the club's Master of the House, stood in the doorway, silver head held high.

The two former soldiers paused on the steps and nodded to each other. Jasper's face had been horribly scarred during an ambush that cost Draven two men, and he wore a length of black silk tied about his hair and a mask to that hid most of one side of his face, including the scarred flesh. "You looking for Wraxall?" Jasper asked.

Ewan nodded.

"He just finished yaffling."

Jasper worked as a bounty hunter and often spent time with the thieves and rogues. He often lapsed into their cant, speaking it as fluently as if he'd been born in the rookeries rather than to one of the oldest noble families in England. At the mention of yaffling—the cant for eating—Ewan felt a pang of hunger in his belly. Was the club still serving or had he missed the meal and would now have to wait until supper?

Jasper slapped Ewan on the shoulder. "You always did have a wolf in the stomach, Protector. If the soup is gone, the cook will always serve you Galimaufrey."

Ewan pulled a face. He didn't particularly want scraps and leftovers. The tracker patted his arm then stared back down the steps. "If I didn't know better, I'd think you only came here to grub."

It wasn't far from the truth. If the club hadn't served meals, Ewan would have attended far less frequently.

He entered and Porter closed the door behind him. "Good to see you again, Mr. Mostyn," the distinguished older gentleman said. "The dining room, sir?"

Ewan cocked his head in that direction.

"Very well. This way."

Although he could have found the way with his eyes closed, Ewan followed Porter through the wood paneled vestibule lit with a large chandelier. A suit of armor stood on one wall and two Scottish broadswords on that opposite. The place looked like the sort of establishment Henry VIII would have frequented. But the object that always drew his attention also made him more than a little melancholy. It was a large shield mounted on the wall opposite the door. A big medieval sword cut the shield in half. The pommel of the sword had been fashioned into what Neil had once told him were fleur-de-lis. A skeleton stared at him from the cross-guard. Around the shield were small fleur-di-lis that marked the fallen members of The Expendables—those who hadn't made it back from the war. The shield reminded Ewan that his lost friends were here in spirit.

Still following Porter, who only had one leg, Ewan was forced to move slowly. Porter's wooden peg thumped on the polished wood floors as he led Ewan past the winding staircase carpeted in royal blue and into a well-appointed dining room. Like the entryway, the dining room was paneled in wood. The ceiling was low and whitewashed, crossed by thick wooden beams. Sconces lined two walls and a fire burned in the mammoth hearth. Four round tables covered with white linen and set with silver had been placed throughout the room. At a fifth table, Neil Wraxall, aka The Warrior, sat with a glass of red wine centered before him. Neil liked order. He liked both giving orders and order in his life. He dined at the club four days a week precisely at noon. He always sat at the same table and in the same chair. No one else ever dared sit in that chair if there was a remote possibility Neil might drop by the club. And if he came unexpectedly, the man in the chair vacated it without being asked. They'd all served under Major Wraxall long enough to know that while he could be flexible when the situation called for it, he preferred routine and predictability.

Neil looked up when Ewan entered. Porter paused, waiting for a sign from the de facto leader of The Expendables. When Wraxall flicked his gaze to the empty chair at his right, Porter led Ewan to it and pulled it out. Ewan sat.

"Wine, sir?" Porter asked Ewan.

Ewan nodded.

"And would you like dinner, Mr. Mostyn?"

Ewan looked at the man as though he'd asked if Ewan wanted to be run through with a bayonet.

"Very good then. I will bring the first course. Mr. Wraxall, more wine?" Porter inquired.

The Warrior looked at Ewan. "Will I need it?"

Ewan shrugged. Neil shook his head. "No, thank you, Porter."

Ewan wasn't certain how much Neil drank away from the club, but he was always moderate in his consumption in The Expendable's company. Once Neil had told him he always kept a bottle of gin beside his bed to calm the tremors when he woke fighting a battle. Ewan had known what he meant. They all had nightmares about the terrors they'd seen during the war. It was the horrors they'd committed themselves that woke them up at night, a scream lodged in the throat.

For Ewan, life in London had gradually begun to seem more real than the memories of the violence and battle. But he suspected it was different for Neil. He suspected Neil was still fighting the battles nightly, hoping to change the outcomes.

For a long while Ewan and Neil sat with only the crackling of the fire to break the companionable silence. They'd spent many nights thus on the Continent during the war against Napoleon—a dozen or more men huddled around a campfire, knowing death would probably come in the morning and willing to make that sacrifice for king and country. If Ewan had to die, he'd wanted to die with Neil at his side. He trusted the man implicitly, and he respected him as much as he respected Draven. When they'd been in the army, they could always count on Rafe Beaumont to break long silences or tension with frivolous chatter. Now Ewan wished he knew what to say to his friend to ease the pain, but Ewan was not good with words. At the moment, it seemed Neil could not find words either.

"Knocked any heads together lately?" The Warrior asked at last. It was more of a command than a question. The Warrior almost always spoke in commands and orders. Ewan smiled, thinking of the pup last night.

"Good," Wraxall said. "Keep in practice. Give me a report on Langley. I should pay him a visit."

"He'd like that," Ewan said.

Neil gave him a wry look. "I'm sure he would. I always lose at the tables. I'll order Stratford to accompany me. Then I'll have a chance."

Stratford was another of The Expendables and known for his skill with strategy. Ewan frowned, thinking of Langley's losses. But Neil wouldn't go to Langley's. Neil didn't want light and laughter.

Porter returned with a white soup for Ewan and refilled his glass of wine. Ewan's belly rumbled again, but he remembered the card. He'd trusted Neil with his life on the Continent. He could trust Neil with whether or not to pay a call on Ridlington. Ewan slapped it on the table before lifting his spoon.

Wraxall picked the card up and turned it in his fingers. "The Duke of Ridlington? What does he want?"

Ewan sipped his wine and met Neil's gaze. Why did anyone seek out The Protector?

Neil drummed his fingers on the table, probably forming a report in his head. "He's a good man. I don't know him well, but I've not heard anything said against him. Do you want me to ask the others to report what they know of him?"

Ewan held the spoon midway between bowl and mouth. Was that what he wanted? A sense of the man before he decided to hear the duke's proposition? Ewan nodded.

"I have other business tonight, but I'll send Beaumont to Langley's with my findings. I doubt he has anything better to do, and an assignment might keep him out of trouble."

Ewan raised a brow. There was plenty of trouble to be had at Langley's, and Rafe Beaumont was a lodestone for mischief. Still, Ewan appreciated his friend's thoughtfulness. Most men would have sent a note, but Wraxall knew how arduous reading was for Ewan, though the two men had never discussed it. Besides, it would give Neil the chance to order Rafe about, and Neil did like giving orders.

Ewan spent the rest of the afternoon in the dining room, then followed Neil to the card room and watched a game of piquet between Neil and another member of

The Expendables. Neil lost, of course. The man was too predictable. It was an enjoyable day, and it took Ewan's mind off Ridlington and the mad female he'd encountered earlier.

Finally Ewan made his way back to Langley's—the return trip uninterrupted by daft women or racing fur balls—and instructed the footmen to fetch him if Beaumont arrived. Of the eleven other surviving members of The Expendables, Neil Wraxall and Rafe Beaumont, were the men Ewan felt closest to. He saw the other men at the club, and he drank or played the odd game of dice with them, but none knew him like Neil and Rafe. He considered them more than friends. They were brothers.

About half past eleven, a footman fetched him, and Ewan stepped outside the club where Beaumont had struck a pose. Ewan was not in the habit of thinking men pretty, but there was no other way to describe Rafe Beaumont, also known as The Seducer. He wasn't feminine in appearance, but he had a perfect face and enough charm for two men. His dark hair and bronze complexion made him the opposite of Ewan's honey blond hair and fair skin.

As usual, Beaumont had a woman on his arm. Ewan's only surprise was that there was but one. "Mr. Mostyn." Rafe bowed with a flourish. Ewan was used to his friend's courtly behavior and ignored it.

"My dear, this fearsome man before you is Mr. Mostyn. He is undoubtedly one of the best men I know. He saved me in the war more times than I can count. Don't let his glare scare you off. He doesn't bite." Then to Ewan. "You don't bite, do you?"

Ewan tried to decide whether or not he was required to answer. Rafe often spoke to hear his own voice.

The woman fluttered her lashes at Ewan. She had reddish hair, freckles, and pretty brown eyes. Her lips smiled broadly. "I could just eat you up, Mr. Mostyn." She winked at him.

Ewan gave Beaumont a look of concern. Unlike Beaumont, Ewan never knew what to say to women. He knew what to *do* with them, but he preferred not to speak while doing it.

"Save your appetite for later, my dear. Would you give Mr. Mostyn and me a moment alone?"

"Of course. I'll wait inside." She looked up at Ewan as though for approval. He moved aside to allow her to enter through the door a footman held open. The gambling hell permitted women, but most were courtesans or women who thrived on scandal. Clearly, this woman did not concern herself with her reputation.

When she'd gone inside, Beaumont sighed. "Hell's teeth! I thought I'd never be rid of her."

Ewan gave his friend a look of incomprehension. If Rafe didn't want her company, why not just tell her so? But then Beaumont seemed to attract women whether he wanted to or not. That was one skill they'd found invaluable in the war.

"Let me think now. If I mess this up, Wraxall will have my head. I'm to tell you Ridlington is an oak. Those are Neil's words, not mine. I don't describe men in terms of foliage, you know. In any case, Wraxall says, no one has a word to say against the duke. Apparently the man does not overindulge in drink, cards, or women. I can't think why Neil should call this a recommendation. The duke sounds like a bore to me, but there you are. Why does he want to hire you?"

Ewan lifted a shoulder.

"Well, don't agree unless he pays you at least double what you make at this club each week. You are worth it, Ewan."

Ewan couldn't have said why, but at the compliment, his throat constricted.

"Now I must be off. I haven't slept in two days, and if I'm forced to drink even one more glass of champagne I'll cast up my accounts. Good night." He slapped Ewan on the shoulder.

"What about…?" Ewan motioned to the hell behind him.

"Good God. Don't tell her where I've gone. I doubt she'll come looking for me. She'll find other amusements." He doffed his beaver hat and strolled off, turning heads as he walked.

Ewan pulled the card from his pocket and read it slowly. Berkley Street at ten in the morning. He'd go, but he wouldn't wear a cravat.

The Viscount's First Kiss

BY
CAROLYN JEWEL

About The Viscount's First Kiss

Viscount Daunt and the painfully shy Magdalene Carter turn friendship into love in their search for a legendary medieval manuscript.

For years, the Viscount Daunt loved Magdalene Carter, the widow of a long-time friend and mentor. She's a brilliant and original thinker whose shyness often paralyzes her, but no one is more knowledgeable about their shared passion for medieval tomes. When he enlists her aid in the search for the legendary *Duke's Book of Knowledge*, a book he *must* find in just ten short days, he hopes to transform their friendship into love.

Sign up for Carolyn's **newsletter** so you never miss a new book and get exclusive, subscriber-only content.

Chapter One

MAGDALENE SAT AT her desk in a good deal of shock. Never once in all the time she'd known him had she experienced the slightest flutter of attraction to him. Now, a mass of butterflies swooped in her stomach. This would not do, she told herself. Not at all. They were friends. Friends. Only friends. One did not have such feelings about one's friends.

"What do you think, Magdalene?" The last time the recently installed Viscount Daunt had called at Plumwood, he'd been Mr. Harry Fordyce, and she had been Mrs. Angus Carter. They had embraced each other as good friends.

He sat on the edge of the desk, one thigh on the desktop, and unfastened a button of his coat. The new Viscount Daunt very much resembled his late father, though many years younger, of course. Medium-brown hair, dark and liquid brown eyes just slightly sleepy at the edges. A sensitive, tender mouth that…

"Yes," she said without moving. Because she couldn't. She wondered if she were ill. Perhaps she was, for she strongly suspected that if she were to stand, her legs would not hold her.

He plucked the letter from her hands and scanned it. A lock of burnished walnut hair fell across his forehead. Good heavens. He was twenty-eight, tall, and well-formed. A man of great vitality. He was handsome. He always had been. She had always known that about him. There was no excuse for her reacting as if she'd never noticed, when she had.

"I do not care for this," he said. "Not at all." He handed back the letter he had originally given to her to read. "I should very much like your opinion."

Friendships had a definite shape, a rationale, a raison d'être. But without Angus, she no longer knew what defined her relationship with the new Lord Daunt. The problem, she decided, was that when he'd come in this morning, she had been distracted.

She'd looked up to see a stranger instead of her friend, and she'd frozen at the impact of *seeing* him as if for the first time. Absolutely, he was a man of astounding good looks. This was nothing new. Except, somehow, it was.

The three of them—Fordyce, ah, but he was now Lord Daunt, Angus, and she—had shared a consuming interest in all things bookish. Whenever Daunt had called at

Plumwood, they'd talked of and about books for hours, and no one had ever been bored. She was very glad to see him again. Of course she was. Glad to see a friend.

Magdalene focused on the page he'd handed her. Her husband had been the love of her life. Nearly two years after his death, she loved and missed him still.

"Well?"

The contents of the letter continued in stubborn refusal to coalesce into words. She was very much afraid that if she looked at him again, she would have more thoughts that betrayed Angus. She returned her attention to the correspondence Daunt had handed over. At last, her brain cooperated, and the letters formed words with meaning. *Italy, odd collection, interested.*

Unfortunately, she could not concentrate long enough to derive meaning from the words or sentences. Her mind scurried off to inappropriate thoughts.

He'd taken care of everything after Angus died. He arranged the funeral, managed all the legal matters, looked after payment of the estate and other taxes due, and took care of endless other details and arrangements. Then he went abroad, in the main to distance himself from his father. They did not get on. Almost no one had got on with Daunt's father. While he was gone, she had tried to learn how to live without Angus.

Daunt had been in America when his father fell ill. The news had taken some time to reach him, and more time had passed before he made his way home to deal with all that one must in such circumstances.

"Well?" he asked again. Quite obviously, *he* was experiencing no difficulty treating her as he always had, with respect and fondness.

"Fascinating, my lord." The honorific required to address him set fire to the bridge between them, and that proved unfortunate. Just when she needed to be moored in the past, she had been marooned in the present where nothing was familiar.

She smoothed her skirt and felt quite drab compared to Daunt's splendor. It was impossible to be around a man like him and not wish to be more fashionable. Her brown frock was comfortable and presentable enough for her solitary life at Plumwood, but it was not à la mode.

"Mr. Mathias Rivett." He tapped the top of the letter and sniffed with the sort of disdain that reminded her of his father. "He's mangled the King's English as only an Englishman can do."

"I suspect he may not be Italian," she said.

He snorted. "I as well."

At last she managed to make sense of Mr. Rivett's letter. She reread the undisciplined script. It was unclear if he claimed to be Italian or to have merely been to Italy. The point, however, was in two words: the Dukes.

Magdalene's hand trembled as those two words sank in. *My God. My God.* She swallowed hard. Daunt would not have shown her this letter if he thought it was complete nonsense. "He says he's found *De Terris Fabulosis.* Is it possible?"

Long before she or Daunt had even been born, Angus had been invited to Florence to view one of the four Dukes, specifically *De Terris Fabulosis,* which loosely translated to *Fabled Lands and Treasures.* The volume documented the location of such treasures as the Fountain of Youth and a city of gold located somewhere in South America. It had been held in the private library of a noted Italian collector now many years dead.

Angus had been thrilled to see the book at all, but the day following his inspection, he found himself accused of theft. A thorough search of his person and his quarters had found nothing. Though Angus had always proclaimed his innocence, rumors that he possessed *De Terris Fabulosis* persisted to this day. He had died protesting his innocence.

If it was true that someone had located *De Terris Fabulosis,* then Angus would be vindicated to each and every bibliophile who'd ever wondered. Most especially, he would be vindicated to those who'd repeated the vile rumors. Her throat grew thick. She hadn't cried in months, and now she was about to lose her battle against tears.

In a flash, Daunt was on one knee beside her chair. He stroked her shoulder and handed over his handkerchief. "There, there, Magdalene. I am sorry to have reminded you of your loss."

She took and released several breaths. At least her nonsensical attraction had been washed away. He brushed his fingers across her cheek, and just like that, another herd of butterflies took off in her stomach.

"My poor, dear Magdalene." His voice had always been lovely, deep yet clear. "I knew you'd want to know."

"Yes, yes, of course, my lord." She was breathless from him being so near. What could possibly be the matter with her? He was Daunt, and she was a widow who interested no one. Most people found her peculiar. Only Angus and Daunt had ever understood her obsession with Medieval manuscripts, for they had shared it. "My lord, stand up."

He sprang to his feet and strode to the other side of the room as if he hadn't been on one knee to her. Which he had, but not for *that* reason. Handsome, vital young lords did not go on bended knee to women like her.

He threw himself on a sofa that was not long enough to contain him. She had grown used to there being three of them. Angus, herself, and him. Now, there would always be one of their number missing. He lounged on the sofa, one booted foot braced on the arm, the other on the floor, Rivett's letter still in his hand. At ease, just like old times, thank goodness. She imagined there was a river between them, impossible to ford.

They had always been familiar and casual here at Plumwood, so his putting his foot on the sofa arm again did not in the least shock her. She did, however, take note of the shape of his thigh. Well-muscled, strong.

My God, how inappropriate.

"I've already replied to him that I wish to examine the books at his earliest possible convenience," Daunt said. "Whether he has all four Dukes as he claims, we cannot know until he arrives. Can you imagine, Magdalene? What a triumph if even one of them is an original! Angus's name will be cleared, and *I* shall have the honor of presenting Professor Peebles with *Liber Ducis de Scientia.*"

He meant, of course, the four volumes of a work that loosely translated to *The Duke's Book of Knowledge.* To those passionate about collecting and studying illuminated manuscripts, as the three of them had been, the work was sometimes collectively referred to as the Dukes.

The Dukes were a compendium of knowledge and information, rightly said to contain the wisdom of the ages. Lorenzo de' Medici himself had commissioned the works. They were completed and delivered to de' Medici in or around 1481. Each text had been written by scholars preeminent in those subjects, and each had been inked and illuminated by sought-after artists.

De Terris Fabulosis was responsible for the launching of no fewer than five ships in search of the riches described in the pages. *De Scientia Naturae Rerum,* or *Natural Science,* had caused a sensation among scholars seeking to understand the world. *De Medicine Arcana* covered the subject of arcane medicine and healing, while *De Motibus Humanis* addressed the subject of human sentiment.

In addition to their literary and scientific merit, each volume of the Dukes was nothing short of art, writ large, and, should they be located, must be considered suitable for display in the august halls of the British Museum. No expense had been spared in the making of them. The volume Angus had seen had been bound in red velvet and embroidered with gold thread. The vellum pages were gorgeously inked and illustrated, with silver and gilt applied by a master artist.

Daunt stood and began to pace. "The club believes it can locate all four of the Dukes." He referred to the London-based Bibliomania Club, of which he was a member. That shivery feeling in her stomach had gone away. Good. "Had you heard Peebles is retiring?"

"I had not heard."

"What? No one wrote you?"

She shook her head. She was isolated here, though while Angus had been alive, she'd never once felt lonely or wanted any company but his. In Badding, however, she'd heard they were calling her the Recluse. No wonder. She'd been to Badding but once since Angus had died.

Peebles, much beloved by the members of the Bibliomania Club, had also been a dear friend of her husband's. Like Daunt, the renowned professor had been a pallbearer at Angus's funeral. She would do anything for either man.

She folded Daunt's letter and placed it to one side. Mentally, she divided the room into the half containing Daunt and the half that did not, with no encroachment by her, literally or figuratively.

"His retirement ceremony is fast approaching. We, the members of the club, are determined to present him with all four Dukes. As we speak, the others are searching for the volumes."

"I wish you speedy success."

"Thank you."

Had his voice always sounded like that? Smooth and warm. Enticing. "Happy as I would be if Professor Peebles were to be presented with such a gift, I can think only of what it would mean to Angus if *De Terris Fabulosis* were found."

"Precisely." Daunt stopped smiling. "*That* is why you must come to Vaincourt." Vaincourt, the seat of the Viscounts Daunt, shared a border with Plumwood. "I shan't accept any response from you but acceptance."

This conversation was more like old times, thank God. Some of her butterflies flew away to bother a younger lady with more reason for the reaction. She clasped her hands on the desktop. He was young, and handsome, and vital, and she was none of those things. For heaven's sake, she was four years older than Daunt.

"Now," Daunt said with a devastating smile, "before I release you to your preparations for your visit, tell me, how is Ned?"

"Ned is visiting my father." She picked up Mr. Rivett's letter and fiddled with the corners.

"Is he?"

"I was as surprised as you are when His Grace took an interest." She was the natural daughter of the Duke of Woaden, acknowledged by him and raised as a lady. The duke had seen to her upbringing, her education, and her financial security. He had even attended her wedding. "His Grace insists that Ned looks like him. *I* think he looks like Angus, but if he sees himself in my son, who am I to disagree?"

"How old is Ned now?" He glanced at her and winked, and her heart sped up. It meant nothing. Nothing. She willed it to mean nothing. "Thirty?"

She laughed. His sense of humor remained as impish as ever. "Six, Mr. Fordyce. My lord. Forgive me. You are so familiar a sight here that I cannot for the life of me think of you as anything but Mr. Fordyce. My lord."

He waved a hand. "Call me Daunt. Please. How did Woaden convince you to let Ned away from you?"

"Quite easily." Daunt knew all her peculiarities, and to his credit, he had never disapproved of her. "He promised to take Ned fishing, and after that Ned could not possibly have been dissuaded from accompanying his grandfather to the very ends of the earth." With the tip of her ungloved finger, she drew a small circle on the desktop. "I miss him terribly. The house is too quiet, and though I am occupied from morning to night, I have nothing useful to do here."

"It can be no bad thing for His Grace to take an interest in your son. The connection will serve him well."

She nodded and smiled against a wave of loneliness and a mother's worry. "Yes. I know it shall. But it doesn't stop me missing him. Both of them. Ned and Angus."

"Understandably." His eyes were soulful, such a beautiful brown. When he looked at her, she felt like the only woman in the entire world. He returned to the desk and took her hand between his. "Your husband was a great and formidable man, and I do not doubt you shall miss him the rest of your life. As will I."

She sniffled. No tears. None. She would not cry. "How kind of you to say so."

"I wish I had been a better correspondent these recent months."

"You had cares and concerns of your own." He continued to hold her hand, but she withdrew it. She sat back and steeled herself against rubbing away the tingle of their contact.

"Are you in need of assistance?"

"How thoughtful of you to inquire, but no. Between His Grace and Angus, Ned and I have no worries for the future." What a lie. She was lonely and bereft, and her son was old enough to visit his grandfather without her. "For now, at least."

"You'll tell me if there is anything I can do." He was twenty-eight years old. A man. A quite compelling man who looked every inch the nobleman he was.

"How kind you are, Daunt," she said with the sunny smile she had learned kept others at bay in the days and weeks following Angus's death. "Are there really two hundred people at Vaincourt for Accession Day?"

"Two hundred? No." The Viscounts Daunt celebrated the anniversary of the day the first viscount had taken possession of Vaincourt. The event had quickly expanded to include celebrations of the solstice, to the point that the festivities spanned three or four days, with dancing and feasts nearly every night. Local gentry from all the neighboring parishes came to celebrate as well. "It's a madhouse there just now, I'll grant you that."

"What of the wagons we saw making their way to Vaincourt?" She relaxed. She had herself in hand. She wasn't going anyplace there were crowds of people. Vaincourt was out of the question. "You don't really travel with an entourage like that, do you? Now that you're a lord."

He flashed a smile that took her breath, a reaction as unsettling as her earlier butterflies. "The very reason my feet brought me here, Magdalene. Those wagons contained books." He spread his arms wide. "Dukes, books, and that letter are why you must come to Vaincourt. I won't have you alone in this house without sufficient protection. You know as well as I that if word has got out about the Dukes, some fool is bound to come looking."

Mentally, she calculated how many volumes would have been on the wagons. Several hundred, she thought. Upwards of a thousand. "How many books?"

"I purchased the contents of three private libraries." He smiled with all the delight of a true bibliophile on the trail of a rare volume. He planted his hands on the desk and leaned over. "Magdalene."

Her mind went blank. Golden brown flecked his eyes. Golden. Brown. And those impossibly perfect cheekbones.

"I have reason to believe that the late Earl of Verney may well have been in Florence at or around the time Angus was there."

"Oh my," she said on a gasp. The Earl of Verney had been an unpleasant man who had boasted more than once that he had no scruples about the acquisition of antiquities, art, or rare manuscripts.

"You must come to Vaincourt," he said. "I need you."

The very idea of being around so many people filled her with anxiety and made her pulse race. She never said the right thing, and she was simply unable to make polite conversation. She never fit in.

"I've put you at the very end of the south wing, as far from the Accession Day guests as you could possibly be. You needn't see anyone at all if you don't care to." He grinned. "Except for me. You must see me if we are to find the Dukes."

"Surely I can assist from here."

"No. You cannot." His smile broadened, and he winked again. "I have located and purchased Verney's entire library, and I can assure you that skullduggery is now afoot." His serious expression returned. "Where the Dukes are concerned, one must presume that unsavory persons shall go to great lengths to have them. I was obliged to hire guards to transport them safely to Vaincourt." He pushed off the desk. "Even were it not for the urgent matter of Peebles, it would be imperative to find the Dukes as quickly as possible." He motioned to the door. "We must leave at once."

She owed him a great deal. So much, she could never repay him. But the thought of Vaincourt during Accession Day made her sick to her stomach. All the noise. The need to say *good morning* or *good afternoon* or whatever was appropriate to the time of day. It was all quite beyond her.

"Have your maid bring your things later."

"Do you mean leave right now?"

"We'll search until evening. I am obliged to make an appearance for dinner, raise a toast to everyone's health. Then back to work." He clapped his hands once. "Time is of the essence."

She lapsed into silence. "Do you really believe one of the Dukes may be at Vaincourt?"

"Yes." His gaze fixed on her, and she was a bit lightheaded as a result. "Someone has already attempted to interfere in my search of those books."

"What?"

"I'll tell you all when we are there. Magdalene, I *need* your help. You are the only one I trust in this matter, and the only person able to tell immediately if we find a genuine Duke."

Her stomach hurt, but she had no choice. Daunt needed her help. "Very well."

Chapter Two

FROM PLUMWOOD, VAINCOURT was a twenty-minute walk along a tree-lined road. They detoured to the cemetery where Angus was buried to pay their respects, so their journey took closer to an hour. On the way, she and Daunt chatted about books and their chances of finding even one the Dukes, let alone all four. She hardly thought at all about having to deal with strangers. With luck and some effort, she could avoid everyone but Daunt.

In what seemed no time at all, they arrived at the two stone pillars that marked the entrance to the estate, one topped by a stone falcon, the other by a bear. The doors of Vaincourt were another five-minute walk past groomed lawns and gardens, many, many times larger than Plumwood. The Accession Day crowds had already begun; people from the nearby villages strolled the grounds in every direction.

The house itself, which never failed to impress when she saw it, was a sprawling edifice of three stories with wings projecting north and south from the original building. They entered via a side door for which Daunt produced a key, and proceeded straight to the library.

The Vaincourt library was lozenge-shaped with two stories of shelves built into the walls and carved woodwork around and between. The geometrically spaced areas of wall were hung with paintings or smaller, daintier shelves of curious items. Three chandeliers provided sufficient light for those reading or perusing the contents. Desks, chairs, and sofas were arranged around the fireplaces at either end, and scattered in between were more places to sit and read.

She came to a stop about halfway in. "May I ask what in the great mysteries of the world you are doing?"

For some reason, he'd cleared out the entire bottom of one of the shelves and left the contents stacked precariously high on the floor. Magdalene reached the first stack of books on the floor and took a slow turn, soaking in the surroundings. Shelves and shelves of books. It was glorious. When she was done, she eyed the stacks of books on the floor. Daunt was no fool. If he was searching the shelves, it was because he had reason to, and that meant only one thing. "Oh. Oh dear."

"Yes," he said. "Exactly."

Once again, she scanned the shelves.

"You begin to see the scale of the problem." He let out an aggrieved sigh. "The books were to be left in the crates and were not."

Indeed, she did see the problem. "They were shelved."

"Randomly, from what I have been able to ascertain. I have located a few from the shipment. Thus far I see no pattern to how they were put away." He gestured at the floor. "The head footman says he thought the man who gave the instructions traveled here with the wagons, but it could just as easily have been anyone. Someone else said it was a woman who countermanded me. Whatever the case, the workers were told to shelve the books, and they did so. If Gomes hadn't been busy with Accession Day, this would never have happened." Gomes was his butler, a former soldier whose bad humor and general unpleasantness had become stuff of legend.

"I presume you gave no such instructions."

"I did not."

"I don't suppose the library catalogue was updated?"

"Of course not."

Magdalene shook her head. There was no need to tell Daunt what he already knew; those instructions had been deliberate sabotage.

"Other than outright theft, one could not find a better way to delay my finding the Dukes than this." He faced her, disconsolate. "The Dukes, if any were in that shipment, may already be gone. I am broken by the possibility, Magdalene. Broken."

A horrible thought occurred to her. "Did this interloper gain access to the crates long enough to examine the contents?"

"If he came with the wagons, yes. If he arrived here under some pretense, perhaps not."

"From whom did you obtain the books?"

"W. Stanley & Co." W. Stanley & Co. was a leading purveyor and auctioneer of antiquities, including books. It was highly reputable. It was impossible that the company had been involved in such a scheme.

Like Daunt, she scanned the shelves once again. Their path was clear. "We have no choice but to proceed as if the Dukes are here."

"Agreed."

"We can but hope." She dusted off her hands. "In the meantime, to work."

Daunt brought over a chair and placed it by the desk. "I'll bring you a stack."

Magdalene cleared her throat. He had brought her here because she was known for her levelheadedness and meticulous planning. "A suggestion?"

"Please." He sat, slumped, on another chair. His hair was mussed, and there was a lock of walnut hair curling over his forehead. "Apply every atom of brilliance you possess to my situation."

She lifted a hand to prevent interruption. The library was huge, but their surroundings seemed intimate just now, with the farther reaches of the space in shadows. She felt a girl, again, finding herself close to a man she admired and who was far too attractive for mortal man. Delightful, delicious frissons of girlish hope and despair swirled through her. This would pass. It must. She shook off the sensation and applied herself to the task at hand.

"We divide the shelves between us. Complete that one, since you have begun there." She gestured to include the panel of shelves he'd been working at. "I'll begin with the adjoining one." She pointed. "You that one. Etcetera."

He nodded.

"Counting the shelves, thus." She turned toward the door and pointed to the rightmost shelves. "Level one, section one, two, three, and so on. Level two, section one, etcetera, etcetera."

"I have the evens, you the odds."

"Agreed. We must also log our progress." She stared at the shelves and then at the books Daunt had taken out.

"I recognize that look," he said. "What is it?"

"From what Angus said, the Dukes are not terribly large. Ten by seven, roughly." She indicated the size with her hands. "Angus told me about a rare manuscript he found hidden inside a butter churn. Another time, he found a quite valuable manuscript affixed to the back of a painting."

"*The MacAllan Register.*"

"As you have realized already, we can presume nothing about the condition of any of the Dukes. They may be in their original glorious condition, or they may have been unbound and left that way, or bound as if it were some other book entirely."

"Anything is possible. Anything."

"The only assumption we can safely make is that it's unlikely the Dukes are smaller." She held up a finger, arrested by a truly horrifying thought. "Unless the pages have been cut."

Daunt blanched. "There are collectors who are scoundrels, as you well know. They think nothing of lying or cheating to get what they want. Then there are those who do not know a rare book from their right foot." He leaned against his chair. "The thought of someone coming here and stealing a book, any book, sickens me."

"I too."

"The thought of someone cutting down—mutilating!—a work of art such as *Liber Ducis de Scientia*, it's beyond understanding."

Magdalene leaned over and squeezed his arm. "If the Dukes are here, we shall find them."

"I do appreciate your enthusiasm."

"I have one last suggestion."

He rested a hand over his heart. "You've done your worst, suggesting the Dukes may have been damaged beyond repair. And for reasons that beggar understanding."

"Every book within our prescribed parameters must be examined, but with luck, the signs of a recently handled book yet remain. Observe the dust, or whether it appears any volume has not been disturbed since it was placed there."

"Yes, yes."

She reached into the pocket of her frock and withdrew the memorandum and pencil she kept on hand at all times. "This, my lord, is why Angus insisted one must never be without a pocket memorandum and a pencil. Allow me."

She sat at the nearest desk, far too aware of Daunt but in control of herself. She numbered the lines. "One through twenty-seven. Bottom floor. Twenty-eight through fifty, top floor, it being smaller." Daunt braced one hand on the desktop to her right and leaned over. She ignored the fluttery sensation in her stomach and drew a narrow column to the right of the numbers. "Mark each row as we complete it. D for Daunt, C for Carter. Here we leave space for notes."

"Why?"

"One never knows." She wrote *D/C* over the narrow column and *notes/remarks* over the other column. "It is wise to document anomalies, anything peculiar, or simply a reminder of a task to be completed at another time."

"I foresee only one problem," he said.

"That is?"

"There is only one pocket memorandum between us."

"I have additional memoranda. I shall make you one modeled after this pattern. This one shall be designated the master." She walked to the nearest desk and rattled one of the drawers. "We require a suitable location in which to keep it. A drawer that securely locks would be ideal. Is there a key?"

He gave her an odd look, then joined her and extracted a tasseled key from the drawer she had rattled. "Behold."

She placed the pencil and the notebook inside and closed the panel. He reached over and locked the drawer. "You'd best keep the key, my lord."

"Very well." He unfastened the tassel and affixed the key to his watch chain.

She tilted her chin to look at him, and she felt another of those peculiar tugs in the center of her chest. "If the Dukes are indeed in this library, they have been bound with some quotidian title that hides the true contents."

He braced a hand on the mantel. "*A History of the Dormouse in Southwest Dorchester Parish.*"

"*Parliamentary Debates 1778 to 1779.*"

He laughed, and when he smiled like that, women must surely fall in love by the dozens. Angus had once remarked Daunt was a favorite of the ladies. She'd just nodded and not given it another thought.

"*Dr. Maxwell's Treatise on the Most Efficacious Methods of Sheep Shearing,*" he added.

"All I know of that subject is a collie dog is required." She was momentarily diverted by the possibilities. "I now have the most ridiculous image of a sheared collie."

"Poor little dog." Daunt straightened his coat and then his neckcloth. "Is it straight?"

"It's only me here, Daunt. I don't care if your neckcloth is crooked."

"I do. *Saints in the Time of Edward II.*"

"It's straight. I promise you." Magdalene propped her chin on her palm. "If you come across that, be sure to set it aside for me."

Daunt shook his head in mock dismay.

"Come now," she said. "You'd do the same."

"I would." Daunt glanced at the pile of books he'd left on the floor. "We shall have to look at every blessed one."

"To work, then," she said.

Chapter Three

AT HALF PAST six, they broke off their search, not having found anything the least Duke-ish in nature. Magdalene logged their progress with Daunt pacing behind her. "Level one, section two, shelf five has a copy of the *Principia* I suspect may be an early edition."

"Really?" He headed for the shelf in question. She remained far too aware of him. It made her feel a girl again, full of impossible hopes and dreams. He returned with the Newton, turning pages. "Hmm."

"Here." She handed him the memorandum, and he used the key fastened to his watch chain to lock it in the drawer.

"I don't know about you, but I'm famished," he said.

The idea of dining with fifty or more strangers was too much to contemplate. "A quiet meal in my room and some minutes to enjoy peace and quiet before returning to the search seem ideal to me."

"But of course." Daunt relayed the necessary instructions to a servant before taking up a lamp to escort her to her room. She easily kept pace with his long-legged stride. It was one of the advantages of being a tall woman.

Accession Day at Vaincourt was worse than she'd imagined and everything she'd dreaded. On their way, they passed a dozen splendidly dressed ladies and gentlemen heading downstairs to the dining room. One of the women was extraordinarily beautiful, with hair the color of gold and a gown of pale pink and blue. As far as Magdalene could tell, Daunt took no notice of her. Soon after that, they were obliged to dodge a giggling woman who emerged from a room and raced down the corridor, an equally elevated gentleman in pursuit.

Daunt drew her closer. "I promise you, there is no one where you are. There's a back way to the library. I'll show you after I've done my duty downstairs."

"Thank you."

They walked several more minutes, took another staircase up, then turned down a narrower corridor than the others. The sounds of revelry and laughter lessened considerably. Left, then left again, and then they reached a corridor that terminated with three steps up to a door painted dead black.

"Here we are!" Daunt opened the door wide enough to admit her.

"Oh," she said when she entered. "What a charming room."

"I did hope you'd like it."

"I do. Exceedingly." The southern wing of the house was distinctly Tudor, and her room was a pristine example of the period. Carved wainscot matched the oak squares on the ceiling. Where the walls were not covered with gorgeously carved wood, they were white plaster with a hint of lavender. The three sets of high diamond-paned windows arched and met in points at the top.

There was only one other door, which she presumed must lead to the bedchamber. On a side table by the windows was an enormous arrangement of fragrant roses, carnations, and wisteria.

"Later in the night, you'll likely hear the owls. They nest in the trees outside your windows." He pointed, though he stayed near the door. His hair was adorably mussed, and a hint of beard darkened his jaw. He wasn't the eighteen-year-old boy she'd met after moving to Plumwood as Angus's bride. Harry Fordyce was a viscount now, a man fully grown, and so perfectly beautiful it seemed unfair. Despite his elevation in rank, he remained as kind and thoughtful as ever, nothing like his father.

"That sounds lovely."

"You are welcome to dine here if you would prefer, of course," he said, "but we could dine in the library. I've given orders that the library is off-limits, so we shall be private. No Accession Day visitors, I promise you."

"Perhaps I shall."

"If you do join me and don't go back the way we came, take those first stairs down, three rights, a left, a right, a right, and you'll come out near the library. It's a longer walk, but a more private one."

"Thank you."

"I'll have Gomes bring dinner for two. If you come, I shall be glad of it. If not, we'll eat your dinner later."

"Oh, so you want my dinner as well. I understand now." His prodigious appetite was always a subject of amusement between them. "Dining in the library does seem the most efficient choice." That was true, positively and absolutely. "Less work for the staff as well. They must be overwhelmed with all these visitors."

Daunt nodded. "I'm to give my toast to the health of the populace at seven. Come to the library at, say, half past seven, and the food will be hot. Does that give you sufficient time?"

"Thank you, I believe it shall."

He bowed and showed himself out.

Now that Daunt wasn't here with his size and beauty taking up her ability to think properly, the room was quiet and soothing. She went to the windows and gazed out at the section of a lake with trees all about, just glimpsed through the trees closer to the house where the light was just hinting at dusk.

She wanted to be at Plumwood where everything was familiar and nothing happened to shake her out of her routine. Here, who knew what would happen? Daunt's good intentions notwithstanding, she might encounter any number of strangers. If she did, it was a virtual certainty that she would say or do the wrong thing at some point.

She rested her hands on the sill and breathed slowly. She was familiar with Daunt. Comfortable. At ease. With him, she could be herself without fear. As long as she kept her new awareness of him under control, all would be well.

Her maid, Tilly, came in from the bedroom. "Did you have a pleasant stroll from Plumwood, ma'am?"

"We stopped at St. John's for a while." She left the window to bend over the flowers and breathe in the scent. St. John's was the cemetery where Angus was buried. "I'm to dine downstairs with Daunt. In the library."

"I know just the gown."

Magdalene knew better than to argue. Her present frock, donned this morning without any thought of calls from viscounts, was not grand enough for dinner at Vaincourt. Before long, Tilly had her dressed in gray silk with slippers dyed to match.

"Hold still," Tilly said. "Let me do something with your hair." She produced a comb and drew it through Magdalene's short curls. With the best made of her fine hair, Tilly draped Magdalene's best shawl over her shoulders. It had once been cream-colored wool but had been dyed black. Over time, the color had faded and was now light enough to pass as a deliberate match for her gray silk.

They both turned when someone tapped on the anteroom door. Tilly put away her comb and straightened Magdalene's shawl.

"Lord Daunt, mostly likely," Magdalene said. "He must have forgotten to tell me something." A stir set up in the pit of her stomach at the prospect of seeing him again. This reaction must be dealt with and dealt with firmly.

Tilly, however, announced someone she did not know, a Mrs. Taylor, who proved to be the woman Magdalene had glimpsed earlier when she and Daunt were on their way here.

She curtseyed to this vision in pink and pale blue silk. With her golden hair and blue eyes, she was a veritable confection of English beauty. "Good day. Evening." What did one say to such a woman? "I am Daunt's neighbor."

"Goodness, you're tall. A giant among women." Mrs. Taylor smoothed the bodice of her lovely gown. "I hope you do not mind I've come to introduce myself. I thought we might go down to dinner together."

"No." She did not know Mrs. Taylor, nor why she'd come here to find fault with her for being tall, or why she wanted to go down to dinner together.

The other woman swept in and kissed the air just above either of Magdalene's cheeks. Her perfume smelled divine. "When I heard you were here, I came immediately. I am convinced we shall be the very best of friends."

Magdalene managed a smile, and that seemed to satisfy the woman.

"Now, when you've changed to something more suitable, I should be happy to show you the house," Mrs. Taylor said. "Shall I wait for you?"

There was a brief silence that threatened to be uncomfortable. She did not do well with strangers. Her pulse was racing, and she had to concentrate on breathing slowly. "I have been to Vaincourt many times."

Mrs. Taylor's perfect eyebrows rose. "Have you?"

"Yes." She did not make friends easily, and on top of that general anxiety, she resented the woman for coming here without warning or introduction. She rarely went out, but even she knew the woman's visit was presumptuous. "The previous Lord Daunt knew my husband. As did the current one."

"Whatever the reason you are here, Mrs. Carter, I must warn you I am determined to shake Daunt out of his doldrums. He simply cannot be allowed to slip into a deeper melancholy."

Magdalene let out a breath. She *would* get through this. "What melancholy?"

"I intend that Lord Daunt shall be sufficiently cheered and entertained and therefore kept from undue depression of his mood while he is here." Her smile was blindingly lovely, but the thought flashed into Magdalene's head that there was some degree of cunning there.

"Undue."

"I have been considering the best methods of entertaining him."

"There are festivities."

"Yes. For the locals, who are so very charming. There *is* dancing tonight. That should be quite jolly."

"The weather was fine today."

"Yes, wasn't it? The young ladies who have arrived so far are not, how shall I say this, first in fashion. But they are handsome, robust examples of the beauty to be found only in the English countryside."

"There are festivities."

"My dear Mrs. Carter." She smiled kindly without actually looking kind, but that often happened to her in situations like this, when she was forced into conversation with strangers with no chance to prepare herself. "Gentlemen are always diverted by youthful beauties arrayed in their finest, Lord Daunt most of all, as I am sure you are aware." She looked Magdalene up and down again. "Perhaps not. Daunt tells me he does not intend to attend the ball."

She lifted her hands and then was not sure she had appropriately conveyed her confusion. Now what?

"You cannot know Daunt well."

Magdalene blinked. "I suppose not." The admission pained her, but one must face the truth with stoicism. "He did not seem sad this morning."

"You saw him this morning? Where?"

"Home."

"What an honor to have Lord Daunt condescend to call on you. And when he is host to so many people!"

"Yes." She was more and more puzzled about the reason for the woman's visit and increasingly anxious that the conversation was continuing in this pointless manner. "An honor."

"He requires entertainment."

"Why?"

Mrs. Taylor grew serious. "Dear Mrs. Carter, if you knew him as I do, you would know that since his father's passing, he is dreadfully changed."

"Changed." She winced. Even to herself she sounded awkward. She never had any trouble conversing with Daunt. With strangers? Such encounters never went well.

"He has completely withdrawn from society." Mrs. Taylor took a turn around the room, stopping every few steps to touch something, the table, a gilt-framed etching, which she set askew, a bird's nest on the mantel.

Magdalene could not stop herself. She went to the etching and straightened it. She also returned the bird's nest to a less precarious position.

"Now he's come here, where there is no one who is a friend and confidante, and where, as charming as the country can be, there cannot possibly be sufficiently elevated entertainment."

"It is Accession Day. There are festivities."

"In London, Daunt entertains constantly. The most brilliant people. Artists and scholars, learned men, beautiful women. But here? There is nothing to keep him diverted. I am gravely concerned."

"Gravely. Yes."

Mrs. Taylor took both of Magdalene's hands in hers and leaned back for another examination of her. A frown marred her perfect features, and while it lasted, Magdalene wondered whether Mr. Taylor remained among the living. Upon the heels of this followed an inappropriate curiosity about just how intimate was the relationship between Daunt and Mrs. Taylor. "Trust me in this matter. I know what's best. Daunt and I have a great deal in common, as I am sure you have guessed."

She seized on that as something to break her out of her conversational paralysis. "Are you a member of the Bibliomania Club?" Perhaps that was how she'd come to know Daunt so well. The club had at least one female member. Mrs. Taylor might be another female member.

The woman's smile reappeared. "He left London directly after the last meeting of the club. Other members have also dispersed. I fear they may soon disband from whatever falling-out occurred. Did Daunt tell you?"

The woman's sly question gave her pause, and for the first time, her anxiety settled enough for her to make a deliberate, considered response. "Tell me what?"

"One worries when one's particular friend leaves behind everyone capable of entertaining him."

Magdalene smiled weakly.

"You *are* in colors again, aren't you?" Mrs. Taylor fingered the edge of Magdalene's shawl. She stepped out of reach. "I do hope so, for I would not wish him to be reminded of his recent loss, and if you are not out of mourning, why, you shan't fit in at all."

"I rarely do." The color of her clothing was completely immaterial to Daunt, of that she was certain. Why anyone else would care was also mysterious.

"Men declare themselves baffled by a woman's interest in fashion." Mrs. Taylor shook her finger at her, then began another turn around the anteroom. "I promise you they understand and applaud the effect." She examined a rather dreadful painting of a dragon poised to devour a knight. "A gentleman may tell you he does not care what colors ladies wear, but it is not true." Mrs. Taylor walked away with the painting listing to the left and stopped near the windows.

Magdalene straightened the dragon painting, and when she turned again, Mrs. Taylor was staring at the flowers on the table. "Those flowers."

"Are in a vase."

Mrs. Taylor's upper lip twitched. "Entirely inappropriate, I fear."

"How so?" Should they be simply lying about on the table? What nonsense.

"They are excessive and the wrong color."

From Daunt's supposedly dangerous melancholy to parties and the colors of ladies' gowns and now on to flowers? "Flowers are the colors they are."

"Yes," the woman said.

If those sly and cunning glances hadn't convinced her, her disapproval of the flowers did. They were not destined to be friends.

"This is not the sort of bouquet one gives a grieving widow."

"Yes. I am." Her heart lurched. She wanted very much to sit down. "A widow."

"Naturally, I inquired about you, Mrs. Carter. You must not be shocked that I know who you are."

"I am Lord Daunt's neighbor." Behind her back, she clasped her hands hard. Her palms were damp. She was better focused now that their conversation had turned to flowers. There was relevant history to relay. "Daunt says Vaincourt's gardens are superior. I dispute this."

"I went for a stroll shortly after I arrived to enjoy the beauty that is Vaincourt. I can tell you categorically that Vaincourt's reputation is well deserved."

"Nevertheless, the gardens at Plumwood are without parallel."

"Plumwood. Do you mean the charming cottage a forty-minute walk from here?"

Forty minutes? Unless the weather was inclement, which it was not now, the walk between Plumwood and Vaincourt never took longer than twenty minutes. "That is likely."

"I agree the gardens there are lovely. What I saw of them."

"You have been to Plumwood?"

"I do believe so. Entirely by coincidence, I found myself passing the most charming cottage. Such a lovely little house. So cozy and rustic."

"Daunt claims Vaincourt's gardens are superior to Plumwood's—"

"I'm sure they must be." Mrs. Taylor seated herself on the only chair. "Vaincourt is renowned for its history and beauty." She considered the flowers, which, yes, must indeed seem excessive to a casual observer. "My dear... You do not understand."

"I believe I do. The flowers are beautiful and extravagant exactly as Daunt intended."

"Daunt makes extravagant gestures whenever he has ulterior motivations."

"He hasn't got those."

Mrs. Taylor laughed, and it was a beautiful, compelling laugh.

"The colors of a bouquet can only come from what is in bloom." Magdalene squeezed her fingers. She'd talked enough. Too much. "Daunt is making a point."

"How droll you are." Mrs. Taylor let her amusement fade. "Perhaps you understand more than I gave you credit for at first."

With that, the conversation took another sharp left. "Droll."

"When he wants something, no gesture is too grand."

"The flowers are a point, not a grand gesture."

"Are you really so naïve?"

"No."

"I hope you do not think he intends to have an affair with you."

Magdalene was too horrified to speak. In a sideways sort of way, she had been thinking that. About that. Not that it would happen, but the remark hit uncomfortably close to home.

"He *is* responsible for those flowers, so I daresay you were an expected guest rather than one who merely arrived."

"You arrived from?"

"London, of course. I must say you strike me as far too sweet and gentle a woman to understand men and their motives."

"Motives. Again, motives."

Mrs. Taylor rose and faced Magdalene from across the table. "Motive is all that matters."

"I do believe I understand the motives to which you refer. I have a son who was conceived with a great deal of motivation."

"With your husband."

"Yes. Good heavens, who else?"

"Do you agree Lord Daunt's interest in you is limited to your knowledge of books?"

Now a sharp right. "Books. Yes."

"And so, my dear Mrs. Carter, given your infamous husband—"

She stiffened. "Infamous?"

"Given your most infamous husband, you must be aware of the very real possibility that Lord Daunt intends to seduce you—"

"Are you mad? You must be."

"Lord Daunt is a rake. As charming and delightful as he is, that is indisputable. Every tolerable-looking woman in London has a story to tell of him."

"Why would Daunt seduce me, then?"

"Oh, you poor, dear woman. You are too precious. You are a widow, and Lord Daunt is an accomplished flirt and an even more accomplished lover. I adore him for both reasons. But surely you see that those flowers prove he invited you here for the purpose of obtaining one of the Dukes."

The reason for those sly looks came into sharp focus. "You mean *De Terris Fabulosis.*"

Mrs. Taylor smiled slowly and with altogether too much satisfaction. "I presume you found the book in your husband's collection."

She made a show of consulting the watch pinned to the bodice of her frock. "You must go now. It was a pleasure meeting you."

"If you're wise, you'll heed my warning about Daunt."

"You must go now." She met the woman's gaze head on.

Mrs. Taylor curtseyed and headed for the door. Once there, she paused. "I hope you will do everything you can to convince Daunt to attend tonight's celebration. His happiness and good spirits depend upon it."

"Good night, ma'am."

When she left, in a cloud of perfume and the rustle of silk, Magdalene stared at the door for some time, very much worried that Mrs. Taylor was a bibliophile of the ruthless, cutthroat sort.

Chapter Four

DAUNT WAS SITTING on the floor in front of one of the shelves of books when Magdalene came into the library. She wore a gray silk that suited her complexion and a gray shawl with fringe of a darker shade. Not deep mourning any longer. She held one end of her shawl and rolled a few strands of the fringe between two fingers.

He liked the color on her. The color made her hair look more definitively brown. A silver watch was pinned to her upper bosom, dangling from a short, silver mesh chain. She looked harassed and out of sorts.

While she closed the door, he reshelved the book he'd just inspected. "*Ave*, Daunt," she said when she was done.

"*Ave*." He blew out a breath to move a lock of hair off his forehead. "Forgive my disrepair." He'd taken off his coat while he worked and was in his shirt-sleeves, hardly decent, even between good friends. "I do not mean to offend."

"You haven't." She stayed with her eyes cast down while he retrieved his coat from a chair that was too far away. "Any man who fills my room with flowers that are almost as beautiful as those at Plumwood may presume a great deal."

He buttoned his coat and grinned at her, quite smug now. "You like them?"

"I do."

He bowed. "I presume, then, that our dispute is concluded, and you concede that Vaincourt has the better gardens."

"I concede nothing."

"I shall try harder to persuade." Good. He'd made her smile.

"Do." She continued into the room. Her hair was all curls, without any combs or ribbons or silk flowers. She looked as if she'd done little but run her fingers through it before she came downstairs. He'd once accused her of favoring the Welsh-comb-style of hairdressing, and she had laughed at him without any embarrassment or denial. From across the room, Angus had winked a confession of his wife's disregard for fashion. "I have recently learned you are a very… charming man."

He turned to keep her in his line of sight as she came in. "I am devastated you did not come to that conclusion years ago."

She blinked, and a shiver of arousal shot through him. "I take it you have not found any Dukes."

"No."

From the corridor, someone tapped on the door, and then Gomes called out, "Dinner, my lord."

Daunt raised his voice. "Come in."

While Gomes supervised setting out their meal, Magdalene went to the shelf she'd been working on earlier and recommenced. A woman of no nonsense and action. He liked that she was tall, given that he was a tall man. An internal energy burned from her eyes and propelled her body through space with emphatic determination. She was no dainty female, and he liked that too. Because she was so slender, her features were sharp. Her face was strong and somewhat irregular. She was only sometimes handsome but was always compelling. When she was among friends, she was full of life and good humor.

By design, he'd ordered simple fare, but even simple fare from his kitchen was sublime. Soup, roast beef, a selection of cheeses, bread, two or three sweets, wine, and a decanter of cognac. As they ate, they chatted about the marginalia in a manuscript she had recently acquired.

"When we are done here," she said, "and we have all our Dukes, you must come to Plumwood to see it."

"I look forward to it." He would, no matter the outcome.

Their conversation continued in that vein for a while, but when they were done and the dishes cleared away and the servants gone, rather than return to the shelves, she stayed at the table with her hands pressed down flat and her eyes on her hands. "May I ask, my lord, about Mrs. Taylor?"

She said the name as if she expected some reaction other than confusion from him. "Who?"

"Mrs. Taylor."

"I'm afraid I don't know her. Or don't recall her, take your pick."

"That is odd, Fordyce, for she seems to know you well. From London, she says."

"We must have been introduced, then, but I'm sorry, I don't recall her."

"She knows about the Bibliomania Club."

"It's not a secret."

She glanced up, and their eyes met. He was always taken aback by the ferocity of her gaze. "I have two lines of inquiry. Perhaps three."

"Very well."

"She says you frequently entertain in London."

He straightened a cuff, then shrugged. "I do."

"She says you are suffering from melancholy." Her eyebrows drew together. "Are you melancholy? I wish you'd confided in me if you are."

"Not that I am aware." His confusion increased.

"Perhaps you do not notice. After Angus died, I did not know I remained in the grips of despair until long afterward when I saw the degrees of my mourning. I had Ned to comfort, you see. What mattered was him. Only now do I see I was not well at all, and that seems such an insidious state of affairs."

He lifted his hands. "I *am* happy. In the main. I don't believe I am in a state of despair. Unless we do not find the Dukes, then I shall be."

She stared at him thoughtfully. "There is more to life than books."

He smiled. "No, there isn't."

"I am serious, Daunt. For quite a long time after Angus died, I was despondent without realizing. Had you asked me, and I believe you did, I would have told you I was perfectly fine. I worry that you mourn your father more than you admit."

Daunt's amusement faded, and he reached for her hand. "Oh, Magdalene."

"You are my friend. If it hadn't been for you, I don't know how I would have survived those days, and now I am worried for you. Someone who knows you well believes you are melancholy."

"How well can she know me if I don't recall her? But never mind that, you think I am melancholy?"

"Not I, Daunt. Though I fear I may have been inattentive."

"You? Never. Very little escapes your notice."

"Mrs. Taylor said you are much changed. She is worried for your happiness. She says you told her you would not attend the ball tonight." She pressed his hands.

"I shall be there long enough to address the assembly. I've told dozens of people that."

"Stay longer, Daunt. See if it doesn't lift your spirits. I can continue the work here while you surround yourself with friends and merriment."

"First, I do not require merriment."

"Is that the melancholy speaking?"

"No. Second, if I attend, so ought you."

"You know I do not care for crowds."

He withdrew his hands from hers. Whatever this Mrs. Taylor had intended, her pronouncement of him as melancholy was pure nonsense. "Are you certain? For I tell you, *you* are much altered. You have been racked by grief."

"Don't change the subject. The topic to hand is you enjoying this evening."

"I shall get immense joy from finding one of the Dukes."

"Go, Daunt." She took his hands in hers, a state of affairs of which he approved. "Attend long enough to refresh your spirits." She waved a hand, then reclaimed his. "From this dull work."

"The work is not dull."

Her mouth twitched. They'd spent long evenings discussing words and when one ought to use one over another. They were comfortable together. She knew him. He did not have to explain himself to her or moderate his opinions or remember to talk less about books rather than more. They were friends, yes, but he wanted more. "Tedious, then," she said.

"I have no desire to dance tonight." He did not know how, or even if it was possible, to effect a change in their relationship without risking their friendship. But just now a future without the two of them as more than friends seemed bleak indeed. "Unless it's with you."

She took in a breath and slowly let it out. "Don't be difficult."

He froze. Half a dozen possibilities whirled through his head, but he discarded them all. She was a straightforward woman who would tell him outright if there was no hope. The problem, as he saw it, was that she did not at present think of him, or any other man, as a potential lover or husband. Until she did, until she'd had the opportunity to consider such a thing at all, any advance from him risked swift rejection.

"She is very beautiful."

"Who is very beautiful? What is your point? Magdalene—" He cocked his head and lifted his hands palm out. "A moment. Have you somehow got the impression that I have some attachment to this Mrs. Taylor? A woman I cannot even recall?"

"You are a man of considerable charm and good looks."

"Thank you." He was Viscount Daunt now. Others were eager and even impatient to be introduced to him. Parents presented their daughters in hopes he would agree to a marriage. He declined all such suggestions. The only woman he wanted to marry was sitting before him, and she would not be convinced by arguments involving rank, wealth, or political connections. "However, I remain baffled as to the identity of this woman."

Her cheeks turned faintly pink. "I don't want us to quarrel."

"We are not quarreling. But I submit to you that any man who declares his love based on a woman's appearance alone has confused love for lust."

She had a habit of listening intently, without expression beyond one of deep thought. That was her expression now.

He continued, rash, reckless, but frustrated that she was so eager to have him in love with someone else. "I know a great many beautiful women. She could be any of them."

"In all the time I've known you, you have never spoken about women you admire. Most gentlemen of your rank and position are married by eight and twenty. Is there truly no woman you wish to marry? I think you must forgive me for assuming the answer is yes, there is."

He crossed his arms over his chest. "Do go on."

"There is a woman whom you love, but you have not secured her because there are impediments."

"Such as?"

"Most likely, a husband."

"That is certainly an impediment." He met her gaze forthrightly. "I do not poach other men's wives, however beautiful the woman might be. I can assure you I have never been the least tempted."

"Oh, that is a relief." That was her way. She debated a point, conceded when necessary, and moved on. "We have now arrived at my next line of inquiry. I am pleased that you are not melancholy and that you are not enamored of Mrs. Taylor."

"Whoever she is."

"I believe she may be here because of the Dukes."

Daunt cocked his head and stayed silent for several long moments. Magdalene's instincts and intellect were superior. If she suspected Mrs. Taylor of nefarious intent, that must be taken seriously. "What facts have you in support of that statement?"

"She asked me about the Dukes and about Angus and asked if I had found *De Terris Fabulosis* among his effects. Ridiculous, I know. Hear me out. I have more to say. I believe it is possible she came here to disrupt your attempt to find the Dukes. She may be using the chaos of Accession Day to her advantage. I suspect she is here under false pretenses and with the express intent of stealing the Dukes."

He picked up his cognac, served just after dinner, and took a sip. "I concur," he said with a grim smile. "She has certainly caused mischief."

"Either she is in love with you, or she means to steal the Dukes."

"Not both?"

That got a smile from her. "It's highly possible."

He was sorry now that he'd been so flippant. She'd taken him seriously. "What do you recommend we do? Shall I close the house and send everyone home?"

"You can't!"

A brilliant idea occurred. He turned it over in his head, looking for flaws and found none.

"What, my lord?"

"I propose that the two of us appear at the ball and see if anyone attempts to gain access to the library. If your suspicions are correct, the sooner we expose our mysterious Mrs. Taylor, the better."

Chapter Five

HIS HEART THUMPED against his chest when Magdalene appeared in the doorway of the ballroom. The dancing was not due to start for several more minutes, and guests continued to stream in. He knew immediately that he'd asked too much of her.

She stood tall and straight, looking as if she were marching to her death. Her lips were pressed together, her jaw was clenched, and she clutched her fan as if she believed she would soon be required to defend herself with it.

She'd changed into a dark blue satin gown that could almost pass as a ballgown. Her shoulders were barer than he'd seen before, but compared to most formal evening gowns, her attire was markedly stark. There was no lace, no bows, just a ribbon underneath her bosom. There was a small ruffle at her sleeves.

Half a dozen gentlemen approached the doorway from behind her, walking rapidly. One of them brushed her shoulder and turned to make his apologies. Magdalene looked at him with a glassy-eyed stare.

"My dearest," Daunt said, hurrying to close the distance between them. He took her arm and slipped between her and the other gentlemen, turning to them with a broad grin. Some of the most beautiful women in Britain had made their interest known to him, and, in his opinion, none of them compared to Magdalene. "Good evening, gentlemen. I hope you're enjoying yourselves."

There were several "my lords" and other exclamations of assent as they hurried in with the swagger and over-confidence of young men intent on the delight of dancing.

When the young gentlemen were past, she peered into the room, stuffed full of the local gentry from several parishes. "How many people do you think are here?"

"Ten."

She replied without a trace of a smile. "My lord. There are at least two dozen."

"A dozen. Two dozen." He guided her inside. They had agreed to make themselves seen, but Magdalene was obviously terrified. "Are you all right? You needn't, you know."

She let out a breath. "I can do this," she whispered. She relaxed considerably when he drew her to a quiet corner.

"Do you see Mrs. Taylor?" he asked.

"Lorenzo de' Medici himself could be here without my noticing."

Daunt bent closer and lowered his voice. "I have news."

She turned her ear to him. "Go on."

"I made inquiries. Gomes says there's no Mrs. Taylor at Vaincourt."

"Here at all, or not staying here?"

"Not a guest at Vaincourt."

"Perhaps she has accommodations in Badding, or she's a guest of someone else. This is most mysterious. She very much implied that she was a guest here."

"Naturally, I have posted additional guards around the library and outside the house. Should anyone gain access, they shall meet Gomes's granite-eyed stare and iron nerve." His butler, a servant he'd brought with him from London, was a former infantryman who brooked no nonsense from anyone.

The orchestra struck up a preliminary note. Several young ladies hurried in and stood nearby with their heads together. He gestured. "Perhaps one of them shall meet one of the young gentlemen from earlier and fall in love."

She was at least partially diverted by the remark, for she managed a smile. "Stranger things have happened at a ball."

He straightened his coat and dusted off a shoulder. "This shall be the first time I've given the welcome speech," he said.

She put her hands on his shoulders and pushed. "Go," she said. "I shall admire your oratory from here."

Daunt made his way to the center of the ballroom. Silence fell, and with one eye on the corner where Magdalene stood, he welcomed everyone to Vaincourt, and with that, he had officiated at his first Accession Day as Lord Daunt of Vaincourt. Pray God that next year Magdalene would be at his side as Lady Daunt.

Rejoining her was the work of some minutes, but he made his way to her. She stood with her back pressed against the wall, quite pale. She'd crushed her fan; it dangled useless from her wrist.

Without a word, he steered her out of the ballroom and did not stop walking until they were several feet along the corridor. He escorted her into an unoccupied parlor. He had elected to open the ball with a waltz, which could be faintly heard. He removed her destroyed fan and discarded it. "You look lovely tonight."

"Thank you."

"I mean it." He swept her into his arms, reckless, so reckless. "Dance with me?"

"What on—" She more or less stumbled into his arms, laughing now that she wasn't staring into the abyss of a ballroom full of people.

"Have you waltzed before?" he asked, even though he'd already begun the steps. The waltz was a dance designed to make a couple intensely aware of each other. He already knew she found him handsome, but he hoped she would think of him as a potential life partner. If Magdalene thought of him as too young, well, perhaps a waltz would introduce her to the possibility that, at twenty-eight, he was most definitely not too young.

He led her on a tight circuit of the room, avoiding chairs and tables. She was tall and bony, and to his discredit, he'd expected her to be awkward. But she wasn't. "You've waltzed before?"

"The duke saw to it I had lessons," she said with a smug smile.

"You learned the waltz?"

"No, of course not. But one year, Angus came home from a trip to London where it happened that he'd learned, and he taught me. I've danced before at the smaller assemblies where I know most everyone." He was intensely aware of her hand resting lightly on his shoulder.

"Do you like to dance?"

"I do." They adjusted to a mistimed section of the waltz with a hop and a bob to fill in the extra beats until the music was back in tempo.

"It's astonishing that in all the time I've known you, I was never at Plumwood when there was dancing."

"How strange that the subject never came up. Angus and I had parties with dancing afterward several times. One does what one can for the local youth. But when you came, why, that was a special occasion for books. Angus and I looked forward to your visits with such eagerness."

He wanted to kiss her. He wanted to hold her in his arms with passionate intent, but despite their impromptu dance and their closeness now, she had given him not one sign that she would welcome such an advance from him.

In the end, he didn't dare.

Chapter Six

WHEN HE AND Magdalene arrived at the library to resume their search for Dukes, the men posted outside reported that no one had approached. Inside, Gomes snapped to attention. "Milord."

"Anything?" Daunt asked.

"Nothing, milord."

Daunt turned and gestured for Magdalene to enter. "You are dismissed. But there's to be someone patrolling the corridors and this portion of the house."

"Very good, milord."

Five minutes later, he and Magdalene were back at work. An hour later, Daunt had to admit to an increasing sense of despair and urgency. They'd made hardly a dent in their search thus far.

They had mutually devised a system for inspecting the books: assess whether a volume was too small to be one of the Dukes, and if not, remove the book in case pages or even whole quires of one of the Dukes were somehow concealed inside.

The top shelves were the most work since they required a ladder, but once he was in rhythm, the work went reasonably well, if not as quickly as Magdalene's. Lack of attention due to tedium was a risk. They both required frequent breaks to stretch or pace.

Tedium was an ever-present and increasing issue, because the contents of his father's library proved to be of little interest to a bibliophile with their particular interests. He only occasionally came across a volume that merited further inspection at some time after they found the Dukes or else failed entirely.

Too often while he worked, his thoughts wandered to that post-ballroom interlude with Magdalene. They'd danced, and he could not say whether that had advanced his cause with her or not. Should he have kissed her? Had he been wrong to dance with her at all? The evidence tended to the negative, for nothing in her behavior toward him had changed.

The clock had just struck the half hour past eleven when Gomes announced himself again with a smart rap on the door. "Enter," Daunt said.

He and Magdalene turned to see Gomes come in with one of the footmen from Plumwood. Per instructions, one of the men outside reached in to immediately close the door.

Magdalene descended the ladder she'd been standing on, her expression a mirror of his own alarm. Daunt turned one of the books perpendicular to the shelf to mark his place before he joined her.

"Good heavens, not again?" she said.

Every so often, rumors about Angus and his supposed possession of one of the Dukes heated up, and some fool attempted to gain entry to the house to locate and make off with the fabled volume.

A rather shocking amount of the time, the would-be criminal proved to be a young gentleman who'd had too much to drink, but once or twice the attempt had been quite serious. The Plumwood staff was well-trained in protection and apprehension.

While Angus was alive, these drunken escapades had been the subject of entertaining conversation after the fact. The perpetrators were inevitably intercepted well before reaching the rooms that housed his collection. Angus had had a set lecture for well-bred young men who'd put their brain on a temporarily liquid diet, but he'd had no compunctions about turning someone over to the authorities.

The Plumwood servant bowed and said, "Yes, ma'am."

"Was anyone hurt?" she asked. Daunt rested his fingers on her shoulder, and she patted his hand. He did not like this, not at all. What if Magdalene had been alone in the house with no one to protect her?

"No, ma'am," the servant said. "Nor was anything taken. Young Jack heard a window break downstairs and went to investigate. The intruder didn't get past the storeroom. We've boarded up the window."

"Thank goodness Ned is not at home."

"Did you apprehend the fellow?" Daunt asked.

"No, milord. He went out the window right quick once he realized he was discovered, I'm sorry to say. He was gone before the rest of us arrived."

"What matters," Magdalene said, "is that no one was hurt."

"Oh, but the intruder was," the manservant replied. "Near as we can tell, that is. There was blood on the sill outside."

Under his fingers, her shoulder radiated tension. "I'll send an extra man or two to assist in guarding Plumwood until this is over."

"Thank you, my lord. That is most welcome." She clasped her hands before her. "Tell everyone at the house to be especially careful. No one's life or safety is to be put at risk. I fear," she said, "that we must expect other attempts."

"Ma'am."

"Beginning now, Gomes," Daunt said, "everyone here is to be on alert for burglars or thieves. Believe nothing you are told except by myself or Mrs. Carter."

Gomes's lip curled. "I trust no one, milord."

"Good man."

When the servants departed, Magdalene returned to the shelves and took down a book. She stood without looking at the volume she held. "I should have anticipated this. I was too focused on Vaincourt." She gestured in a motion meant to encompass the entire library. "I assumed, wrongly, that if indeed Mrs. Taylor is after the Dukes, she would concentrate her efforts here when, in fact, she made it perfectly clear she was interested in *De Terris Fabulosis* and that she wrongly believes Angus had it."

"Why only the one volume?"

She scowled at the book in her hands. She opened it and fanned the pages. "Nothing." With a deep sigh, she returned the book to the shelf and took out another. "I also wrongly assumed she knows the Bibliomania Club is searching for the Dukes, but I now believe she hoped I would tell her why the members scattered to the winds after your most recent meeting."

"I'll have the servants on the lookout for her. Tomorrow," he said, "I'll have them scour the guests for injured women."

"Do you really think she attempted the break in herself? She might have hired someone."

"Anything is possible." Daunt smiled. "Half the women here shall be limping tomorrow."

"They did not have the most graceful Lord Daunt as their partner."

"I'll take that as a compliment."

"It was meant as one." Her cheeks turned pink. She made a face at the book. "People ought to be honest and forthright. They should not tell lies. They should not pretend to befriend someone or imply they are in love when they are not."

"You expect too much of our fellow men. And women."

"She must think me a fool to believe even half of what she told me. The only reason I listened to her at all was my concern for you."

"My supposed melancholy, you mean."

"I suspect she was lying about everything except her interest in *De Terris Fabulosis*."

"Likely."

"I am obliged to consider that possibility." She looked at him, eyes snapping with anger. Her fingers around the book turned white. Daunt took it from her. "If I didn't believe she'd steal something else while she was there, I'd let her search Plumwood as much as she likes. Angus does not have *De Terris Fabulosis* or any other Duke."

He curled a palm over the nape of her neck and pulled her close. "My dear. Whoever she is, whatever she intends, know this: Foolish people believe foolish things."

"You only say that to make me feel better."

"Yes, but it happens to be true." Daunt did not move when she took a step closer and laid her forehead against his shoulder. More than anything, he wanted this to mean more than her need for comfort, but he did not entirely trust his ability to assess the wisdom of doing anything but holding her close.

After a few moments, she looked up with that fierce expression he knew so well. "There is only one way to end this, Daunt, and that is to find the Dukes."

"Indeed." He released her, and for a moment, she stayed where she was. Too near for him not to be perilously close to losing his head. He would not act rashly.

"Thank you for being kind to me, Daunt."

"You deserve nothing else."

"You as well." She gazed at him, and had she been any other woman, he would have kissed her.

He set her back, and they returned to searching for the Dukes. An hour passed with no luck. From time to time, they exchanged idle conversation, but it was distracting for them both. In the main, they worked in silence.

Magdalene was now nearly three-quarters of a shelf ahead of him. She finished her fifth shelf and took out her pocket memorandum and made notes. "I have finished level one, shelves one, three, five, seven and nine. Nothing. You?"

"Level one, the evens through six, with eight partially done." They weren't making enough progress. Hands on his hips, he calculated the hours that going through the rest might take. It might as well have been a hundred years.

They worked in silence another hour, with neither of them saying a word. They logged their progress and examined books; turning pages was becoming a numbing experience.

Not long after the clock struck one, she stepped back from the shelves she was inspecting, stretched, and yawned. "Would it be too much trouble to ask for coffee? I brought a supply, if you haven't any on hand. Tea will do, otherwise, but you'll find me fast asleep on the floor without refreshment of some kind."

He returned the book he'd just checked to the shelf and yawned too. "I sent Gomes to Badding to be sure we had coffee on hand for you."

"Did you really?"

"I knew you would be here and that you prefer coffee. Having some to hand was the least I could do." From the angle between them, he had a view of her sharp cheeks and her nose. She was not, by any measure, an attractive woman, and yet, there was such determination in her, such ferocity that he could only imagine what it would be like to kiss her, to take her to bed. "You shall be pleased to know I have everything on hand to make your coffee *à la Turque*. Exactly as you like it."

"What a brilliant, brilliant man you are."

"Make a note of that in your pocket memorandum."

She took out her pencil and opened her memorandum. "Lord Daunt," she said as she wrote, "is brilliant."

"Twice over."

"Twice over."

He rang for a servant, and when he'd made the request, he said, "I'll have Gomes make coffee a standing order until we've found the Dukes or run out of time."

"Excellent idea."

They went back to work, this time chatting about the books they'd found or discussing a title that deserved a closer look when there was time for such a digression. The coffee soon came with a tray of food both savory and sweet. They sat, and she rested her head on her folded arms. "You do the honors," she said. "I'm too tired."

He served them both, and after some coffee and a few bites of food, she returned to her more usual state of alertness. "Do you want the last bit of ham?" he asked.

"No, thank you."

"What about the cheddar?" He ate the ham.

"That *was* a good cheddar," she said.

He walked to her side of the table with a portion of the cheese. He held it up to her mouth. "Here."

She leaned over and ate it. He held her gaze longer than was absolutely necessary. Too quickly, she flipped a page or two before closing the book she held. She returned it to the shelf and selected another. Her fingers were long and slender. She still wore her wedding ring. "I owe you an apology," she said.

"For what, pray tell?"

"For believing for even a moment that you and Mrs. Taylor were lovers. It was wrong of me." She spoke quickly and to the books before her. "It's just that she's quite beautiful. I don't mean to pry. Forgive me, Daunt."

"There is nothing to forgive. I have had lovers in the past, though not half as many as you are imagining right now."

"Only a hundred, then?"

"There might have been a hundred and fifty." He took a breath. "Magdalene. My dear. Allow me to answer the other question you are not asking me." She lifted her eyes to him. "I am careful, always careful."

"Angus said women adore you and that you adore them."

"I do." Magdalene always approached a subject head on. The tendency led to blunt conversations he so enjoyed having with her. Now, though, the subject was personal, and there was a good deal of risk in proceeding. But perhaps the bigger risk lay in taking no chance at all. "None of that means I am profligate or indiscreet or intemperate. I am none of those things."

She opened a book so the pages would fan out. She had more to say, he could feel it. Softly, she said, "Do you have any children?"

Her question was a door left ajar that had been tightly closed until now. If he went through that opening, the personal intimacy he'd always wanted was within reach. His truthful answer might destroy all his hopes. He could lie. A lie would be easy. A lie would protect them both.

"I have a son," he said. "He's a year younger than Ned. He lives in Sussex with his mother. I acknowledged him from the start. There was no question of that. He'll start public school soon."

"Do you see him very often?"

"Several times a year."

Her eyes stayed wide. "Do you love his mother?"

"I've never loved any of them," he said. This was not the time, most assuredly not the time, to tell her he'd only ever been in love with her.

She replaced another book on the shelf, but left her hand on the spine. "Have you ever been in love?"

"Yes."

A smile curved her mouth. "I'm glad to hear that. I should hate to think you'd never been in love. Tell me about her. What's she like? Is she beautiful? The woman you love, I mean. Why haven't you married her?"

"Where to start with all that?" He did not bother to check more books. "She is amusing and accomplished. Her intellectual gifts astound. She follows her own path through life. Her character is unassailable, but she does not care what anyone thinks about her varied interests. There's no subject she is not interested to learn about and capable of mastering should she put her mind to it."

"I think I would like her a great deal."

"I've never met a more fascinating woman in all my life."

"Have you known her long?"

"For many years." He held her gaze. "Is she beautiful? I suspect I know what others would say, but I say she is."

"Does she collect books?"

"She does. Our interests there intersect quite neatly."

"I do not understand, Daunt." She drew her eyebrows together. "You adore her, that's plain. *You* are handsome, and generous, and amusing. I cannot imagine any woman not falling to your considerable charm. Why aren't you married?"

He shrugged. "She loves someone else."

"Oh." She let out a soft breath. "I am sorry. What a foolish woman she must be."

Chapter Seven

IT WAS JUST past eleven at night, though Daunt was rapidly losing track of night and day; they'd slept no more than five or six hours in the last twenty-four At present, he and Magdalene were seated at one of the library tables, finishing off the meal Gomes had brought. He breathed in the aroma of Magdalene's Turkish coffee. They had found many of the books maliciously shelved, but none had been one of the fabled Dukes.

There had been no further attempted break-ins at Plumwood. Whether that was due to the potential injuries of the perpetrator or to the additional guards he'd sent was not entirely clear. There had been attempts detected at Vaincourt. Privately, he worried that this Mrs. Taylor—or someone else—may have located one or more of the Dukes before the books arrived at Vaincourt.

Magdalene, relentlessly cheerful and optimistic about their situation, took another sip of her coffee. "Which do you think we'll find first?"

"Which do you most hope to find?"

She pursed her lips. "To find any of them would be thrilling, but to answer the question posed, *De Scientia Naturae Rerum.* What might we learn from past observers of the world? You?"

"All of them," he replied. "However, I should like very much to read about the past understanding of how and why we feel as we do. Why did de' Medici's scholars believe we feel as we do? Why do we fall in love with one person and not another?"

"Ah. *De Motibus Humanis,* then. I agree, the subject is a fascinating one. Would you make one of the potions, and if you did, would you drink it yourself or give it to another?"

De Motibus Humanis reputedly contained recipes for the purpose of altering or affecting emotion. He did not believe for a moment that such a thing was possible, but it was amusing to speculate, particularly with Magdalene. "If we agree the recipes are efficacious, the moral answer is clear. One may not alter another's emotions without the subject's consent."

She nodded slowly. "One must ask if there is a difference between administering a potion and flirtation or seduction."

"The difference seems plain to me. Were I to flirt with you or attempt a seduction, you would be aware of that fact. Your ability to resist, or your desire to succumb, are not negated by my actions."

"Would you not agree that some persons are expert in persuasion, while others are susceptible?"

"I would. A potion administered without consent leaves the recipient powerless, and therefore, that action is morally repugnant." Daunt finished off his pudding. "What would *you* do? Assuming consent, potion or no potion?"

"If I were in a situation in which the emotions between myself and another were unequal when in the normal course they ought not be, such as with people bound by matrimony, I would seek to change my own feelings. Therefore, I would consume the potion."

"In this scenario, are you the party more in love than the other? Or are you suggesting you would seek to move from love to hatred?"

"Marriage is a partnership."

"Even in hatred?" Debate with Magdalene was always intellectually stimulating, and that had got wrapped up in the state of his heart where she was concerned.

She laughed. "No, but if I hated my husband, hypothetically speaking, I believe I would take the potion myself and transform my hatred to love."

He shuddered. "To live a life of delusion? No, thank you."

"Would it be delusion?" She tapped her fingers on the tabletop, one after the other. "After all, if the recipes found in *De Motibus Humanis* indeed effect a change in the consumer's emotions, then it seems to me there is no delusion."

"But why do you hate this husband of yours? Is he cruel or intemperate? Does he neglect you?"

"I do not know!" She threw up her hands. "He's not a bibliophile."

"Horrors," he said with a smile. She returned the smile, and there were parts north very much affected.

"Indeed. The only thing worse than a husband who is not a bibliophile would be his infidelity."

He let that sit between them a breath too long. "In such a case, you would agree to having love imposed upon you by artificial means?"

"The hypothetical before us is a marriage in which I actively hate my husband. What recourse would I, as his wife, have in such a situation? I would be almost entirely subject to his whims. Where I live, what funds are available to me, whether there is to be intimacy between us. I should think it would be a good deal simpler to be in love with one's husband rather than all but powerless to escape him. Therefore, I might well prefer a potion that transforms my hate to love." She put down her cup. "A horrible predicament, to be sure. For a woman, such an unequal situation is fundamentally different than it is for a man. Women have few, if any, remedies."

"I withdraw the hypothetical."

"Too late. The point was to create a set of conditions with but two options—for me to live with a man whom I hate, or to have the opportunity to drink a potion that transforms hate to love. I submit to you that in such a case, I would consider drinking the potion. I had rather be in love than not."

"Do you want to be in love again?" He held his breath while she considered her answer, for his future now hung in the balance. Better to know and find a way to move on if there was no hope for him.

"Well." She clasped her hands before her. "I confess I am at a loss as to a proper answer. Hypothetically, yes." Hypothetically. The weight of that response pressed on his heart. But what of you?" she asked. "You say you are in love with a woman who does not return the sentiment. Would you take a potion to cure your hopeless love?"

"No. I would not."

"Why not?" She looked genuinely puzzled.

"Suppose," he said slowly, "suppose I am in love with you."

She met his gaze head on without the slightest indication that she realized she was the woman in question. "Very well. Suppose you are."

"In the situation I have described, I cannot make you fall in love with me simply because I wish it."

"True."

"But from that it does not follow that I wish not to be in love. My love for you is justified. A potion that takes that from me must necessarily take away my ability to perceive all the aspects of you that are worthy of my love and regard. I submit to you that such a result would be a tragedy."

Her smile faltered. "My greatest wish is that you find the love you deserve, for there cannot be a more gallant, steadfast man than you."

"Thank you."

"Nevertheless, I maintain that a potion would be a far simpler to the problem of unrequited love." She picked up her coffee again. "Think of it. Rather than flatter and send flowers and rack our brains with ways to hint at our affections, we simply say, 'I should like for us to be in love. If you agree, please drink this.'" She offered him her coffee. "Simple and straightforward."

He took her coffee, drained it, and set it down. "How long before it takes effect?"

Magdalene burst into laughter. "Oh, Daunt. You do amuse me."

They went back to work shortly after that. At two o'clock, he looked over and saw Magdalene on a ladder, her forehead pressed against the books. He coughed loudly, and she came awake or out of whatever reverie had engaged her.

He descended his own ladder and walked to her, hand extended. "My dear. Perhaps it's time we retired for the night."

She looked down at him and blinked several times. He held his breath, for he saw quite clearly that she had momentarily mistaken his words for an invitation to retire together in the improper sense. He stayed as he was, hand extended, perfectly willing to have that misunderstanding in play.

"Yes," she said. "Yes."

He assisted her to the floor and briefly enfolded her in his arms. "It does us no good to work until we are stupid with sleep."

She laid her cheek on his shoulder. "When even coffee cannot refresh us, it's clear that what we require is a potion to keep us awake and alert."

"Without *De Motibus,* sleep must be our remedy."

She took a step back. "As ever, you are correct. If only coffee were a more perfect potion. I am exhausted at the same time I am absolutely wide awake."

"I won't have you falling off a ladder. You might break your neck."

The blue ribbon threaded through her hair caught the light from a nearby sconce. Daunt found himself once again in that peculiar space between all that he knew about seducing a woman he wanted as a lover and his inexperience with courting. He almost wished he did have a potion to relieve him of his misery.

He held out his arm. "I'll see you safely to your room."

Chapter Eight

MAGDALENE PUT HER hand on Daunt's arm and allowed him to lead her along the corridor, leaving behind a locked door and the servants engaged to guard the library, one inside, two outside the door, and another three patrolling outdoors. At the top of the stairs, she glanced in the direction of the main section of the house and said, "I do believe your first Accession Day is a success."

Daunt said, "Only if at least three people are asleep in one of the card rooms or dining rooms."

"Does that happen often? People falling asleep here?"

"If you serve copious food and liquor and provide sufficient and diverse entertainment, someone is bound to be snoring in a corner somewhere. Shall we have a look?"

She nodded, because there, unlike at the ball, there was no one but them present. Daunt led her down the corridor that would take them to the main section of the house. He poked his head into one of the smaller parlors before the front one. In here, several tables had been used for various card games. On another table were two pairs of dice and a cup. A second cup had fallen on the floor. A chess game abandoned with white set to checkmate in five was on a table near the fireplace. In the back of the room stood a roulette wheel, and there a portly gentleman snored into the pillow of his folded arms. Chips and markers were scattered everywhere.

"You see?" Daunt said as they withdrew. They found two more gentlemen asleep in another parlor, one facedown on a sofa, the other underneath a table. "That's three."

"By your criteria, we must pronounce Accession Day a resounding success. But I must ask, was there any doubt?"

Daunt shook his head. "Always."

The sincerity of his response struck to her soul. Daunt uncertain of his abilities or worried that he might not meet his father's high standards was entirely new to her. "*I* had no doubt. I do mean that."

"It's kind of you to say so." He said this with a smile that set off another flock of butterflies.

Their friendship did have a new shape, and it behooved her to discover what that meant for the two of them. In the previous version of their friendship, there had never been this sort of intimacy, nor the potential for it.

He had done so much for her. So much. Now she had the opportunity, perhaps, to be of some assistance to him. More than anything, she did not want him to be unhappy, and it seemed to her that he was. She stopped walking and clasped her hands behind her back to prevent herself from brushing his hair off his forehead. "Your father was a great and terrible man."

"I am aware."

"You are not him. *You* are kind and generous. Your soul blazes with all that is good and decent." Every word she said was true. Every word felt to her as if she was discovering this truth only now. She had known without knowing that Harry Fordyce had been her friend. Not a friend because she had been married to Angus, but a friend in truth. If she stayed here, looking at him, she would cry, and he would expect an explanation for her tears, and all she had was this bundle of tension in her chest that she did not understand.

She took his arm again, and they ended up, she had no idea how, in the music room. Habit, perhaps, given that she had spent so much time here when she'd been nursing his father in his final days.

They separated, and for some time she felt the previous Lord Daunt's presence so strongly, the tension in her resolved to the frustration and resentment that his caustic temperament inevitably had caused.

Daunt walked past the harp, a hand extended so that his finger sent a muffled, plaintive series of notes floating into the air. She stayed where she was as her emotions dissolved and reformed. She was grateful to have his friendship. He understood her, with all her flaws and oddities. He reached the piano and slid two fingers along the polished top. In this moment, he looked a good deal like his father. At rest, he had his father's stern beauty.

"A beautiful instrument, no?" he said softly.

"It is, my lord." The house was quiet; there was only the faint sound of the wind moving the shutters and the occasional settling of timbers. Like his late father, Daunt was a man of considerable presence. Doubtless he'd age just as beautifully, though, it was to be hoped, with a good deal more of his generosity intact. She imagined his hair turned from walnut to snow, nearly as thick as it was now with him in his prime.

She had the oddest sensation of a new kind of loss, a future sadness over what would not be. Would she be near when Daunt was old? Would their friendship still thrive in the coming years? Whatever the answer, his future wife would be by his side, for it was inevitable that he would find a woman who returned his love, maybe even the woman he loved in such secret.

She too ran her finger along the top of the pianoforte. She wondered at the identity of Daunt's love. She must be from London, a woman of the nobility, no doubt. "I wish we had a piano as fine as this at Plumwood."

"I'll send you this one."

"Oh, heavens, no. You absolutely may not."

"No one here plays half as well as you."

"That's not so."

He gave her a look, and again she was completely off kilter. "Come play whenever you like."

She pushed his arm. "Don't be so awful."

"You smiled." He sat on the bench and held out his hand to her. She sat beside him and flipped through the music that had been left out.

"I happen to know you play beautifully." She ignored the butterflies in her stomach at the two of them sitting so close. Apparently, the old saws about lonely widows were true. She *was* lonely. She *did* miss the companionship of marriage, and now she was nostalgic over a possible future in which she and Daunt were more than friends.

He placed his fingers on the keys and played a chord. "Thank you."

The feelings were there, undeniable, unwelcome, and inappropriate. Not just that; they were inconvenient. He was in love with someone else. Whoever this woman was, he loved her with a rare passion.

"Before your father was too weak to be moved from his room, the servants would bring him here, and I'd play for him." She glanced at him and saw his surprise. "I don't suppose I ought to be surprised he did not tell you."

"Nor did you in your letters."

"I'm sure I did. I told you I was calling on him."

"Yes, you did write that."

"Toward the end, he lost his sight. It soothed him to listen to me play."

"It was kind of you to visit him at all, let alone give him a private concert. He was not the easiest of men to like."

She placed her hands on the keys and pressed one so gently there was but a whisper of sound. "I did not mind."

"I was greatly relieved when I received your letter. I feared I would not arrive home in time, and I thought, thank God, Magdalene is there. She'll manage everything." He played another chord, and she played one on her side, answering his melancholy tone with a lighter trill from a tune popular with children.

"I did not recognize the servants when we arrived here," she said. "Everyone I knew from your father's days is gone."

"After decades of service to the family, they deserved a pension." He played two notes with thumb and forefinger, middle C and E. "He was not the kindest of employers."

"No." This was quite true.

"Gomes has been in my employ for some years now." His voice was mellow, low and velvet-edged. "I've often thought he and my father would have got along." Daunt removed his hands from the keyboard. His shoulder brushed hers. "Curmudgeons the both of them, through and through."

"What shall we play?" She played a scale and then another, limbering her fingers. Better to concentrate on music than Daunt. Her state of mind just now was not conducive to being a good friend to him.

"Do you require sheet music?" His voice returned to that soft, silky tone. Lord, his voice alone was a tool of seduction, more effective than any potion.

"Let's improvise." She played another scale, and Daunt, who knew the game from so many evenings at Plumwood, played a complementary series of notes. "Variation on this. What do you say?"

For several minutes, they played four-handed, and it was just as delightful as it had always been. He was an inventive musician who followed her lead, and they were soon breathless with laughter and the exertion of overplaying all the motions.

As one, they stood, she slid her arms under his to take over his side of the piano, and she ducked while he lifted himself up, and they switched sides. Their concert ended on a series of trills and chords and him singing nonsense words.

"Oh, that was great fun.," she said when she had her breath back. "I'm so glad we played."

Daunt leaned an elbow atop the instrument and put his chin on his palm. He regarded her serenely. He was very good at disguising his thoughts, a fact that made it difficult to know whether he was at ease or pretending to be at ease. "Play something you enjoy. I'd love to hear you." He laid a hand over hers. "You needn't, if it pains you."

"No. I don't mind." She chose a passage designed to challenge her fingers and her heart. Music Angus had loved to hear. "Something to lull us to sleep," she said.

When she finished, Daunt said, "I might just lay my head down here."

"Or you could sleep on the floor like that other poor man."

"The servants will get him upstairs, never fear."

For nearly ten years, she had lived happily as the wife of Angus Carter. Content and happy and in love. Daunt had been her friend, and they had got along famously. She appreciated his fine mind, his humor, and, if she were honest, his good looks. But now that she was a widow of nearly two years, there was a hole in the boundaries of their friendship, and she was passionately in fear of doing something that would upend the delicate balance of whatever their friendship was turning into.

She played Haydn, then Bach. Several times, Daunt let his head roll back, whether his eyes were open to gaze at the heavens painted on the ceiling overhead, she did not know. She had slipped into a state where there was no distinguishing between herself, the instrument, and the music. Notes, and tones, and themes, and all the beauty to be called forth came from her soul to translate with the touch of her fingers.

When, at last, she had come to the point when her hands must be still, she looked at Daunt and said, "Tomorrow is two years to the day since Angus left me."

Quiet lay upon the room like a shroud, and her heart shrank when she understood she'd said something wrong. She often did, but not with Daunt, and now she had.

He put a hand to the side of her face and left it there. "Magdalene. Dearest. Your grief pains me."

She could not look away, and she got trapped in Daunt's eyes, and the moment became inappropriate, and it continued with her loneliness and her regard for Daunt, and their friendship right here, in this very moment, hung in the balance. She leaned away. "Forgive me." She shook her head. "Forgive me."

His hand stayed on her cheek, warm and intimate, and her longing to be touched sprang back to life. "The only thing I shan't forgive is you not doing what you'd like."

She wanted to kiss him. She wanted the comfort of touch and the shivering anticipation of intimacy. But she did not dare.

He did, though. He dared.

Chapter Nine

DAUNT'S KISS WAS every bit as expert as she'd imagined. His lips were soft, but the pressure of his mouth was firm, cajoling rather than insistent, which she found charming and stirring both. She'd been married, for heaven's sake, none of this was new to her, but Daunt's reputation for mastery in the art of seduction made her worry he would find her deficient. She was not the woman he'd secretly loved for so many years. She could never measure up to that paragon.

He was so different from Angus, many years younger, of course, and, well, he was Daunt. His arms tightened around her. Lord, but his kisses were stupefying. Her body responded wholeheartedly. She was used to Angus, and Daunt was taller and broader through the shoulders, and everything was different. Her entire life was changed without Angus. He'd taken her heart with him, yet here she was in another man's arms and glad to be feeling alive.

He pressed one hand to the side of her throat. His fingers curled up and around to the back of her head. She relaxed against him and granted space to the desire snaking through her. The heaviness in her breasts, the aching need to be touched there, the shivery damp between her legs, all that she'd thought she'd lost when Angus died.

Daunt's tongue moved into her mouth, and she responded, oh, how she responded. In kind, and from there, she lost her ability to do much besides react and marvel at the discovery that it was possible to feel like this again. His hand on the side of her throat stayed there, but there was just the slightest pressure. Bringing her forward, toward him.

Then he moved his other hand to the side of her face, and the most astonishing need continued to build in her. What was left of her wits whispered a warning not to make more of this than was warranted. He was a rake, and very good at it, a master of seduction, and it was too easy to mistake physical longing for something else.

He drew back, eyes closed, head tilted back. She ran a finger along the curve of his lower lip as she studied his face, so familiar to her, yet not at all. She brushed her finger along the line of his cheek. "Look at you. Such a lovely man."

He turned his head and nipped at her finger.

"Please don't apologize or say it was a mistake," she said. "Even if you think it was."

He ran his hands down her back all the way to her bottom, and her head filled with images of him naked—her admittedly fevered state supplied an astounding level of detail. "I do not kiss indiscriminately or without intention."

"Never?"

His eyes darkened. "In my wild youth, yes." He shook his head. "I wish Angus had shared less about me on that point. My youth is firmly behind me."

"He made the remark in passing."

"I wish I had spent more time with you and Angus."

"You would have been welcome, you know that."

"I know." After several seconds, he said, "There are reasons I did not."

"Oh?"

"Another time," he said, still holding her close. "I'll tell you another time."

"It's not as though I could not guess that ladies find you attractive and long to be in your embrace."

"Do you? Long to be in my embrace?" Her stomach swooped away. He did know how this was done.

"Yes," she said, because it was true.

"I am relieved," he murmured. He bent his head and kissed the top of her shoulder, and that rocked her to her core.

His focus returned to her, and she melted against him. She didn't care about tomorrow. As to the distant future when they were old and gray, well, she would have this memory to sustain her. "Kiss me again, please."

He released her bottom and returned to kissing her, and she responded. Angus was gone, he was gone, she would give anything if he weren't, but she wanted Daunt's kisses. She wanted his arms around her, the warmth of his body, the shiver of increasing arousal. She'd been dead inside for too long, and he reminded her there was more than grief in her world. Being here, looking for the Dukes with him, had shown her that.

Presently, he leaned back. He toyed with the trim at the bodice of her gown. "I am between mistresses, by the way."

"Am I to commend your abstinence or inquire whether the position is open?"

He kissed her on the mouth once, quickly. "You keep me honest."

"Well, which is it?"

"Neither of us is an innocent. We are here in the midst of Accession Day at Vaincourt, the home of the Viscounts Daunt, where, I can assure you, all sorts of connections are made."

"Do you mean to offer me the position on a temporary basis?"

"Are you interested?" he said with a wicked smile.

She laughed, and he kissed her shoulder again. His mouth was warm, one hand tight around her waist and holding her close, the other sliding along her collarbone.

Daunt put his mouth by her ear and whispered in tones that melted her resistance, "My love, *are* you interested?"

"You cannot possibly expect me to answer that question when I am nothing but a mass of desire."

Abruptly, he stood and hauled her to her feet. She stood, dazed, thoroughly kissed, thoroughly aroused. He swept her into his arms and carried her to a sofa near the fireplace and the harp. He laid her down, braced a knee on the sofa, and stripped off his coat. He stretched over her and kissed her again, hard and fast.

Yes, she thought. This. She wanted him to keep her from thinking. She knew she made everything more complicated than necessary, even this, when passion ought to be the least complicated thing in the world.

He drew back and stared down at her. She did nothing when he took a handful of her skirts and pulled up. "I wish you were naked, but this will do." He put his hand on her knee, and she relaxed to give him the view he wanted. "Lovely," he said. His attention moved to between her legs, hungry, she thought. He looked at her as if he meant to devour her. Another shiver of arousal slid through her. This would happen. He would. And she would allow him.

"You'll have to withdraw," she said.

He nodded once and put his hands on his trousers' fastenings. He pushed her knee to one side, and she committed every moment to memory, the intense awareness of her body, the longing, the uneasiness of the unfamiliar. As he slid his hand upward, she closed her eyes—as if that would change anything. His movement was gentle and confident, but when he reached the apex of her thighs, a moan escaped her lips.

The intensity of her reactions increased, most especially between her legs. The tips of his fingers slid over her, then pressed in. She was wonderfully wet and aroused. He stroked once, then again, and then he lowered himself and pressed his mouth to the inside of her thigh.

She tried to say something, but she could not recall her own name, let alone his.

In a low voice, he said, "Do you want me to stop?"

She shook her head.

"Not enough," he said in that same low voice. "I need an answer from you."

"Do not stop."

He pressed his mouth to her thigh again. "I want to make you shiver with delight. Shall I?"

"Please, yes."

He kissed her between her legs. There. Right there, and she surrendered to the sensations of her body. She opened herself to him and the pleasure of his mouth on her, and then her body peaked, and she was lost to physical sensations she hadn't felt in far too long.

She lay back, racked, out of her mind with pleasure and lust, and she rested a hand on his shoulder. "More," she said. "More."

He settled himself over her, adjusted her skirts again, and slid inside her, and the sensation of his cock inside her, stretching her, inside her, Daunt was inside her, and he felt so bloody wonderful—*she* felt wonderful. Her breath hitched, and she lifted her hips toward his, and my God, my God. To be physically close to someone again brought tears to her eyes. She was beside herself with lust, out of her mind with pleasure. Tears welled up, stopping her breath.

"Hold me," she said when she had the words. "Don't let me go."

"Never," he said. He'd only just made her come, and she was about to again. His hips moved against hers, and he propped his hands on the sofa on either side of her head while he moved inside her. A hard thrust that she answered. He slowed, locking gazes with her.

"Magdalene. God, Magdalene, this is paradise." He drew a trembling breath. "I... I adore you. I adore you."

Chapter Ten

SHE WAS NOWHERE in the house. He'd confirmed that by his own observation from the windows of his room. He'd happened to be staring at the approaching dawn, berating himself for the way things had got out of hand in the music room.

It was happenstance that he'd been at the window when she walked out of the house. No servant walked with her, and if these were usual times, it would not matter. Plumwood was close. But there was a housebreaker lurking about.

He donned coat and hat, snatched an umbrella against the uncertain weather, and headed out. Plumwood wasn't far, a walk straight north. Twenty minutes away at the least.

Except she did not continue to Plumwood. She turned east to the cemetery. He followed.

A thousand years ago, a church had flourished here, but it was long since fallen to ruin and scavenged for rock down to the foundations. The locals continued to bury their dead here, and that included Angus Carter.

In his head, he rehearsed the words he would say to her and the way he would say them. Gentle, reproving for coming out here alone and unaccompanied, kind because, after all, no one, not even Angus, had been able to make of her anything but a version of what she was.

The sky was now distinctly gray at the edges. Morning birds had begun to stir, and farther away, livestock commented on the coming dawn. There was dampness in the air, but he enjoyed the cold; he always had. From his window, he had formed the impression that she had a sturdy coat, and he'd seen the trailing end of a scarf, caught by a breeze before she captured and wrapped it more firmly around her neck.

He knew her location, but he would have found her in any event. He came over the slight rise at the northeast corner and saw her with her back to him, facing Angus's grave. Daunt stayed where he was. Across the field, a man drove his sheep, while the sky turned pink, pale orange, and wisps of palest blue threaded through the gray.

How was it that this awkward, bloody genius of a woman, of no particular beauty, could seize his soul in her hands and bring him to tears? He loved her. Last night—this morning—he'd made love to her, and now he was terrified she would not want that again. How could he live if she did not want him the way he did her?

She faced him, and he did not say any of the words he'd rehearsed. She'd stripped away all the polish and boredom of his existence. He walked to Angus's grave and stood there, head bowed.

A breeze fluttered her hair. He took off his hat. When he was capable, he said, "Angus wrote to me before he died."

"I posted the letter."

"Did you read it?"

She shook her head.

"He asked me to look after you."

She smiled. "I know. He told me." She drew her coat close.

"He said you would grieve too much."

"There are not enough years in eternity for my grief."

"I should have come to you sooner."

She gave one last look at the headstone and said, "I'm glad you did not. You would have found me quite tiresome."

"No."

"Are we all right, Daunt? After what happened?"

"Of course." He gave her his arm as they headed toward the cemetery gate. They weren't, though. He did not see how they could possibly be all right.

Chapter Eleven

THE PIT OF Magdalene's stomach hollowed out at the sight of empty library shelves and the mass of books that had been summarily tossed on the floor. Daunt stood beside her, silent while she took in the scene. Whoever had done this had stood on the second level and let books fall where they might, including all the way to the bottom floor.

She took several steps forward and bent over one of the piles. The damage was appalling. The spines of some of the books were broken, and books that had landed open and facedown on the pile had pages that were bent or torn.

She looked at Daunt, quite sure that she wore the same grim, ashen expression as he. "What sort of hell spawn treats books like this?"

"If I were to answer you, my language would be unfit for your ears and unworthy of a gentleman."

"Do you know how this happened? Were there not servants on guard?"

"Gomes and another servant arrived to relieve the men stationed here. Both the servants outside the library were on the floor and insensate. They appear to have been drugged. When Gomes opened the door—it had been barricaded from the inside, but he is nothing if not resourceful—he interrupted our thief in the process of wreaking the destruction you see before us."

She put a hand over her heart. "He captured the culprit?"

"Alas, no. He escaped that way." He pointed to one of the windows. "But not before bashing Gomes on the head."

She gaped at Daunt, but he was not as shocked as she that anyone would resort to violence because of a book. "Is Gomes all right? What about the other men on guard? What happened to them?"

"Gomes has a black eye and sore ribs. One of the men who was drugged has awakened and says he remembers nothing from the time he left the servants' common room until the moment he awoke in bed. The other did not get off as easily. He received a brutal blow to the head. The surgeon says he'll likely survive, but one never knows."

"This is horrible, Daunt. Just horrible."

"It is." He gripped her shoulder, and she put her hand over his. "I've told Gomes to take the day off, but he has refused thus far. Since I know you will ask, the room was dark, and Gomes did not get a good look at our intruder. He did insist that he got in several blows of his own, and I can assure you that if Gomes landed a blow, the recipient feels it as we speak. Badly. Whether he took anything when he fled, we cannot know, but Gomes is certain he did not have a satchel or bag."

Magdalene felt more than a little ill. She went closer to the decimated shelves. "It's mostly the ones we haven't done yet, isn't it?" she said.

From behind her, Daunt said, "Yes."

She kept her back to the damaged books, but it wasn't any better not seeing. She *knew* they were there, broken and abused. Daunt rubbed his face several times, and she wondered how long he'd been up. She knew for certain he hadn't slept any more than she. "One of the Dukes would fit in a coat pocket," he said.

"If he found it, there's naught we can do."

"I ought to have posted more guards. We ought to have gone through the books like this."

"What? Throw them around like this, do you mean?"

"We'd have been finished in half a day."

She took his hand in hers and ignored the shiver of electricity between them. "It would have killed us both to do something like that, and well you know it. We are up against a true villain, a man who does not scruple to break the law or risk another man's life, or"—she gestured—"this."

"He is after the Dukes, after all." His fingers tightened around hers, and he drew her closer, then pressed a finger of his other hand to the center of her forehead. "I recognize that look. What thoughts are whirling about in that brain of yours?"

"Our intruder must have seen the book he is after."

"How so?"

Painful as it was to look, she gestured at the jumble of books covering the floor. "One man could not have examined every one of these books, not with the necessary care. He *must* know the condition of the book he is seeking, the size, the color, and the binding. We may therefore assume, my lord, that any Dukes that were once or still are in this library"—she held up a hand to stop him interrupting—"are not in their original condition. They have been re-bound, and he knows what they look like."

"The question is, did he find them?"

"Gomes interrupted him. Therefore, he fled before his full task was complete."

"Or he was interrupted just when he found it."

"That is a possibility," she said. "I presume you have someone on the trail of our housebreaker."

"Of course," he said.

"No true bibliophile would do this."

He picked up a book that had been damaged by a much heavier one falling on it. Half of one page was missing. "A philistine. A barbarian."

"One wonders whether we should continue to consider Mrs. Taylor a suspect," Magdalene said. "She may well have come here because of a false conviction that *De Terris Fabulosis* is at Plumwood, but is she so devoid of humanity that she would do something like this? That was not my impression of her."

"I do not know. No one but you has seen this Mrs. Taylor. We know nothing about her. We do not know if she has accomplices who did this, or if this is the work of someone else entirely."

She brushed a lock of hair off his forehead. He went still, and she let go and stepped back, horrified that she'd taken such a liberty. She stared at the pile of books, at anything but him. When she had herself under control, she said, "I do not see that we have any choice but to proceed on the theory that he, or she, was not successful."

Chapter Twelve

THEY WORKED THE rest of the day and all the following day with scarcely a break for meals. Both of them worked faster, going through book after book after book with relentless urgency. Ironically, their criminal intruder may have done them a favor. In the jumble of books, it was plain that some of them, being open, were not one of the fabled Dukes.

Daunt had never in his life been so on edge about any woman. He'd held her in his arms and brought her to completion, and he still had no idea if he had any chance with her at all. Today, after all that had happened between them, she was behaving exactly as she had the day before. Now was not the time for an interrogatory on the subject of the events in the music room. After all, she had not told him that night meant nothing to her. He'd waited all this time, he could wait a little longer.

At ten o'clock, well before Gomes was scheduled to bring their coffee, Daunt closed the last book. He turned to Magdalene.

She stood nearby, hands clasped under her chin, eyes wide. "This," she said softly, "this is most disappointing."

Quiet fell again, but he broke it. "Perhaps they were stolen before the wagons even arrived."

"Always a possibility. If that's so, there is naught we can do." Magdalene turned in a slow circle, scanning the shelves and the stacks of books that had been tossed onto the floor.

"Magdalene?"

A deep crease appeared between her eyebrows. "You are certain one or more of the Dukes were in that shipment?"

"Not absolutely, no. But Verney once boasted he had one of the Dukes."

"Did anyone believe him?"

"He was a madman by the end. No. But when the club members engaged to locate the Dukes... I should have known better than to pay attention to the drunken ravings of a man more unpleasant than my father." After days and days of work, they had nothing. Worse than nothing. "I've failed him. Angus. Peebles, and everyone else too."

"You haven't, Daunt."

"I could have helped one of the others, but no, I had to go haring off after Verney's collection when I knew it was possible he never in his life saw one of the Dukes, let alone possessed one."

Magdalene chewed on her bottom lip the way she always did when she was thinking. He doubted she was aware of the habit. He loved her earnestness and her utter dedication. He always had and always would, no matter what happened between them.

"What?" he asked.

She stared at the ceiling for a time, then, slowly, returned her attention to him. "When they brought out the books after they were delivered here, did they empty all the crates?"

"Yes. Of course they did." His belief in her intellect was all that kept him from despair. "That was the whole bl—dashed problem."

"You're certain?" She held his gaze, and for that space of time, it was like old times, when he'd known his feelings would never be returned. Theirs was a friendship based on respect, admiration, and their connection with Angus, and he could never, never tell her the state of his heart. "You purchased these books in a single lot, correct?"

"Several combined as one."

"We have been through all these books, and there is not even one Duke. Not rebound. Not disguised as another book. Not hidden inside a larger one." She held up a hand. "Bear with me. We cannot stop looking simply because it's possible one or more of the Dukes were stolen from this room. Not when there is still time and not when we do not know it for a fact."

"Agreed." He sighed deeply. "I tell you, the thought of going through all those books to confirm we did not miss anything fills me with dread."

"You are not alone in that reaction. Before we recommence that search, let us consider other possibilities."

"What possibilities are those? That there are no Dukes and never were, that's one. Verney never had any of them, that's another. He did, and they have been stolen. Yet another."

"Possibilities, yes. But let us consider the ones that make our continued search worthwhile." His response to that was a nod. "Suppose," she said, "the workmen who shelved the books were sloppy in following their unexpected instructions?"

"What is your point?"

"Suppose the Dukes remain in their original binding. Red velvet, not morocco leather." She gestured at the shelves and the floor. "Not like these."

"Are you suggesting the Dukes were removed from the shipment?"

"Another possibility, yes, but an unprofitable inquiry given our situation, as in that case there would be no point searching. I feel certain that the employees of W. Stanley & Co. would know better than to remove anything from a lot duly purchased." She plucked a book from the shelf in front of her. "Morocco leather. A spine with gold lettering." She took out another and held up both. "Aside from size, they are similar. They are instantly identifiable as books."

"I cannot fathom where you are headed with this. Yes. They are books. I bought an entire shipment of them."

"Think, Daunt! Apply your intellect to the problem at hand."

"I'd rather we applied yours."

"It's possible that those tasked with unpacking these books would not have shelved something that did not look bookish to them." She lifted the volumes she held. "That, my lord, is why I ask you if you know for a fact that every crate was emptied and that every book was, in fact, placed somewhere in this room. In the lots you acquired, do you know for a fact there were books and only books?"

His eyes widened.

"Surely you recall the candlestick affair?"

He did indeed. Angus had purchased a lot of books and had them shipped to Plumwood. One of the crates had included a pair of candlesticks, a circumstance that had led to a great many jokes and puns about literature and light. "But what has that to do with Dukes? It is abundantly clear that candlesticks are not books. Shelving a pair of candlesticks would have been absurd."

She replaced the two books. "You make my point, Daunt. You or I would have immediately seen that a Duke, even in its original condition, was a book, and books are to be shelved. But would the workmen who were instructed to shelve the contents of the crates have come to the same conclusion?"

"My God."

"By chance," she asked, "are the crates still in the house?"

"I have no bloo—not the slightest notion."

"In storage, perhaps?"

Daunt led the way to the back of the house, then downstairs to the area where the workers would have stored the boxes, if they'd kept them. The seventh storeroom they inspected was full of wooden crates.

He went in as far as he could, given the contents, and hung his lamp from a hook in the ceiling. He rubbed his hands together to ward off the building cold. "But are these the correct crates?"

"Yes." She spoke with certainty.

He whirled to face her. "You say that because?"

"Observe the markings." She pointed to a crate with *WS&Co* printed on the side facing her. "W. Stanley & Co."

She scanned the room slowly. "I believe we are safe in assuming the crates arrived at Vaincourt and were unloaded at the back of the house. We do not know at what point your original instructions were countermanded, but I think we may assume the crates were brought here first. Regardless of ensuing events and their order—were the crates taken to the library, emptied, then returned here, or were the books uncrated here and carried upstairs?—we are free to employ a brute-force method in ascertaining the contents."

"Empty crates are light."

"Therefore, we shall easily learn if there are crates that are not empty."

"If there are any." He did not want to take heart when there was every possibility they would find nothing.

"Keep heart, Daunt. We shall leave no stone unturned."

They stood side by side, staring at crates stacked the height of a tall man. "Let's start here," he said, pointing to a stack to his left. One crate, though, sat apart from the others on the stone floor.

"Let's," she said.

Daunt gave the crate a gentle push with the toe of his boot; it moved backward easily. "I doubt there's anything inside."

"Shall I hold the lamp?"

"Not necessary. I'll let you know if you should." The lid came off easily since it had been pried open already and was merely resting on top. He peered inside.

"Well?"

"Wood shavings." He plunged his hand into them and felt about for anything left inside. "Nothing."

"And the one behind it?"

Indeed, there was another crate behind that one. He reached around and pulled it toward him. "This one is heavier." Like the other, the lid was merely resting on top. "Not empty," he said with some excitement.

"How heavy?"

"Not very." He dragged the crate closer to the lamp. It too was filled with wood shavings. Magdalene went down on her knees on the other side, writing in her pocket memorandum.

"'Located crate with additional items from W. Stanley & Co. auction house.' Proceed, my lord. I'll note the contents while you call them out."

Without doing much besides pushing aside some of the shavings, he saw a jumble of items. The first item he withdrew was a much-folded length of cloth. "Measure of fustian," he said, brushing off shavings. She wrote that down while he extracted another item and held it up.

Magdalene spoke as she wrote. "One vase, likely Chinese, painted with dragons, background pale green. Approximately fourteen inches high by twelve inches at its widest, wouldn't you say, my lord?"

"Yes."

"Carved dragon, green material. Suspect jade," she said when he brought out the next item. "That's very pretty."

"Consider it yours. The vase too, if you'd like it. Oh, and look here. Another vase." Daunt reached in and took out a candle snuffer. "Looks to match the first, but I'll remove the smaller items first." He withdrew several more items, placing them carefully on the floor around them while she logged each one as it came out. Daunt let out a laugh and held up a pair of ceramic candlesticks. "A match for the pair you and Angus found?"

"Don't you dare try to foist those off on me."

"That's odd."

"What?"

Daunt lifted out the other vase. He tipped the vase upside down to shake out wood shavings, and a dull *thunk* sounded. He and Magdalene shared a glance. "Don't get your hopes up," he said.

"Perhaps during transit something worked its way inside?"

Daunt squinted, then shook out more shavings. Another *thunk* sounded.

"Can you see what it is?"

"No." He reached in and made a face.

"What if there's a spider inside? My God, Daunt, don't break it!"

He glared at her over the vase. "Kindly do not bring up the subject of spiders when I have my hand in a confined space."

"My apologies."

"Something wrapped in cloth." His pulse kicked up, because whatever was in there was at least roughly book-shaped.

"Do be careful."

After some manipulation, he withdrew a cloth-wrapped package. His pulse raced despite knowing the odds were high that it was nothing. He handed the package to her, and she took it with a reverent expression. "It's roughly the right size. If, after all this, we've found one of the Dukes," he said, "it's you who should see it first."

"As you said, we mustn't get our hopes up." She brushed off the shavings clinging to the outer wrapping, then unwrapped the bundle.

His heart skipped a beat when he saw a flash of red and gold. No. It couldn't be. Could it?

Magdalene drew in a sharp breath. "Daunt."

"Is it?"

She opened to the frontispiece and read the title. "*De Medicine Arcana.*"

He took a slow breath and calmed himself. He did not want to overreact or make undue assumptions.

"Daunt, oh, Daunt, look. Heavens, my hands are shaking, I'm that overwrought."

Gently, he took the book from her. He closed it and examined the red velvet binding shot through with gold embroidery. There was simply no doubt that this was one of the de' Medici Dukes. "Magdalene. Magdalene, Magdalene, my love."

"We've done it," she whispered. "We've found one of the Dukes."

"We have indeed."

Her eyes were open wide. "What about the other vase?" She reached for the vase, peered in as he had, then put a hand inside. Her eyes opened wide.

"What?" he said.

"There *is* something in here." She reached farther in. "It's jammed in here tightly, but..." She manipulated her arm. "Yes, yes. Ouch!"

"Are you injured?"

She shook her head. "No, but—" Again, she moved her hand. "I've got it." She pulled out her arm and withdrew another cloth-wrapped package. This one was bulkier but the same size. "Here," she said. "You open it."

He accepted the parcel and opened it. He saw the same maroon and gold, the same delicate stitchery. He opened the book and read the title in a shaking voice. "*De Scientia Naturae Rerum.*"

The cover was in poor condition. The gold thread looked to have been picked out. Large sections of the velvet were damaged or worn smooth. The back of the binding was in only marginally better condition. In addition, there was some damage to the tops and corners of some of the pages. The frontispiece was torn. He turned, with great care, some of the pages and saw the gorgeous italics script, illustrations in pigments that retained astonishing vibrancy.

Magdalene looked over his shoulder. "How beautiful it is."

"Yes. I am humbled to hold in my hand something so beautiful." He picked up the cloth it had been wrapped in and carefully folded it over the delicate volume. "I've no idea if we will be lucky enough to find the other two, but let's see what we find."

Magdalene nodded. "Yes, let's."

It was the work of several more minutes, involving the inspection of every single crate to confirm there were no more Dukes to be found here. Magdalene stood with her hands on her hips. "That's disappointing," she said.

"Disappointing?" He faced her and took her by the upper arms. "We've found two of the Dukes. Two of them. If it weren't for you, I'd still be going through books upstairs." He tightened his fingers on her and brought her close. "You. Because of you. I could kiss you for being so brilliant."

The silence took on a peculiar weight.

She waved a hand, and he caught it in his and held her palm against his chest. The room shrank to half its former size, a fourth, an eighth. There was not room for both of them here. The quiet unsettled him, but he couldn't think what to say.

"Magdalene," he whispered. "Oh, Magdalene, I do love you."

Chapter Thirteen

THE MOMENT SEEMED impossibly delicate. The faintest disturbance of air might end the echo of his confession. She did not draw away, but neither did she fall into his arms and confess she too loved him.

She licked her lips, and he could see she was considering what to say or do. "Daunt." He brushed his fingers over her cheek and brought her closer. She swallowed hard, and her cheeks were flushed. "It is exciting, Daunt. I too am overcome by our discovery."

He kept her hand in his and took one of her curls between two fingers with his other, and then he kissed her, a short kiss, soft and gentle, and accepted by her. He kissed her cheek, then her forehead. "Magdalene, oh, Magdalene, I love you. I have loved you for years knowing there was no hope. But now." His throat thickened with the fear that he was too soon with his confession. "I love you still, that shall never change. But it is my hope that one day you find me worthy. If that's impossible, tell me. Tell me, and I promise you we shall be friends as we have always been."

She drew a trembling breath, then gripped his upper arms and gazed into his face. "I do not know what I should feel. It is too much. All of this, you, the Dukes, everything. It's too much."

"All I ask is that you consider me."

"I've been so lost without Angus. He was my anchor, and—" She pushed away from him and retreated until her back was pressed to the wall. Her gaze remained fixed on him. "I've always known you are attractive, but now I *know* it and... and... I should not have these feelings about you. I never thought I would be one of those lonely widows men are so eager to seduce."

"No. No, Magdalene. That was never my intention."

"I thought if we made love, I would be satisfied, and we would go on as friends." Her eyes went wide. "I *was* satisfied. I was, oh, Daunt, never think I wasn't."

"But?" His life was in suspension.

Her eyes glittered with incipient tears, and that tore him to pieces. If she loved him, if she had any feelings for him but those of friendship, would she be on the verge of tears? "I thought Angus would be the only man for me. These feelings—" She ran her fingers through her hair. "These *feelings...*"

"I knew it," he said softly. He would retreat. He had overstepped. He must retreat, and he must do so gently. "A Welsh comb."

"What?" Her gaze fixed on him, puzzled.

"Most ladies of my acquaintance arrange their hair with combs and pins and silk flowers. One hundred strokes with a brush every night before retiring. But not you." He ran his own fingers through his hair. "This, perhaps a ribbon, and you are done."

"Oh. That. I just don't see the point."

"It's fetching."

"My God, Daunt. Do not do this to me."

He went to her because he could not stand to see her so unhappy. He put a hand on her shoulder. "Magdalene. Don't be unhappy. I never intended to upset you. We shall be to each other what we have always been."

She wiped her eyes. "I don't know what to do with these feelings. He's dead, Fordyce—Daunt." She rested her forehead against his shoulder and gripped the front of his coat. "He's gone, and I miss him every day, and now there's you, and I want to make love to you again, and if that's so, did I ever really love Angus?"

"You did. You know you did. You still do. Nothing changes that."

She wrapped her hand around the back of his neck and brought him to her for a kiss. Not a peck, nothing chaste. He opened his mouth, and their tongues met, and Lord, but he might not survive this. He was here on this earth once and only once, and this was the woman he wanted by his side for all the days left to him.

He had no experience with the emotions tangling up inside him. The prospect of having the woman he loved was overwhelming; the prospect of losing her devastated. A soft moan escaped her lips. He was by no means a perfect man. He had his flaws like any other man, but if it was within his power to make her happy, he meant to do that.

Slowly, he pulled back, but she left her arms around his shoulders. "My dear." He took a breath and settled himself. "Sweetheart." He whispered the word at the same time he drew a finger from the underside of her jaw to the top of her shoulder. "Please, please tell me I have not mistaken your intent. You did mean to kiss me like that?"

"I've been dead inside for so long, and now I am not, and I..." Her finger slid across his lips. "I want kisses and whispered endearments and a man's strong arms around me, his breath warm, my hands on his skin. Someone who will look at me as if I matter." She lifted her head to his, and her bosom pressed against his chest as he bent to kiss her. Nothing held back this time. Lips touching, his tongue sliding along the inside of her mouth, and then the same from her.

He set his hand in the curve of her lower back. The longer he held her, the deeper he kissed her, the more powerfully intimate their embrace became, and the more uncertain he became of her mood, of her feelings for him, of what she thought this encounter meant.

He was the one to break their kiss, and he was pleased to see her dazed expression. "Magdalene..." He trembled with the possibilities. He kept his arms tight enough around her that she would know he intended this embrace. She tightened her arms around him. "Later," he said softly. "Later, when you are prepared, when you've had time to consider, we can speak again."

Chapter Fourteen

"HAVE YOU GOT the Dukes?" she asked.

He patted his pocket. "It's time we got some sleep."

"Yes. Yes, I daresay you're right." She retrieved her pocket memorandum and her pencil from the floor, and he took the lamp, and they were on their way upstairs. He walked her to her room and, well. He was weak. He went inside with her.

Her maid came into the anteroom when they entered. Without looking at her maid, Magdalene said, "I do not require assistance tonight."

The servant looked between him and her mistress, then curtseyed. "Yes, ma'am."

When they were alone, he said, "May I stay?"

"Please."

Yes. She said yes, and he wasn't about to wait for anything to bring them to their senses. He took her hand and led her to the bedroom. The moment he shut the door behind them and secured the lock, he led her to the bedchamber.

He sat on the edge of the mattress and pulled her between his spread legs. He kissed her again, and it was as satisfying as the first time. He wasn't a rake kissing a woman he hoped to seduce, or a courtesan he'd paid, or his mistress.

She had a ribbon in her hair, and he removed that. "So soft in my fingers," he whispered.

She let out a breath. He stripped her off, buttons undone, hooks unfastened, ribbons untied, garters removed. He was greedy to see her, intent on touches that would make her moan and soften against him, and that would convince her there was no other man in the world who could please her.

She was a tall woman, her height in her legs, slender but in no way delicate. He drew his hands down her body, from her shoulders to her waist, then up until he covered her breasts. "Oh, Magdalene, you are so very beautiful. Don't. Don't shake your head like that. You are."

"Don't try to flatter me about my looks. I cannot possibly believe you."

"Somehow, you've got a wrong impression of me."

She took a step back, but he leaned into the space between them and grabbed her fingers. She stopped, head tilted just so.

"Don't," he said. "Don't ask me to leave." That was selfish, and he was ashamed for putting himself before her. "Forgive me. Forgive me. If you don't want me here, I'll go." He sat up, or attempted to, but she threw her arms around him and pulled him back to her. "You're sure?"

"I am," she whispered.

He slid his hands down her body. "Whatever you want from me, you shall have it."

"You."

He kissed her collarbone and then the ridge of her cheek. "Suppose, my dearest heart, that we discover we can be friends as well as lovers?"

"Suppose we discover the opposite?"

He shrugged. "There are former lovers of mine with whom I maintain friendships to this day."

"How many?"

He turned onto his side and brought her hand in to kiss the tips of her fingers. "I love you," he said over the voice in his head screaming that he'd just made a fatal mistake. "I love you and want you, and if you never return my love, then so be it. I'd rather you reject me than live my life never having told you of my feelings."

"Daunt," she whispered. "Don't say such things. Don't tell me lies, not even pretty ones."

He met her gaze straight on. He slid his hand down her stomach, over her belly, to her mons. "A bed this time. Come to bed with me. Let me kiss you everywhere. Caress you everywhere. Later, if you tell me we cannot be lovers, I shall take my disappointment elsewhere."

"Oh," she said when his fingers delved.

"You're wet," he whispered. "I want to make you wetter yet." He slid his other hand the length of her spine. "Shall I? May I try?"

"Yes," she said on a breath. "Yes, please."

He laid her on the mattress and stretched himself over her and kissed his way from her shoulders to her breasts, and there came a moment when she surrendered to her body. Yes, yes, Lord yes, but he wanted this. He took her nipple into his mouth, and he did love the shape of her, the taste of her. He loved that small sigh, and then her gasp and the moan that came. He continued downward to the apex of her thighs and set himself to kissing her there, licking, stroking with his tongue, absorbing the taste of her and her reaction. With his free hand, he stroked the inside of her thigh, pushing enough to make room for him.

She came without reserve, shuddering, calling out, and then she sat up and worked at the buttons of his waistcoat. "Help me," she said.

"With pleasure." Before long, his clothes were off, and he splayed himself over her, and she ran her hands down his back. He fell into the siren call of arousal, and he pushed aside all this uncertainty about their future. She had agreed to this, they were in bed, and she was touching him, and Lord, but her fingers were clever. That slide of a finger over his nipple, the softness of her, the press of her mouth to his skin.

Her hands wandered over him, and he lay back while she continued to touch him. She took pleasure from him, adored him with her mouth, her hands, and fingers, and he was nearly beyond enduring any of it. At last, though, he put his arms around her shoulders and held her while they kissed, and she'd learned something of him, for this was better than before.

"Please, Daunt," she whispered.

"Yes, my love?" He turned them over so that she was on her back and he between her legs.

"Put your beautiful prick inside me."

"I am yours to command."

She pressed her head back and laughed. "Oh, yes, my very own viscount to see to my pleasure. Yes. Now."

The curve of her mouth drew him in the way it always had. Whenever she smiled, he wanted to be the object of her pleasure and desire. He pushed up on his hands and adjusted himself, allowing the anticipation to fill him.

She slid her hands down to his low back and arched against him, and he pressed in, in, and in, and she was warm and soft inside, and this was Magdalene, whom he had loved and admired for too many years to count. She met his thrusts, the roll of his hips, and pressed against him as if she could not get enough.

He quickly reached the point where all that mattered was the quest for their mutual pleasure. She came first, calling his name, "Daunt, yes," and finishing with an incoherent cry.

He was close, so close. The base of his spine quivered and he withdrew, and she held him close, pressing herself against him so that his cock was between them while he spent.

Chapter Fifteen

THEY'D FOUND TWO of the Dukes; what a triumph that was. The satisfaction and excitement of that permeated him as Daunt lay beside a sleeping Magdalene. He drew her close, and she sighed and curved her body against his.

In fewer than twenty-four hours, he must meet with the other members of the Bibliomania Club. He hoped and prayed that the others had succeeded in finding the remaining Dukes.

Magdalene stirred, and he was immediately diverted from the subject of Dukes. "Do you hear the birds?" she asked, voice muffled from her being mostly beneath the sheets and covers.

He hesitated. Did she realize she was not at Plumwood and that he was not Angus? "I do," he said. "It's one of many pleasant ways to awaken."

"It's why I so love this room." She turned over and opened her eyes and slowly smiled. His heart thumped when she pressed a hand to his cheek. She shivered once. "Good morning, my lord."

"Are you cold?" He slipped out of bed to avail himself of the water closet and afterward stopped to add more coal to the fire.

"Did you sleep well?" Magdalene asked as he headed back to the bed. She was sitting up now.

"I did, and you?" He had a clear memory of last night, including telling her yet again that he loved her. She had not replied in kind.

"I can't recall the last time I slept so well." She drew up her knees and wrapped her arms around them. "Hurry back, Daunt. You'll catch your death."

"I am not cold." He set his hands to his hips. "Are you thinking of returning to sleep?"

She looked him up and down with undeniable appreciation. "What a specimen of a man you are, sir." She held out her hand. "Come here."

He rejoined her in bed and slipped his arms around her. She came in close. There was hope in that, wasn't there?

"Did we really find not one Duke, but two? Or was that just a dream I had?"

"We did indeed." Lord, he was in Magdalene's bed, in her arms, and she did not look sorry that he was here.

She sighed. "I do wish we'd found *Fabulosis.*"

He wrapped his arms around her and pulled her close. "The two of us know he did not make off with the book."

"You have always been his unwavering supporter. Have I told you how much that meant to him? And to me."

"Perhaps one of the other members has found it."

"Write to me if they have, Daunt. Please?"

"That goes without saying." He leaned down and kissed her, a long and tender kiss that she returned.

When they parted, she said, "Heavens, you kiss divinely." Under the covers, she pressed a hand to his chest. "You're warm," she whispered.

"So are you." He pressed a kiss to her shoulders. This time, he knew better than to blurt out his feelings. She needed time. It was her nature to come at new things slowly. She had not decided against him, and he chose to take hope from that.

Her hand wandered downward, and for some time, he was highly diverted, and then something more. She still wanted him, surely that was an appropriate conclusion to make of the night's events. He hadn't been at all sure what the morning would bring. Would she explore his body like this if she regretted their intimacy? She pushed him onto his back, and he complied.

"Magdalene." He cleared his throat. "Magdalene, my love..." She slid down, and then her mouth was around his cock, and he was entirely erect, and all too soon he could not think of anything but her mouth and his cock and the fact that the woman he loved was in bed with him. Orgasm robbed him of thought and words, and that might well be for the best. She might not welcome another inept declaration of love.

She laid her head on his chest while he floated on the edges of bliss. Physically, he was sated, but his uncertainty about their future remained. He'd confessed himself too soon. He'd rushed her when she needed time because that was how she was. Careful. Reflective. Considered.

He set his hand on her shoulder and kept the sheets and blankets around her. Even with the fire built up, there was a morning chill in the air. "That was a most excellent start to the day," he said. "But if you want to sleep, do."

"I'm not at all sleepy."

"In that case, I could return the favor." He kissed the top of her shoulder and draped an arm over her waist, but someone tapped on the door. From the other side of the door, a female voice softly called out, "Mrs. Carter?"

"Tilly," she said to him.

Daunt sat up. "Shall I hide behind the curtains or under the bed?"

"Don't be ridiculous. Neither. She brings me chocolate and a brioche every morning."

He relaxed. There was hope to be had from her acceptance of his presence here. "Do you think she's brought enough for two? I'm ravenous."

"I'll share." She raised her voice and said, "Come in, Tilly."

The servant opened the door and focused on a corner of the ceiling, her cheeks bright pink. "My lord. Gomes says to tell you there's a caller. A Mr. Rivett."

He and Magdalene exchanged a startled glance. Rivett was the shop owner who'd written claiming to have a complete set of Dukes. "Please tell him I shall be down shortly. Offer him anything he likes."

"Yes, my lord. I'll have your breakfast shortly, ma'am."

When Tilly closed the door after herself, Magdalene grabbed his upper arm. "Rivett is here!" She practically leaped out of bed. "Oh, Daunt, we cannot keep him waiting."

He gathered his scattered clothes, and Magdalene helped him dress. "He cannot have a complete original set of Dukes," she said while she folded his neckcloth and tucked it into his coat pocket with the Dukes they'd found last night.

"No. But he might yet have something interesting."

She patted the outside of his pocket. "Where will you put these?"

"There is a safe in my rooms." She nodded and tucked his watch safely in another pocket. "I shall meet you outside the front parlor in, say, forty minutes? Does that give you enough time to dress?"

"Another Welsh comb for me. Now go." She pushed him to the bedroom door. "Tilly!"

Daunt had quite the trek from Magdalene's quarters to the north wing where his valet awaited. He locked the Dukes safely away, gave himself a quick bath at the basin and, with the assistance of his valet, made himself presentable.

Magdalene was waiting outside the parlor when he arrived. He kissed her hand, and together, they entered.

Chapter Sixteen

As Magdalene followed Daunt into the parlor, a dark-haired, slender man in his middle years stood, a leather case held flat against his chest. He bowed deeply to Daunt. "Good day, my lord. Thank you for seeing me."

After seeing Magdalene to a seat at a desk, Daunt acknowledged him with a nod. "Mr. Rivett."

"At your service, milord."

Her seat gave her an unimpeded view of Mr. Rivett and Daunt. She settled her shawl around her shoulders, mildly anxious about this encounter with Mr. Rivett. She kept her hands clasped on her lap and concentrated on taking deep, soothing breaths. Daunt's presence had much to do with her relative calm.

"I appreciate your writing to me," Daunt said. "You've certainly traveled a long way. I hope your journey was uneventful."

"How kind of you to inquire. Yes, milord, though I am glad to be back on English soil."

"You do not live in Italy?"

"Oh, no." Rivett was well-dressed but travel-worn. His hair bore the obvious impression of a hat, and his boots were dusty. "I travel the Continent whenever the business calls for it, which it often does."

"That business is?"

"Quintas & Rivett, purveyors of rare and curious items, established in the year of our Lord 1753." He bowed. "We are located on Noncet Close, near Duke Street, London. We recently opened another shop in Hampstead Heath."

"You deal in rare books, do you?"

Magdalene racked her brain for any recollection such a shop. Quintas & Rivett had no reputation as a dealer in rare manuscripts else she would have heard of it.

"If the subject matter is suitable, we might. In the main, however, books are not an area of interest for me. My customers had rather see what is gruesome and bloody. Relics of the saints. Mummies and bones. I've sold my share of nooses to a certain lord. Burial shrouds of infamous murderers, begging your pardon, ma'am. I don't mean to frighten you."

She let out a breath. "I am not frightened, sir."

"Stories of the macabre and tales of the depraved sell quite well."

"May I ask how you came to contact me about the Dukes?" Daunt asked.

To her left, a flash of light caught her eye. She looked, but all she saw was the flowered wallpaper and the closed door to the adjoining room. A glance at the window provided no explanation for the shift in light. There were no clouds to cause the light to change. How odd.

"I bought a shipment in Florence, you see," Rivett was saying. "When it arrived at Noncet Close at last, these books"—he patted the leather case—"had been included. I thought they were interesting, though not for customers of Quintas & Rivett. I made some inquiries, and it happened that two of the men I spoke to mentioned you were looking for one of these books."

"Oh?" Daunt said.

The flash to her left distracted her again. She looked again. The keyhole was dark; there must be a key on the other side.

"Here now, I'll mangle the title, for it's not in English. *Terra Cotta Fablosia* or some such thing."

Magdalene sat up, and Daunt said, "*De Terris Fabulosis?*"

"That sounds more like it." He nodded to himself. "Is that the book you've been searching for?"

"I confess, Mr. Rivett, I am astonished that none of the men you spoke to offered to buy it."

"Oh, but they did. Every blessed one of them. I thought to myself, if these men offer me good coin sight unseen, what might your lordship offer?" Rivett placed the leather case on the table, his hands resting lightly on top. "I warn you, though, I'm not inclined to sell just the one. They came as a set of four."

"I shall represent to you that it is a certainty that two of those volumes are not genuine."

Magdalene stood to take a closer look at the interior door. Indeed, the keyhole was dark, but there was a very peculiar sense of motion. She stayed to one side and bent to have a look, but there was nothing, now. Had she imagined there had been? There was movement and then what was unquestionably someone's eye.

"That said, in the matter of rare books," Daunt was saying, "I prefer forgeries and copies are removed from commerce. Less confusion for the serious collector and less chance for the new or inexperienced collector to find they've paid good money for a bad product."

Rivett's eyebrows shot up. "I make no representations about the books except that they were shipped to me from Florence. Others have said they might have value and that you are looking for one of them."

"Did your experts authenticate these books?"

"No, milord. I merely described what I received." He tapped the leather case. "Collectors always surprise you with what they find interesting and valuable." He smiled. "I've made a good living from the fact, milord. Some book smaller than your hand, and there's a fellow somewhere who'd sell his own mother to have it. A figurine that looks like nothing, yet someone pays a hundred pounds for it without blinking. These books, I can see why someone would be interested. They're colorful, and if nothing else, there's value in the gilt and silver."

"There's gilt?"

"It's why I asked around. Pictures like that, all colorful, and there's someone, somewhere, willing to pay ready money."

There was no possibility of the set being genuine, but nevertheless, excitement stirred in the pit of her stomach. At least two of those books could be genuine, after all. And if Rivett was wrong about what he had, the books might be something else of interest.

"May I see them?" He held out his hand, and Rivett handed over the case. "Did they arrive in this case?"

"No, milord. But I'm willing to sell you the case too, if you're interested."

Daunt chuckled and handed the case to her. "Would you do the honors?"

Based on the Dukes they'd already found, the case was approximately the size required to hold four such volumes. She glanced at the door and saw another shift in the light from the keyhole. She slid the books free of the container Mr. Rivett had put them in.

"They are the right size." They'd come out upside down, but it was instantly obvious these were not in original condition. They were each bound in leather, not red velvet. She turned over the topmost one and examined the binding. "The workmanship is exemplary, meticulous, even." From the corner of her eye, she saw Rivett smile.

"Go on, my dear," Daunt said.

Magdalene opened the volume and was obliged to hold back a snort. The pages were a heavy-grade cotton rag dyed to approximate the color of vellum. No one with any expertise in such manuscripts would be fooled for a moment. Her initial impression was that these were meant to be copies. She agreed with Daunt. Even a copy of a Duke was interesting, but it was best to have them all in the possession of an honest expert.

Other than the materials, the similarities between this and the Dukes they had already found were striking. The frontispiece was lettered in the same style, with the primary title, *Liber Ducis de Scientia,* and the title of this volume, *De Motibus Humanis,* matched that of the two genuine Dukes. This struck her as an improbable coincidence, unless whoever had created the copy had, indeed, seen at least one of the originals. The illuminations on the interior pages were lovely, colorful, precise, and, at times, piquantly amusing. "Exquisite," she said, with true appreciation of the work that had gone into creating this copy. "Truly, this is artistry."

Rivett's smile turned to a grin. "Did I not tell you they were pretty?"

"Such meticulous work." She picked up the second. "One can imagine a scribe with his pots of ink and pens bent over the pages long into the night."

"Which volume is that?" Daunt asked. He'd planted himself in line with the door such that from where he stood, he could see only that four volumes were before her.

"*De Motibus*, my lord. Someone spent hours, nay, days, creating this."

"In your considered opinion, are they genuine?" Rivett asked.

She put down the book. "I am sorry to say that this one is not."

"Well, now, that's a disappointment. What about the others? Have a look at *Terra Cotta*. That's the one his lordship is interested in, and if you ask me, it's the prettiest of the four."

Daunt sighed and picked up *De Motibus*. He paged through it, taking care not to bend pages. "As forgeries go, this is quite good."

"We do not know that it is a forgery, per se."

"Point taken."

Magdalene looked at the next one. *De Scientia Naturae Rerum* was another meticulous copy. The content was not immediately recognizable to her as some other text, and the subject matter did address the natural world, though she still did not doubt this was a historical text presented as if it were a Duke. "If he'd used vellum, I think this one might have fooled many an experienced collector." She took the next book from the stack and opened it. "*De Medicine Arcana*."

She opened to a page of meticulous italic script. The drawings and illuminations were equally deft. The colors were a bit too bright, and the paper was, well, paper, rather than vellum, but someone had worked quite hard at achieving the correct color. "The work here is really lovely. I wish I knew who did this."

Daunt withdrew two notes from his wallet and put them on the table with his forefingers holding them firmly down. "Twenty pounds for the four of them, taken permanently out of circulation."

Magdalene looked at the door, and again, there was another shift in light. This time, she was convinced there was someone on the other side of that door.

Meanwhile, Mr. Rivett eyed the bills. He took the near ends between thumb and forefinger. "I won't say as I'm not disappointed, milord, but twenty pounds in my pockets that weren't there this morning is a fine thing." Daunt lifted his hand, and Rivett took the money. "I'll be on my way, then."

"If ever you come across a book you think would interest me, please contact me. It's been a pleasure."

Rivett bowed once. "I'll do that."

When Rivett was gone, Magdalene put a finger across her lips and walked to one side of the door. She pointed at the door and then at Daunt and mimed opening it. "My lord. He believed us when we said his books were not genuine."

Daunt held her gaze and said, "My darling Magdalene, you were impressively clever. He'll never know the truth."

Her heart turned over in a most peculiar fashion. The endearment, the way he looked at her, his trust in her broke through the wall she had put around her heart.

Before she could begin to understand what that meant for her, he opened the door in one smooth motion.

"Oh!" A woman tumbled to the floor with a thump. She had blond hair and, if that weren't enough, she recognized her perfume.

"Mrs. Taylor?" Magdalene closed the door firmly, while Daunt extended a hand to the woman and helped her to her feet. He maintained a firm grip on her arm. With her free hand, Mrs. Taylor brushed off her skirt. Her lower right arm was bandaged, and there was a small spot of red blooming on the linen wrap.

"Identify yourself," Daunt said.

"That is Mrs. Taylor, my lord."

He studied the woman and shook his head. "I've never seen you before in my life. Again, I say, identify yourself."

"Why should I tell you anything?" She attempted to free her arm of Daunt's grip. "You're hurting me."

"To avoid jail?" he said.

Mrs. Taylor, or whoever she was, blanched.

"Would you mind telling us what happened to your arm?" Magdalene said.

"Nothing."

"Madam, it behooves you to be forthcoming with us. Accession Day is concluded. Had you been admitted via the front door as would any other caller, you would have been announced. Therefore, I must conclude that you are not here by permission. The authorities frown on trespassers and sneak thieves."

Mrs. Taylor pressed her lips firmly together.

"The Chinese dragon," Magdalene said.

Mrs. Taylor said, "What do you know about that?"

"Enough to infer more than a few things. When my husband examined *De Terris Fabulosis*, he translated one passage, a text describing an exquisite Chinese dragon carved from jade and guarded, it was said, by two real fire-breathing dragons. He did not, as I suspect you know, have the opportunity to translate the portion that described where one might find the dragon."

Daunt lifted his eyebrows.

"It is the best of the alternate explanations for her interest in *De Terris Fabulosis*," Magdalene said in a gentle voice. "She is no bibliophile at all. She collects artifacts from China." She returned to the last of Mr. Rivett's Dukes. "Am I correct, Mrs. Taylor?"

"You're mad, both of you. I was here for your celebration, I admit that. I meant to leave, but I became lost."

Daunt leaned over her and said, "What is your connection to the late Lord Verney?"

She pressed her lips together again, then burst out with, "He stole from my father. Papa collected items from China, but he soon became enamored of genuine Chinese items. From the very earliest age, I assisted him. He'd read Mr. Carter's translation, and he wanted to find that jade dragon too. He prepared to travel to China."

"On the basis of a book written nearly four hundred years ago?" Daunt said.

"He was obsessed. To finance the trip, he arranged to sell some of his collection to Lord Verney. His lordship took the pieces and then refused to pay. In fact, he denied he'd ever seen them. Six months later, Papa was dead of a broken heart."

"What were those items?" Daunt asked. "If you could describe them in particular, that would be most helpful."

"A pair of vases painted with dragons. About this high." She indicated with her hands as best she could, given that Daunt still restrained her. "They are green. There are two dragons painted on each vase. The third is a jade dragon. About the size of your hand. The tail curls up and over its head, and there is smoke coming from its nostrils. One clawed foot is lifted."

Daunt took a step back and released Mrs. Taylor's arm. Magdalene nodded, for she knew exactly what he was thinking, and she agreed, wholeheartedly. "Mrs. Taylor," he said. "I cannot condone your actions here. You have been foolish and foolhardy. Magdalene, would you call for Gomes, please?"

She did so, and when the servant arrived, Daunt gave the necessary instructions. They waited in silence for Gomes to return with the carefully packed crate. Gomes glared at Mrs. Taylor when he put down the crate then withdrew in an equally stony silence.

Mrs. Taylor burst into tears when Daunt opened the crate and took out the first of the two vases. "Oh, oh, Papa."

He placed the other beside it and then withdrew the jade dragon. Her tears continued. Without comment, he handed Mrs. Taylor his handkerchief.

Once her tears abated, she approached the table slowly. "May I?"

"You may," Daunt said.

She picked up the dragon. "I thought I'd never see them again."

"You may have them, on one condition."

"What?"

"That you swear on your father's honor and your immortal soul that you shall never again attempt to deceive anyone nor steal from them."

She hugged the dragon to her. "Thank you," she whispered. "Thank you."

"Do you so promise?"

"I do. I do, my lord."

Magdalene herself was close to tears. The gesture was everything that was superior about Daunt.

Mrs. Taylor turned her tearful face to her and said, "I am sorry for deceiving you. I apologize to you for that. My lord, I judged you as no better than Lord Verney. I was wrong, and I apologize."

"But why," Magdalene asked, "did you want *De Terris Fabulosis*? Surely you do not intend to travel to China yourself?"

She wiped her eyes. "Lord Verney bragged to my father that he knew the location of the jade dragon. How could he have known that unless he had the book himself or Mr. Carter had shown it to him? When I learned that Lord Daunt had acquired Lord Verney's library, I thought it was my only chance. I hoped that if I found that benighted book, I might also find the items he stole from my father."

"You may go, Mrs. Taylor," Daunt said. "And please do not be offended if I tell you I hope never to see you again."

"None taken," she said, still tearful.

When Mrs. Taylor was gone with the crate and its carefully packed items, Magdalene walked to the table. "What an absolutely extraordinary day."

"Indeed, my love." He picked up *De Motibus* and opened it. "I wonder if we have the necessary ingredients for a love potion."

"*I* should like to see a real dragon. I wonder if *Fabulosis* gives a location for the dragon that we could find today."

"There is but one way to find out," Daunt said with a nod at the remaining volumes.

"Would you travel all the way to China?" she asked.

"For a book, yes. For any other treasure, unlikely."

She picked up the last Duke. *De Terris Fabulosis* was different enough from the others that her pulse skipped a beat. Like the others, the binding was leather, but were those smudges at the top of the pages remnants of red fabric? With her heart beating hard, she opened the book. The pages were vellum, not paper. The pigments of the illustrations were gorgeous and precisely the hue and saturation one expected. Some pages glittered with silver and gilt. "My lord."

"Have you found the passage Angus translated?" he asked.

Magdalene held the book tightly against her chest. "Daunt." She could scarcely speak. "I am shaking again."

"What is it?"

"Daunt, this one is genuine."

"I beg your pardon?"

"*Fabulosis* is a genuine Duke."

Chapter Seventeen

MAGDALENE WATCHED DAUNT examine *De Terris Fabulosis.* Carefully, he turned pages to expose a map of the world as it was known in the time of de' Medici. "Exquisite," he whispered.

"See here?" she said. "Remnants of the original binding."

"Yes."

"Oh, Daunt, I'm still shaking," she said.

He turned more pages, with her looking over his shoulder. As with the other two they'd found hidden in the vases, the writing was meticulous, the illustrations beautiful and colorful. "Directions for finding El Dorado." He turned more pages. "An illustration of the Fountain of Youth. The island of Amazons."

"It's beautiful, but Daunt, we have sent Mr. Rivett away."

Gently, he closed *Fabulosis.* He knew exactly what she was getting at, she knew that immediately. "Twenty pounds is by no means fair compensation for a treasure such as this."

"No, sir. It is not."

"I'll have my secretary send him a suitable sum."

"It's only fair." Tears burned in her eyes.

"Consider it done. What is it?" he asked. "What's made you so sad?"

"*De Terris Fabulosis* was in Italy all this time."

He cupped a hand around the back of her neck and brought her close. "Indeed it was."

"Oh, Daunt." She clung to him.

"Vindication is sweet, my love. I, for one, look forward to announcing how and where we located it. Don't cry. Please do not cry."

"I am not crying."

He used the side of his finger to wipe away her tears. "Of course not." Slowly, he closed the cover of *Fabulosis.* "I wish Angus had lived to see this day."

She pressed against him, trembling inside. "Thank you. Thank you, thank you, thank you."

He patted her back, and she melted against him. "If not for your efforts," he said, "we might not have even one Duke, let alone three."

"We would have this one. Mr. Rivett said several people told him you were looking for *Fabulosis*. You have been looking for the book for years."

"I thought the more who knew, the better the chance the volume might come to light."

"All this time, you too were attempting to clear Angus's name."

"But of course."

She gripped the lapels of his coat. "Professor Peebles's retirement is fast approaching. How soon must you leave for London?"

"Today," he said.

"Professor Peebles will be so pleased." She did not want him to leave her, but she had no choice in that. "Give him my regards, won't you? Then come back and tell me everything. What he said when he saw them. His expression. Everything."

"I shall." He ran a hand along the edges of the binding. "Three Dukes," he said. "And they are spectacular."

"Kiss me again, Daunt. One more time."

His smile broadened. "Of course, my darling."

He did exactly that, and this kiss was less tender and a bit rougher, more an expression of his need this time. She threw her arms around him and kissed him passionately.

Their kiss rocked her to her soul. Daunt had broken her open and changed her forever. He'd pulled her from despair and shown her how to live again, how to love again.

"With you," he said when they parted, "it's always my first kiss."

"For me, as well."

"My heart pounds every time you're in my arms. It's a wonder you put up with such boyish ways from me."

She was transformed. No potion, no seduction had wrought this change in her. "Oh, Daunt, what have you done to me?"

His eyebrows drew together. "Kissed you witless?"

"Is there a love potion in *De Motibus*?"

"There is."

"And have we the required ingredients?"

He laughed. "What if we did?"

She pressed a hand to her heart. "If we do, would you consider taking it?"

He shook his head, then slowly, his amusement faded. "Say that again."

"Would you take the potion?"

"Why, Magdalene?"

She sat on the nearest chair in a boneless heap. "You said you were in love with someone else. I knew your heart was not available, and now—" She made a helpless gesture. "I apologize. I should never have asked."

He crossed his arms over his chest. "No," he said. "I would not drink the potion."

"No. No, of course not. It's just ..."

"Just?"

"I've fallen in love with you." She took a steadying breath. "I know you are in love with someone. Please. Do not let this come between us."

"For such an intelligent woman, you have come to a remarkably wrong conclusion." He brought her to her feet and took her head between his hands. "*You* are the woman I love. I have loved you for years. For years. I've waited for you, lived in fear you'd love someone else and—"

She could hardly get her mind around the idea, but there it was, growing in her. "You love me?"

"I have been saying as much since I came here. Magdalene, I love you madly. I admire you. I respect you. I adore you. You are the only woman I want by my side."

Her eyes opened wide, and she let out a laugh. "Oh my heavens, Daunt." She threw her arms around him. "Daunt, say that again."

"I love you. We do not need any potion, my love, for I already adore you."

"Again, say that again."

"I love you with all my heart and soul." He lightly gripped her upper arms. "I'll love Ned too. I'll be the best possible father to him."

She pressed her hands to his chest. "I'll love your son too. Never fear that."

"When I am done in London, and Peebles has been presented with our Dukes, I'll call on your father. I'm quite sure His Grace will want settlements to properly protect you."

"Yes, yes, yes, Daunt."

"As soon as we may, for I tell you, I am looking forward to a lifetime of first kisses."

"You shall have them, my love," she said, her heart overflowing. "As many as you want."

About Carolyn Jewel

Carolyn Jewel was born on a moonless night. That darkness was seared into her soul and she became an award-winning and USA Today bestselling author of historical and paranormal romance. She has a very dusty car and a Master's degree in English that proves useful at the oddest times. An avid fan of fine chocolate, finer heroines, Bollywood films, and heroism in all forms, she has two cats and two dogs. Also a son. One of the cats is his.

Visit Carolyn on the web at:

carolynjewel.com

Twitter: @cjewel

Facebook: facebook.com/carolynjewelauthor

Goodreads: goodreads.com/cjewel

Sign up for Carolyn's **newsletter** so you never miss a new book and get exclusive, subscriber-only content.

Books by Carolyn Jewel

HISTORICAL ROMANCE SERIES

Sinclair Sisters Series

Lord Ruin, Book 1

A Notorious Ruin, Book 2

Surrender To Ruin, Book 3

Reforming the Scoundrels Series

Not Wicked Enough, Book 1

Not Proper Enough, Book 2

Other Historical Romance

How To Find a Duke in Ten Days

Dancing in The Duke's Arms

An Unsuitable Duchess, from *Dancing in The Duke's Arms* Anthology

In The Duke's Arms, from *Christmas in The Duke's Arms* Anthology

Christmas in The Duke's Arms

One Starlit Night, novella from *Midnight Scandals* Anthology

Midnight Scandals, Anthology

Scandal

Indiscreet

Moonlight, A Regency-set short(ish) story

The Spare

Stolen Love

Passion's Song

PARANORMAL ROMANCE

My Immortals Series

My Wicked Enemy, Book 1

My Forbidden Desire, Book 2

My Immortal Assassin, Book 3

My Dangerous Pleasure, Book 4

Free Fall, Book 4.5, a novella

My Darkest Passion, Book 5

Dead Drop, Book 6, a short novel

My Demon Warlord, Book 7

OTHER PARANORMAL ROMANCE

A Darker Crimson, Book 4 of *Crimson City*
DX, a *Crimson City* Novella

FANTASY ROMANCE

The King's Dragon, a short story

EROTIC ROMANCE

Whispers, Collection No. 1

The Sinclair Sisters Series

Lord Ruin

He hunted for beauty. He wasn't prepared for love.

"Entertaining, satisfying and sensuous." (All About Romance)

There's a reason Ruan Bettancourt, the Duke of Cynssyr, has obtained the nickname Lord Ruin. In London for the season, his plan is to marry the most beautiful debutante on the marriage mart, and he always gets what he wants.

Spinster Anne Sinclair is sensible, strong, and overlooked. On a night in which she vowed to protect her sister from the infamous Lord Ruin, she never expected to end up in bed with him.

Forced into a marriage neither of them wanted, Anne and the Duke believe they have no hope of passion or love for the rest of their lives. When the rogue falls completely for his tall, bespectacled wife, it's up to him to convince Anne to relinquish her heart.

Lord Ruin is the first book in The Sinclair Sisters saga, a series of Regency historical romance novels. If you like captivating, naughty, angst-ridden heroes and intelligent, complex, spine-steeled heroines, then you'll love Carolyn Jewel's steamy series.

Read Lord Ruin

Chapter One

London, 1818

CYNSSYR GLARED AT the door to number twenty-four Portman Square. "Blast it," he said to the groom who held two other horses. "What the devil is taking them so long?" He sat his horse with authority, a man in command of himself and his world. His buckskins fit close over lean thighs, and the exacting cut of his jacket declared a tailor of some talent. A Pink of the Ton, he seemed, but for eyes that observed more than they revealed.

"The Baron's a family man now, sir." The groom stamped his feet and tucked his hands under his armpits.

"What has that to do with anything?"

A handbill abandoned by some reveler from one of last night's fetes skimmed over the cobbles and spooked the other two horses, a charcoal gelding by the name of Poor Boy on account of the loss of his equine manhood; and a muscular dun. The groom had a dicey moment what with the cold having numbed his fingers but managed to send the sheet skittering to freedom.

"Man with a family can't leave anywhere spot on the dot," the groom said.

"I don't see why."

The door to number twenty-four flew open with a ringing crack of wood against stone. Of the two men who came out, the taller was Benjamin Dunbartin, Baron Aldreth, the owner of the house. He moved down the stairs at a rapid clip, clapping his hat onto his blond head as if he meant to cement it in place. The other man gripped his hat in one hand and descended at a more leisurely pace. The wind whipped a mass of inky curls over his sharp cheekbones.

"My lord." The groom handed Benjamin the reins to the dun. Before the groom could so much as offer a leg up, Ben launched himself into the saddle without a word of greeting or acknowledgment. Most everyone liked Benjamin. With his good looks and boyish smile, it was practically impossible not to. At the moment, however, Cynssyr thought Ben did not look like a man who cared for the family life.

"Come along, Devon," Benjamin said to his companion. He spoke with such force his dun tossed its head and pranced in nearly a full circle before Ben had him under control again.

Cynssyr's green eyes widened. "Have you quarreled with Mary?"

"Certainly not," said Ben.

"Well, you look like you've been hit by lightning from on high and still hear the angels singing. What's put you in such a state?"

"None of your damned business." The dun stamped hard on the cobbles, and Ben swore under his breath.

Cynssyr's bay snorted, and he reached to soothe the animal. "I should say it is, if I'm to endure such behavior from you."

"Devon!"

"Is this, by any chance, about Devon's letter?"

Ben's neck fairly snapped, he turned so quickly. "What do you know about that damned letter?"

"He wouldn't let me read it, but it must have succeeded. Camilla Fairchild is too young to be looking at a man that way." Cynssyr's mouth quirked and with the slight smile his austere features softened. When he smiled, he was about as handsome as a man could get, a fact not lost on him. He knew quite well the effect of his smile on the fairer sex.

Devon reached the curb in time to overhear the last remark. Coal-black eyes, at the moment completely without humor, slid from Ben to Cynssyr. "Disgraceful, ain't it? Her mother ought to set the girl a better example." He, too, accepted the reins of his gelding from the groom. He glanced at the stairs.

"Do you think she will?" Cynssyr managed, quite deliberately, to sound as though he hoped she wouldn't. Christ, he hoped not. He fully expected to soon discover what Mrs. Fairchild's backside felt like under his hands. Soft, he imagined. Energetic, he hoped.

"You ought to know better, Cyn," Devon said. "Even Mary said so."

"You will be relieved to know that at lord Sather's rout Miss Fairchild's passion was as yet untempered by experience. I merely provided her some." His smile reappeared. "A regrettably small amount, to be sure."

"You know, Cyn," Ben said, "one of these days you're going to miscalculate and find yourself married to some featherbrained female who'll bore you to tears."

"What else have you done, Devon, that's made him such wretched company?" Cynssyr kept one eye on Benjamin.

"Not one word," Ben said, glaring not at Cynssyr but at Devon.

Devon stopped with one foot in the stirrup to gift the world with affronted innocence. "All I did was—"

"Not one!" Ben turned a warning glance on him, too. "Not a word from you, either, Cyn."

Dev shook his head and mounted, exchanging a glance with Cynssyr who shrugged and found himself still mystified.

Only when the three were long out of earshot of the groom and riding toward Hyde Park did Ben speak. "How dare you?" He took a crumpled sheet of paper from his pocket and thrust it at Devon. "How dare you!"

"My personal correspondence is none of your affair." Devon, who had never expected to come into his title, could nevertheless exude more condescension than ever his father had managed, and the previous earl had been a master.

"Give me one reason I oughtn't call you out."

"Now see here," Cynssyr said, more than a little alarmed.

"Frankly, Cyn, if you knew about the letter, I ought to have satisfaction from you, too." Ben turned back to Devon. "Well?"

"I asked permission to court her when we were at Rosefeld for your wedding. But I had not the proper credentials then." Devon laughed bleakly. "I am Bracebridge now."

"Four years ago," Cynssyr said, "Camilla Fairchild was all of what, twelve or thirteen?"

"Good God," said Benjamin. "Not Miss Fairchild."

Devon snatched the crumpled paper from Ben's hand. "I won't lose her a second time."

"Lose whom?" Cynssyr drew even with Devon. "What are you two talking about? Devon, I thought your letter was for Miss Fairchild." Two women out for a morning walk stopped their stroll to stare at the men riding by. Out of pure habit, Cynssyr gave them an assessing glance, which made Devon laugh.

"Have you declared yourself?" Ben waved at the paper in Devon's hand. "Besides in that note of yours, I mean."

"If not Miss Fairchild, then whom?" Cynssyr said, by now more than a little annoyed. "Miss George?" When that got no reply, he said, "Not Miss Willowby. Oh, please, no. If it's Miss Willowby, I forbid it."

Devon slid the note into his pocket. "She has not the slightest idea of my feelings."

"Good God."

"Now that she is here in London," Devon said, "I mean to change that." He pulled back on his black, waiting for Ben's dun to draw alongside. Once again, Cynssyr found himself maddeningly excluded. "With your permission, of course."

"It isn't my permission you need be concerned with," Ben said. "It's her father's."

"The old man can bugger himself for all I care." The black-as-the-depths-of-hell eyes that even Cynssyr, who knew better, sometimes thought devoid of life flashed with a violent fire.

Benjamin grinned.

They were at the Park now, off the streets and onto the riding paths. "Would one of you," said Cynssyr, "please tell me what the devil you're talking about?"

"Dev thinks he's in love."

"That much I gathered." He looked over at Devon. "In love with whom?"

"My sister-in-law," Ben said, throwing up one hand. "That's who."

Cynssyr gave Devon a look. "Which one?" He moved out of the path of a fat gentleman on a white mare. To the best of his recollection, there were four Sinclair sisters and Benjamin had married one of them. That left three. And, if memory served, the Sinclair sisters deserved their reputation for beauty. Ben's wife, Mary, was among the most beautiful women of Cynssyr's rather vast acquaintance. He almost didn't blame Ben for marrying her.

"I don't *think* I'm in love."

"The youngest? Miss Emily?" His green eyes flickered with interest. "If she turns out half as beautiful as she promised, she'll cause a riot at her debut."

"No. And stay the hell away from Emily, Cyn."

"Then it must be the brunette. Lucy." The name rolled off his tongue replete with his recollection of ebony hair and features of heartbreaking perfection.

"No."

"You mean the eldest?" He could not for the life of him summon an image of the eldest Sinclair sister. "That's impossible. I don't even remember her."

"Blonde? Gray-blue eyes. Yay tall." Ben indicated an inch or so below his chin which meant a tall woman, perhaps even an ungainly one. "You'll meet her tonight at the ball. Meet her again, that is."

"Why don't I recall her?" Cynssyr glanced at Devon.

"And by the way," Ben said. "Stay away from Lucy, too."

"Why?"

"Because when it comes to women, damn you, Cynssyr, you're a rogue, that's why."

"Mama begins to despair. Perhaps I ought put to rest her doubts of a succession."

Ben snorted. "I'd not curse any of my sisters-in-law with you for a husband."

"Now that," Cynssyr said, "wounds me deeply. When at last I marry, I expect I'll make a most excellent husband."

"Hah," said Devon.

"*Et tu, Brute?*"

"You can't even settle on what woman to seduce tonight."

"If not for Napoleon, I'd likely be years married. A positive dullard, like Ben here." But Napoleon there was, so Cynssyr wasn't married at all. Love, naturally, would have but a limited role in any marriage he contracted. The war had burned out his capacity, if ever he'd possessed it, for such saving emotion.

"A dullard?" said Ben, spoiling his attempt to appear insulted by breaking into laughter. Devon rolled his eyes.

"Whatever you two think, I'm quite aware I need a wife. A man of my station requires a wife, as my desperate mother so often reminds me."

"God help the woman fool enough to marry you," Ben said.

"Why not one of your sisters-in-law, Ben? It seems an excellent idea." Dozens of suitable candidates were thrown his way every season, this one being no different from any other since the war. But he'd not been able to bring himself to the sticking point with any of them.

"No."

"I'll reform." He grinned. "I promise."

"You'll reform when hell freezes over."

A faint memory tickled at the back of his mind. He tapped his temple. "You mean the spinster, don't you, Devon? The eldest. The one with the spectacles."

"Blond hair, gray-blue eyes. Yay tall," Benjamin repeated.

"What was her name?"

Ben's blue eyes chilled another degree. "Anne."

"Gad. I still don't remember her. Except for the spectacles." He looked askance at Dev. "I have never understood his taste in women."

"You truly want to marry Anne?" Ben asked Devon. Curiosity and relief lingered at the edges of the question, but hearing him, no one could doubt the seriousness of the matter. No doting father could have sounded more cautious.

"Yes."

"I meant to introduce her to Declan McHenry," said Ben, looking thoughtfully at Devon. "Or Phillip Lovejoy."

"I'd be obliged if you didn't."

"Good God, you are serious, aren't you?"

"It's been four years. I am done waiting." Amusement brightened Devon's brooding eyes and made his severe mouth curve in a surprisingly warm smile. It did interesting things to his face, the way severity gave way to warmth. At times like this, when he saw Devon smile, Cynssyr understood exactly why women went so eagerly to his bed.

If Devon had really decided the Sinclair spinster was the woman he wanted, then the matter was done. He would have his way. The why of it mystified him. Even as plain Devon Carlisle, he could do far better than some dried-up female who wasn't even pretty enough to bother taking off her spectacles. As matrimonial material, the earl of Bracebridge was nearly as sought after as he himself. Nearly. But, not quite.

"Enough. No more blather about love and marriage, you two," Cynssyr said. With a flick of the reins, he steered his horse past a fallen branch then cantered to the edge of a meadow where he waited for Ben and Devon.

"Jade," Ben accused when he reached the meadow.

Cynssyr flashed a brilliantly arrogant smile. "The trouble with you, my lord Baron Aldreth, is you love your wife. And you, Devon. For shame. You disappoint me. You disappoint all our sex, falling for this Miss Sinclair."

"Love," said Dev with one of his wry grins. "A most heinous crime."

"Love." Cynssyr lifted one brow in the supercilious disdain he usually reserved for certain rebuttals in the Lords. "You mean a man's delusion he's not been robbed of his freedom and a woman's that she's gained hers?"

"Exactly," Devon said.

"How can you trust your judgment now?" He lifted his riding whip, but brought it down on his boot leg, not his horse. "Fools the both of you." So saying, he urged his horse to a gallop. "Anne Sinclair," he muttered. He heard Devon and Ben thunder after him and gave his horse its head. They had no chance of catching him now. Only the best horseflesh found its way into his stables. He had the best of everything. Wine. Horses. Women. Friends.

He wanted to roar with disgust and dismay. Devon married. What was he to do with himself then? To the devil with spinsters who set their caps on marriage, he thought as the chill wind whipped past him. "To the very devil with her." Thus did the duke of Cynssyr, so deservedly referred to as Lord Ruin, dismiss the woman with whom he would soon be desperately in love.

Read Lord Ruin

Made in the USA
Lexington, KY
10 October 2017